GIOVANNI'S GIFT

GIOVANNI'S GIFT

Bradford Morrow

VIKING

VIKING
Published by the Penguin Group
Penguin Books USA Inc., 375 Hudson Street, New York, New York 10014, U.S.A.
Penguin Books Ltd, 27 Wrights Lane, London W8 5TZ, England
Penguin Books Australia Ltd, Ringwood, Victoria, Australia
Penguin Books Canada Ltd, 10 Alcorn Avenue, Toronto, Ontario, Canada M4V 3B2
Penguin Books (N.Z.) Ltd, 182–190 Wairau Road, Auckland 10, New Zealand

Penguin Books Ltd, Registered Offices:
Harmondsworth, Middlesex, England

First published in 1997 by Viking Penguin,
a division of Penguin Books USA Inc.

3   5   7   9   10   8   6   4

AUTHOR'S NOTE

Like Pandora, I was given a box some years ago, and like her, I opened it and marveled at its contents. The characters and events which sprung into fictional life as a result of my transgression are purely the products of my imagination and do not represent the actual histories, thoughts, or actions of anyone, living or dead.

Grateful acknowledgment is made for permission to reprint excerpts from "Even Better Than the Real Thing" written by Paul Hewson, Dave Evans, Adam Clayton and Larry Mullen. Copyright © 1991 PolyGram International Music Publishing B.V. Used by permission. All rights reserved.

LIBRARY OF CONGRESS CATALOGING IN PUBLICATION DATA
Morrow, Bradford,
Giovanni's Gift: a novel / Bradford Morrow.
p.   cm.
ISBN 0-670-87292-X (alk. paper)
I. Title.
PS3563.O8754U5   1997
813'.54—dc20   96-34024

This book is printed on acid-free paper.
∞

Printed in the United States of America
Set in Fairfield Light
Designed by Brian Mulligan

For my aunt and uncle
and for Martine

GIOVANNI'S GIFT

I

THE NIGHT MUSIC

For good unknown, sure is not had, or had
And yet unknown, is as not had at all.
In plain then, what forbids us to be wise?
Such prohibitions binde not.

—JOHN MILTON, *Paradise Lost*

$IMAGINE$ a scene of rural serenity, a night scene. Dinner is over, the embers in the stove are dying. Outside, the air is perfumed by the sweet scent of alfalfa. Above the mountains surrounding this faraway place, the stars are a menagerie of silver flickering motes, phosphorescent droplets in the cold black infinity of space. Some cottonwood seeds, down here below, borne aloft in their own little clouds, mime their star cousins. They rise on a soft breeze above the darkened field whose coarse grass you wouldn't want to roam across barefooted. Imagine them, and imagine that the ridge beyond the creek is blackened by the night and that the meadow which stretches between is sunk in blackness, too. The amber dogtooth moon rests behind that cradling ridge but soon enough will bestir itself and rise, sometime after those who live here have climbed the stairs to their warm and familiar room, where maybe they will read a page or two before extinguishing the lamp and drifting off to sleep. Crickets will continue to make their humdrum song, one sustained percussive note rendered over and over, as the sleepers begin to dream country dreams. It would be hard to fathom a purer vision of people at peace in the natural world.

But look again, imagine just a little further, because there is more.

When the unwelcome visitor, who was quite awake at the wheel of the car, reached the end of the rough mountain road, the crickets fell quiet and silence descended upon the valley. Later, when Edmé— she who was upstairs asleep beside her husband, Henry—described to me that first night of the grotesque visitations, she remarked how the nocturnal creatures that usually made such raucous music were oddly subdued. She awakened as if by premonition, sometime after the intruder cut his engine, parked, and presumably began his furtive hike up through the south field. Aside from the clock in the kitchen downstairs, whose pendulum measured out seconds and chimed hours with mechanical rigor, the house was hushed, drowned in thick quiet, so that inside and out tranquility reigned. Edmé fluffed her pillow, turned on her side, and closed her eyes again. But the silence insinuated itself into her thoughts and kept her from falling back asleep.

"That's when I should have known things weren't right. When I should have figured out that someone was probably out there."

Meaning: in the country, silence is the harbinger of change. Then, her voice darkening like the very night she described, she told me of the deafening music that brought her, in a single swift movement, to her feet. She and Henry faltered past chairs and a bureau bathed in shadow, toward the window on the creekside wall of the bedroom. Though they could not see one another, each knew what a look of shock would be there if they could. As they crawled to the rectangular opening that was only faintly brighter than the murky room, both were awed by the bewildering volume of the music, by its nascent violence, its forthright chaos. Night would never be like it had been in the past. Both of them intuited this, too.

They looked into the open fields, the near meadows, but were able to see nothing out of the ordinary. Staring into nothingness, as their eyes reconciled the dark and pupils dilated, they listened. Once they could begin to make out forms, they worked hard to see. He studied the near yard for movement, and she the brambles along the creek. But no one walked defiant across the yard; no one was to be observed running under the pendant river willows. All was utter pandemonium, despite the physical stillness of the scape. The music, this unholy racket, harsher than anything either of them had ever heard, persisted with bludgeoning drum and screeching voice, so that from every corner of the world outside their window, it seemed, the air filled to bursting. Maracas and cymbals sizzled, and the thrashing bass pounded in an upheaval of sound. She said she may have screamed, but the music—what seemed to be music, though since misshapen by its amplitude it brought to mind industrial noise, like an exploding ironworks—was so tumultuous that neither she nor her husband could hear anything else.

And then, as suddenly as the music began, it ended.

One of them said, —Jesus. But neither moved.

Their hearts beat hard, as the reverberations, aftershocks really, of the music throbbed in the valley, diminished, and finally succumbed to the palpable quiet.

Crickets chirruped again as if nothing unusual had happened. The barn owl shrilly sputtered. Several birds, thrushes or Steller's jays, traded boughs and issued echoey cries of protest, but soon they quieted, too, and the night reverted, as if on ungodly cue, to its original rich calm.

Edmé and Henry listened for retreating footfalls in the cut field grass, or the crunch of pebbles along the walk, or muffled laughter below them in the gauzy bushes that ringed the house or from behind the small outbuilding which stood at the corner where two irregular drystone walls converged down toward the whispering brook. Nothing. Flashlight cradled in one hand and his old Remington in the other, Henry made a brief search beyond the near periphery first and then moved on out past the tract of stubbly ground that was illuminated by security floodlights. Edmé stood on the east porch, in her white bathrobe, and watched his progress as best she could, calling his name whenever he ventured too far beyond the

margin made by the powerful halogens that shone from the eaves. As
he wandered back up toward the house, he turned now and then
to look behind into the darkness. Still, nothing. In a shocked daze
he climbed the stairs and together they went inside and for a time
sat unspeaking at the kitchen table. The peace was punctured only
by that steady cadence measured out by the wall clock. It was two-
twenty.

—Should we make a call? she said, finally.

He didn't respond. She understood why, but spoke again.

—See if Noah wouldn't be willing to come up and look around?

—I don't know, he said in a soft voice. He was studying his hands
as if they might hold some answer.

—We ought to at least let him know what's going on here.

—But we don't know what's going on.

—It couldn't hurt to call.

He caught himself tapping his thumb against the tabletop. The
rhythm of the music still pulsed in his memory, in counterpoint with
the pendulum at his back. —Well, he said, and folded his fingers
into a tight knot, hands merging then pulling apart and relaxing out
flat before him. —In the morning, maybe. They seem to be done for
tonight.

The pot whistled, the clock struck the half hour. Chamomile tea
from hops that grew wild in the meadow, and hard spoon-biscuits.
After they put the dishes into the sink, they bolted the three doors,
drew the curtains on the first floor, and climbed the wide stairs back
to the bedroom.

By sunrise it all seemed illusory. Though they weren't ones to be
easily spooked—they were accustomed to both the pleasures and lia-
bilities of solitude—they did make a search of the grounds for evidence of the anonymous intruder, but found nothing, not so much
as a broken branch in a juniper berry bush, or a trail of crushed grass
that might lead down to where the road ended by the main gate, a

swinging metal horsegate a couple hundred yards below the house, down where the road that led to Ash Creek ended. Maybe they had suffered a simultaneous nightmare? Neither raised the question of telephoning Noah, the sheriff in town.

What was most fascinating about their reluctance to seek any help, Aunt Edmé told me later, was how it seemed to be the result of their unwillingness to acknowledge, in the fresh light of another dawn, that it had happened at all. She explained to me, "We just managed to forget, by afternoon the very next day, how upset we'd been, how frightened, shocked even, we were by the *strangeness* of it all. We just kind of decided without saying so that, no, nothing had happened."

Nothing, in any event, that would warrant Noah Daiches coming over. It would take more than loud music in the middle of the night to persuade Henry to ask Noah for help. Not that there was an unbridgeable rift between the two men; just that Henry had developed a tactful if grim resistance to Noah because of the incident with Giovanni Trentas some three years before, and neither Henry nor Edmé wanted to reopen that scarred wound. This night music did not, of itself, point backward in time to Giovanni's misfortune. Therefore, my aunt and uncle found it logical to believe that what had happened to them just now would never happen again, was a freak occurrence. Some kids had gone berserk, say, in the middle of the night, were driving around high on drugs, maybe, just driving with no particular destination in mind, with nothing in mind *at all*, which was possibly their usual state of mind—or state of non-mind—only to arrive at the end of a dirt road, where they decided purely randomly to harass whoever happened to be asleep in that house up there. Why not? Just for kicks, what the hell.

Yes, this was one way to discount what happened. No doubt there were other explanations, equally viable. In the tacit way husbands and wives have of reaching agreement about certain matters, without

ever coming to an explicit resolution, Edmé and Henry Fulton deval-
ued the madness and hostility of the music and carried on, a stubborn pair of hopeful stoics.

Life went forward. Men came with rigs and over the course of the
next couple of days hayed both the meadow below the house and the
larger meadow across the creek, leaving behind great cylinders, raw
spools of yellowing green, here and there, to dry in the sun. Both
Edmé and Henry helped with this process. In another few days they
would come back, to load these bales onto ricks and convey them
down the road. No money changed hands between my uncle and
these fieldmen, one of whom happened to be Noah's brother. They
took the hay off, did a neat job of it, three times a year, and for the
effort got feed for their livestock. It was a perennial ritual and gave
my aunt and uncle a meaningful connection to their land. Moreover,
the men had known Henry's father, admired him, back when Ash
Creek was a working ranch. They'd known Giovanni Trentas, too,
before the mishap, or whatever one would call it. Trentas had been
Ash Creek's caretaker during the years when Edmé and Henry lived
out on the coast, and the men would encounter him from time to
time in town, with that daughter of his, named Helen. She was a
pretty girl, they concurred, almost a woman really. She certainly had
always seemed older than her years, and stayed by Giovanni Trentas's
side at all times, as if she were his child bride. Sometimes when he
would go quiet as an empty jar—living as he had for so many years
on his own, taciturnity was a habitual quirk of his—Helen was seen
to pick up the conversation where it had been left off. They were an
inseparable pair, father and daughter.

While Noah's brother, Milland, and the others might not have
encumbered themselves with the admiration for Trentas that they
had always held for Henry's father and Henry himself, neither did
they openly dislike him. They did express to Edmé their regret at not
being able to attend Giovanni's funeral. And, Henry told me, Milland Daiches had asked him, once, what would become of Helen,

now that her father was gone. Henry no doubt declined to respond, having always thought that Milland was not altogether *there,* so to speak, and not someone he would care to see Helen involved with in any way—not that Helen Trentas had ever seemed to be one in need of protection.

Midweek the following week, after life seemed for all the world to have settled back down into a peaceable routine, the intruder returned. This time Edmé slept and Henry was awake when the chaos began. Lying in their bed of carved mahogany, he first heard a gust of wind rustling the dry bushes below, then rose and moved to the window in five smooth steps and looked out, just as he had looked out that window many times in the past, noticing how the leaves of the grant lilac seized moonlight which pooled under the strew of clouds over the mountains. The leaves shivered, gathering that light like greedy children who hold out their palms for sweets. There was no murderous figure standing in the middle of the yard gazing defiantly up—although the scarecrow in the garden might have seemed to wave its sackclothed arm at him; there was nothing he could see that was out of place. Minutes passed. He breathed in, out. More minutes, and then he was tired. Just as he began to back away from the window frame, tempted to give up and try again to sleep, he heard vague human murmurs, a man with a deep voice and maybe even a lisp, followed by the blunt *cluck* of a switch being thrown. The second invasion of their solitude was under way.

This music was different from the other night. Where first the music had been rock and roll, this was orchestral, a brooding tone poem—Richard Strauss, *Tod und Verklärung,* Edmé recognized— but once more pushed through speakers with such sheer belligerence as to render it primeval. Like the birth of some nasty new universe out in the kitchen garden.

Henry was prepared this time. He pulled on his trousers under his nightshirt and slid into his wellies. With twelve-gauge, already loaded, in hand, he made his way downstairs in the dark, and stole out onto the side porch that paralleled the creek some hundred yards away. Standing for several moments in the pitch black, he tried to get a precise sense of where the music was coming from. He grasped the shotgun, cheekpiece of the thing up against his heart, as he studied the nightscape before him. A haze filtered the light, and he blinked as if to clear it away. As he glimpsed his land he saw it wasn't black outside, and yet it wasn't light, either. The fields, walls, barn, vista, every familiar landmark—all awash in music—had been robbed of detail and visual nuance. The moon, high overhead, had leached the sky of pigment. If he hadn't been quite so enraged, he might have thought he was having a vision.

He trained the gun on what seemed to be the source of the noise, and thought for a moment about how the world out there seemed afflicted, in some way unhealthy, as if it had been wounded and some metaphysical physician had wrapped it in medicinal vapor. He pulled the trigger. The blast, which under other circumstances would have seemed loud, was weirdly faint, enveloped as it was by music. Since the mouth of the barrel had flared bright, giving his position away to anyone who might be watching, he strode, careful not to catch his knee against any of the old Adirondack chairs arranged along the porch, to the corner where the front adjoined this side veranda. He stood at the head of the staircase that led down to the foreyard and, having noted the music was drifting toward the south, shot in that general direction a second time. The report echoed through the valley and up into the gorge above the falls. The music ceased.

Henry swallowed what felt like a small stone going down his dry throat. Silent, Edmé came up next to him, and together they waited.

The smell of powder tasted bitter in the dewy air. Henry was a man comfortable with guns. When he pumped the twelve-gauge to eject the spent shell, he felt a momentary surge of power, only slightly edged by the horror of having just unloaded live ammunition at a man. Edmé whispered, —Look there.

—What? he asked.

—See that, down by the gate? They're gone now.

She was sure she'd seen double red taillight eyes blink down beyond the lowest meadow. They listened, but their ears were ringing from the cacophony of music and gunfire. Then they heard the engine of the car traveling away from the ranch, down the dirt road, which was nothing more than a pair of furrows hedged by wild grass, larkspur, and thistle.

Henry squinted, thinking, This is Tate doing this. Nobody else could be so hateful.

It was a thought he would keep from Edmé.

An hour eased by, maybe more. Certainly, the moon had moved down the sky. A shower of meteors brought them back to themselves, a fine cascade of silver threads, and Henry saw that the world had been returned to its subtle nighttime colors, its cobalt and Prussian and blackberry blacks. They sat side by side under the eaves until dawn conjured other bands of the spectrum, pinks and saffrons, to dye the horizon. She went into the house and made coffee. Her back was numbed by the long watch.

—Now will you call Noah? she asked, when at last he followed her inside. He propped the shotgun against the wainscot, and took his chair at the table. Sunlight decanted through the window at his back. His irises, hazel in most light, were ebonized by shadow that morning, and his blinded eye, a whole story unto itself, had a wedge nicked from it that made one iris pearlescent along its bottom. My uncle was still a handsome man, with broad high cheeks and aquiline nose distinguished by a fine, raised, whitened ridge, the result of being broken in a fall. His uncombed hair caught the dawn in such a way it might have seemed like haloed flax.

He ran his hands over his face. —What the hell do they want?

But though neither he nor Edmé knew, as the trespasser hadn't yet left behind a message or any evidence of wanting something, Noah Daiches never heard from them that day.

The third occurrence, and what Henry witnessed the following night, finally helped both of them grasp that what was happening at Ash Creek was not some innocent mischief. This night visit had an unexpected twist, like a signature in invisible ink that would slowly materialize so it might be read, a specific denouement that followed the music, and it had the effect of breaching what was left of Henry's confidence that he could protect himself from the malign will of others. My uncle had endured debacles over the course of years, my aunt had been forced to cleave to idealism during times of trouble, yes. But the crudeness of the third visit threw into question, surely, any orthodoxies such as *One reaps what he sows* or *You get what you deserve.* No one deserved this, he believed. Nobody sowed seeds this rotten.

They slept a wakeful sleep over the course of the warm close day following their vigil. They worried about the shots fired into the dark, anxious that someone might have been hurt. Doing this was against every rule Henry had ever been taught as a boy when learning from his father the gospel rules of wielding firearms. Never shoot unless you can clearly see your target—it was the first tenet of gunsmanship. That law he had surely broken, and through the long day Henry drifted in and out of a dull regret about it. He should have fired into the air. The music maker, whoever he was, couldn't clearly see Henry there on the porch, camouflaged by darkness, and so wouldn't have had any idea whether he was drawing a bead right on him or not. A shot at the moon would have been as effective a warning as one in his direction. The second shot had also been unnecessary. After all, he was apparently withdrawing down the gentle rise, presumably running away. Nothing justified firing at a man in retreat, no matter what sort of reprobate thing he had done to you. And while, yes, the music was malicious, terrifying to the two of them, without explanation or reason, as they could see it then, it was nothing so criminal as to merit being shot in the back.

These thoughts bothered him. He shared them with Edmé, who

said, simply, —They had coming to them whatever would've happened to them, and that put his mind at ease, at least a little.

The weather turned sultry, unusual in these high mountains, and especially so given that the month had been marked by cool nights. Now the evening was whitened by haze. Whenever a draft shuffled through the trees, wheezy as if with asthma, the leaves would quiver in gratitude. The windows were left open to draw what cool vesper air rose from the gorge hollows and lively creek. Doors, however, were bolted, the new household habit. His twelve-gauge was leaned against the bedroom wall, whose papered pattern was a series of formal urns from which an abundance of fanciful sun-faded blossoms teemed. Full moon only a week away, the waxing light outside would have been quite intense had the sky been clear, but clouds gathered as summer mist lay upon the valley.

The music broke in on this large silence which ranged around them, and again the middle of the night had gone mad.

My uncle listened not in disbelief so much as contempt before descending the stairs once more. Behind him, he heard her say, in an exhausted voice, —Don't go down, just let it finish, and as he walked out to the second-floor landing he answered, —Go ahead and call Noah.

The outburst seemed to originate now from a different place. Rather than from below the house, it flooded the dark from a knoll above. Some rock song, unidentifiable to Henry and if anything even more raucous, eerie, wanton than before.

—Henry, she cried out.

But he had vanished downstairs.

At the northern end of the long veranda the hill adjoined the house along the back. Scraggly bushes cluttered the sheer ascent, and squarish blocks of stone, granite and igneous chunks, tumbled scree, jutted here and there, wild outcroppings decorated in every cranny by corsages of thorny flowering thistle and stubborn foliage. Without benefit of light, he made his way up the snaking path toward the summit of the first knoll, where the recorded voice taunted and the synthetic beat persevered, and though Edmé had gone out to the edge of the porch and even pursued him a little way up the trace, she thought the better of following, so returned to the veranda.

All the house lights remained off. She didn't know whether Henry had taken a flashlight with him up the steep bank, but if he had she saw that he wasn't using it to make the climb. Not that he needed it—his feet knew the trail as well as his eye. The path veered, zigzag-ging within the natural curves of the cliff face, and she squinted up-ward into the shadows, tracking its meanderings in her mind—Edmé knew the path nearly as well as Henry—but failed to catch sight of him. She ran back inside the house, then returned to the porch with her camera, which was fitted with a telephoto lens, a one-hundred-thirty-five millimeter. Pressing her eye to the viewfinder, she scanned the miniaturized yet magnified horizon for movement. She calcu-lated that Henry must have reached the first bluff, a flat stony field covered with scrub.

Cottony fog was punctuated by drops of lukewarm rain, heavier than drizzle, but not an outright shower, a *spitting sky,* as Henry might jokingly have referred to it in other circumstances. His face ran with sweat, and he drew deep breaths through pursed lips rather than give himself away by gasping, though he might surely have wanted to gasp, as the night bore down on him and the rain had the odd effect of seeming to sponge away all the breathable air. The darkness was more comprehensive than on the previous nights of disturbance, and Henry was grateful for that, since he assumed he could read the myriad natural obstacles in these woods better than any stranger, and therefore lightlessness served him, gave him the advantage. Still, he hesitated, knelt, collected himself, got his breath back, before pressing forward toward the locus of music. He guessed two hun-dred yards, three at the most, separated him from the trespasser.

Best, he thought, to circle around behind on the creek side—the creek twisted through an endless series of small but furious falls in the gorge below him, just east, off his right shoulder, as he negotiated the narrow footpath along the cliff rim—in order to avoid walking straight into the clearing where he assumed the man, or men, awaited him.

Edmé lit a candle. It gave off a strong scent of fennel as she set it down on the telephone stand in the kitchen by the door. She flicked through the pages of the address book until she found Noah's number. She lifted the handset and ran her finger around the rotary to connect his exchange, wondering whether anyone would be at the station at this hour, though imagining that of course someone had to be there, if not Noah himself, because didn't problems like this occur most often at night? When she raised the handset to her ear, she heard nothing. When she tried to disconnect—tapping the plungers over and over with shaking fingers—she disbelieved the banality of her gestures as much as the fact that the line was dead.

What did they think they were doing? Edmé might have said it aloud, —What do you think you're doing? but found she didn't have sufficient breath to get the words out. She snuffed the candle, and the kitchen filled with a fennel perfume.

As for Henry, he too smelled smoke, but not of candle wax and wick. Rather, of burnt birch, he guessed. Punkwood. Bitter and rotty— not resinous like pine, nor a clean burn like oak. He knew at once what it meant, and it served to raise in him an even greater resentment than he'd already felt. How dare they burn a fire on his land? They'd known enough about surviving in the woods in stealth to gather soft wood in order not to make any noise with an ax, known, it seemed, that birch bark will start damp. The winds up here were apt to shift in frivolous ways, so Henry was not certain exactly where the fire'd been set. He continued up toward a small pasture quite near, ducking under the low-slung boughs of tart blue spruce and ponderosa, which gave off their own spicy scent that mingled with the aroma of wet smoke.

He was more careful now to proceed unhastily, defensively. A wary calm came over him, a fine sharp focus. A few steps taken, he took a few more.

Then, beneath the din, he could have sworn he heard Edmé calling his name, —Henry? faint as a reverie. But, well, no. The voice couldn't have been Edmé's, could it? Surely she wouldn't make such a mistake as calling his name, and risk betraying to the music maker that his victims had separated. Edmé wouldn't want him to know that she and he were confused, frightened—although of course it was the truth. If ever, Henry thought, there was an instance where the truth would *not* set him free. He breathed hard, moved forward.

Clothes soaked through by the rain, which had let up some. They were heavy and clung to his thighs and back and made his climb harder. A new song saturated this high corridor, and echoed off massive tablets of ancient earthbones, as he once told me they were, stones coerced to the surface by volcanic shoving and unveiled by antique masses of glacial ice. Henry heard the words

> *You're the real thing,*
> *Yeah the real thing.*
> *Even better than the real thing*

which made him wonder, though only for a moment, How can anything be better than the real thing? But the slide guitar cut through that thought like shears through tired old ribbon, and so he kept moving forward toward this real thing, getting higher and higher just as the music did, finding that his heart beat hard, inarguably to the rhythm of the bass and drum, as he heard

> *Gonna blow right through ya*
> *Like a breeze*

or something to that effect, and more than ever felt unconnected from any sense of explanation for what might be happening here, or why. One matter he did comprehend, however, was that he was very near the origin of his grievance. The backlit limbs, slack under the weight of August, danced, it seemed, up ahead of him. He considered shooting a warning into the air overhead, but reasoned he had the best opportunity of forcing matters to a less violent resolution if he maintained his anonymity under this shroud of night and seized for himself some advantage of surprise.

Then he saw them. Two of them.

A man dangled aloft with arms limp at his sides and legs stiff, hung by heavy rope from the crooked thick limb of an old oak there, one of the trees that had withstood many winters, had endured for generations, one of those trees that ranchers referred to as a wolf tree, because when all others failed you, if you were being pursued, this one would be there for you to climb and escape the predator's fangs. The other, whose movements were at first not much more emphatic than his companion's, or whoever, stood near the hanged man, visible in the flickering light of the fire. He wore a half mask that did not hide the crazed look set upon the barely visible features of his face—his mouth, the eyes seen through the cutouts of the mask. The two were framed, from Henry's vantage, by jagged, spiky leaves, and by twigs and many tesserae of saplings and wild hedges, on the opposite side of this meadow, a hundred feet distant.

Before he had the least chance to speculate upon what this could *mean*—one person hanged and with luminous spikes driven into his pale skull from forehead over crown and down to the base of the neck, the other with an insipid grin seizing his lips—Henry found he had stumbled headlong into the clearing, his own damp head swimming with confusion, in a state closer to terror than he had ever felt. In the low surge and dance of what small fire was left, Henry stared agape at the living figure as it strode toward him now with such quickness as to seem inhuman, then halted beside the hung man.

With a nonchalant flick of the wrist, fingers touching the knees, he set the suspended body in motion, so that it swung, stiff and surely lifeless. The intruder said not a word but returned with frank delight Henry's shocked gaze, and then, taking several steps oddly backward away from the other, who stood with his shotgun half raised, offered Henry what could only be called a condemning smile. The music all the while continued, louder than Henry could bear. He put his left hand up to his ear, for a moment dropping his concentration. As he did, the figure leapt backward, crashing into the thicket on the far edge of the clearing. The silver crate or box, from which the music seemed to emanate, the fleeing man had been seen to snatch from the ground in one swift flowing movement as he sprinted into the tangle of woods. And there had been something else, too, inanimate and accusatory, which the trespasser had waved in the air before him, and which Henry witnessed in the dying light, before the figure made his escape.

Henry did not pursue him, nor did he fire any shells into the air, still reverberant for another few moments before all was a fresh calm and the forests on either side of the gorge swallowed up the last echoes of music. When he approached the hanging man, whose unpliant form still swayed to the beat of gravity's measure and no other, the recognition that its clothing was Henry's own came as a last insult. Plaid shirt, charcoal wool trousers, silver buckled belt—all had been stolen from his house apparently, to be brought up here for this. And the mannequin—for the hanging figure was not dead but constructed of rags, bound in white cotton to resemble the human form—had painted upon its blank countenance a childish rendition of a skeleton's skull face.

Henry unyoked the effigy and pulled it down. The thick rope he afterward cut with his pocket knife, having climbed into the wolf tree and edged out on the limb to get at it. He stood for a long time by the fire whose flames devoured the stuffed figure and lariat, and stared at its playful oranges and crimsons, until the thing burned itself out, was reduced to ashen junk, to nothing.

OVER THE COURSE of my thirty-three years, my aunt had never asked for help. Edmé was a woman of prodigious independence. She was stoic, both she and my uncle were, always had been. It was not a matter of pride—though they were proud, after their own modest fashion—nor did it have anything to do with arrogance. Their manner was the result of a life lived simply, with detachment, and far enough away from the frenzy of success so as not to be ruined by its needs. This was how I always saw it, anyway. Independence was for them the greatest *sine qua non,* the very last thing they would ever relinquish.

Yet when Aunt Edmé telephoned me at my small flat in Rome, to apprise me of what had been happening during this past year at the ranch, I heard in her story, or behind it somehow, a cry for help. This was new. Nothing I had ever heard in her voice before. I offered to come visit, as it had been a while since I'd seen them, and although I didn't say so, such a trip wouldn't involve much of a sacrifice on my part, as my own affairs were not in the best order. But I sensed her immediate withdrawal.

"We're all right, Grant," she said. "These past few months have been quiet. Just, like I say, all of a sudden they seem to be back to their old tricks, and we wanted to let you know, in case."

"In case what?"

"Just . . . in case," the words assuming the flat reserve of her part of the world.

"Edmé, why didn't you mention this before?"

"Tell me, Grant. How's your lovely Mary?"

"Well. I've been meaning to call you about that."

"About what?"

Silence. Then, "I guess it just wasn't meant to be."

Even before the cliché faded into a faltering explanation and her response that she hoped we would find some way to work things out, a wave of regret, a savory nausea, passed over me. Aunt Edmé was not going to pry. It was not in her nature. She presented another question, innocent if poignant: "How is your work going?"

I had no better answer to this than to her inquiry about Mary.

My work, I thought—this hodgepodge of translating, of private tutoring in English, of clerking in a bookshop, not to mention the ridiculous opportunity I'd recently been offered at an import-export firm—and muttered something by way of bringing this brief conversation with Edmé to an end. My God, I thought. My expatriation, my doomed marriage, my general absence of bearings and direction—these were not issues I felt it was possible to discuss with this beloved woman, who never had the least acquaintance, so far as I knew, with any of them. After we said goodbye, I found myself twisting the nose off a loaf of bread I had bought early that morning at the *alimentari* downstairs from the studio where Mary and I had lived this past half year. I lifted the bread to my lips and then, unable to eat, laid it on the table by the window. Looking out across the roofs of Rome, I saw the cupolas and domes here and there in the distance, and my mind went blank. What followed was a moment of thorough paralysis, an inertia of both body and spirit. What regret, what longing, what physical loneliness overwhelmed me as I stood alone in this room, nor would it have helped if I could have scolded myself for feeling so suddenly low. I had had my chance with Mary. There was no disowning that hard fact.

Rome was the end of our brief but troubled road. Mary and I came here hoping the eternal city would either restore our love or collaborate in the final throes of this marriage gone wrong. Why it seemed to us that Rome would be a better place than elsewhere to follow matters through to their inevitable end is now a mystery. Maybe it had to do with our belief that here in a city so inundated by ghosts, the deliverance or death of our love might happen with greater ease in the vast drowning wash of its history. The end would come quiet as a sigh underwater, was what we thought. Such was the peace we'd sought, and such was the peace we found, though both of us were aware that hidden within this small triumph of discretion was our great failure.

The marriage had gone well enough in the beginning, three years earlier in New York, where we met. An impetuous consortium of two, it was us against the world, the same way many must feel, encouraged by passion and the intuition that nothing can destroy an intimacy, a synergy this strong. We met one night, then again late the next afternoon, and by the third evening, after we'd spent the entire day in one another's arms, I was absolutely sure she must be pregnant. It seemed impossible to me, to both of us, that such erotic yearning and relinquishment could have any other result. She called me husband, and I called her my wife. Not for even the briefest moment during those nights and days together did any remnant of the larger, more cynical world, which would have seen us as perfect fools, break in on our selfish ecstasy with one another.

We shut ourselves away from the city. Day and night became emptied of meaning. Once in a while we would wander out into the whirlwind of urban life, into streets swarming with people going on with their innumerable pursuits, but we felt detached from all we saw, except when looking into one another's eyes. I have no memory

of what we might have said to each other about what was happening
to us, though no doubt we felt as if we'd managed to accomplish the
impossible. That we had left this world behind.

Not some summer romancers, we fell in love under gray skies,
walking hand in hand past Chinese families gathering ginkgo berries
in the park, where within weeks the leaves would come down off the
branches of the trees under the torrents of November rain. We
kissed in dark corners and were scandalous in the back seats of cabs
that carried us in the middle of the night from my place to hers. We
made love in a corridor outside her door one impatient evening and
were nearly caught by one of her neighbors, but felt that a kind of
wholesome purity graced our every pleasure. Nothing could touch
us, we believed. Ours was indomitable love.

We were married down at City Hall before Christmas. By first
snow, an obstetrician was able to confirm Mary was indeed pregnant, and though we had predicted it, the disclosure caught us off
guard somehow. How it transpired that after such a brief passage of
time both of us had come not to want this child—at least "not now,
not yet"—remains mysterious to me. I'd wager it will always linger in
both our minds, the question of why we decided to go ahead with
the abortion. I held her hand and looked into her eyes and saw the
depths of her pain that day, as she lay under a sheet in the small recovery room in the clinic. We never discussed it after that.

I can picture Mary with such ease (her animated face and pale
cream skin framed by dark-brown short-cropped hair, resembling
with uncanny exactness the bewitching boy with pouty lips and
haughty feather in his cap in Caravaggio's *The Calling of St. Matthew*,
which hangs not far from here, in the San Luigi dei Francesi) and
would imagine she'd describe these final months in terms not unlike
my own. Because, even when we stopped agreeing about many things,
we continued to acknowledge that when we made our decision not
to have the baby, it was the beginning of the end of everything. And
though it took several years for miraculous beginnings to come to a

sorry end, it can't be said we didn't fight what simply happened to have been irrevocable. Rome was our last chance, as we saw it. We came, we tried to recapture our recent past, but the heat was gone. What kindled in its place was frustration, joyless and accusatory. Nothing we did was enough. Or, that is, nothing I did. For her part, I know she tried. But for mine, by taking up with a pretty young wanderer I met by the Barcaccia—a fountain, centered in a basin as oval as Mary's face, that depicts a flooded ship from whose marble hull water cascades through cracks and breaches—I put reconciliation out of reach for good.

Unaware of what I was doing, or why, I picked up this girl, took her home, and so delivered the quietus, as they say in the old romances. Coitus as quietus: Mary found us in bed, of course. Dreamily, cruelly, I made sure she would. And though I was furious, in my way, that she had the audacity to make the sanest possible move, which was to get away from me, from this monster we managed to become, I'm not the kind of person who would wish her harm or bad luck or anything of the kind. For her it had become life or death, really. And she thought to try life once more. For me, just then it hardly mattered which way it would go. The only decision I was able to come to was that I would make no decision. I would give myself over to the whims of chance. And if Rome was to be my little finale, all I could say was, it might have been worse.

Not that my life had been all that grand or theatrical before. Nothing much had ever gone on with me. No super-wicked skeletons rattled in my cupboard. The troubled road I mention has to do with an untidy personal life, would be a way of putting it. I'd been in another marriage before this, one between youngsters that was never intended to survive. That and the tenuous but persistent affair with a woman named Jude constituted the extent of my serious intimacies. These three mark the cardinal compass points of my adulthood. Mary—my second try at matrimony—gone. Daniella, wife the first, vanished into another improbable marriage, which has taken

her away to Jerusalem with her Protestant missionary husband, dedicated to retrieving for Christ as many Jews as possible. And Jude, always there but not there. North, south, east. An incomplete survey
of an unfinished journey, not a map one could follow with any hope
of *arriving* somewhere.

In the dusty Forum one day not long after Mary had abandoned
me, standing near what remains of those broken, evocative statues of
the vestal virgins, listening in reverie to the hundreds of bells ringing
the noon Angelus, I realized that there are times when loss is as easy
to embrace as gain. This can happen only when hope is properly subdued, hope being a great troublemaker, with its cry of *Try, try again*
and *Give it another go.* Hope was nicely becalmed that afternoon, as
if the music of the bells had purified me. In my heart I felt a peace
almost as sweet as any after the ecstasy of love. I'd failed anew,
which was in itself nothing new.

But before that? before I met Jude on a train spiriting across
France some years before, each of us living out of knapsacks? before
Daniella first said hello to me in New York, downtown at the Quad,
and asked me if I wouldn't mind moving to the left or right, as I was
blocking her view of the cinema screen? before I met Mary?

My life began in the maternity ward of Columbia Presbyterian,
July 9, 1962. My mother and father were, even for their day, quite
young to be parents. Maria Teresa had a dark Piedmontese beauty:
olive-black eyes and black hair fell straight around her subtle face in
such a way that unveiled the trace of Turkish blood which complicated her family tree—something Muslim, something Byzantine there.
Her manners, as I imagine her, were those of someone far more mature than a girl of just twenty, back in the early and still somewhat
innocent part of that uninnocent decade. First generation, she was;
the wild child, the nonconformist daughter of a diplomat—not the
ambassador's daughter, but that of some mid-echelon aide in the
Italian consulate in the city.

Likewise, my father's father had affiliations, whose meaning and responsibility I never much bothered to understand, with the foreign service, and spent a lot of time shuttling back and forth from New York to Washington, with trips overseas between. My parents were introduced in those same grand, marble mansionette rooms where so many others in the diplomatic corps met. Maria Teresa had just turned eighteen. Matthew Morgan—freckled and sandy-haired and bony—was himself in the last month of his eighteenth year. They formed their youthful confederation within a matter of days, an act that would be repeated by their son. For my parents, love at first sight—never a guarantee of permanence, as they too learned—perhaps came as an acknowledgment of mirrored isolation, the product of their general unrootedness. Or maybe theirs was at first a rarer love, unaffected by any sort of individual need. Either way, neither of them was still a virgin within a week of their introduction. So my mother confessed, in her charming way, to a nosy son who often doubled as her confidant and friend.

Both grandfathers of each family were temporarily engaged with work at the United Nations for those first years of the sixties, and I'm not straight on the details of who represented whom or in what capacity, or any of that stuff. So far as any of it mattered to *my* life, it was their momentary permanence, their provisional *staying put,* that made my entry into this world even possible. For this reason, I've always harbored a real envy toward anyone lucky enough to be born in a place, grow up there, get married and go on living there, thrive and suffer and eventually get old and die—and, yes, be buried there. Yet those few people I've met who knew what home means, by my definition, either hate it or don't appreciate it for the fateful gift it is. The thought of being able to visit your parents in the old neighborhood, stay the weekend in your childhood bedroom, know what's happened to friends through the years, up and down the block, seems like a dream come true. This is why Ash Creek, as my uncle's ranch is called—taking its name from the brook that cuts it down the middle—has always held such an important place in my heart, even though it's true that Uncle Henry himself had to venture away from it to see its real virtue. *Domi manere convenit felicibus . . .* never was there a saying whose wisdom was more eternal: *Those who are happy might best stay at home!* Even in Rome, where those words were first uttered, such an adage failed to find its way into my experience.

My father, not so unusually, would follow in my grandfather's footsteps. In every way, I might add. Which is to say that his work *worked him,* so to speak, as he and his youthful family were condemned to follow him to points around the world. He never quite rose, just as my grandfather never rose, to a position of sufficient prominence that he could make a demand of his superiors for a permanent post somewhere, an assignment that might give his family the chance to set down roots. He lingered in the middle ranks, in the same murky professional substratum where grandfather Ernest had lingered for decades, never catching the break that would allow him to stop being shuffled from one place to another. We went where the political winds carried us, and no more complained than do fallen leaves blown down avenues in Vienna, or London, or for that matter Caracas, where we passed one brief autumn after the advent of some vague cabal, some assassination, some wrestling of power by this clique from that.

My own childhood neighborhood was a cobbling of capitals. Most of them were here and there in Europe; some I've named already. No need to set down the rest of these cities, or the dates when we lived in them, and when we moved. They are something of a blur, anyway. Whenever I try to look back over those days of tutorials, or playtimes in the embassy yard behind thick walls, for whatever reason, I can't arrange the details into any kind of total pattern. It's all a disarray of half-remembered boulevards, of old statuary and mustard-colored buildings and manicured lakeside parks. It is a disorder of faces, some mustached and some mascaraed, leaning down to greet me in foreign tongues or mutilated English—*How you do you do?* or *Please meeted you,* or *Hello do you?* The only significant—that is, *telling*—pattern I can see is the blur, the smudge.

I knew, from as early as I had the means to fathom such things, that my parents' marriage had become, if not loveless, quite cool, and it was when I intuited that they stayed together less for their own happiness than for mine, I turned into a masterful little manipulator. It became of utmost importance to me that I please both my father and mother at any cost. Thus, I became *a good boy,* in the sense that I went out of my way not to be bad—whatever *bad* meant at the moment. I understood in my immature heart that the way to keep them together was to make them love me, above all, so that any consideration of breaking apart our fragile family would be seen as impossible. They'd damn well stay together, if only for my sake.

And this was how I grew up, carried around from place to place by a couple who themselves had been ferried and flown and driven in cars that never belonged to them, living in temporary rooms their nation gave them, and so forth. Only when I reached the age of eight or nine did my parents realize it would be healthy for me to have some exposure to a more stable environment, a place where I'd have a summer room I could (sort of) call my own, no matter where diplomatic work took us during the rest of the year.

My father's sister, Edmé, had met and married a man named Henry Fulton, an architect who made his career out on the coast, and the two of them had often expressed a willingness to have me as a summer resident on Henry's family ranch, where they spent their summers in the western mountains.

The first time I wandered up into their lower meadow, careful not to brush against the brash razory leaves of stinging nettles, short of breath in the meager alpine air, running up toward their ranch house with the shiny roof, I was thoroughly exhilarated. Here was a life unlike anything I had ever known. Sky bluer than any blue I'd seen, clouds more magisterial than any skyscraper or other man-made wonder, and beneath them, the ranging mountains and green valleys forever changing hues as the day aged. Sometimes, during low moments in my later years, I would find myself wondering whether my adult dissatisfaction and disenchantment weren't made keener whenever I considered the serenity my aunt and uncle and their place inspired back when I was a kid. Childless themselves, these two spoiled me with long days of honest work and honest play—of mending fences, helping with chores, building a treehouse; of evenings at the table in the kitchen playing cards, or out in the yard, stargazing, learning from Henry the names of constellations. When, in September, I returned overseas to whatever city my parents were situated in for the year, they understood, just watching my behavior, that the summer visits to the ranch were a good idea. They continued without interruption until I went to college.

My uncle had woven those three months' absence from the office into the rhythm of his work year because, he once told me, he needed distance to understand what was near at hand. And he was good enough at his art that he got away with doing things his way. He might have risen to greater prominence in the world of architecture, perhaps, if he hadn't marginalized himself with this annual retreat. But no one could say that he marched at someone else's orders, just as they couldn't claim he failed to carry his own creative weight even from a distance.

And so here I stood, newly alone in Rome, further away than ever from the serenity of those summer days, having just enjoyed my only cherished moment of the week—a moment in which often I caught a blind glimpse of old serenities—when the bells in every church and cathedral of Rome began pealing the noon Angelus. Back from the Forum, there in my cramped apartment, the bells still rang in my head, with the same clarity as when I heard them just an hour ago. I threw my head back and closed my eyes to the world and simply basked once more, if one can be said to *bask* in the tintinnabulation of church bells, relished the pure strength of history. Maybe this slow drifter who was I, this mangler of marriages and failer at any number of things, managed in this one weekly ritual only to produce the most shallow, false sense of bliss for himself. But it didn't matter to me. I loved the afternoon of the Angelus anyway, even though I knew that no one pulled on the ropes in those ancient campanili on my behalf. That was as it should be. Why should any bell resound for one who'd whittled away at every last thing that might once have had personal significance, until so little was left? I didn't harbor the slightest sorrow, however, that none of this soulful magnificence of bells was in my honor. I took the music into myself like a sacred drug, reveled happily every Sunday in the vast pealing of those bells, and for hours afterward I belonged to the continuity of history here, somehow, and to Rome itself.

That day when Edmé called was no different. After the Angelus itself ended, and the ringing was silenced and faded in invisible wreaths of sound, following the gray circling of pigeons startled from their roosts, I returned in no great hurry from Palatine to Pantheon to our, I mean *my,* flat. The telephone had been ringing when I unlocked the door, and I had that curious conversation with Edmé.

The moment of paralysis and memories by the window didn't last long, however profound it had been. An idea formed in its wake. My birthday had just gone by the month before, gone by like so much else, and the time had come for me to remedy my small misery by doing something affirmative. Any move, it seemed, would be the right move, given my current conditions. And the imponderable cry for help I detected in Edmé's voice gave me direction. The fact that hubris may have tarnished my altruism, my grand idea that maybe I could help straighten out the matters of others even if I couldn't remedy my own, didn't occur to me then. Instead, I was committed, even joyously overwhelmed by this fresh purpose which rose up, as I say, into my personal emptiness while I continued to stare at Rome's rooftops that Sunday afternoon.

Having packed some clothes, I walked downstairs to look for presents, then splurged on a cab to the airport, where I boarded a flight which would take me away from Rome. I had left, on the kitchen table where my landlady would find it, rent for the balance of the month, and a note instructing her to keep anything of mine she fancied and give away the rest to friends, charity, or the garbage men. I apologized for the abruptness of my departure but wrote, *É l'ora di andare* . . . the time had come to move on.

THE HOUSE at Ash Creek stood miles from the nearest neighbor, a man named David Lewis, who was even more reclusive than my aunt and uncle. It was the only dwelling on earth I knew which remained just as it was when I was growing up. That my fondness for the place has endured over the years, has even grown, proves my parents made a brilliant move when they decided to deliver me into Edmé and Henry's hands during those summers years ago.

Ash Creek has taken on some of the rousing grandeur of myth in my absence, and has remained for me a kind of blessed sanctuary, a refuge *in potentia,* an asylum to which I might retreat whenever my life had gotten, well, impossible. Even though I haven't visited there all that often as an adult, my room with its narrow bed by the creek-side dormer window means solace to me. Its sage and chestnut geometric stencils chasing up the walls and across the sloping, angled ceiling. Its Morris chair—almost my namesake chair—with an old russet leather pillow for a backrest. Its Chinle Indian blanket worn thin and agreeably faded, there on the plank floorboards. Its little desk still the repository of drawings I made of flowers when a kid, annotated with great care as to habitat and species. These signify *home* like nothing else in the world.

Once, when I asked my architect uncle how he managed to

envision corridors and alcoves and rooms for a building that only existed in his head, before he began to lay them down in lines on a vast
sheet of blank paper, he said, —Close your eyes, Grant.

I closed them, and said, —Yes?

—Now think of a chair, he said in his deep, familiar voice.

I thought of my chair, its armrests and how the cool dark seat was
hollowed to fit my body. —Okay, I said.

—You're sitting in the chair now?

—Yeah.

—So stand up, and then sit down again.

All right: I stood, sat.

—Feel the floor under you?

Yes, I could feel it.

—Picture the floor. And picture the wall in front of you and the
ceiling over your head.

I did what my uncle asked me to do. The wall was sage, olive,
chestnut, with abstract repeating patterns, just like in my bedroom
upstairs. So was the ceiling.

—You need some air in the room. Make a window or two in the
wall, nice big rectangular windows for the sun to come through.

I did, and the sun shone through, altogether quite real.

—Now stand again. And walk out the door into the hall.

In my mind, I did. I found myself standing just outside my bedroom, on the landing, where I leaned against the lathe-turned newel
post and gazed down the stairs along the curve of the railing.

—You outside the room? he said, interrupting my fantasy.

—Yeah.

—Well, hold on, wait a minute, he said. —How'd you get outside
the room?

—Through the door? I half answered, half asked.

—I don't remember mentioning a door. Where'd that door come
from?

I opened my eyes. —I don't know. It was just there, I guess.

—Just where it needed to be for you to walk out of the room, is that right?

—That's right, I said.

—Well, that answers your question. You created a door where there needed to be a door: that's how I do it, too.

But what I didn't tell him was that the door I walked through was not the door I imagined but the one he had imagined years before when he built the house and that bedroom in it I so cherished. What I did learn that day, because of the imagining game we'd played, was that Edmé and Henry were the principal reasons I loved the house.

Some might consider Ash Creek a lonely place. Indeed, few ever came out this way—no matter what hour it was—and, until the night visits began, none came without being heard or seen miles before they reached the hillside. This was just what Uncle Henry had in mind from as far back as when he was a boy making sketches in his head but not really knowing why, having been born on this same land and grown up in a house that once had stood not far away. Its particular setting displayed the same concern some wise Clovis predecessors ten thousand years ago might have shown, and that was with an eye toward assuring that he have a dominant view over the long, narrow valley, day or night, so that no one could appear here unexpected.

The house was traditional, arts-and-crafts inspired but with western details; William Morris crossed with Zane Grey. An honest and well-made building, stone covered with stucco and whitewashed, it had dark-green wooden shutters at every window, which were stayed with old brass hardware. Graceful plump copper rainspouts snaked down the gables from that tin roof made steep in order to prevent birds from nesting in its niches or joints. In deference to its rural solitude, there was no formal entrance to the place, though a staircase with varnished driftwood railings and river-stone risers and flag steps would get you up to the porch that wrapped two and a half sides of the house, supported by carved, weathered pillars of local ash. The edifice nestled so naturally in the landscape that one might think it had always been there. You would never guess it was occupied by someone completely conversant with the postmodernist nuances and varied postulates of contemporary architecture, unless you entered Henry's studio and saw there his maquettes of unbuilt dream palaces in odd shapes and bright colors.

Naturally, they hadn't been expecting anyone that first night the music came harrowing their peace. They rarely expected people. Not that these members of my family—all the family I have left now—had always been ascetics, solitary mavericks, or whatever. My uncle, as already mentioned, had lived a life veritably the opposite of this seclusion. He had migrated to the West Coast, where he made his name and money, and returned on his fiftieth birthday, having had enough of urban engagement—the war of ambition, as it had become for him.

With Edmé, he had circled the globe more than once, by rented car or hired *tuktuk,* by horses or caravan of camels, by airplanes— sometimes quite rudimentary, such as the retired military carrier flown among Andean peaks in Peru, three of four props turning over, the cargo door but an open void secured by a single rope, beyond and below which were marvelous blue, windy vistas—and all kinds of ships, from trawlers to liners. During those journeys, they traveled way off the trodden paths of holiday tourists, so that they knew the back streets of Comayagua better than the avenues of Paris, knew Buddhist wats in the mountains of Burma better than any Catholic mission in southern California, knew firsthand the folk architecture of Chad, unrenowned beach villages of Cyprus with their contiguous Moorish hives of bone-white dwellings interconnected by narrow twisty stairs carved in cliffs, knew the astute shanties atop stilts in coastal Nicaragua and Madagascar. They had seen more examples than most of the handiwork of man at his best. That is: engaged in erecting houses, shelters where families could sleep, work, worship. Their travel had been a passion fully indulged and had the effect of making both Edmé and Henry come to appreciate the old truism about the sweetness of home.

This past decade of relative solitude at Ash Creek was the simple consequence of a decision made one afternoon in his lair of glass and burnished steel, with its view of Coit Tower and the bay beyond. He had gone into the office early that morning, with the idea of finishing the redraft of a museum extension. It happened, he said, in an instant. He laid his pencil down on the drafting table and walked to the wide window. An orange tanker with rusted white deckhouse was churning laboriously toward port, out in the choppy waters of the bay. Gulls, aft, hovered like dirty rags dangling from invisible wires in the air behind the radar mast. As he stared at the slow progress of the ship, the idea formed in an almost physical, palpable way before him. He was finished, he thought. What he had wanted to do was accomplished, and anything more would be redundant. He had the chance at an unusual, spiritual symmetry in that he could bracket a part of his life with the same quickness and surety he had shown a quarter century before, when he'd marked his path, so to speak, with a decisive open bracket. It made sense he could arrive so abruptly at the terminus of his career, insofar as he had come upon it just as suddenly.

Henry had left to attend state university more at the bidding of his father than from any personal desire to leave Ash Creek, had done well enough there in classes but developed no ambition as such to go out and make some brilliant mark in the world. That is, not until he discovered the religion of architecture. There was a time he was fond of telling the story of his revelation, but he'd always suspected no one quite *got* it with anywhere near the impact he intended to communicate.

—One winter day, he would begin. —Deep in January, snowing hard, just plain bitter cold. One of those days where no matter how many layers of clothes you were wearing, the wind cut right through to your bones. Just after sundown, everything had gone sparkling

deep blue, a blue that seemed to radiate *right out* of the snow. As I
walked toward the library down at the far end of the commons I noticed the building was glowing, gold orange, like a melon color, and
all the windows were glowing, too. I kept walking, and as I did I
don't know how it happened but I began to see the larger planes of
the building. I'd never noticed the columns along the front before,
never saw how they were finished at the capitals and at their bases,
and how they carried their weight so effortlessly, so that you *wouldn't*
notice really. Masses, I saw. Forms. And how each part of the building, no matter how big or small, extended away from the central entrance, had its part to play, like a role in the drama of the whole
building. Well, I completely forgot about how cold it was. I found
myself tramping in the snow around every side of the place, just
bowled over by how many decisions somebody'd made, one after another so interesting, and how they all added up to the good old *school
library!* It was my only brush with the divine.

This was inevitably a moment when Henry, normally taciturn,
even shy, having revealed, as he saw it, his soul to the person listening, made either a new friend or whatever the opposite of a friend
might be. Not necessarily an enemy, but someone who would fade
back into the prodigal world of people and more people. He wasn't
altogether wrong in believing that more often than not whoever
heard this story of falling in love with architecture, his January
epiphany, would nod, smile, even allow, —That's a good story, before moving the conversation along to some other subject, and so as
time went on he told it less and less often. Edmé, a rapt young
woman with brown eyes and an abundance of chestnut hair gathered
into a French braid, had listened too, of course, when he first told
her his miniature fable, and she would happily tell you that hearing
it might have marked the moment she fell in love with *him*.

Then, after so many years of finding his own way to make those
masses harmonize, allow verticals to carry and distribute weight
without effort, coax materials and colors and forms to work, each in

roles that satisfied him, he'd come to this revelation that he had ful-
filled, or nearly, whatever need had been born that winter's evening
outside the campus library. I say nearly, because another architectural fantasy remained unfulfilled, one that had less to do with com-
missions and the construction of buildings. Designing the perfect
city was a project that had obsessed him from as far back as he could
remember, and if he got the designs right—so that harmony between
nature's needs and those of man could be discovered on his drawing board and in his models—then maybe the day would come when
he would see it made an actuality. This was nothing he spoke of
with his colleagues, who'd have scoffed or condescended, he assumed. Even he sometimes thought the project a folly (or *folie*), but
nothing would come of never giving it a chance. He would fix up the
studio across the creek from the house, then, and move toward theo-
retical design on his own. Yes, he thought: it was time for him to finish properly his other life, the one he'd known as a boy and had
eloped from—or been benignly evicted from by his father—not three
decades before.

Other considerations drew him to return to Ash Creek, too. Giovanni Trentas, for one. Henry had some difficult obligations to attend
to, he knew; unstated promises, but promises nevertheless. Time had
come to begin keeping them, or at least begin to assess whether they
could be kept.

Edmé, as I would later piece together from the puzzle which lay
before me, was meant not to know of any alliance between her husband and Giovanni Trentas, and initially resisted all this suddenness.
She had looked forward to their visits every summer to Ash Creek,
where their retreat from the world was as absolute as they wanted it
to be, but the melancholy vision of giving up city life altogether for
country was summed up when she said, —We'll go mad all alone out
there. We'll start seeing things, start talking to trees and rocks. We
have the perfect balance now, let's don't ruin things.

—You're looking at it backwards, Henry countered. —It's a

chance at freedom, more freedom than we have now, to travel, to do whatever you want. I see it as a beginning, not an end.

—As the beginning of what?

He thought about this, looking out over toward the lights of Berkeley across the bay, where he had completed his graduate work and gone on to establish his practice with a firm in the city, looking at this place that had been their principal home for so long. —If we find that it doesn't work out—

—You mean, if it doesn't work out for *you.*

Henry had no viable response, and said as much. He could only repeat that, for his part, he had reached an end, and could think of no other alternative.

—If you want to stay, he began to offer, but Edmé did not.

The firm, in which he was a partner, granted him an extended leave, but refused his resignation offer. Henry stuck around long enough to finish the projects that were close to completion, and consulted in the transfer of designs in which he had some personal interest to others who had worked with or under him. Within a few months they had closed the house, shipped everything to Ash Creek, and left by car for the long drive to the mountains.

Together Edmé and Henry began this third and probably final act of their lives, far from any crowd urban *or* rural, and set about living it, making a point of never getting in people's ways, nor on the other hand allowing others to insinuate themselves into their routine. For half a decade, all had continued without incident. During winter they often persisted in their informal investigation of the world; during summer they hibernated at Ash Creek. Giovanni Trentas continued to help Henry with the running of the place, though now of course the ranch was more a ranch in name than in function. He and his daughter had taken a cottage in town, and though she was seldom seen here, Giovanni himself remained a constant, congenial presence.

Life was good. Better than they might have expected. Indeed, life for them might have been considered ideal, idyllic, utopian. Especially to someone like me, whose path seemed, by comparison, random and vagrant—as if I were living up to my name, Grant the vagrant, Grant the migrant, Grant the nomad without a cause, gazing enviously at any crusader who at least carried a map and had some sense of objective, of bearings and goal. Not to mention a welcome place to return to when the road got foul.

MEMORABLE FOR its sculptural, resolute edges, Noah Daiches's face was that of an arbiter. Its every facet was taut, hard, firm, and his forehead soared above blue eyes that resembled a pair of turquoise earths, bright as the waters of the ocean as seen in photographs from the moon. His red-brown, fine hair seemed forever unruly, though it was freshly trimmed. Burnt-umber thin lips rarely lifted into a smile. His head was long, cheeks profoundly sunken, and deeply furrowed crow's-feet fanned out into his temples and down so far as to almost touch upon his sharp jawline. Likewise, his body was long—rangy, as some would have it—with sinewy arms and long strong legs. His clothes were invariably khaki and he wore a run-down leather flight jacket on the warmest days. Many respected him, though he had his detractors, who read his solemnity as contempt.

—Noah, Henry said, having walked down to the gate, a few hundred yards below the house at the bottom of the mowed meadow.

—Morning, Henry, Noah said, taking his outstretched hand. —I hear you had company last night?

Henry shrugged his shoulders, half embarrassed, and allowed them to fall, saying, —Come on up.

Together they climbed the mild rise of the field, which gave off a slight peppery scent in the daybreak air, Noah waiting for Henry to begin some clarification of why Edmé was obliged to call, the morning after the intrusion, from David Lewis's house. Seeing he was reluctant to talk, Noah simply asked, —You recognize them?

—No, said Henry.

—How many were there?

—I just saw one, but it felt like there might have been more.

—How's that?

—I don't know. You know how you can feel people's presence.

—Not really. I don't have a third eye like some of us, said Noah, voice edged with a mild trace of sarcasm.

—You mean a sixth sense.

—Third eye, sixth sense. Edmé says the phone's dead.

Henry walked alongside Noah and said nothing; he and Noah had grown up together in so far as they were the same age and attended the same rural school, a clapboard structure that stood on the grass shores of the river and now, though its roof leaked and windows were boarded, bore a historical landmark plaque which designated it the oldest one-room schoolhouse in the region. This freedom to gibe came from so much shared history. Here was a childhood friendship that had never matured, and just beneath its surface, just at its edges, some of the comical cruelties of youth lay in wait. The cynicism, the taunts, the derision—neither of them could help himself: it was like some game begun with a boyhood bout, like a hundred-yard dash across the schoolyard that evolved into a subtle lifetime marathon.

—Maybe the storm knocked the service out, Noah said.

—It wasn't a storm. Mild rain is all. The line's been cut.

Henry pointed with his hand to the right as he spoke, gesturing over toward the creek, which widened down beyond the gorge. The two men deviated, still side by side, toward an enormous old barn with rusted tin mansard roof and adze-hewn boards that once had been painted flat red though the paint had since been flayed by

weather, so that what remained was silvery plank siding. Along the
back of this structure, white birches and mountain willows and cotton-
woods curtained the runoff brook, which burbled in its pristine bed
of smooth brown stones. Harrows, an old jeep with a mildewy canvas
top, a vintage tractor crumbling into metal dust. They walked past
these. And they walked around behind the barn, along a narrow
natural corridor between it and creek trees, and then Henry halted.

—See that, he said.

Noah glanced at where he indicated with a nod of the head.

The line dipped at the corner of the barn, before the far end of its
catenary curve lifted back high to an impromptu pole that had been
fashioned of a dead, defoliate, and limbed tree farther down the hill.
Henry said, —I keep meaning to raise the line here. It's my own
damn fault.

—You don't even have to stand on nothing to get at it, said Noah,
who squinted at the earth directly beneath where the black cable
had been snipped away from the green glass insulator attached to
the low eaves.

They both looked closely but could see no footprint.

—I'll call the phone company for you when I get back to town,
said Noah.

—I'm sure Edmé already did.

Continuing up along the bank of Ash Creek, they passed the
stone springhouse and veered left toward the foreyard.

—Was it kids, you say?

—The one I saw might've been a kid; he wasn't too tall. It was
hard to tell—he had a mask on.

—Nobody you recognized from around here?

—I never saw the mask before, if that's what you mean.

Henry continued to play with the idea of whether or not he
should mention the effigy, the hanging, the skull head, the thing
dressed in his own clothes. He hadn't mentioned it to Edmé, in
part not wanting her frightened more than she already was, not to

mention that she'd wondered aloud, before going to town this morning, about whether it'd been a mistake to move to Ash Creek, that maybe she'd been right to be reluctant. —Listen, Edmé, this kind of thing happens anywhere you live these days, he'd argued.

But also, he had to admit at least to himself, as he'd later confide to me, once all the secrets had been laid bare, that he was somewhat embarrassed—was that the word?—certainly unnerved, by that vision in the high meadow the night before. Perhaps it had been a rash move to burn it, after all, but it seemed the best way to *get it behind him*. As if by obliterating it and keeping the matter to himself, it *almost* didn't take place. Henry did have some idea why that effigy hung in the tree, but sensed it was premature to discuss it with Edmé, Noah, or anyone else.

Noah paused as Henry undid the latch that held the yard gate to the fence post and swung the gate aside, a movement that set clanging the cluster of sheep bells attached to the rounded gate newel.

—A mask, you say.

—Well—

—I guess it's one of those things where you had to be there.

Henry said nothing as Noah walked into the grassy yard still damp from the night shower. Now he wished Edmé were here to buffer Noah Daiches. But after having made her call to Noah, she had gone into town, to buy supplies while the sheriff was up at Ash Creek, so that Henry wouldn't be by himself, though of course this was not something she would ever tell her husband. The two men crossed the yard, along the ground floor of the house, passed the double doors that led into the cellar, and climbed the craggy stone stairs which were excavated into the steep bank at the northern end of the yard.

—I'm assuming, telling from what Edmé said, it was up here, then? Noah asked, as they mounted the wide cool stone steps.

Henry said, —Let's go.

One after the other, for the trail was not as wide as a bridle path, they scaled the sheer slope, Henry first, although Noah knew the way well, had known it for years. There were many trails that would take a hiker up away from the house and back into the endless rugged woods, but this one was used most. If you stayed with the trail along the quasi-perpendicular gorge, overgrown with thicket on either narrow side, the strait path eventually descended until it paralleled the wild creek, with its clutter of monumental boulders and many virginal deep pools holding grayling and trout. Farther up was superior hunting: elk, bear, and mule deer. The two of them had in the past forged their way miles upstream into settings so elementary, so rigorous and fierce and sacroscanct, so uncivilized, as to seem brutal, even though it was they who'd carried weaponry and entered the inhuman forest with the intent of killing. After what had happened back in there several years ago now, maybe not quite that long, Noah hadn't been back up to walk this trail with Henry, and were the truth to be known, Henry didn't trek far up there much anymore himself, though once it had easily been his favorite part of the world. What before he had loved in it—its primitive shadowy floor caped so deep in pine needles that when you walked on it you were buoyed by its sponginess; its trees that died never by the hand of a chainsawer but by lightning or simply felled by rot from old age; its sudden inexplicable meadows paved by thick grasses and decorated with mountain flowers, columbine and tiny rock-blossoms—he now found foreboding, though he would never admit this to Edmé, let alone Noah. He could hardly admit it to himself. For one flickering instant, his imagination connected that earlier tragedy—well, not a tragedy really, was it, but a personal disaster for him, and of course the ultimate personal catacylsm for his oldest friend—with these present disturbances. Less connected them than vaguely considered them at the same time, over the course of a dozen paces up this first rise. The death of Giovanni Trentas and the presence of a masked hangman surely had no connection other than place. And even regarding place, if one were to think about it, the terrain higher up, beyond where he'd encountered the kid last night, up where he had found Trentas, or what remained of Giovanni Trentas, might as well have been on a different world compared to the gracious banks, meadows, knolls down here at the mouth of the gorge, so dissimilar were they. Thus, the twelfth step taken, these discrete ideas proceeded in opposite directions, having never truly formulated as more than physically contiguous. As they dispersed from his thoughts, Henry slowed and turned to see that Noah had paused below him, had hands on hips, and was talking.

—What are you, deaf, man? Couldn't you hear me?

Henry said, —What?

—Damn it, Noah said. —I was telling you to hold your horses.

—You're getting soft, Daiches, Henry said.

—Listen. Who called who for help?

—At least I can walk up a hill, man. You sit too much.

Neither smiled; it was the genus of humor that involved neither laughs nor smiles and was premised on mild diminishments that were leveled one man at another.

Henry looked down past Noah and admired the way the morning light was reflected off the roof of the house. Bright as a mirror it glittered, just the converse of this back gable, which was sunk in profound shadow. He liked the many various angles and pitches of the roof, and how the graceful column of blue and gray stones rose from the foundation along the back wall to form the chimney, rising above the peak, and could remember with satisfaction how he managed to build that chimney and the enormous hearth inside, one stone at a time, cut from his own crude quarry on the other side of the creek. He never grew tired of admiring that house, and the other structures, too, which was something he could not say about all the buildings he had designed and seen built here and there in the world. Nor did he tire of what he saw out beyond the collection of buildings, green and gray-brown bluffs and the snaking tangle of trees hugging the creek as it meandered the valley, which widened and gradually flattened out, while spreading downward and on toward the great valley beyond, and the farther range even beyond that, some hundred miles away.

—All right, let's go, said Noah, who had begun again to climb.

Within the quarter hour they'd arrived at the clearing that had been the scene of Henry's encounter. The hasty indentation in the ground, where the trespasser had made his fire, shed flecks of white ash into the air as a faint breeze stirred. Having looked around the circumference of the fire site for prints, Noah walked the perimeter of the clearing, hands in his pockets, eyes on the ground. No prints: whoever it was, was good. Or else it had rained just hard enough to wash away any evidence. Henry dragged a crooked stick through the fire pit, probing for coals, hoping Noah wouldn't look too carefully at the ashes where minuscule bits of the cloth mannequin lay unburnt.

—Which way d'you say he took off?

Henry raised the stick and pointed at a breach in the shroud of foliage centering the west margin of the clearing.

—You follow him?

—No, said Henry.

—Well, I'm going to take a look.

Noah strolled over to the breach and entered the forest on the far side. Time passed, then from some way in, he called back to Henry. Henry dropped his stick beside the pit and followed the voice.

Crouched beside an object on the ground, Noah asked, —This yours? when Henry reached him. The shoe, a man's, but smaller than would fit either Henry or Noah, seemed pathetic beneath a stand of prematurely turned quaking aspen. Its buckle iridesced and the leather was stiff, as if it had been exposed to weather through many seasons. Not only did it look utterly foreign in this diffident and fluctuating shade, but its style was strangely anachronistic. Hurled languidly out of the human universe, it ended up here, collecting rainwater and fallen leaves, useful to no one, though once, somewhere, its leather had been tanned, measured, sewn, fitted, and the finished object placed in a nice shop window, where it was admired and bought. No doubt its owner had polished it back in the days when it was worn. Henry, who made it a habit to avoid the empty sentiment of such philosophical wayfaring, caught himself considering the shoe a perfect analogue for human endeavor, then snapped out of it, glancing into Noah's eyes, which were frankly staring into his.

—I don't think so, Henry said, remembering suddenly there'd been a question asked of him.

—You sure?

Henry said, —No, of course it's not mine.

—Does it look like what the guy was wearing last night?

—I don't think so, but I couldn't say for sure.

—How'd it get up here?

—You tell me.

The search became cursory and oddly reluctant after this absurd discovery, both having arrived at the same thought that they were not accomplishing much. No more words were exchanged, so that as they wandered about, purpose diffused and some edgy haze of defeat clouding any ability to observe, the only sounds they heard were of their own rubber-soled boots breaking fallen branches underfoot, the dead measure of breezes hissing in the high boughs above them, and the piercing random lament of some distant mourning dove. Without agreeing to give up, at least not verbally, they circled back toward the house from over west, down a gradual series of meadows that in Henry's father's day had been used for cattle and sheep, through ruined drystone ingresses whose single pole gates had long ago decomposed into mulch, having found aside from the pile of warm ash no trace of any trespasser. Noah considered the discovery of the forlorn single shoe to be barely of enough interest to warrant carrying the thing back down with them. He did, though, hoisting it aloft to one side of him at the end of a stick, carrying it as you would the dis-eased remains of a dead animal, like a rabid squirrel, say, depilated by rot and stiffened by rigor mortis.

Noah agreed to black coffee at the long kitchen table. Edmé had not returned yet. They spoke of other things, what was going on in town, of mutual friends, who was not healthy and who was. And afterward, Noah left, walking himself down to his car at the old steel horsegate, the shoe in a paper sack.

—We'll just see how it goes, Noah'd said.

And Henry had nodded, wishing for all the world, once again, that he and Edmé hadn't divulged to Noah or anyone else—now the neighbor whose telephone Edmé had used might know, too—what had happened. He should have foreseen that nothing worthwhile would have come of a visit from Noah. Not because Noah was un-willing to investigate—he had come, hadn't he? and promptly. But rather because he knew himself well enough to recognize it wasn't in his nature, nor even possibly in his best interest, to accept help. He decided, if that kid, whoever he was, whatever he wanted, was brazen enough to turn up here again, it would be far easier for Henry to shoot him than ever make another search of the premises with Noah.

He was overreacting, sure, but couldn't help himself. From the kitchen window he observed Noah backing his car until it faced the rutted lane that would take him down along the creek for several miles, where it widened, fed by uproarious tributaries, and became a deepening river, even as the dirt lane widened into a road and inter-sected a county highway to town.

The car quickly disappeared into scrims of greenery. It was early afternoon. He took a tomato from the windowsill, I imagine, where Edmé had laid out a row of them to ripen in the sun. After rinsing the dirt off its bright-red skin, under the cold column of spring water from the tap, he wrenched off the pliant stem and bit into it. The tomato tasted rich and sweet and earthy. At once, his mood light-ened. He walked down the stairs, across the foreyard, and past the rows of squash, beans, carrots, peas, in the kitchen garden, through a paddock of waist-high grass that led to the rocky beach of the creek. In spring, when it had warmed enough to melt the high snows, these copious stones were burnished in cold water. By August the creek had receded, leaving a treacherous beach for the walker to negotiate. Henry knew which stones would hold his weight without rocking and which wouldn't. He crossed the creek not on the narrow footbridge but by leaping from rock to rock, and climbed the path on the far shore. There were two Henrys who lived at Ash Creek, he thought, as he finished the tomato, which he'd eaten like an apple. The primitive, juvenile, rustic Henry who lived in the tiny rivalries of youth and who moments ago could contemplate the pure barbarism of such a violent response to the boy who taunted him. And then there was the Henry he was more accustomed to, the Henry who had matured, he supposed—and this was the Henry who walked toward the glass and cedar studio that rose into view.

Here it was that he worked for several hours a day, continuing to draw buildings for his megalopolis, his Taliesen of sorts, the utopian city that obsessed him, more and more fanciful structures that would go into his supercity which would very probably never be built. Here he sat down to gaze out at the wild waters of the creek and reflect on what Giovanni's shoe—for he had come to believe that this was what Noah Daiches had discovered up on the hill, the shoe that the intruder had waved over his head the previous night before he lit out into the woods—could possibly imply. That is, what it could mean beyond the fact it disproved for once and all that the left foot of his friend's corpse had not been removed by some poor famished animal come upon the body and taken it for a lucky gift of nature. The shoe had not been there a week earlier, when last he had hiked through that nearby stretch of woods. It was a problem for both Henrys to contemplate.

TWENTY-THREE HOURS was how long it took for me to arrive at this sleepy little bus depot bathed in the dusty light of dawn. Delays and circling and connections and sitting and more sitting, all the usual tedium of travel. Hours of marching beside others under the anemic fluorescents of airport terminals, with eyes too weary to see. Hours of overhearing monotonous exhausted voices of fellow travelers in concourse after concourse. Moments of temporary resurrection as I washed my face, somewhere, during a layover. And then back into the demimonde of voyagers.

When I arrived finally at the last of these airports, a vast sprawl of runways carved into the high plains, I decided against any more flying. I still had quite some distance to cover, but it was better accomplished without leaving the earth. The bus departed the city, followed the highway up into the foothills and then into the mountains as the sun went down, so that we were soon shrouded in a consummate darkness punctuated only by headlights descending the sinuous canyons. The steady lament of the engine lulled me to sleep finally, before we crossed the continental divide, passing through places like Hideaway and Troublesome, so when I stepped down out of the warm interior of the bus and got my first breath of chilly mountain air, I was very awake.

On my face must have spread the most unguarded smile of boyish recognition. I retrieved my suitcase from the baggage hold and set out to find a café that might be open at this early hour, walking through the heart of my favorite childhood town, and as I did, warm euphoria flooded through me. Such a welling of elation, so very present and palpable despite my fatigue—such *happiness*. These were unexpected passions, which I hadn't experienced in some time.

The main street had changed, of course. The proliferation of gift shops implied what I already knew, that I was not returning to the same simple paradisal province I'd known as a child. The old five-and-dime was replaced by a store in whose windows was outdoor gear: designer mountain-climbing equipment; crampons and carabiners and bright-yellow nylon rope; a tooled-leather golf bag filled with fresh irons, wedges, woods; fancy saddles and fly-fishing tackle. Here was a natural foods store, its window papered with handbills advertising nutritional retreats and reflexology seminars, and within were bins of organic nuts and shelves of herbal tinctures. Gentrification had not completely seized the day, but I could see it was beginning to make inroads.

The bank building, with its corner entrance and its great round clock extended like an inefficient awning above, was, on the other hand, just as it always had been, massive blocks of local granite piled two stories high—still the tallest edifice in town. I passed by its sturdy facade, then entered the café next door, sat, ordered coffee, asking for what had been on the brewer longest, in hope of getting something black rather than the usual American transparent brown, coffee miming tea, then settled to consider what next to do.

Ash Creek was way too far from town for me to walk. I doubted there were cabs here, and the bus wouldn't take me any closer. In fact, I had no choice but to telephone my aunt and break the news that I'd not abided by her wishes, as she had expressed them when we spoke just yesterday in Rome, and that I had come. I could offer to check into the local hotel, I thought. Though, of course, that wouldn't make much sense, given I'd come to see Edmé and Henry, and to learn what I could about the night visits. The giddiness I felt at being back in my cherished childhood haunt began to fade.

As it happens, my apprehension was misplaced. "Grant, how wonderful," Edmé said. "One of us will be down to pick you up in an hour. Just stay where you are."

Whether it was the caffeine from the third oily cup of coffee that rekindled my confidence; or whether it was relief at Edmé's reaction to my impetuous trip that brought me careening into their solitude, wholly uninvited; or my awareness, however impudent and gauche, that the waitress, whose name was May and whose hair was the fiery orange of the earlier sunrise, had taken notice of me . . . whether it was any of these things that caused my self-assurance to swell, I don't know. But I was grateful for this quaint spirit of hope that visited me again as I sat there, for this hope that coursed through me like pure adrenaline.

My past did not have to dictate my future, I thought. How unique it might be to climb out from under the usual *guilt quilt,* as Mary used to refer to it: that steadfast melancholy, for want of a better term, that blanketed me day in and out, and had—with the exception of those first giddy months we spent together—for many years. It was what some people refer to as a glimpse, this moment. Here, now, the loyal guilt quilt had lifted, so that I sensed maybe there was something possible for me, that I might start anew, invent someone fresh in this body of mine, here in this place which no one whom I had ever harmed called home. Maybe, I thought, there could be life after Mary. Maybe I could find some way to reassemble all these tangents into some kind of coherent existence.

Even for the illusion, I was saturated with gratitude. I paid my bill, left a tip on the table, said goodbye to May, and stepped out onto the sidewalk. The clock on the bank read eight. Already, the

town was quite alive with people. May, Mary—May's name was
Mary, but shy one crucial, growling letter—it wasn't long before she
and the hope I'd been feeling were gently erased.

Henry, not Edmé, retrieved me from my muddled musings.
"That's all you brought?" he asked, swinging my leather bag into the
back of the car. "That's it," and I climbed in beside him, and we took
off for Ash Creek.

"You look well," my uncle glanced at me sidelong.

"I do?"

"You could use a haircut. Other than that—"

"You look well yourself," twisting my hair, which did hang down to
my shoulders.

"You've got to be tired. Edmé's making up your room."

"Thanks for letting me stay on such short notice—I mean, on *no*
notice."

"We're always happy to have you, Grant. You know that."

The conversation continued along these simple lines, my uncle
and I never having developed over the years much skill at make-talk.
As we spoke, I marveled at what I saw outside the window.

The sun was higher now. It spread a lazy light across the wide valley, a vast moraine many millennia ago and now a fertile expanse
of green crisscrossed by serpentine glacial streams. Small hanging
glaciers and sparkly ice faces clung to shadowy crevices and gullies
in the highest ranges surrounding this great bowl. Snow that never
melted, centuries-old slush. Magpies alit on barbed wiring. Cattle
grazed in the distance. The world was constituted of primary and
secondary colors. The bright-yellow center line of the highway, the
black of the road itself. Green upon green out across the valley and
into the sierras below timberline. Purple ridges and spires and sum-
mits. And above all this, blue. Blue-from-some-god's-palette blue. I
was awed.

Discourse between me and Henry revived once we turned off the

paved road and got onto the rough narrow winding track that edged
the marshy mountain delta where Ash Creek split into fingerlets,
then rejoined, finally to spill its racy waters into the wide, slow river
out on the broad plain. We needed *things* in order to connect.

"What's that?" I asked.

He looked to where I was pointing. "Sandhill crane," he said. "We
see a lot more of them than we used to."

"That's good," I said.

"Is it? They're only here because of a freshwater lake some developers got it in their head to dig near here."

"I thought architects loved development."

"I'm hardly an architect anymore."

"You think your night visitor's been hired by some developer to get
you off your place, maybe intimidate you into selling?"

Henry cut me off, subtly but firmly, by just not answering. I
glanced over at his profile as we were jostled by the thousand ruts
and washboarding of the road, and saw there his firmness, his Fulton
self-possession, a kind of stern restraint I had always admired in him
but also feared.

"The road's bad as ever," I offered by way of apology, and he
warmed again, remarking, "Just the way we want to keep it, all but
washed out."

"That's one way to hold traffic down."

Behind us rose a great cloud of road dust. We passed the Lewis
house, which was set far back off the narrow lane, in a meadow of
wildflowers and tall grasses. His gate was closed, padlocked. Soon
we reached the lower gate to Ash Creek, and I got out, unhooked it,
and allowed gravity to take hold and swing it down until it cleared
the road edge. Henry pulled through and braked again, once above
the gate. I rehooked the chain over the post, heard the crashing
cataract of the creek, hard by the road, whose sides were waist high
in yellow scrub. Another mile and the second gate came into view,

with its cattle-guard grating and aluminum rails. Once more he stopped, and I stepped out, drew back the same bolt I had drawn many times before, the bolt that held the gate in place, and stood aside to let my uncle drive through.

Above, at the top of the meadow, embraced by a windbreak of pines, was the house. My home on top of the world, or *almost*-home.

AUGUST LAST YEAR, that year before I made my visit, had dissolved into September. And in the wake of Noah's search of the woods above Ash Creek, September passed without trouble into October. The quaking aspens quivered in acre-long clusters across the faces of the mountains, as Edmé would recall, and between them the deep green of conifers lapsed black under the heavy shadows thrown by goliath thunderheads that would crop up in the skies, toss down wind and rain, and then fold up into nothing, or crumple beyond the peak-teeth above timberline. The nights grew cold; frost would come before Halloween.

Edmé and Henry, I gather, had by this time utterly dismissed the night music as the preposterous gambit of some youngster whose notion of fun was different from that of others. Although Henry did not reveal to Edmé anything about the hanging, and also chose not to mention to his wife the discovery of Trentas's miserable shoe, his exclusion of such information did not affect life much, since the passage of those untroubled weeks into months made it possible for Henry himself to begin discounting these details. Perhaps he had leapt to the wrong conclusion; maybe it wasn't the dead man's shoe after all, maybe the effigy strung up in Henry's own clothes was truly the work of some rowdy who didn't know the difference between simple mischief and outright, ugly perversity. Henry hadn't slept much those nights before making the search in the dark up on that knoll at the mouth of the gorge: was it possible, being frazzled, he had hallucinated the whole thing? Time passed, and as it did he couldn't help but begin to question himself on these points. He, moreover, had convinced himself that it had been wise not to fill Edmé in on various particulars. No need to frighten her. So that, when Noah had called a few days after the incident back in summer, to inquire whether there'd been any more trouble at Ash Creek, Henry remarked, —Nothing to report.

—I guess it was a prank, then. There's more goes on in the back hills than any of us would care to believe. I don't know why you two don't consider taking yourselves out of quarantine and coming on down here to live with the rest of us.

—Don't care for the company, Henry said.

—I'll try not to take that personally.

—Why not? It might do you good, said Henry, in his flattest intonation. It was a way of speaking that allowed him to turn askew some trifling bit of humor in such a way that it cut just a little.

Noah ignored this and said, —You given that shoe any more thought?

—What am I supposed to think about it?

—All right, have it your way. Let me know if our friend shows up again.

—I think you're right about it being a prank.

—That's refreshing.

—What do you mean?

—That you'd think I was right about something.

—Noah.

—Yeah?

—Let's forget about it, Henry said, and they talked a little about hunting season, the hunters who'd begun to arrive as they did every year, and so forth, before saying goodbye.

After Noah had left the ranch the afternoon of their walk high
into the woods, Edmé returned with supplies from town, including
rolls of high-speed film for her camera and two boxes of fresh shells,
one for Henry's twelve-gauge, the other for her own rifle. Having put
the food and other things away in cupboards and refrigerator, she
decided to walk down to the creek and over the narrow bridge to the
studio.

Edmé read his half-averted face, on entering this rustic sanctum,
so unutterably different from his former work spaces, with the exception of his beloved draftsman's table, the same table he had
drawn on since graduation from architectural school. Henry's face
told her it had not gone well with Noah.

—Didn't find anything, she said. Verification, not question really.

Without raising his eyes from his drawing, he said, —Even if
there had been, Noah would've seen right through it. And I don't
mean in the sense of seeing through a ruse or like that. I mean—

—Henry, I know what you mean.

She walked past the oak drafting table, as I imagine the scene,
past Henry intent upon an elaborate sketch, fat-pencil in hand creat-
ing a hatchwork of black on cream, to the bay of windows overlook-
ing a series of waterfalls. In a landscape of magnificent perspectives,
instances of nature displaying the balanced asymmetry and material
urgency that human architectural imaginations coveted and strove to
invent, this scene was her particular favorite. Its disruption of massive blocks of stone, like scree knocked loose by some great giant.
The swift white descent, throwing spray over the receptive pool,
rippled the skin of the mahogany-colored water. The constant shimmer of light, never twice the same. The waggle and twitch of droop-
ing boughs, kicked into motion by eccentric gusts created by nine
waterfalls stepping down the gorge mouth. Bobbing of rotted logs,
and taloned roots exposed along the rocky shoals. The declivities,
the variance of flora, those cottonwood cotton balls lofting seeds
here and there over the face of it all, miniature parachutists con-

signed to the whims of warm coastering thermals and cool, rising waterfall mists.

Whenever she wondered about the decision they'd made those years ago—one year for each of the falls—she had but to come over here and stand at this window. The studio was a crude but solid shanty, built by Edmé and Henry with their own hands exactly as he pictured it in his dreamy boyhood. It was, as he called it, his monument of antiarchitecture, not one nail in the building, with every joist and beam embracing mortise and tenon, the roof a jigsaw of handhewn cedar, the interior forever warm in winter and cool in summer. And, then, there was the kinetic living photograph of a window that caught in its glass the rollicking falls. Still, those few who had been invited across the creek to visit the studio never failed to ask him why he didn't fix the place up a little, and Henry's response was always the same. He liked it the way it was.

She said, —So beautiful, and left him to his work, that day last year, having brought Henry over some lunch. She returned to their house across the creek, where she wanted to develop some shots from their most recent foray abroad. Maybe later she would collect flowers for a bouquet that would brighten the kitchen table—an act that would help to dispel the intruder's presence at the ranch. Maybe she would fill the kitchen with the smell of corn bread. But whatever she did, before the sun had lowered into the serrate haze of trees along the western ridge, the man from the telephone company would have come and reconnected the line, and, for that day at least, life at Ash Creek would return to normal.

Now, a year later almost to the week, in the wake of more visits which had come in the middle of the night, I stood by the window in the studio where she had stood, having just taken a long walk with Edmé up into the gorge then come back down along the opposite bank, emerging just above Henry's studio—stood there as captivated by the natural scene outside the window as she had been last August.

"For all its magnificence, all its beauty, there isn't a single vista in Rome that can touch *that*," I said, gesturing over toward the many falls, craggy stones, multitudes of greenery outside.

"It's a different kind of beauty than you find in Rome."

Like Bellini on acid, I thought. His *St. Jerome in the Desert,* say, but without the scrawny saint, and instead of all those jagged out-croppings of barren dry rock, a vast roiling of cold water, an erupting of verdant trees. We had come inside, hoping to find Henry, but the studio was empty. During our walk, Edmé brought up the inevitable questions about Mary, my work, my aspirations, and so on and so forth—essentially rehabilitating all the subjects I had managed not to elaborate upon during her call to me in Rome. I confessed to her this time, even mentioning the wanderer of the Barcaccia and my insane flagrancy with her, since it seemed to me of no particular value to equivocate.

"I'm not very good at marriage," I said. "Some people seem to be able to do it, like you and Uncle Henry, and other people don't."

"Maybe you need a break from one another. I know you love Mary."

"How could you not love Mary. Everybody loves Mary."

"People love you, too," Edmé said.

"Mary doesn't. Not anymore. It's not just a matter of having some time to ourselves, either, I don't think."

"Well, we shall see. Things, as they say, do have a way of working themselves out. And what about the translation jobs and tutoring and all. That sounded like very interesting work."

I didn't want to laugh, but did. "Let's just say this isn't the zenith of my career, the pinnacle of my love life, as good as it gets." Edmé laughed, too, though not as disparagingly as her nephew, who con-cluded, "It's safe to say there's room for improvement."

Here in the studio I marveled at the miniature city, or whatever it was, the masterful maquettes that were situated on every available flat surface. "You'll have to get your uncle to explain what they are,"

Edmé answered, in response to my question about the colorful organic sculptures and masses of drawings attached to the walls and piled on several drafting tables.

I said, "Doesn't Henry worry someone will break in here?"

"He hasn't said anything to me if he does. Besides, why would anyone want to break in? What's to steal—some architectural ideas, some models in progress, some books?"

I had no answer, except that I wanted to broach the topic of this fresh round of night visits with her, and thus far, having been at Ash Creek for several days now—days and nights undefiled by loud midnight music or any other unusual episode—I'd been unable to get either of them to discuss the matter. In a way, I sensed I'd made my embarrassing confession, and now it was Edmé's turn to offer some revelation about what had been happening, what it was that provoked that barely perceptible cry for help I heard in her voice over the line in Rome.

"I suppose the answer to that is just another question: Why would somebody bother you at all?"

"Don't think your uncle and I haven't gone over that question more than once."

"I told Henry the other day that I thought maybe it was some developers wanting to intimidate you, get you to let go of the place."

"Well, it wouldn't be the first time that happened around the valley. You probably don't remember the Posners. Over on the other side of town. They had a good-sized ranch. Your uncle and John Posner used to be pretty good friends. I think they were over here quite a bit some summers when you were a boy."

"Maybe so," I said, trying hard to remember. "I think so, yes," not wanting to let Edmé shift away from the subject.

"They had a lovely place that happened to be below state lands and above property that was owned by some consortium of development people who had it in mind to connect the upper land with the lower and turn it into another ski resort. I guess they had it all worked out with the state. So all that stood in the way of this thing coming into being was the Posner family. I know they turned down quite a lot of money for the ranch. And then their barn burned to the ground. They lost a whole string of thoroughbreds in that fire, I remember. But the arsonists did a good job. Henry says they were professionals."

"They never got caught."

"No."

"What happened to the Posners?"

"They held out another year or so. But the harassments went on. They had a dog that had been like a member of the family, and after that dog disappeared, they settled. They got more than the land was worth, at least."

"And now the place is all pistons and lifts and fake Swiss cottages?"

"The lease deal with the state fell through, is what I heard. But I don't know. This kind of thing never went on out here when your uncle was growing up. Not when you were young, either."

"But wouldn't that discourage them, the developers? That the deal failed over there?"

"Those people never get discouraged, Grant. You tell them no, and they don't say, Well, okay, we'll go elsewhere. You say no, and they hear *maybe*. You say maybe, and they hear *yes*."

"So you think these night problems are—"

"I don't know what they are. Something tells me no."

The creek hissed and gurgled beyond the studio window as we sat for a moment, and then I asked, "What tells you no?"

"I have no answer for that," which was at least the beginning of a conversation about the visits, I thought, however elliptical was its conclusion, or non-conclusion. "You know, you really should get your uncle to show you these designs," she said, diverting us back to Henry's futuristic city.

We walked back to the house, where we found a note from Henry indicating he had gone to speak with David Lewis about repairs on the lower creek bridge, which were needed to prevent the rickety patchwork of boards-over-timbers from collapse. Edmé suggested I walk down the road to the bridge and visit them, and so I did. In no hurry, I sauntered along, thinking how happy I was to have reforged my perennial friendship with Edmé, to have talked a little, revealed some and learned some in return. Henry was not about to share so easily such conversation with me, at least not about things as abstract or conjectural as love and fear. So I told myself as I strolled down the scruffy road, hearing only the music of crickets. He had always been a restrained man. Shrewd, prudent, one who kept his own counsel. And yet his taciturnity seemed more pronounced than I remembered in times past. It would have been easy—maybe even proper—for me to worry that my crashing into their generally peaceful lives, in the hopes of helping people who had not asked for help, made them a little less than pleased with me. But, in fact, paranoia aside, Edmé and Henry had not been unwelcoming.

To the contrary, I thought—as I saw Henry waving at me from some distance below, walking back up the road, his conference with Lewis apparently over—every hour, it seemed, had been filled with congenial doings, reminiscent of those days when I lived with them during my boyhood summers. Hadn't Henry and I climbed those Bellinian rocks outside the studio window just yesterday? and fished the quiet pools there, brown oases amid the deranged white bubbling where the cold water tumbled from cliff to cliff? Hadn't we caught trout just as we did when I was a child? small spotted brook trout that fought like salmon, and which, when we had a whole mess of them, my uncle and I cleaned with knives, side by side on our knees in the pebbly shoals down nearer the house, flinging their entrails into the icy current?

We had. And before that, Edmé had me out there helping her in her garden. I had never appreciated what a wizard she is, at heart, how whatever she sets before herself to do, she does; how impressive and daunting is Edmé. The garden looked like a little Eden of tilled dirt and sturdy vegetables. A natural-born naturalist, she coaxed from the ground plants that were not supposed to thrive in the brief season which defined this zone—tomatoes and pole beans and favas—and kept a sophisticated root cellar in rotation, stocked with shelves of beets, potatoes, carrots, rutabaga. I noticed at lunch how skilled a vintner she had become, had even figured out how to extract decent liquor from mountain blueberries and juniper. After we had finished eating, we walked through the house to the back door to make our way down to the gardening shed. On the way, I noticed a remarkable photograph of a street scene in Beijing, a black-and-white print of a legless boy wrapped like a bust in silken drapery, who stared up into her camera lens with a look of angelic resilience. I realized that never had I seen Edmé in this light before: she was an artist just as accomplished as Henry. Landscapes and street life, karsts and deserts, businessmen and monte dealers, prostitutes, couples in love, greengrocers and graffitied storefronts—she captured so many different people and places in her shots. The house at Ash Creek was hung with prints of scenes from every corner of the earth. Edmé's genius and Henry's smile, when we met on the creek road, put my mind at ease once more. I was in the right place, whether or not I'd come here for the best reasons.

As ASHAMED as I am to admit it, by the last uneventful week of August I began to doubt the extravagant stories I'd been told about the night visits. I kept these growing doubts to myself, but began wondering whether maybe it was some animal that had caused the trouble. Perhaps my aunt and uncle's imaginations had gotten the better of them, I began to think—although it was true that the year before, in new frustration at a second wave of pre-winter visits, at Edmé's insistence they had quietly hired a mercenary soldier who staked out the place for a month, or six weeks, dressed in his fatigues, his face blackened with military greasepaint. He had more than one encounter with the night visitor, even pursued him using a nightscope of some sort and shot at him, but never caught him, and quit. My aunt just yesterday showed me the photograph she had taken of this young guy with hard eyes, crouched with rifle at the ready, earnest and muscled, smiling for the camera. I couldn't explain away his skirmish with the intruder, but nevertheless found myself a little skeptical.

This changed. After dinner one night, we sat on the porch and watched the bats come out from under the barn eaves to begin their ballet of feeding. We smoked our evening cigarettes—Uncle Henry joined me; Edmé didn't—and had glasses of musty port, then decided to call it a day. Before going upstairs I remembered something. Edmé owned a set of the writings of Nathaniel Hawthorne, a present her mother gave her when she was a girl. The books, bound in leather with gilt edges and gold-stamped on the spines with fanciful acorns and ornate flourishes, were kept in a bookcase in the front room. Over the years I had worked my way through Hawthorne, a project that was now nearing completion. From the beginning, back when I was in my early teens, Edmé had me sign my name on the endsheet of each volume I read, and so I developed a special fondness for *The Marble Faun,* as well as his other books, and every so often would take down one volume or another and look at how my signature had changed over the years. Sentimentally inspired by the port, maybe, I went to the bookcase that night, and so took to bed a volume entitled *The Wonder Book for Girls and Boys,* thinking, This is just your speed, Grant.

The fact is, *The Wonder Book* enthralled me. I read about the Gorgon, Perseus, and Danaë—who reminded me of Jude, for no reason other than that I missed her and remembered the time I'd brought her to Ash Creek, where she slept with me in this small bed, her strong, supple limbs woven around me and her warm breath on my neck. In the yellow lamplight I learned how some unrighteous people set Perseus and Danaë adrift in the sea, where they floated in a wicker basket until they reached the isle of Seriphus. Perseus grew up to be a handsome youth, and so forth, and as he did, the evil king got it in mind to send him on a treacherous enterprise, where he would likely be killed—at which time the king could have his way with helpless Danaë. What the king dispatched Perseus to bring back to Seriphus was the head of Medusa, a Gorgon with snakes for locks of hair, a monster who if she looks you in the eye will turn you to lifeless stone forever.

I might as well have been six, given my impassioned response to the text. The description of Medusa's brazen brass claws, scaly iron body, and venomous tongue was spellbinding. On the road to

Gorgonia, or Gorgonzola, or wherever, Perseus encounters the god
Mercury, who goes by the name of Quicksilver. The two discuss the
boy's plight, and Quicksilver advises him how it were better to be a
young man for a few years than a marble statue for a great many.
And when I read this I was reminded of the Forum and all its
broken, bloodless statuary, and how I had felt just a few days earlier
more at home there with them than anywhere else. Not so healthy,
that kind of attitude, I thought, and fingered my hint of a beard, the
stubbly mirage of a vandyke, and decided that tomorrow I would go
into town and get my hair cut short and face shaved at the barber-
shop. At worst, it would be another childhood reminiscence made
real: I wondered, for instance, if they still had their barber's pole that
revolved in its glass case like a pirouetting candy cane. My mind
drifted away from Perseus as now I studied the abstract designs on
the ceiling wallpaper, which resembled—what else?—the manifold
faces of scary grotesques.

And so, here I was, in bed alone, at night, in the middle of
nowhere, as they say, feeling apprehensive as a result of reading a
children's fantasy. I would be a liar not to admit to skittishness
whenever I heard something outside in the dark. That in my hands
was a comfortable narrative from another age did nothing to assuage
these real fears conjured by the unusual sounds—unusual to me, at
least—produced in the woods outside my window: sounds of yawn-
ing branches and tittering leaves, the susurrus of the stream like
white noise. It was so quiet, compared to those months of living in
Rome, where the noises of a cosmopolitan city rose all night from
the streets, offering me their false sense of community, even of
fellowship. But still, the dread that sometimes seized me when I
was a boy, fear that someone was watching me, had not died with
my childhood. The dark forest was alive out there, no matter what
adult rationalizations I was able to bring to bear against it.

My eyes were closed, the light still on, and I awakened myself
when Hawthorne fell from my fingers to the floor. I rolled over and

pulled the cord to extinguish the lamp. Same white noise of the creek, same white noise of the crickets, my own breath deepening as I drifted toward sleep.

What prevented it was so faint as to be unreliable. Sometimes a song will come to mind and you will listen to it, absentminded, letting it continue almost as if it were background music to your thoughts. And sometimes you will let that song go on for longer than it should, until it becomes annoying and moves from background to the fore, so that those other thoughts are scumbled like soft aural paint under a palette knife, until you admit that you have to force the song out of your mind.

What was happening to me was not unlike one of those irritating moments when the song in my head had subtly moved from the back to the fore. I suppose that my eyes were open now, when I pulled aside the blanket and sheets and swung my legs around out of the bed. The music was not in my imagination but truly wafting in from the open casement window. The softest, most ineluctable music, sweet and distant. I peered out into the night and found myself finally coming awake. Surely I couldn't have been asleep for more than a few minutes, I would have thought, but a glance at the glowing hands of the alarm clock there on the bedside table proved me wrong. Several hours had passed. The clock read twenty before three.

I saw nothing out the one window and so crossed the room to the other, the dormer that overlooked the creekside field. As I did, I felt my heart racing; I drew deep breaths in and blew out. Scanning the dark, I saw not one but two needles of white light bobbing slowly across the field on the far side of the stream. The music faded in and out of earshot. It was buried by the rushing water and complaisant chirring of crickets, then it reemerged, vague and very out of sync with the world up here on the hill.

This was it, I thought. This was what I had come for, wasn't it.

For just the briefest instant, a voice within might have asked why—
now *why* have you come here for this?—but if that voice spoke, I
didn't heed those words.

Instead, my whole concentration was focused on the field. The
lights disappeared behind a thick stand of trees, I supposed, since
they were suddenly gone from view, and so I took advantage of this
interval to grope in the dark for my clothes, get into them as best I
could, buttoning my shirt as I crept down the staircase to the first
floor of the house. I was careful not to knock down any of Edmé's
framed prints, whose glass glowed like rectangular ghosts, but was
negligent of my shoestrings until I tripped, making a crash and
catching my temple against what turned out to be the corner of the
breakfront (aptly named, under the circumstances). I touched my
forehead, feeling for dampness in the dark, but there was no blood
there, so, head throbbing, I stood again and listened, hoping I hadn't
awakened my aunt and uncle—assuming they weren't already roused
by the soft music of the night visitors. Hearing nothing, I made my
way to the front door, opened it slowly, and stepped outside onto
the porch, knelt, tied by touch the shoelaces. Palming the smooth
irregular handrail, I made my way down the steps to the pebble walk
that would lead to the gate. That is, it would have led to the gate had
I followed it. Instead, I walked due east rather than south.

The field was far more dewy than I might have imagined. My
trousers were wet from cuff to knees by the time I reached the
chicken-wire fence that enclosed the garden. I wondered whether
it hadn't rained a little during the night for the grass to be this
drenched. Step, then step, then another step, then another, raising
my foot high and carefully placing it out ahead of me, I continued
toward the creek.

Only when I heard the voices behind me, whispering, calling my
name—or was that an illusion? was it the creek making human
sounds, as it sometimes does?—while at the same time I saw the

lights again, across the creek, up toward the studio, did I realize it hadn't been all that wise for me to place myself between Edmé and Henry and their antagonists.

Gunfire shattered the empty night. This is rich, I thought, as I buried my face in the stones on the stream beach. Beautiful, perfect.

An eroticism resides at the heart of panic. Where have I read about the wondrous erections some men experience when they are about to meet death? As if death were the vixen of vixens, and the only way to pass beyond the pale was through this literal final surge of orgasmic life. The hysteria I felt there, lying beside the not-still waters of the cold brook, inspired at the same time heightened awareness and a nonsensical madness of sorts. My mind twirlygigged and fussed with all kinds of little things that didn't matter and never would matter. As I heard the laughter and shouts from across the water, even dared to raise my head to see, some hundred yards away, the flashlights of the intruders jerking as if seized by spasms, bounding across the upper field for some brief distance before being extinguished, I found myself thinking about Mary. Yes, Mary. Wondering where she had gone. If she had already found for herself my replacement. How could she have left? and so forth. Found myself daydreaming—nightdreaming, rather, though very awake—about what Mary would think if she could see me now, here, soaked through from dew and the splashing creek, not quite crying, but not quite not crying, either. Mary, I was thinking, maybe you would take a little pity on me if you could see me here—

And then it was I heard the voice breaking in on my miserable fancy, the loud voice, my uncle's voice, in a fury so harsh that I hardly recognized it, blurting out, "Stand up, get up, *get up*," as he discharged from his shotgun another blast straight into the sky, the report of which echoed back from the gorge and hills even before I was able to climb to my feet, screaming, "It's me."

"Jesus, God," I think he said before he came up and threw an arm around me. "I thought, you know, you were . . . you better go back to the house," and went on toward the footbridge.

Instead, I followed him as best I could across the creek and up the path into the ghostly meadow. "Henry?" I cried out as softly as I could, having fallen behind and wanting to avoid any chance of mistaken identities again. He didn't respond, but I heard him exclaim, "Jesus," once more as I ascended the brief acclivity of mud just by the cantilevered edge of the studio, smelling in the mist the floral cedar, which mingled with the aroma of my own sweat. He was standing beside the studio entrance, at the uppermost gable of the building, and had his flashlight trained on something there. When I reached him, expecting to witness who knows what, I stood at his side and stared, too, at the empty space where the door used to be. They had extracted it from its hinges, removed it entirely from where it had hung. A quick search inside disclosed they'd taken nothing else but the door.

"What would they want with a door?" I asked.

My uncle hushed me, said, "Listen."

We stood together in the hollow, at the empty sill, and heard the raw whine of an engine turning over, then turning over again before catching, as if fed by a dying battery. Although we could not see the main gate from the studio—lush undergrowth which Henry had often meant to cut and burn blocked the view—we could hear the rattling shocks of the car as it plunged down the road, away from Ash Creek, back toward the valley.

A cursory search up into the meadow, following their tracks in the heavy grass, failed to give us any answer about what they might have done with the door, but I believe that by walking together for those long minutes in pursuit of an explanation for what had happened, we were relieved temporarily of the burden of trying to answer the more difficult question of why. "We'll find it in the morning," my uncle said, finally, and we retraced our path to the house, which was brightly lit and looked welcoming, familiar, and safe against the pitch-black night that embraced it. That Edmé had brewed black tea was pleasing, too, unless you paused to think about what it meant. Which is to say, why make a pot of tea unless you feel assured that things will fall back into place? What bothered me, as I sipped the tea with my aunt and uncle in the kitchen, was the insight that the preposterous had become reasonable, the abnormal become normal for them. In my naïveté, I asked myself, How can we sit here like this? How could someone be expected to put up with such brazen contempt? How should I have answered, really, that question Edmé first asked me when I climbed back up the stairs to the bright veranda, around whose white halogens moths and midges and all sorts of other airborne insects hovered, the simple question, "Are you all right, Grant?"

"I'm all right," is what I had said. But I wasn't *all* right, and moreover understood that nothing was all right here. "I hadn't realized Henry was shooting in the air, so I took a dive half into the creek in case he thought I was someone else," I continued, by way of explaining my soaked, muddied, torn clothes. When I ran upstairs to change, I glanced at myself in the mirror and saw that the welt on my forehead was already purple; my hands, too, were cut and mildly bruised.

". . . their way of declaring you have no secrets you can keep from them," I overheard Edmé saying, as I came back down to the kitchen—a comment which all these months later I would find myself plumbing for deeper meaning than I might have guessed just then.

"What's that?" I asked, taking a chair.

Edmé answered, "I was just telling your uncle why I think they took that door off. Since they didn't steal anything valuable and didn't vandalize anything in the studio, they just wanted to make a little gesture. It's how they seem to do things—crude but subtle.

Here, put this on your forehead," and she handed me a dish towel bundled with chipped ice.

I thanked her, pressed the ice pack against my temple, and glanced over at my uncle, who had said nothing. What would remain with me during the day that followed was not my trivial injury, nor the eccentricity of the vandals' performance, nor even thoughts of what Edmé could have meant by her interpretation of the stolen door. What would return to me was the blanched cast of my uncle's face *in response to* that interpretation. I had known Henry Fulton for many years now but never had seen his eyes turn that blankly inward in their gaze, nor the corners of his mouth draw into such a scowl. That look would return to me, as would what we found, instead of the old door, down at the main gate the next morning, when Henry and I walked there.

As we approached, we could see that the intruders in their hurried exodus had left the gate wide open. But they'd left something else, too. A piece of paper was tacked to the gatepost. It waved lazily in the light breeze that ranged up the valley. We could make out the black lettering scrawled across the paper, even before we reached the gate.

Tell the truth, the note read.

LABOR DAY had always meant change at Ash Creek. And change had always been marked with a feast. In times past, the party was a farewell to their friends and acquaintances, before they returned west for nine or ten months, to their reengagement with city life. But when Henry reached his *crise de coeur,* his *crise de croyance,* or whatever precisely it had been, and he and Edmé moved to the mountains permanently, they found the Labor Day feast habit was impossible to break. And so when September came around, Edmé made all the invitations by rote, and both found themselves preoccupied with getting things ready for the annual event. I found myself caught up in these preparations and even excited at the prospect of the great party, which I'd always been forced to miss as a boy, because I had invariably been shipped back overseas for the beginning of school.

The kitchen smelled sweet with zucchini bread, and tart with homemade gazpacho, days in advance of the party, and I helped Uncle Henry clean the year's worth of stray leaves and other debris that had drifted into the enormous barbecue which he used only on Labor Days but which otherwise stood, like some squat cenotaph of cement and brick, in the upper corner of the yard. The grill, fashioned from an old steel bed frame and blackened with char, we chafed with wire brushes and washed with cheap vegetable oil. I made a pile of split wood behind the venerable structure, then asked how long the barbecue pit had been here. "I built it back in the year they discovered fire," he said, without the slightest grin on his face.

Which made me laugh a little, but also wince. And this is why. Because I loved my uncle Henry, wanted to laugh at his jokes, no matter how ridiculous or flat they were, and because he had become for me as much my father as my own father had been. Because I didn't want him to be wicked or wrong in anything, to have any faults, to err—be human, I suppose, is what it comes down to in the end. Why not? For the same reasons most sons want to believe their fathers are, at least to some essential degree, honorable, benevolent, noble, and so forth; are *good*—like daimons who perhaps will be there for us when we sons make such a mess of things. If my father were still alive, I might well have been spending this month with him and with my mother, too. But they died, my parents, in the most archaic possible circumstances, aboard a cabin cruiser that sank. Perished with a delegation of people in, of all places, a harbor, in calm water, October 1988, seven years ago next month. They died in "suspicious circumstances," given that the passengers were representatives of countries some of which were involved in political enterprises not popular with what my father called *the fringe*. Nothing was ever proved, though some men were arrested.

Was it callous of me not to develop any interest in vengeance or the quest for justice? My orphaning affected me differently than Jude thought it should. Jude, who I was living with at the time in New York, wanted to see me sue the government for negligence, or something like that. But what I felt was mortal resignation more than outrage or inspired grief. All I saw was that my parents were gone. They who had stayed together for my sake for a number of years, then found something valuable in one another again, after I wandered off to make my own life, so that their marriage was renewed and rejuvenated for at least a time before the accident. Now it was dissolved in murky water, and I was alone. That is, except for Edmé and Henry.

When I brought Jude here to meet these surrogates, I had built up such an impossibly fabulous image of my aunt and uncle that Jude might fairly have expected to meet divinity; I worshiped them both. And Jude, I remember well, was not disappointed. For all my devoted embellishments, she found my aunt to be, —Amazingly *sane,* which was, in Jude lingo, a compliment of the highest order. And as for Uncle Henry, she had no compunction in assuring me that if he were just a few years younger and unmarried . . . well.

Which brings me, circuitously, to my wincing. I winced because that morning when Henry and I walked back up to the house after the discovery of the *Tell the truth* note, I sensed that I'd witnessed a flaw of some kind in my uncle, a deficiency or even worse; that something here was more wrong than I might have suspected. Nor was my apprehension diminished when Henry folded the note, slipped it into his shirt pocket, and asked me, in a voice thinner than usual, "Grant, I'm going to ask you not to mention this to your aunt."

"No problem," I said.

"It's something I have to take care of myself."

No problem, I thought to say again, and I wanted it not to be a problem. However, for the few days subsequent to that single oddest pact my uncle and I had ever made, I felt awkward whenever he and I were alone together. Maybe I was afraid he would again take me into his confidence, which now I did and didn't want. But my nervousness passed away under the incremental currents of other things that seemed to rise, one after another, into view, distracting me in such a way that Rome seemed farther away in space and further in time than it actually was. My past was beginning to look simpler than my present.

First among these other things was Mary's letter. My heart began to pound when Edmé handed it to me, having driven as she did every several days down to the end of the creek road, where the rural route mailboxes stood, battered bright mini-Quonsets secured to a crosspost that resembled the skeleton of a crucified puppet. Mary knew me too well, I thought, as I thanked my aunt, left the house, descended the steps, and walked west toward the high saddle of grass and scrub where I could be alone.

The envelope didn't have a forwarding notice on it from Rome; no—she had known to send it directly here, had known I wouldn't last long by myself in Italy. I found an outcropping of rock to sit on, and faced east so that it was possible to look down across the cradle of the valley which the creek bisected, see the great barn several hundred yards below and the house to its left, and the other buildings, even the cabin where my uncle was born, near the gate, a ramshackle structure that had not been lived in for half a century but which in its way was the spiritual nucleus of Ash Creek. Tucked into the foliage on the opposite bank, Giovanni's own small hut stood, and I could even see a corner of the roof there from this high vantage. I inhaled, looked down to what I held in my hands, exhaled. Enough of what lay before me; let's see what was gone.

The letter was handwritten. Blue ink on white paper. I hoped, I must admit, that Mary would offer some chance for reconciliation. A breeze from the valley breathed on my cheek.

Dear Grant, it read, *I figure this is where you might be, and if not, assume Edmé will forward it to you in Rome if you're still there. As for me, there's no point in being coy. The postmark is right. I'm back in Seattle. What goes around comes around, right? Bainbridge Island is where I need to be for right now. All the old familiar faces, and all that kind of stuff. What I imagine you are also seeking. I am writing to tell you I don't feel so hurt as I did before, and I feel bad about some of what I said that night in Rome. I was hurt, as you well know. I was angry and lashed out. You are and always will be someone I love—*

Here I glanced up into the midafternoon light playing across the fields, noticed briefly the darker patches below me, where the bales of hay had been removed onto old wagons and taken away about this time yesterday. Ambiguous as to whether the hope I had just felt for the words of reconciliation I probably now would read was wise or foolish, I wondered: Did I really have the courage to work things out with Mary? Then I read what followed.

—*someone who will always live in my heart, despite what's happened. But as you seemed to figure out long before I did, love just isn't enough to hold us together. I have hired a lawyer. He's a nice guy.*

My own arrogance made me quiver with revulsion for having so completely misread her pledge of love.

I've told him that we don't own very much, we aren't "thing" people. That we don't have any property really to contest. He says it isn't very orthodox for a couple seeking divorce to share the same lawyer, that it can be seen as a conflict of interest and all, but I told him we aren't very orthodox and that we have no interest in conflict. You know, like that. He needs something in writing from you, though. Or if you want to give him a call, I'm enclosing his card. I propose we just split the filing and whatever other legal costs there are. I don't want anything of yours, and it is my guess you are of the same mind. Grant, I'm sorry this didn't work out for us and am willing to accept part of the blame. I know you think that if we had the baby those years ago things might have turned out different. But there is no saying now. What's done is done. There were some wonderful moments that I'll always cherish, and it's those times I want to remember. The rest will fade into dust, as it should. All I want back now is my freedom. It's a sad thing, but for the best. I know I'm not telling you something you don't already know. Let's keep things simple by making any other communications through the lawyer. Please give my love to your aunt and uncle. And, Grant—take care of yourself. Love (a hard habit to break), Mary.

Freezing hot and scalding cold was how I felt. As if I had a fever. When I rose to wander back down to the house, a dizziness forced me to sit until my head stopped swirling. Got up again, and a sere riptide of unidentifiable sentiments carried some ruptured part of me away with it, so that I might have sworn the person who descended the hill was not quite as whole as the one who had climbed it. I wrote a letter to her lawyer that night, informing him that whatever Mary wanted was agreeable with me, warranting that whenever he required my half of the retainer he had only to write me in care of Ash Creek and the money would be forwarded straightaway. I set forth the somewhat contradictory position that because I loved Mary, I had no intention of disputing any details of the divorce—though I did hope he might be able to file on grounds of incompatibility, or irreconcilable differences, or whatever was permissible, something that suggested our mutual failure rather than blamed the collapse of the marriage solely on me. The glue of the envelope, needless to say, tasted bitter when I sealed the letter. Edmé and Henry, bless them, got nearly as drunk as I did that night, and were both blustery and outrageously sanguine about how bright my future would be, once I got over this and was able to move forward with my life. Not one of us had a bad word to say about Mary.

For all the hopeful inebriation of the prior evening, the next morning found me under an extravagant cloud of defeat. Nursing my hangover, I borrowed the car and drove into town to make good on my promise to myself about a visit to the barber. My blue mood brightened as I entered this little realm of remembrance. The tile wainscots, mirrored wall, burnished chrome, and the brown vinyl of the classic swiveling chair. The polychrome bottles of tonic, oil, pomade, and the metal combs marinating in indigo liquid; all the elixirs and instruments of the trade standing in rows magically doubled by their reflections in the mirror. These sights and perfumy smells, the echoey quiet, and my old barber's words, "What can we do you for today?"—yes: *you for*—combined to make me feel, though an outsider, at home. As I sat in that chair and was shrouded in a white shawl, I caught sight of myself, however, in the mirror, and this spell of comfort was broken. I found myself bewildered about who was staring back at me.

"Well?"

I snapped to, said, "I want to look different. Just take all this hair *off*. And let's go ahead and shave this, too," running my hand over the sparse growth on my cheeks and chin.

"You got it," he said, and went to work.

How sunken my eyes appeared. My nose seemed more bladelike, my lips narrower, pallid, more downturned than how I'd maintained them in my imaginary self-portrait. My green eyes were liquidy this morning, and reddened along the rims. And my skin was darker than usual from being out under the sun, I supposed, a component that gave me my only real intimation of health. No doubt the binge of the night before didn't help matters, but this Grant who began to emerge, as the backcombed tangle of hair fell to the marble floor, was someone I—like the barber—had a more difficult time identifying, accepting as being *me*, than ever in the past. Christ in heaven, I thought.

The barber went about his business. His friends, retired men who whiled away the day with him discussing whatever motes of gossip happened to be in the air, disappeared behind their buntings of newspaper. Soon he finished, laid hot towels over my face, shaved me with a straight edge, talcumed me, finally lifted away the sheet. I couldn't bring myself to look again in the mirror.

"Say, you're Henry Fulton's nephew, aren't you?" he asked, as I paid.

"No," came out of my mouth, and immediately with that lie arose my recognition that I was involved in some process I felt uncomfortable with—something to do with resisting the burden and responsibility of *belonging* somewhere.

"You look just like him. He used to come in here years ago."

"Sorry, you're confusing me with somebody else," I said, thanked him, and left for the post office to certify the letter, and after, driving back toward Ash Creek, across the base of the vast bowl, away from town, nestled against one wall of mountains, toward the east-

ern range, I discovered that what I understood about myself was not
unlike this concomitant emptiness I saw before me. Maybe it was
the most insipid epiphany of my life, and one almost impossible to
describe. Nevertheless, its upshot was this: Apart from the night visits, which still held angry fascination for me, and other than those
three words scribbled on the piece of paper my uncle and I kept hidden from Edmé, nothing much held me here. However vague or subtle were those compulsions to stay, the freedom (*that* word again) to
leave had even less purchase on me. I didn't want to become my
uncle's keeper, so to speak; but my own life was so stalled that by de-
fault I thought I would stick around for another week. Certainly, see
the Labor Day feast through. If nothing arose to suggest I should remain, I would take off. Toss a leaf in the air and see which way it
drifted, then follow. In a life notably disconnected, never had I felt
so extrinsic, so scattered.

And yet, look at Edmé coming down to greet me, and to help me
carry up to the house the couple of boxes of food and drink I had
bought for the feast. Look at the wide smile on her marvelous face,
look at that endless strand of hair that has come loose and hangs ele-
gantly, tracing the edge of her face down to the long, narrow neck.
Just look at how bright is the red of her sleeveless blouse against the
green of the woods behind her, how sharp blue her jeans are in con-
trast to the yellow of the mowed field. She walks with vivacity, and
says, "The new Grant, I like it," inspecting me from the side, her
hand on my shoulder. "I like it."

And I think, modifying my earlier impression, Well, not *everything*
is adrift. No, not by any stretch.

The nights before the party passed without any disturbance, and
Uncle Henry measured, cut, glued, braced, planed, and hung a
plank door to replace the one that had been stolen. I already had
gleaned some understanding, by watching this process of violation
followed by recovery, about how it was possible to then move toward

a kind of defiant refusal to dwell on the night visits, almost to forget they happened. It made sense to me. Time passed, and some of the acts that transpired in its fragile embrace passed, too.

Why the name of Helen Trentas, which appeared at the end of the list of those who were attending the Labor Day feast, caught my attention is not hard to explain. She had always been a figure of mystery, to my mind. Given that her father, Giovanni, had been my uncle's dearest friend, as I have said, I have always found it a bit odd she wasn't more a presence or part of life at Ash Creek when I was there. But Helen Trentas was always elsewhere. —Helen's with friends in town, I would be told, or, —She's not feeling well today, but wanted so much to come meet you. For years running, she had been sent to stay with some uncles or other relatives of the Trentases in the small town of Velletri, in the Alban hills near Rome, a fact which sometimes made me think that if I ever met her, it would more likely occur in Italy than in the States. There had always been something that prevented me from encountering this person whom I might have considered a distant cousin in the extended family of Henry and Giovanni's friendship.

But on Labor Day afternoon that would change, it seemed. Also, I would have the chance to see some others I had met in years gone by, such as Noah Daiches, whom I went hunting with when I was in my teens, alongside Trentas and Henry, on my one abortive attempt at that lurid sport. There was David Lewis as well, with whom I had only the most passing acquaintance, however nearby he'd always been.

The early clouds that had festooned the peaks of the mountains burned off by noon, and I found myself in a genuinely good mood, as if the celebration of the end of a disastrous summer might be just what I needed in order to make my way into the promise of fall. The kitchen was a tumult of cooking, Edmé presiding over all manner of pots, bowls, and cups, cutting strawberries, preparing cold bean salad. We had decided that since the clouds had been replaced by a hard blue sky, the festivities should be held on the lawn below the long porch. Henry and I carried several folding tables out from the cellar, spread them with tablecloths, and set up chairs around them. Bottles of Coke and beer were stood in big buckets of ice, and bottles of wine were left on a table in the shade. We lit the fire and went together down to the creek, where we caught a creelful of small trout to add to the mixed grill of ribs and chicken. And by three that afternoon, the cars began to arrive and guests colorful as chips in a kaleidoscope could be seen coming toward the house. Children ran; dogs chased one another. Men and women walked with baskets of fruit, potato salad in bowls covered with foil, cold casseroles, various other contributions to the feast. There must have been a couple of dozen people who turned up for the gathering: some friends of the Fultons, others who had worked here from time to time, though mostly in times past, and even others who were friends of friends. I met more than I would ever be able to attach names to, though a pair of identical twins, Sandra and Andrea the poor girls were called—who would, by the time they reached school age, metamorphose into Sandy and Andy—I accompanied, along with a little boy who seemed mute, to the stream, which they proceeded to lash with willow limbs. "Take *tha'* an' *tha',*" they cried together, whipping the fast surface of the creek until one of the dogs mindlessly tumbled forth from the thicket of brush, across the bristling shoal, to splash headlong into the water, soaking the twins, who began to cry, then laugh, before they ran back toward the house, while the boy and I trailed behind. The adults stood in groups with their drinks and talked while the other children, some rather old for such games, I might have thought, played tag, their hair gussied up with crepe paper removed from the decorated tables, skipped and howled, kicked a ball in the sunlight back and forth across the divoted field, raising marl chalk like djinns' mist. The place was converted from calm to hilarity within a matter of a quarter hour. The valley filled with pleasant shouts and shrieks and squeals. The radio, which Edmé brought out onto the porch above the lawn, played some improbable classical music, like unidentifiable Berlioz or a piano trio of Arensky or some such, which would later give way to country western, once someone who cared one way or another about such matters had drunk enough to slip up there and change the station.

She who interested me most showed up last.

She came walking up the mild rise like a dark Botticelli, her feet not planted upon a seashell but veiled slightly in ocher dust, long hair neither rosy blond nor configured so as to hide her but willowy auburn flowing over one shoulder, which itself was covered in embroidered drapery, a dress that swirled below the knees and was cinched at the waist by an old Navajo belt with hammered silver disks. A potpourri of necklaces, clay and silver, hung around her neck, and a pair of ankle boots completed her funky, elegant outfit. She seemed familiar to me, of course, from a photograph that was taken half her lifetime ago—a framed photograph of a dark-eyed little girl who stood boldly holding hands with the men on either side of her, Henry on her left, looking straight into the camera, Giovanni on her right, gazing down at her with pride. The photo was in my uncle's studio, on a shelf otherwise laden only with books of his trade, and as recently as the day before, when I helped Henry rehang the door, I'd studied that image of the girl in the antiquated pinafore, blouse with a lacy collar, and floppy ribbon which gathered her hair just behind one ear. I knew at once who she was, then, this woman walking up the hill, and although I can at times be very shy, this was not one of those moments. Midsentence, midword, I found myself abruptly carried away from a dialogue with somebody's cousin or nephew, caught as if by some invisible thread, and I walked to the gate at the fence that divided lawned yard from field, then through it to meet her in the meadow. She was carrying a paper bag, and I said, "Can I help you with that?"

She smiled, and handed it over. Her eyes were not black, as they'd appeared to be from a distance, but were the darkest hazel. They were eyes in whose gaze one could discern a spectrum of spirits at play—here was a young woman who even before she spoke one could see was simultaneously wary but fearless, haunted but pragmatic, virtuous but mindful of what might be seen by others as forbidden. I was so swept away that I had literally to shake my head to clear my thoughts. She looked at me straight on, without blinking, with such disarming boldness that I found myself staring hard elsewhere.

"I'm Grant," I said, glancing askance, "and you're Helen Trentas, aren't you."

We walked side by side toward the house. The partygoers made a genial conversational medley of voices and laughter in the mild air.

"I can hardly believe the curse is finally broken," she said.

"Sorry?"

"I thought there must be a curse some witch placed on us a long time ago that barred us ever from meeting." She smiled sidelong at me, and I saw again the sweet ominousness, that formidable spirit that flashed there: how else to put it other than that I sensed, however capricious or infantile or fervent it may seem of me to say so, that we were *meant* to meet, and this afternoon, not a moment before. Her mention of witches and spells seemed to me appropriate, given the swelter my head was in.

"You've introduced yourselves," Edmé said, taking the bag from me with one hand and extending her other hand to Helen. "How are you, Helen?"

"Edmé," Helen said, and kissed my aunt on the cheek.

I was struck by the formality of these gestures and tones.

"You didn't need to bring anything," Edmé said, looking into the bag at a couple of bottles of chardonnay and some freshly picked mint with small stalks of purple flowers at the crowns of each.

When we three strolled to the table covered with red checkered oilcloth, where Edmé set Helen's bottles beside the others, I asked her what she would like to drink, poured her some wine, and refilled

Edmé's glass, and Helen and I moved out into the crowd. Her presence at my side was bewildering, somehow, I must admit—it was as
if I were telescoped in time backward, back toward some fresh juve-
nility that caused me to scrutinize myself, my gestures, the way I
would lift my glass to my lips and drink, the way I'd swallow. It was
not something I was used to, nor was it particularly desirable, since I
envisioned these Labor Day revelries as a chance to unearth some
clue, maybe witness something suspicious and thus discover who,
and what, was behind the night visits. Helen Trentas sweeping me
away into dreamy postadolescence would not, of course, do much
for my capacity to focus. In fact, she was saying something to me,
asking me what brought me out to my aunt and uncle's. "I'd heard
you're living in Rome."

"I was," I said. "But now I'm not really living anywhere."

"Is your wife here? You're married, aren't you? That's what I
heard."

"You heard a lot."

"Actually, I tend to hear very little."

"Because no one tells you or because you don't listen?"

"Both," she said. "You still haven't answered the question."

"My wife and I are in the middle of a divorce."

She looked down, and said, "I'm sorry."

"It wasn't meant to be"—again that commonplace, the same I had
offered Edmé the week before from Rome. "That is, it's something I
don't seem to be very good at—"

"Marriage?"

"Well, that too. But I meant, explaining why we broke up."

Helen Trentas said, "I didn't ask for an explanation. I just said I
was sorry."

We walked into the crowd, and I smiled to see Edmé taking shots
of the children, even as she shepherded her guests, made sure they
had drinks, told them which table they were to sit at. Henry tended

to his work at the brick pit, where Helen tentatively embraced him, and he her, saying, "You look beautiful this afternoon."

"Sometimes the eye of the beholder's blind."

"He's right, though," I said.

"That's enough of that," she said, and as she did, I inferred something fundamental about Helen Trentas: she was, for whatever reason, a catalytic person, one who provoked change, some sort of reaction from others, whether she intended to or not. I don't even now believe my wobbly imagination was telling me lies, or manufacturing half-truths, when it speculated that others in the immediate group had moved either *toward* or *away from* Helen and me, as we made our way up the slight rise toward Henry, where he stood between the postern of the garden and the grill. It was subtle, the movement, and continued through the course of the afternoon.

What brought it to mind just then was that I couldn't remember ever seeing Henry Fulton happier. A remarkable contentment spread on his face as he stood there, his arm around the shoulder of his late friend's daughter. As interesting to me, though, was how Helen Trentas returned his affection only to a point. When Henry asked her, "So how has everything been?" her answer of simply "Fine, I guess" carried within it some message that I could not understand. She seemed to me relieved when someone, whose name I failed to get, joined our group to continue with the discussion about national politics, about which I was completely in the dark.

As this person talked, capturing at least superficially Helen and Henry's attention, I stared with abandon at Giovanni Trentas's daughter, glancing away only whenever those eyes of hers darted toward me. Soon enough, my uncle asked me to tell the others to bring their plates, the feast was ready.

"I'll come along with you," Helen said.

"You don't think Grant can handle it himself?" my uncle asked.

"Who knows?" she laughed. "I'll find out."

"Very funny," I said, as we walked to Noah Daiches, who was standing with his wife, Martha, and announced supper, then moved along to the next group. David Lewis (whose mane of black hair was drawn back into a ponytail, a small embodiment of liberalism quite untoward in this part of the world) stood with a woman whose silk cardigan and flounced dress seemed *haute* among all these jean shirts and dirndl skirts, among bola ties with elaborate slides—lapis, coral, turquoise—and great silver aglets that sparkled like bantam stalactites at the ends of woven leather cords. This woman, whom I had not met yet, gave me her hand and introduced herself, and as she did I noticed Helen drop behind me some, almost as if she were reluctant to speak to "Mrs. Tate, Willa Tate, and you are?"

"I'm Grant, Edmé and Henry's nephew."

"Good to meet you, Grant. Hello, Helen," Willa Tate said, gazing around my shoulder.

Helen nodded, I saw from the corner of my eye.

"How have you been?" Willa continued, as if I weren't there.

"All right," Helen said.

"I wish we saw you sometimes up at the house. You know you're always welcome. Won't you come for dinner sometime?"

"Thank you," was all the response she made.

"Time to eat." I smiled at Willa and noted the shiver about the dark painted lips and some sadness that toyed at the periphery of her eyes, which were dark and shaped like lilac leaves, open and of an intelligent arch. Her hand, after she let go of mine, left with me an impression of physical strength. Her even voice was edged, guttural, perhaps with a cigarette rasp, although she seemed not to smoke. She was a handsome woman, with pale, fragile skin whetted by time and tautened by willfulness, or so I guessed. A force, a presence, Willa was anything but willowy.

Helen Trentas, who had seemed diffident and unsettled during their exchange, was once more poised the moment Willa said, "Again, very nice to meet you, Grant," and left us.

The company sat at many different tables, the children sitting on blankets laid on the grass. At the two tables nearest mine, Edmé headed one, Henry the other. I may as well admit I was crestfallen, to use that nice old word, when Helen Trentas, demure but smiling her half-smile at me as she drew back a chair there, sat at Henry's table in the upper yard near the grill, along with Martha Daiches and David Lewis, rather than my own. These three tables, at the edge of the others, were arranged so that Edmé's was closest to the foot of the stone steps that led up to the house, Henry's was above, and I sat with my back to the garden and the creek beyond, which rustled like raffia. David Lewis's wife, Jenn, Milland Daiches, and Graham Tate—called by his surname only, it appeared—sat with me. Over Milland's shoulder I could see Edmé talking with Willa Tate, while Noah listened, passing the bottle of wine as the purple shade of the house began to envelop them, the afternoon creeping steadily toward evening. David Lewis's black quirt waggled at me, while he engaged Helen Trentas and Martha Daiches in conversation, as Henry looked on, now and then oddly staring, or so I thought, at Helen. For myself, I was soon enough drawn away from my little dreary fantasy of disappointment, into a dialogue I did not really want to have with Tate, toward whom, within minutes of shaking his large hand, a hand in which my own seemed frail and worthless somehow, I developed a dread which might have been irrational, had I not been prepared to dislike him during a brief conversation I'd had earlier with Edmé. Labor Day, she'd told me when Henry was out of the room, was the only time during the year that Graham Tate and Henry Fulton were willing to stand together under the same sky. Every other day, she went on, they had difficulty acknowledging each other's presence.

What was the conflict? I asked, and then Edmé seemed to want to back off. She conceded that the enmity was old, involved misunderstandings, she insinuated, between the two of them that dated back to days when they were growing up in the valley here. It was a story for another time, maybe, she said. But she wanted me to know, in case Tate used the occasion of my visit to some advantage. I'd nodded, but wondered what Tate could possibly say or do to gain any edge over my uncle through the likes of me. Edmé finished with some mention of Tate's obscene wealth, and how she suspected he always had it in mind that to take Ash Creek away from Henry would be a fine piece of satisfaction. "How could that ever happen?" I asked. She said, "It couldn't," though again I had to wonder at just who this man was and how he might fit into any theory about the night visits.

So now I had shaken his hand and sat with him to eat. I'd intended to watch his interaction with my uncle, but failed to see if they'd even spoken. "I understand you've just come from Rome," he said to me, however, removing the fillet of one of the trout from its skeleton of white bones no thicker than whiskers.

I said yes, coming forward from my wash of thoughts.

"We visited Rome some years ago," he said. "Willa seemed to like it."

"And you?"

"Me, I found Europe depressing, nothing more than ruins, ruins and ruins, restored ruins, ruined ruins. A vast graveyard compared to where we live. Imagine a whole continent smelling of mildew and diesel exhaust. Even their air is full of death—"

"Mildew is alive, actually," I whispered.

"And what about the saints and bishops behind glass in the crypts of the cathedrals? They call us barbaric, but what sort of civilized people would want to worship in a place where putrid old skulls and bones are on display?" Deft, he lifted the moist spine and crispy head of the trout free of the other fillet and laid it aside. My eye followed the golden-black roasted eye of the fish and for a moment I marveled at what amazing things that eye had seen during its brief time alive in the creek, then smiled to myself at Tate's deboning a dead beast in order to feed on its flesh, while diatribing about the ironies of spiritual nourishment occurring in a church full of bones. Tate apparently could read my mind, and said, "You find that amusing, I gather, but both civilized *and* barbarous men have to eat, don't they, Grant."

"I don't understand what you mean."

"You probably think I'm an isolationist or uninformed or what have you, but if you give it some thought unprejudiced by centuries of their continuous self-aggrandizement, you might see there is something to what I say. Not that we, in this country, are all so much more refined than they in Europe. It's just that here we *know* we're savages, and there they believe otherwise, and for myself I prefer the pure to the hypocritical savage. A little less vicious, somehow, less wicked." Tate finished his wine, then said, "I didn't like Rome," which I understood to mean, among other things, that he didn't like those who *came* from Rome recently, either. I turned to Jenn Lewis, and asked, "Have you ever been to Europe?" hoping to bring in another point of view that might dispel the sudden quiet that came over our quartet by the garden.

"No, I haven't," she said, and Milland Daiches said, "I haven' neither. I'm no traveler. Never was. Other places just don' interest me. Why go somewhere where nobody knows you and you don' know nobody?"

"My mother's family came from Italy," I said. "So maybe I can't be objective about it."

Tate asked me how long I intended to stay at Ash Creek, and I said I wasn't sure. "Well, I think it is good of you to visit your aunt and uncle, them being up here alone so much."

"They're doing *me* the favor of taking me in."

Jenn said, "Good people, Edmé and Henry."

Milland Daiches, I noted, remained quiet now, childlike, as if waiting for direction from Tate, who poured more wine, tipping the bottle toward the glasses on the table with a carefulness that oddly brought to mind an acolyte setting his lengthy candle to the wicks of other candles on an altar. His argument about Europe was of course absurd, as he forecast I would judge it; though there was just enough of a flicker of truth to it, if you maneuvered yourself around to his singular perspective, that I found him more unnerving than before. Prejudice need not be slapstick or vaudevillian to be prejudice, I thought; buffoonery comes in various guises, sometimes in the robes of priests, sometimes the gowns of academics, why not in the sorrel tweed of a local power? Because, as it would become more clear to me, Graham Tate was powerful, and yes, as Edmé'd said, was wealthy, and his opinions were monolithic and often given as fact. The near hour we spent in one another's company on the lawn, seated side by side at the Labor Day table, made me come to a troubled respect for him. He certainly had an appetite for wine and food as well as dogma.

Whatever formality there had been to the supper now began to fracture, as desserts were brought down and laid out on the long table, and the shadows stretched out like phantasmic auras of giants over the grass and dying flowers and rustling loosestrife. Kids rushed in clusters up and down the hayfield hill, trying without success to get a kite to rise into the warm evening sky. There were breezes, but they were wayward. Down and up the children ran again, but no sooner did their paper wing begin to gather some height than it would turn over and head in a steep descent to crash nosefirst into the soft turf. The country music was on the radio and someone who had brought a guitar began to sing and play along, exuberantly, in another key. I was standing, listening to David Lewis's wife, Jenn, discussing something, I cannot remember what, with someone, I cannot remember who, when Helen Trentas appeared at my side and said, "You having fun?"

"Tell me," turning toward her, I asked, though I knew the question was clumsy, "who *is* Tate?"

"That's not an answer. I don't have an opinion about Tate. Or, let's put it this way: I try to refuse to have an opinion about him. How's that? Did he give you his speech about the Old World?"

"He seems not to think much of any place beyond this valley."

"Since you'd just arrived, I imagined that was what you would hear. He likes to throw people off balance. I've heard the same speech, of course. Because I've been there, and he never has."

"But—"

"He said he's been there, right?"

"Yes, with Willa. But why would he lie about such a thing?"

"Because that's his nature."

I looked at her, waiting for more, but seeing she had nothing further to add, said, "Tell you what, let's go help those kids get their kite flying, why don't we?"

We walked down away from the party, into the field, where it was markedly quieter.

"No, wait. I have an even better idea," she said. "You want me to show you something I'll bet you haven't seen?"

The children would get along fine without us, I said, and went back for a bottle of wine and two glasses. I caught up with Helen, who had strolled down past the barn toward the shaky, half-rotted trestle bridge that the tractor used to be able to cross pulling behind it a fully laden wagon but over which one now trod gingerly, with a legitimate fear the whole structure might collapse beneath one's feet. We crossed, Helen first, then me, running on tiptoe, holding our breath and arriving at the far side bursting with laughter. She raised her index finger to her nose, and started through a meadow of spent lupins whose spires, only last month, must have been brilliant with yellow blooms, and pink, and violet. The lowering sun cast a rose tinge over the woods along the ridge crest. She led, and as I followed I took in the fluency of her movements, her boyish hips on her lean frame moving so easily in counterpoint with her swinging arms as she climbed through the meadow and into a sparse stand of aspens that edged the forest. I could smell her hair, and I admired how agile she was as she placed one foot then the next at just the right rocky flat when the grade became steeper, and the children's voices were left behind, as well as the guitar and singing. I concentrated on following in her footsteps exactly and even tried to mimic how I imagined she was breathing, just ahead of me there.

We didn't talk, but heard the robins and other thrushes making their plangent calls, announcing the onset of dusk, as they did every evening whether someone was here to listen or not. This was a piece of the land I did not know very well; for some reason, my feet had always carried me either up into the gorge north of the house, or west over the saddle ridge, or south downstream where the road stretched out toward the valley. There were cliffs here, not all that steep, nor formidable, really, but which required an effort to ascend that my urban sloth simply didn't want to engage all that often—actually maybe never, come to think of it—and so, although I had spent years traipsing the wilderness around Ash Creek, none of the geography Helen Trentas and I now hiked was familiar to me. "This is incredible," I called out to her, as she'd ranged ahead of me a hundred feet. She didn't hear, maybe. She didn't respond, at any rate.

There it then was. A lush virgin pasture of grasses that had never been mowed since the beginning of time, whose surface reminded me of the sea, with fixed waves, ripples, swells. Out toward the edge of the meadow, from which we could see the vast valley stretching away for what seemed hundreds of miles, was situated a cemetery, with a tumbledown wrought-iron fence that ran perhaps twenty feet by twenty-five in a rectangle. An iron gate, attached by only one of its hinges, permanently ajar, faced the meadow.

"I knew about this place, but you're right—I've never come up here before," I told Helen.

"You'll probably think I'm morbid, but this is my favorite spot in the world."

"Why morbid?"

"The graveyard. My father's buried here. And so are your great-uncle and aunt."

We entered the little cemetery, wading through swales of thick grass that had grown up around the gate.

"I haven't been a very dutiful daughter this year, I'm afraid," she said, as she knelt down and began to tear away some of the long growth that concealed the lettering incised in the white tablet of stone. I read the inscription,

GIOVANNI TRENTAS

BELOVED FRIEND AND FATHER

7 September 1933 – 23 August 1992

and stood away from where Helen knelt. She laid aside slim sheaves of grass and patted the grass that remained over the bed itself with a gentle protectiveness that made it look like she was trying to comfort the man who lay below. I turned away while she seemed to whisper a prayer in Italian, the sound rejoining my past and present as I noticed the valley had begun to gather light, pulsating glowy dust-red light, almost as if it sensed that by doing so it might stave off the absolute darkness of nightfall. Wind whistled in the trees. The birdsongs came less frequently. And suddenly Helen turned toward me, still sitting with one knee akimbo and the other bare where her embroidered skirt had fallen away some, and said, "Wouldn't it be *wonderful* to be buried here?"

"Well, I guess if you have to be buried, this would be a better place than most," and with that, I leaned against the hip-high fencing and uncorked the bottle—all this talk of death, I thought; let's live while we're still alive.

"But of course you have to be buried somewhere in due course," taking the glass from me with one hand and reaching out with the other to take mine, as I helped her up. "I just mean, given the inevitable—"

We walked the few steps over to the other headstones in this private plot, those of Wesley and Rebecca Fulton, my great-uncle—Henry's father, who was laid to rest here in 1965—and great-aunt, who lived on for another decade, as well as that of Henry's brother, seldom mentioned since there was so little about him to discuss, a boy who died aged ten, of meningitis. I recorked the bottle, set it down, and tore away some of the tangle around the stones of these people I never knew but toward whom I felt a blood attachment. I sensed Helen watching me and now liked the feeling of those eyes on me, and thought for a moment how strange that sensation was, since I never liked people watching me, then came up with an idea.

"I want to come up here again," I said, "like tomorrow or the next day, with Henry's string mower or a scythe or something, and straighten this place up a little. You want to join me?"

"Sure," she said, and although I had gotten what I wanted, I thought to myself, You're too much, Grant, asking someone on a date—a date of *sorts*—to do a little sepulchral gardening.

I asked Helen, "Tell me a little about how your father . . . unless, that is—"

"I don't have a problem talking about it. I don't know how much Edmé and Henry have told you, but I'm sure he was murdered."

"What?"

"There are some who don't think so, but I do."

"Why would anyone want to kill Giovanni?"

She looked at me with a face clouded by unreadable ambiguity, and said, "Why? Forgive me, but why ask why? It matters a lot less to me *why* someone does something hateful, especially when what's been done is irreversible. If he was murdered, who by and how are questions that can answered. Those are the questions that keep me up nights."

"You know who did it?"

"I have my ideas, but no, I don't know for sure."

"What happened to him?"

"He didn't have any enemies, but he didn't have many friends, either—your aunt and uncle, me, we were his friends. Willa and he were pretty close. When they found him up in the gorge, he'd been away for a couple of days, which was not all that unusual. He did that. He'd go off for days, when I was older, of course, would just come up into these woods. He was a hermit at heart, loved going off like that with nothing more than a bedroll, some coffee, his rod. He knew these woods really well, they were his favorite place on earth, so I never worried about it when he took off into the hills. It was the *way* they found him, with his foot gone, that made me realize things weren't right."

"Can I ask, where is your mother in all this?"

"Her? Long gone." Helen said these few words with a distinct new tone of voice: flat, detached.

"You mean dead?"

"I mean long gone. She ran off on him."

"On you, too."

"I shouldn't hate her, I never even knew her really, but I do hate her," she said, with magnificent ferocity. "I'm glad she's gone. Anybody who could do that to him, I never want to see her. Margery. Like in that nursery rhyme, 'See-saw, Margery Daw.' Ugly name, don't you think?"

"If you say so."

"I say so."

Silence hovered over us there for a few moments before I asked, "You must have been really young when she left?" but Helen seemed to be thinking about something else.

When she looked up at me, she said, "Look, I'm a bit of a bastard, all right? Let's change the subject. Why don't we talk about you?"

"Because you're more interesting than me."

"Why should I believe that?"

"I thought you didn't believe in asking why, but all right. What do you want to know?"

"You'll tell me whatever I want?"

"Why not?"

"First question—"

"You only get three."

"First question. Why did you always avoid me when we were growing up? How come this is the first time we ever met?"

"That's two questions. Answer is, I didn't avoid you—I've always assumed you had other things to do; at least that's what they told me, whenever I asked about you."

"You asked about me?"

"Of course. Now you have one more question."

"That's not fair." She laughed, her face brightening with the most remarkable swiftness before she grimaced with concentration. "I'll ask my other question when we come back. I'll ask my other *two,* in fact."

"If you say so," realizing the exchange had come to an end. We sat, two pixillated waifs who had drunk more than perhaps we should have, our backs against the eastern length of filigreed black barrier, as the clouds that towered out toward the west punched up their sunset tangerines and silvers and neon golds. After a silence, I added, "I hope you don't think I'm being insensitive, asking about your father, but I *am* curious—that is, I mean to say, if he was murdered, wasn't there an investigation or something?"

Helen didn't answer, sat instead with knees up and head leaning back against the iron crosspost, staring at the clouds, and didn't seem to mind that I now studied her in the feverish light. Rather, she appeared to have withdrawn so far into herself that I doubted she had even heard my last question (how I hoped she hadn't), and so I didn't say anything more but took advantage of this withdrawal, or whatever it was, to run my eye down the gentle curve of her profiled forehead to the delicate dark brow and then to follow the straight projection of her nose. It was more sensual, in its way, how I felt looking with total absence of inhibition, than if I were touching the profile my eye traced. Her philtrum was pronounced, where the angel touched her just above the lips, as the fable has it. And her lips themselves were somber, the lower lip very full, and the chin was modest but strong, with the slightest hint of a cleft.

She simply didn't move, for minutes that accumulated one upon another, and neither then did I. Her ambiguous serenity forestalled my making any stupid mistake like coming out with the usual crap that one asks another in a moment such as this, like, *Penny for your thoughts,* or, *Was it something I said?* I glanced over at the clouds to see if something was there, a vision of some god descending to earth, or a visitor from another planet, that would make her so rapt, but of course I saw nothing but a diminishing day. When I did reach over, and with my middle finger tucked her hair behind her ear, she turned to me without blinking and looked me in the eye more deeply than I could recall anyone ever doing before. Our kiss came almost as an afterthought to this eroticism of the eyes, this real passion of openly looking, but it was a kiss made just with the lips and tongue and teeth, and had nothing to do with arms or bodies crushing together in any kind of embrace. The kiss continued for a long while before Helen Trentas climbed to her feet, offered me her hand, said, "We need to be getting back."

I'm not sure, but I don't think I said anything, because I wasn't able to say anything. Nor did we talk, though I held her hand for part of the way back across the cemetery field until we reached the tree line, where again she led and I kept up with her quick pace, from rock to rock and on down the knoll. As we hiked, my head was obviously aswirl with Helen Trentas, but I also found myself wondering how they managed to get a body *up* this declivity in order to bury it. Something to remember to ask, I supposed. I pictured a moment in the future, the remote future, when I might have to carry Uncle Henry up this rough path, or dear Edmé—no, my mind was not steady, nor was it full of romantic thoughts as perhaps it ought to have been. And when I recognized this, I glanced ahead at the form of Helen Trentas and marveled at what had just happened between us. Where was all this going? It didn't matter to me. I could smell the perfume of her hair, and nothing much mattered more than that.

The woods filtered out dusk so that in here it appeared to be false night, with columns of sun shooting horizontal through the blindering leaves over there, and over there. The way out seemed much longer than the way in, which was fine with me, though it made no sense, as we surely were walking more quickly downhill than up.

But then the aspen grove appeared before us, and the meadow after. Just before we reached the clearing, Helen turned around and said, "Thanks for letting me show you that," to which I was going to say something like, Thank *you* for . . . whatever I was going to say, who knows what abstracted palaver, except that what I saw beyond her—fire not of sunset but crisp flames reaching from the ground toward the sky rather than vice versa—made any response unthinkable as we both looked across the creek, and began to sprint, me in front of her now, as quickly as we could.

The ranch house was not on fire, nor the studio, nor the barn. I crossed the bridge and joined the others who had already formed a haphazard bucket brigade from the creek up the bank to the oldest building on the land, a one-room house that was sunk in desuetude already, was almost entirely overgrown by greedy saplings and vines— which burned like black coily snakes—and whose roof had long ago collapsed. What burned swiftly to the ground was a structure that had no practical value whatever. Henry himself hadn't bothered to raze it for the simple reason of sentiment—it was the place where he'd been born, the first building erected at Ash Creek.

"How'd it start?" I shouted at Noah Daiches, who stood next to me at the dousing end of the line. The fire was nearly out already, and had apparently burned in a burst. Smoke and miniature orange rafts of hot ash flowed toward the pale first stars.

"Don't know," as he tossed an emptied bucket behind him to

someone who jogged it back down to the creek for refilling, then reached out to take the full pail from me.

"What a shame," half to myself.

"What?" he shouted back.

"I said, What a shame."

"Yeah, shame," he said.

The fire flamed out to smoldering char within an hour. Beyond its initial eruption, apparently, it had never burned so hot that it did much more than blacken the surfaces of the timber. But the old edifice was sufficiently gutted so that Henry would decide, within the next week, to ask the fire company to come up to the ranch and finish the job somebody had started. That is, assuming someone had deliberately set it. Assuming the crackling and hissing of fire was a form of night music.

EARLY MORNING. The first downstairs, I filled the kettle with water and lit the gas burner with a match. The blue flame tinged yellow reminded me of a celestial crown, but the kind only fallen angels would dare wear, since their heads are already on fire. I felt a little out of plumb, felt muddled, bemused; and in some sort of contradistinction to this, euphoric and bright as the sun on the chrome handles and trim of the stove. As I sat at the kitchen table and stared at the pot, two images turned over, projected before me on the nebulous screen that hung, in a way, between my eyes and what they should have seen. The images are predictable: Helen Trentas's beautiful head, and the flames of the fire stabbing the ultramarine dusk. As I made my coffee, I began to come around. What little I had accomplished thus far this morning, I realized, had been in a sleepwalk. Only when I ground the java beans did I actually awaken.

Edmé found me on the short veranda that looked out to the east field, toward the gate. Two blue spruce taller than the house framed our view of the blackened cabin, which continued to smoke. From a limb of one of these spruces a red squirrel was scolding us for disturbing it, issuing sharp cries of *chip-chip-chip*. Dew lay, ephemeral fluid crystals, on every surface out there in the natural world.

"Morning," she said, and sat beside me, her cup in one hand, and in the other what appeared to be a decorative vintage cigar box, whose gold and brilliant green edge glistened in the dawn light. The box was wrapped round and round with ribbons, some of them old and some newer.

"What have you got there?" I asked.

"You and Helen seemed to get along last night," she said, and sipped her coffee.

"Yes."

Edmé said nothing for a moment, then went on: "We've got a lot to do today, dealing with what's left down at the old cabin after that fire."

"Just let me know how I can help—"

"Your uncle's devastated about it. What's more, I can tell you—I don't know how to say this to you, Grant, but your uncle—I believe you can count on his not being very supportive of you and Helen—"

"I don't understand."

"You two went off together for quite a while."

"She took me up to the cemetery."

Edmé heard eagerness betray the actorly control I attempted to lace into my tone of voice like some kid who hoped to get away with denying the obvious—and it wasn't in fact quite clear to me *why* she needed to forewarn me about Helen Trentas and my uncle Henry, or why I was hiding my agitation, or ardor, or whatever, but it was rather clear to both of us that I had every intention of circumventing his wishes, if this was what they were going to be. She said nothing, so I simply asked, "Why would he care one way or the other? Plus, it's not like we aren't adults, first, and second, we haven't done anything."

"I'm just telling you what I think would happen if you brought it up this morning, is all."

"Understood," I said, uncomprehending.

"I want you to have something." She set her cup on the wide arm of the Adirondack chair, lifted the cigar box, and handed it to me.

"Giovanni asked me to keep it in a safe place for him, and I've kept it for three years. He gave it to me a month before he passed away. I think you should have it now. Don't ask why, I don't know exactly why—but *here*."

I took the box, waited for her to continue.

"When I asked Giovanni if he wanted me to have Henry put it in his safebox he said no. I sensed he didn't want me to show it to any-body. I haven't, but the thing makes me more uneasy all the time. It may sound silly, but I'm superstitious about it."

Edmé was all riddles this morning.

"What's inside?" I asked.

"Giovanni told me everything that ever meant anything to him he kept in here. I thought to show it to Noah when he was looking into Giovanni's death, but I didn't. The investigation didn't last very long—they closed the case so fast it seemed like a sham to me—and I didn't want his life, or death, to seem part of a sham. Mind you, I'm not asking you to open it. I don't think that you should, but, well—it's yours."

"Thanks," I said, wondering what was the point of having a box you couldn't open.

"Why don't you take it to your room, put it away. I'd just as soon your uncle not know about any of this. He's got enough on his mind."

"All right," and I got up and left her there on the porch. The con-tents shifted from one side of the box to the other as I climbed the stairs. I closed my bedroom door behind me, gently, and opened the mirrored door of the armoire with the firm thought of following Edmé's instruction to the letter, even though I could make no sense of it, by hiding the box in my bag which was stowed within. As the mirror sprayed reflected silver light around the room, I caught just a glimpse of the colorful ribbons—plum, green, puce—held between my hands in the mirror face, and thought what harm could come from having just a look at what was inside. A myth like the one about Pandora loosing evil sprites across the earth as the simple result of her being curious was just that, a myth, a fable. And besides, hadn't all the evils that there were in this world already been set free? What more harm could possibly be done?

I sat on the edge of the bed, and began one by one to untie the ribbons that shrouded the beautiful, if a little tattered and soiled, old box. Outside my door, I could hear my uncle on the landing, then descending the stairs. For a moment, but just for a moment, it occurred to me to wonder why my fingers rather than those of Helen Trentas were the ones touching these many ribbons.

Unbound, the antique wooden box was beautiful. *La Flor de Fontella,* it read on the ornate lid, *Fontella* over and over again. On its top was an oval portrait of a brown-eyed beauty with cocoa hair partly covered by a lace head shawl and with a red rose that matched her red velvet bodice, trimmed in white and cut low at the breasts. She wore a smile of perfectly modest yet just as perfectly frank sensuality. Above her floated the legend with the name of the Havana-filled cigars that once were kept inside. Giovanni had carved a little niche out of the center front of the lid and driven a brad into the panel, which served as a latch.

As I turned this latch, and lifted the lid, the perplexities that had arisen in this place I had always considered far above the world's welter came to mind in an absurd litany: *Tell the truth*—"Grant, I'm going to ask you not to mention this to your aunt"—*tell the truth*— "I'd just as soon your uncle not know about any of this"—*tell the truth*—"Say, you're Henry Fulton's nephew, aren't you?" the barber had asked, to which I replied "No." The night visitors themselves seemed detestably misguided. After all, if they so badly wanted my uncle to tell some kind of truth, why was it they had to make their desire known in such wicked and skewed ways? As I sat there in this little room I knew so well, I came to the firm understanding that in

my attempt to escape the patterns of self-created crisis that had become so habitual in my life, I had only managed to enmesh myself in
a fresh complex of troubles. Troubles that seemed less easily solved
than any I had managed to create. Troubles that only a week before
were attractive for being so distant and separate from my own, but
which by now were moving toward the heart of what was left for me
to love.

II

THE PARADISE
OF CHILDREN

"What can it be?" thought Pandora. "Is there
something alive in the box? Well!—yes!—I am
resolved to take just one peep! Only one peep;
and then the lid shall be shut down as safely as
ever! There cannot possibly be any harm in just
one little peep!"

—NATHANIEL HAWTHORNE,
The Wonder Book for Boys and Girls

HE HAD just celebrated his tenth birthday when his parents put him aboard the ship with his older sister so that they could make the ' crossing before the weather turned bad, and before the war got even worse than it already was. They added the name Sam to his papers, in the ingenuous hope that such a good, common name might make his acclimation in the new world easier. After all, wasn't it true that all the men over there who weren't named Joe or Harry or Dick went by the name of Sam? If not, who was Uncle Sam with the goatish beard, top hat, and pointing finger they had seen once in a magazine from overseas? Yes, Sam would be his new-world name, they agreed. And therefore Giovanni Sam Trentas was settled aboard ship with his sister, Paola, unable to speak a word of English, and rather unsure of the reasons he was being deported, although his mother had explained to him, and more than once, that she would follow, his father would follow, and soon they would all be together again, reunited in a place called Coeur d'Alene, way out west in America.

Paola herself spoke only passable English but, unlike her shyer brother, more than made up for whatever shortcomings she might have with the language by employing her natural vivacity, her gift for lively pantomime, to make her thoughts understood. She cherished her new role as her brother's substitute mother, as she saw it. Slender, dark-haired, with green eyes that were said to be her Valle d'Aostan maternal heritage, with long hands and legs and neck, Paola was an irreverent but naturally graceful sixteen-year-old who could pass for a decade older than she was. I can imagine them, she and her brother, wandering the decks during the voyage to New York, perhaps being adopted by another family on the overcrowded ship whose cargo included not just refugees from fascist Italy but livestock. Cattle, sheep, chickens, a menagerie of domesticated animals. I can picture them sharing meals of *baudin* and *filoncini,* red wine and *frutti secci,* which made the crossing tolerable as they were pressed together in cabins, all their possessions tied into unwieldly bundles stacked in every corner, hoping against hope this choice to leave their homeland was the right one. I can understand that though she had been told to call her brother "Sam," she either forgot or else decided Giovanni was still *Giovanni*—or else *Gianni,* as she called him, despite what had been typed on his emigration documents. Either way, the nickname never took hold, so that by the time they dropped anchor in New York harbor, everyone who had gotten to know Paola and her brother cried out to him, —*Arrivederci, piccolo Giovanni! buona fortuna e stammi bene!* When the two were processed through New York immigration, one of the customs officers did refer to him as Sam Trentas, but that was the last time either the boy or his sister heard the name used, with the single exception of my uncle Henry. When Henry heard this story, he then and there adopted "Sam" as his own nickname for his friend. Giovanni always liked that, too, that his friend had a special name for him.

The train trip took nearly as long as their ocean passage. A woman who is only referred to as the Signora in the little diary of their voyage—presumably kept by Paola, but present in Giovanni's box and hence my extrapolations—accompanied the children as far as Chicago. The children continued on alone, and were met at the train station in Spokane, then driven across state lines back to Coeur d'Alene, along the immaculate river there, through the green and red and brown unspoiled mountains of Kootenai County. Giovanni must have been awed by the Bitterroot range, its snowcapped peaks and the great lakes that had collected in the deep ravines of this northern scape. There is preserved in the box a photograph of the clapboard house, whose every eave is hung with gingerbread trim and which, though the photograph is black and white, was clearly painted in several shades. A black dog barks at the photographer from the porch of this house, and is blurred somewhat in the faded image, which gives him a ghostly look and elongates his bared fangs, but otherwise the house has about it the look of comfort, even gaiety. The woman who took them in was one Marie-Alexandre Ponset, a friend of the Trentas family from their days in Aosta, in northern Italy, indeed the only friend they knew in America, and it would seem that while Giovanni could at the time speak no English, Marie-Alexandre conversed mostly in French. The babel of many voices speaking in several languages around the table at dinner in Coeur d'Alene must have been something to hear. Until he managed to learn some English, or even a little French, I would think young Giovanni was forced to spend quite a lot of time in his head.

Lost in the mercenary sump of time past are years whose activities are largely unaccounted for, years whose daily doings must have seemed so significant to those who lived them, years of adjusting to a foreign culture, of striving not to feel forever like an outsider, of playing with children who made judgments upon one because one dressed differently and spoke with an unlikely accent—the years in which Giovanni grew up and came of age. I am unable to account for all kinds of personal history. There was nothing in the box that explained why the Trentases failed to keep their word and follow their children to Coeur d'Alene. A letter written in bad French and posted from Aosta, enclosed in the black-bordered envelope that was traditionally used to convey the news of a death, begins with the phrase *Il ç'est avec grande douleur que je vous adressé la présente lettre* . . . and goes on to express the sender's condolences on the passing of their mother. The letter seems to suggest, though in subtle terms, that had she not gone south to Rome, not allowed herself to be swept away by the promise of a better life elsewhere, she might have lived longer. But other than that extraordinary bit of inbred philosophy, nothing.

Or, rather, much that went in many directions: for while the box gave me little about specific events in Giovanni's childhood days in the Bitterroots, it was a cornucopia indeed, of preposterous stuff collected hither and thither in the years that followed his departure from that tidy, prim house by the lake. The box was the repository of fragments from another age.

Here was the ticket for a dance recital.

And here, the recipe for dandelion wine.

Here was a pair of rusted spinner hooks in a folded paper case.

And here, the calling card of one Maurice Oser, *Controller of rats, mice, roaches, vermin.*

A carefully typed column of numbers I read up and down until I figured out they were meant to show how, by saving one dollar one day, and then two dollars on the second day, four on the third day, eight on the fourth day, and so on, doubling the number of dollars you save for each new day of the week, you will have amassed in a few weeks over a million dollars.

Here was a packet of rolling papers—*Papiers Mais, Bestest 200 leaves, Verdadeiro papel Francez*—and another of the Prince Albert brand.

Subscriber's receipts for *Country Home, Automobile Digest, True Detective,* I found in the box, together with a printed flyer for *Présure lactique Suisse,* beneficial in the treatment of *l'anémie, la gastralgie, la dyspepsie, le diabète, la constipation,* and *les effets pernicieux de l'alcool.*

Half a sheet of foolscap was here—or maybe only a third of the original leaf of paper—ripped roughly from top to bottom down its center. The leaf was densely written on in a small hand, black ink. Since it was only a scrap, which I had tried hard without success to read over the next days, and because a couple of feathers had fallen out when I unfolded it, I assumed it was meant to protect these feathers: two beautiful feathers, grayish brown with white fuzz.

A little black leather change purse lay beneath the feathers, an old purse holding ten Italian lire, two wartime pennies struck in some cheap alloy, and a handful of several dozen copper pennies—which, as I weighed it in the palm of my hand, made me think, He couldn't go far on *that*.

This handsome brass cylinder, with a plunger at one end and nipple at the other, was the largest talisman here, something whose use I could not fathom, at least on first scrutiny.

Photographs and keepsake cards in abundance.

A miniature diary for 1942, which I leafed through with hope of discovering what Giovanni had done before his emigration from Italy, but in which I found not a single mark other than the letter S—as ornately drawn as a treble clef—penciled in the addresses section at the back.

An amusing booklet, printed on cheap paper, whose cover was illustrated with a man wagging his finger at two women and a gentleman who resembled Fred Astaire, all of whom were laughing merrily, beneath the banner: *Dr. Miles New Joke Book.* "What's the idea of the Smiths taking French lessons?" I read. "They've adopted a French baby, and want to understand what it says when it begins to talk." Jokes such as this were interspersed with advertisements for products such as Dr. Miles Anti-Pain Pills and Dr. Miles Nervine.

And so Giovanni's box, it appeared to me, was a little museum of whimsical curiosities which allowed me some glimpse into the life of this man my uncle had so dearly loved and who knew Helen Trentas from before she could walk or speak. His treasures offered me the chance to envision the history of one who had always been peripheral in my life, a man I never saw as having much to do with me, one whose voice I could for some reason remember, but whose face and figure I recalled only after discovering a formal portrait of him, standing beside an unlikely plinth, his arm settled upon its capstone with an elegance that seemed inherent.

Still, this stuff allowed me only a patchwork portrait. And while it might have been sufficient to satisfy my curiosity a few brief days earlier, now it was not. Now I wanted to know everything I could about the life of this immigrant.

And I was not to be denied. Hidden beneath the gewgaws and bric-a-brac were the letters which would give me my clearest insight into the life of Giovanni Trentas. That morning, the morning Edmé placed the box into my hands, I did not, of course, read them, if only because there wasn't enough time for me to do so and still make any pretense of abiding by my aunt's opinion that I not open the box at all. Nor did I go through its contents just then and touch each of the objects catalogued above with the reverence of a credulous sleuth. All I did was crack the seal, so to speak, then put the thing away, as I'd been asked to do, before returning to the porch, where Henry had joined his wife in a debate about the cause and meaning of the fire. My attentions were divided, though, as I heard Edmé's words "No one would dare—"

"Why not?"

"Somebody would be bound to see them, all those people around. It's just too risky."

"Nothing risky about it," Henry scoffed. "If anything, it seems all too convenient."

"I don't understand."

"All those people around make for good distraction, that's what I'm saying. Besides, Edmé, listen—face facts. It *did* happen, and the timing, right after we'd opened our place to the community, the mockery of it . . . ," and his voice descended into a whisper until we could not hear him anymore, although his lips continued to move. We three sat, as if suspended in that image, quiet and saddened by the allusion. Then my uncle turned to me and spoke again. "Grant, did you notice anybody missing from the party when the fire first started?"

Before I opened my mouth, Edmé intervened. "There were so many new faces, how would Grant be able to tell whether someone had slipped off? What's more, it was getting dark by then."

For my part, I shrugged my shoulders. "You're sure somebody actually set it?"—coming back into the present, out of the curious wonderment of the box.

Henry said, "Well, what caused it otherwise? You think it was a case of spontaneous combustion?"

We had spread plastic tarps over the tables overnight, because after the fire had been extinguished no one had the stamina to begin putting party things back in order. I took this as my opportunity to sidestep my uncle's understandable animosity—not really directed toward me, as such, but dangerous to be near in any case, I sensed—and so I left them there on the veranda and went down into the fore-yard to see where to start cleaning up. The tarps were bright blue, and the lawn looked strangely populated by these shiny mounds. As I pulled the covers off, wet with dew, and laid them out across the fence in the upper yard to dry, my mind went back to Giovanni Trentas and what an awful ending he'd met just up in the gorge there. The beautiful small boy he must have been, who had come and made his way in a country foreign to him, who had worked hard during his life and raised his daughter in the absence of a wife who'd left him—that *that* long road would carry him to such a butchering, and the horrid disfigurement of his body besides, seemed to me, as I breathed in the soft morning breezes which moved through the trees and over the grasses, appallingly unfair. No one deserved such a fate as that, I thought. And the idea that whoever had done this to him was alive and well, as able as I to breathe this sweet air, caused a deeply unsettling indignation to come over me. It was as if I could hear Jude's disembodied voice again, chastising me for not pursuing those who'd been responsible for my parents' death that evening so long ago, telling me that here I had in some way a fresh opportunity, one not to miss. So far as I can tell, it was during these moments by myself, before Edmé came down to join me, that my passion to discover who it was that killed Giovanni Trentas was born.

I remembered a book about the origins of consciousness I had read some years before, a book I was able to understand in only a limited way but in which I found an unforgettable line. *The most primitive, clumsy, but enduring method of discovering the will of silent gods is the simple recording of sequences of unusual or important events.* Other than the fascination the words held for me in their proper context of mythology, and of the genesis of religious rites, my interest in the idea was purely intellectual. That is, I believed then that these words would never have any direct impact on my own life. And yet, now look: I find myself writing this chronicle, like a primitive looking for direction from a great, or small, unnamed power. As I stood there that morning, however, I sensed that the will of silent gods was not confined to deep history. Even the most obscene myth and nastiest god manifest themselves here and there every day. All we have to do is notice them.

As I walked down to meet Helen Trentas by the gate, I believed that whatever problem Henry might have with my fledgling friendship with this young woman, I would find a way to change his mind, to convince him there was no harm in it. Indeed, quite the contrary.

If it was because he thought it a little precipitous of me, even capricious, to show an interest in another woman so soon after Mary and I had gone our separate ways, I wouldn't be able to argue convincingly that he was wrong. Assuming what Edmé said was true, that I could expect Henry not to be supportive of me and Helen—and there was no reason to believe otherwise—I understood such a response, more likely than not, would arise from his fear that someone might get their feelings hurt. I know my uncle loved me, and I could tell from the way he embraced her, spoke to her at the Labor Day party, that he was devoted, in his way, to Helen. It made sense he might be concerned about the two of us, even apprehensive. It was not like I boasted some sterling history in this regard. My uncle and I hadn't seen all that much of each other this last decade. Why should he give me any benefit of the doubt? Here I was, separated from a woman he and Edmé had certainly liked, a woman I met and married in very short order, and not so long after I had visited Ash Creek with Jude, an entirely different kind of person from Mary, and

one quite plainly I adored. What right had I to come breezing into
their lives—heart before head, glands before heart—and promptly
entangle myself with Giovanni Trentas's daughter? A good question,
and one for which I had no ready answer.

"Hello, you," she said.

"Hello again," I said.

She was dressed this morning in denim: a faded denim shirt with
sleeves rolled back and jeans worn smooth and a little frayed along
the cuffs; brown box-toe work boots, also well worn in; and her hair
was pulled back into a ponytail. The sky was not overcast, though it
seemed summer had somehow given way to autumn, just after Labor
Day, there being a bite in the air that only last week had not been
present. I took Helen's hand, since it was presented to me as she
said hello, and leaned forward to kiss her but, sensing a subtle withdrawal or hesitation, gave her a rather chaste fraternal kiss on the
cheek. Helen Trentas was no easy read, I thought. "You ready to do
some work?"

"That's why I'm here," she said, cheerfully.

"You probably know better than I where Henry keeps tools for this
sort of thing," and we walked up the slight grade to a shed next to the
barn, where there hung, on pegs, a scythe and a rake, and on a work-
bench that ran the length of the small building lay a pair of clippers.
"What's this?" I asked, pointing at a great zero of heavy iron, a mam-
moth contraption with rusted jaws and teeth, to which she answered
without a moment's thought, "A bear trap. See this? This is the anchor, this staked chain, that keeps the animal from getting away
once you have caught it, and this is the spring bow, and this is the
opposing spring, and this disk is called the trigger pan. The bows are
pulled apart, you place a piece of meat on the pan, the bear releases
the springs by tampering with the bait, the trap teeth and chain hold
the bear until you come the next morning."

"And kill it."

"Kill it, of course. Why trap a bear and not kill it? Unless you want to train it to walk on its hind legs in the circus."

"Have you done that? Trapped a bear and killed it?"

"With my dad and Henry, a few times, sure. Back when your uncle kept livestock here, one bear could do a lot of damage. They had to take care of things, so they'd set a trap or two."

"Jesus," I said. "Is it awful? I mean, just killing it in cold blood like that?"

"What choice was there?"

We had left the shed by this time, and walked together down to the ruined bridge. "I don't know," I answered, feeling suddenly immature, or unsophisticated, or what have you. "I've never killed anything."

"Henry told me you're a good fly fisherman."

"I'm all right at it."

"Then you've killed."

"Trout? It's just not the same."

"Not the same? You're probably one of those people who believes someone can be a vegetarian and still eat fish and poultry. Flesh is flesh, killing is killing."

"Look, trout don't feel. They have the most rudimentary brain stem, not even a cortex, I don't think. Mammals have brains, therefore feelings, emotions. They have warm red blood like us. I'd just think that their closeness to human anatomy would make it much more emotional, harder to look them in the eye and shoot them."

"Don't look them in the eye, then," Helen finished as we made our way into the copse at the top of the east meadow, and from there climbed up the steeper slopes.

Strange girl, I thought, following, doing my best not to feel overwhelmed by her.

As the sun baked the crispness out of the air, we performed our task in the most curious silence, a mute calm that was fragile and edged by paradox. The fragility arose from the fact that though we desired to speak to one another, get to know each other better, the sober stark purity of the small cemetery forbade it, somehow, this morning. A visual caress, a frank kiss, seemed further away than they had the other evening, when the wine encouraged me and the embracing dusk covered us. The paradox I sensed arose from how physically close Helen and I were up here, alone, side by side cutting overgrown orchard grass, raking, trimming with the long stiff shears around the headstones and the fence—and simultaneously how distant, as I say. I could hear her sigh and groan when she worked; could smell her perspiration, saw out of the corner of my eye the bead of it run from her temple down over her cheek, all of which I found erotic, despite my efforts to dampen such sentiments, given where we were and what we were doing. Eros and Thanatos, as equivocal bedfellows as ever. They were with us in this mountain meadow, as we labored with little sense of the passing time. If we traded more than three words, I'd be surprised. After what must have been hours of hard work, the cemetery began to emerge from under the years of growth. A great pile of cut grass had been raked together outside the fence and remained to be burned or moved to a place out of view where it could rot into yellow mulch. Otherwise the job was finished, and we agreed that the small graveyard looked beautiful. Glancing up at the sun, I could see that the day had dwindled well into afternoon.

Helen said, "Follow me." She'd brought with her a knapsack and in it lunch—olives, sandwiches, sun-dried tomatoes in oil, a mason jar of water, Anjou pears. I watched her hands, mostly, while she unpacked. We sat, ate, at the edge of the high field, some distance from the cemetery, looking out over the valley. "Thank you," I said, as she presented me with a checkered napkin.

"Thank *you*," Helen remarked. "You don't know how many times I wanted to come up here and do this. I couldn't ever face it by myself."

"You don't strike me as the kind of person who'd be spooked by anything."

Helen looked away when she said, "You don't know me."

Startled once more by her forthrightness, I kept my mouth shut.

"I'm spooked by all sorts of things," she said, drinking water from the jar. "I'm completely superstitious, something I inherited from my father."

"Superstitious about what, for instance?"

"Wait a minute. I'm the one who has two questions coming."

Again, I said nothing.

"All right," she said. She uncrossed her legs, pulled off her boots and socks, dropped the latter into the former, and set them away from her before crossing her legs again, now barefoot. "Second question. Tell me, why are you here?"

"I thought you didn't care about why things happened. Isn't that what you said?"

"That was then, this is now."

"All right. But what makes you think I have any other reason to be here than to visit my aunt Edmé and uncle Henry?"

"When someone answers a question with questions, it generally means the answers would be questionable, if you were able to hear them. So in a way you've answered your own question. If you were only here to visit, you would just've answered my question by saying, I'm only here visiting and that's all."

"Too complicated for me. What's in that water, anyway? Listen, I'm here in part because I didn't have anywhere else to go—"

"Yes—and?"

I told her that there had been things happening down at Ash Creek, in the night mostly, that Henry was loath to discuss with anyone. He and Edmé didn't really know who was behind it, or why it had been going on, and so I asked her to keep this to herself. She held my gaze steadily as she crossed her heart with her forefinger, and waited for me to elaborate, which, though I knew I should not,

I did. The night music, the other aberrant facets of the twilight siege—much of which still had not been fully revealed to me by Edmé—I narrated to Helen Trentas, who sat there rapt, while she listened: not so much shocked, or agog, as such, than engaged fully, as if she were memorizing each mite of data I could provide. "You know all about this already," I said.

"Nothing of the kind," she contradicted, with such force that I found myself offering an apology.

"I might stick around for a little longer, if they'll let me. Not that they need my help, God knows—I'm not *that* patronizing—but just because . . . I don't know," and I wondered whether I should add that my interest in remaining here had also to do with her.

"You're curious," she said.

"Who wouldn't be?"

"No, I don't mean you are *curious*. I mean *you* are curious."

"Me? curious?"

"I don't say it as an insult; it's a compliment really. Most people are neither curious about things nor curious per se, and I think you're both."

Who was this woman? I thought, with faint regret at having told her what I had about the episodes at Ash Creek, a sudden paranoid worry that I had made a mistake.

"I have one more question, but I'll save it."

"Why do you get to ask all these questions?"

"Only three, just like in the fairy tale," she said. "I'll save the third one for just the right rainy day," leaning forward toward me, having taken a bite from the pear that she'd been tossing gently from palm to palm. Her face was very close to mine and I studied the flecks, slivers, specks of variant colors in her irises, and the distension of her pupils as she moved into the small shadow my head cast upon hers under the lowering sun, a warm afternoon sun that must have been about halfway along in its descent through the blue elliptic. She tasted of musky pear when her mouth opened on mine, and she kept her eyes unshut, looking into my own with an urgency that suggested to close them would be a kind of travesty, or betrayal, or even a hypocrisy. And so, although she was blurred, I focused on the buttery light on her skin and on her dark drift of hair, glistening with reds and prismatic greens, even golds and oranges. I could hear us each breathing through our noses with a steady rhythm that had become congruent, so that we inhaled at the same time and then slowly let out the air, paused, and breathed in again, as if metamorphosing into a single person.

We kissed for what must have been a very long time, before my hands—which had touched her back and her hip, had come to rest on her thigh after tracing her side, caressing her breast beneath the thick, smooth surface of denim—before my hands found themselves on the grassy earth, supporting our weight as we shifted and lay down. Our fingers began to loosen buttons and belts and pull away clothing, and when we were both naked from the waist down and I moved on top to enter her, she finally closed her eyes, turned her head to the side. On her face was a perfect fusion of ecstasy and anguish. My hands on her shoulders, my elbows dug into the unpliant ground cushioned only by long waves of heavy grass and tiny flowers, I lowered my head to kiss her at the side of her coral-brown lips, in which a twining of her hair was caught. "Is this all right?" I whispered, surprised at how breathless my voice was, and when she moaned *Yes,* I did enter her, and the softness of her was beyond anything I'd ever known.

We were simply meant to coalesce, it would seem, just there. My left cheek pressed into her right cheek, as if we were slowly dancing. Her arms splayed, wrists up above her head, freely vulnerable but somehow powerfully *sure*—because such a gesture of relinquishment indicated trust, and such trust came solely from choice, and such choice was hers because she was ardent and strong—she loved me back with the same vitality I gave to her. As we moved with each other, her suppleness and élan merged beneath me, in a way that seemed to have little to do with our rhythmic plunging bodies, so that my skin on hers was as if charged by an order of spiritual electricity that raced down my bristling spine. When I finally strayed onto my side, facing her, close, our nostrils taking in the same small air, though there was a vast universe of air surrounding us and moving in breezes over us that we might have seized if we wanted, the world went temporarily obscure.

A little black ant, delicate and harmless, awakened me, as it made its way across my forearm, sometime later. Helen was already conscious, again with her dark eyes on me, although she had not pulled away an inch from where we had been when I blacked out before. You are beautiful, was all that came into my mind when I saw her there, studying me, a look of magnificent knowing innocence on that face. Then, I said it aloud, "You're beautiful," and she said to me before a moment had passed, "You are, too." When we got up to stand on the tangle of our clothing, began to gather ourselves together to return to Ash Creek, I was sorry to relinquish the joy of that tiny mutual paradise we'd briefly created.

Lunch detritus in the knapsack, scythe over shoulder like the figure of death, rake slung beside it, we juggled the sundries and tools in such a way that we could hold hands, leaving the meadow behind. My instinct, a suspicion which spread through me like dye spilled in water, that we had been observed in secret, maybe from the verge of the clearing, just within the curtain of trees, didn't come over me until we were well down into the dappling shade that struggled with sunlight in the lower woods. I stopped suddenly, and Helen stopped also. "What is it?" she asked.

Wary, I looked back up the path to scan the complex of trees, rocks, leaves, flowers, behind us.

"Grant?"

Of course there was nothing to see. I say "of course" because even now, knowing what I know, this premonition remains ambiguous to me. "I'm not sure," I answered Helen then, and half smiled at her.

"Is someone back there?"

"Maybe," I answered, and yet if the questions were put before me now—What proof do you have you were being watched? what proof is there that such a feeling was not the result of your own sense of, like, guilt or paranoia or even something else?—I'm not sure I could answer any better than before.

"Shall we go look?"

"No. Let's get back," I said.

We continued down through the forest, and though the sensation remained with me, I turned my attention to asking Helen when I could see her next. "I'll be away for a few days—there's a thoroughbred show I have to ride in," she said. "That's what I do, you know, work at a stable, training horses. You'll have to come by sometime."

"I will."

We reached her car, down by the main gate, knowing we were within view of the house, and somehow sensed, though without saying as much, that we had best shake hands. So we did, and afterward I traipsed halfhearted, faintly out of sorts, toward the shed to rehang the antique apparatus and stare for a moment at that rusted but potent bear trap, trying and failing to imagine Helen raise a shotgun at the growling head of the poor beast caught in that iron jaw, while she studied it with the same sweet holy eye that had so recently stared into mine, before pulling the trigger that would send its brute and terrified soul hurtling into the next life.

MA BIEN aimee soeur et beau frère, il-y-a quelque jour que j'ai reçu votre letre . . . , I read, behind the closed door of my bedroom, hearing the steady noise of the creek through the window, thinking I should go downstairs soon to help Edmé set the table for dinner, but not before despairing of my ever making much headway with the clutch of letters written in patois . . . *tante belle cose* . . . some kind of northern dialect, written to Giovanni many years ago by a friend of his family's. The handwriting was spidery, the ink blotched and paper browned. What emerged from the correspondence was this above all: that Giovanni Trentas and his sister were consigned to the care of friends, left to continue on alone in their new providence in part because of the sudden death of their mother and in part because of the disappearance of a father who seemingly was caught up in the nasty politics and dark war of his day—a fragment of biography derived from these other missives from Aosta and Rome. Trentas senior appeared to be a gunrunner for the *partigiani,* the antifascist partisans, a fact that Edmé would later corroborate, though she herself would say Giovanni was never quite clear about the hard facts of his father's deeds and ultimate fate. What was clear, from the letters, was the boy's abandonment, whatever the reasons, to the currents of life in bucolic Coeur d'Alene, where he learned the ways of a new culture.

The letters from overseas were interesting, but did not really offer me, or at least so I thought, anything about the Giovanni who was my uncle's friend and my (now) lover's father, and so I turned to the next, much smaller bundle of notes, which were folded, and secured with a paper clip.

These were more like bits of old confetti swept up from the gutter in the wake of a forgotten parade, so exhausted was the paper and faded the writing. They were also immediately more provocative. The first was merely a scribbled note, penciled on a tiny scrap, *When he goes I can come to see you but not before. I don't want him to see me. Until tomorrow, then.* Unsigned, I saw: anonymous to me but so close to Giovanni that no name was needed. Or was the sender afraid it might fall into other hands?

I turned to the next, written on notebook paper with bristly edge where it had been torn from a spiral pad,

> *Dearest, Not tonight I am afraid, and not tomorrow either. I am sure they do not know but it is not good to take the chance now. I am hoping you enjoyed that little present though it was nothing very much. I am sorry for all this trouble. I love you.*

What was this? I thought, and began to open the next note but was interrupted by a knock at my door. Hastily, I slid Giovanni's box under my bed, where it would be hidden by the dust ruffle, and said, "Yes?"

"Dinner," answered my uncle Henry. I opened the door and we walked downstairs together. When he asked what I had been up to today, that he hadn't seen me around, I didn't deceive him in so far as I said I spent the afternoon gardening the cemetery with Helen. Needless to say, I didn't elaborate beyond that, and his apparent reaction was far less negative than I might have presumed. Indeed, he said, "Thank you for doing that."

"It's a paradise up there."

"I haven't been to pay respects to Giovanni and my folks for a while. Everything is all right?"

"Everything's fine."

Centered on the kitchen table was a simple bouquet of late-summer flowers arranged in the small Venetian glass vase I had brought as a present the week before. The vase reminded me of Rome, the unassuming gift shop where I bought it, and prompted a consciousness of how much had happened since then, since the Sunday of the Angelus bells. The disaster wrought with Mary, the presentiment that all was winding down toward a vortical black hole for me, my several decades in the world having amounted to a great big zilch, a grand naught, a goose egg, what have you—this polluted vision of myself had shifted some in these past few hours. Here at Ash Creek, where one might have imagined less rather than more would be going on than in Rome, here I had managed to immerse myself into not just my own new life but the lives of others. The leaf I'd planned to toss in the air to see which way the wind blew, so that I could follow it if all else failed after the Labor Day feast, seemed to have floated downward and come to rest just at my feet: I was where I should be, not just because of my interest in Giovanni Trentas's death, and in his daughter, too—but because I felt at home here with my family. I was in what might well have been an inappropriately agreeable mood—inappropriate because it was fringed by some ugliness and antipathy I couldn't yet fathom—and enjoyed the conversation, about nothing in particular, that evening more than any we had before, gathered around their hospitable table.

After dinner, after our customary smoke and drink on the porch, Edmé excused herself, saying she was tired, and Henry, too, proposed to turn in early. The thought of going upstairs to read more of *The Wonder Book* did not, tonight, attract me—my God, not at all—

and I asked Henry if I could borrow the car, go down into town, have a drink somewhere. I wasn't tired, I told him.

The headlights cast their momentary luminescence over myriad forms, glazing everything in flat white, as I drove along the creek road. This water spruce stump naturally took on the fleeting persona of the crouched assassin, that carcass of spindly driftwood assumed the appearance of some fantasy anorectic about to jump to a sudden suicide under the very car I steered, I who was perhaps as wired by the smoke as by the thimbleful of cognac, indeed maybe just *wired* period. The centerline of this rough mountain road consisted of grass, resolute thistles, clusters of brave Shasta daisies that survived the occasional thrashing of the underside of passing cars. An effort was required of me to keep from being mesmerized by the blanched fur of it. The turnoff and bridge across to the Lewis house awakened me from my reverie. I glanced over my shoulder and could see that they were home tonight; yellow light streamed from windows on both floors. A bird, perhaps a pygmy owl, since it seemed smaller than the barn owls I had seen in the past, flew with brilliant dispatch across the lit breadth of vista before me. Soon I reached the main road, and during the trip into town encountered only one other soul on the highway, a pair of headlamps traveling in the opposite direction.

Downtown at night. Some words in neon along the main street. No pedestrians. A truck, a couple of cars. Streetlights on each corner burned a hallucinogenic green-pink, their luminous globes hung from vintage poles which resembled tall cast-iron fiddlehead ferns. The three traffic lights suspended across the main street on span wires were set on timers and simultaneously changed from yellow to red, at which point I braked and ran my eye up and down the deserted rows of storefronts and businesses, saw the drawn shades of second-floor apartments, and couldn't help but marvel at what different compromises we all have to make in this world, what disparate places we each draw comfort from. I drove slowly, and though

I did, the business district soon disappeared behind me. Solid rows of pane-glass and block-granite buildings gave way to darkened hedges and, behind them, lawns; at the end of brick sidewalks rose ornate Victorian houses. Porch lights, which drew crazy insects as usual, made a mellow pooling over shrubs and trellises. Beyond this neighborhood of stately older houses was a gas station, the pumps bright under the island fluorescents, and beyond that were bungalows and a trailer park cozied behind a low wall overrun by tendrils of night ivy. Soon I found myself back out into the countryside, where, a mile down the road, I reached the Hotel St. Clair, a carpenter's gothic of clapboard and fire escapes—an old depot which had fallen on hard times since the afternoon my uncle took me there to have my first beer, the summer he deemed I had come of age. Nostalgia overwhelmed me as I pulled into the dirt lot where I parked. Music came from a side door, which stood ajar.

Within the smoky (I inhaled deeply) tavern were perhaps a dozen people. Some sat on stools, others stood or leaned against the long varnished bar; several men were engaged in a game of pool on a three-quarter table in a back room. I recognized, unexpected, the face of Noah Daiches, and considered for one moment quietly turning and leaving, though I would have no reason not to have just the opposite reaction to his presence here, not really—to walk up to him, a familiar face in a crowd of unfamiliar faces, and greet him. Either way, such thoughts were without much value, since Daiches saw and addressed me before I could have fled. "Grant, what brings you down here? Little slow on the hill?"

"A little," the warm sensation of my nostalgia having faded.

"What are you having?" He offered me the stool next to his.

I sat, and said to the bartender, "Scotch and water, then."

Noah continued, face grim, at variance with his words. "Nice party other day. Edmé knows how to do things right."

"She does."

My drink was delivered and money taken from the crumpled heap that lay, a miniature damp accordian, before Noah Daiches. "Thank you," I raised my glass and Noah raised his. Those crow's-feet at the corners of his eyes deepening and lips lifted toward though not fully up into a smile, he said, *"Salud."*

Nodding at his money, the emptied glasses by his hands, I asked, "Your night off?"

He turned his sculpted head to me. "You must miss being— where was it you were? Rome, you said?"

Lighting a cigarette, I translated easily his remark and sensed he was right, of course, and had in fact bought along with my drink a right not to be questioned by the likes of me. I said, a little meekly or apologetically, "I try to never miss wherever I'm not. I'm here, so why miss there?"

"That's a good philosophy, I guess. Easier to say than live by, I'd expect."

"You're probably right. I'm sure I fail more than succeed, but I try, anyway."

"Good, good. So, how *are* things up at Ash Creek, then?"

The question was not offered casually, or as mere pleasantry, but rather with swift, unsettlingly direct nuancing, which is to say it seemed to me a specific inquiry about the continuing siege there. I offered him the bland "Fine," while thinking perhaps the St. Clair hadn't been such a great idea.

"When I didn't hear from Henry yesterday about following up on that fire, well, I was a little surprised. He decided it was some kind of accident, did he?"

"It was too bad, that fire," I said, and looked over into Noah's blue eyes and then back down at my hands, cupped as if in prayer around my Scotch.

"Could have been worse. Your uncle was lucky there were so many people there at the time to help out." He paused. The country music on the jukebox had stopped, and the television suspended over the bar down at the end by the front door softly burbled above the voices of the laughing men and the prattle of ivory on the table beyond the alcove festooned with bags of nuts, chips, pretzels. Some game was being broadcast. I glimpsed the blinding green of the playing field, and the small figures that chased one another around, now and then abruptly enlarged to fill the screen with huge misshapen shoulders and radiant helmets that resembled scarabs dancing some surreal fandango.

"Football," I said to Noah.

"Very good," and for once a smile broke on his lips.

I thought to say, Isn't football played during the winter? but reconsidered, wisely enough, and simply said, "I hate sports," as if it needed any further explaining.

"Myself, I like lacrosse. Nobody around here but me likes lacrosse. They all say it's a game for foreigners, but I like it."

"That's the one they do on the beach?"

Noah said, "Well, if you say so. Sure, why not."

"Whatever. I really do hate sports."

"What do you like, Grant? You strike me as the kind of person who likes—let me guess—books, museums, culture."

"Do you think it was an accident?" ignoring his question.

"The fire? No, I don't see it as an accident. Even if there hadn't been any of these problems up on the hill, I'd have a hard time seeing how that fire could've got itself going."

Here was territory I both wanted badly to enter and feared embarking into with Noah. Perhaps the Scotch weighed into my choice of pursuing it, perhaps not, but I did fare forward. "Somebody might just have carelessly flicked a cigarette, or look, there were a lot of kids at the party. I was thinking maybe some kids had gone down there to sneak a butt. God knows, I used to do that when I was younger. Edmé still frowns a little on my smoking, I think, though now I don't bother to hide it anymore."

Noah Daiches himself was rolling a cigarette even as I spoke, and I watched him with haphazard attentiveness, as you can always tell a lot about someone who rolls by the *way* he rolls his smoke—the degree of deftness, whether he has to lend all his concentration to the exercise or no, if a leaf of tobacco is spilled by a wayward forefinger or heavy tongue. Noah'd done this many times before, I noted; he was dexterous and paid little mind to what he was about, rolled himself a perfect cigarette, lit it, drew the strings of his pouch, and tucked the red packet of rolling papers in one of the pockets of his leather flight jacket. *Papiers Mais,* I saw—the same brand Giovanni Trentas used to use, I recalled from my earlier quarrying in his box. Printed on the cover was a stalk of golden corn bound with a red ribbon. One ear was partly shucked, laying bare its rows of kernels and threads of silk.

"*Très elegante.*"

Noah pulled the packet back out and said, "This paper's the best. Friend of mind up in Vancouver gets them for me. You must know how to roll. Everybody in your generation knows how to roll *something.* Here . . ." and I took one of the papers, stubbed out my own, and clumsily rolled another with Noah's tobacco. That this man and Giovanni Trentas used the same unusual paper begged a question, I might have thought, which would have to be asked—but asked of someone else. Before I could think about it further, Noah spoke. "Edmé tells me you and Helen never met before."

"Helen Trentas? No, yes it's true, we hadn't."

"I wouldn't have believed it if she didn't say so. You looked like old friends the other day."

"She seems like a nice person," once more as blandly put as I could manage—again from the suspicion I was being subtly quizzed, though I could give no rational reason why Noah Daiches would want to glean anything from me. "Very beautiful," I added.

Noah said, "I suppose."

We sat unspeaking for a few moments and I weighed whether one did such a thing, plunged ahead with questions whose legal meanings were beyond one's competence to fathom, and the substantial significance of whose answers would probably also remain unclear. Blind to the hubris of gypsying ahead into places where I didn't really belong, there to solicit responses from people I did not know, to try to find the answers to questions I wasn't sure about—good Lord!—yet what did I do but stumble forward, with the arrogance of a true Pandora.

"Her father, Giovanni," was what I said, "I remember him from my days up at Ash Creek. He's the last person I would ever expect to wind up like that."

"Like what? We're all going to wind up like that someday."

"Murdered? I don't think so."

There, I thought. For better or worse it was on the table. Not that I expected much back for my effort. Daiches signaled the bartender, who refilled his glass.

"I meant deceased. Whoever said he was murdered? Did Helen tell you that?"

"You mean he wasn't?"

"We weren't able to substantiate any such thing. He died of some kind of trauma, if I remember. Coroner concluded he fell to his death."

"What about his foot missing?"

"You're up in the woods and you die, and when I go up there to re-cover you, chances are better than even you'll have more than a foot missing. You've put in some time up at Ash Creek. You ought to know how many animals live in the wild."

"I know—"

"Well, where's all their cadavers? You think every time some mule deer goes and dies, his friends get together and bury him nice and neat? Only reason the woods aren't piled with rotting carcass is be-cause out there they eat each other. And what the scavengers don't want, the maggots'll take. And when the maggots are done, then the microbes set to it. Fact is, if your uncle hadn't found him so soon after he passed—what was it, just a couple days—we would have found a strew of bones and hair, nothing more."

All this notification was offered to me with the flat, assured vocal hues of one who wasn't to be messed with. My sense of Noah's superiority in the matter of forensics and such—I mean, other than at a funeral, I had never even seen a dead body—did prevent me from debating him. It did not, however, inspire a shyness that would forbid my asking another question.

"You think his death has anything to do with these new problems up at the place, these night visits?"

"Why would it?"

"I don't know. I just think—"

"What did you say you do for a living, Grant?"

"I didn't say."

"If you'll pardon me, you sound an awful lot like some private investigator who hasn't got his license yet."

Silence from me.

"Look. That was a shame, what happened to Trentas. Must have been kind of an awful ending. Coroner's report suggested his heart wasn't that good. The body was quite scarified, at the base of a slant where it looked to have taken the fall, etcetera. He didn't have too many friends, kept pretty much to himself, serious fellow. Nobody I know had a thing against him, though, either. We didn't need some long-drawn-out investigation to conclude it wasn't a wrongful death. That's what's in the report if I recollect, and beyond that it was case closed. I am aware his daughter thinks otherwise. Which is again not uncommon, but even Henry didn't think there was any foul play involved. So far as these night intrusions go, your uncle only lets me know what's going on when it suits his fancy. None of my business unless he wants to file a complaint. I don't suppose he told you that last time he called me up there, all we found was an old shoe— Milland . . . Tate . . . look who's here—"

I turned, saw them both, the latter with jacket and bola tie, looking rather more formal than any of the others here, and said hello. Milland actually clapped me on the back, offered me a sooty smile, and asked me how goes it. Tate was sullen, I thought. Or else contemptuous. Or maybe indifferent. Either way, these men had a lifetime of commonality that made me feel more than ever my being both out of place and out of my league. These were not mere country boys, I recognized, with the possible exception of Milland. They might not have had the upbringing or education I did, but Noah and Tate were, I knew, astute, manipulative, complex, rough men. Around them, I couldn't help but feel like some inept boy.

If Tate and Milland hadn't arrived when they did, I wonder if I would have pressed on with the next question that had come to mind for Noah, regarding the note Henry and I found attached to the post, the night someone removed the door from the studio. Henry had sworn me to silence with Edmé, but never mentioned that I keep the note a secret from anyone else.

All things being equal, maybe it had been best that I missed my chance. As it was, I stood, thanked Noah again for the drink, shook hands with Milland, and pivoted to say goodbye to Tate but saw that his back was turned to me. He was involved in conversation with someone else. Once outside, I happened to look over into the taproom through one of the side windows, where I saw Tate speaking to Noah Daiches. His gestures seemed emphatic, and though I could view him only in profile and from some distance, he seemed to be annoyed. I wondered whether this change of demeanor had to do with me. I had the distinct sense Graham Tate considered me a nuisance, a mild inconvenience of some sort. But why?

I was probably paranoid, I told myself hopefully, as I climbed into the car, fumbled with key and lights, began my drive home. The dewy moon was full above me, above all of us, and shed a carpeting of light over the mountains and the valley they embraced. Tate more likely than not was barely aware of my existence here, I concluded. His annoyance was directed at someone else.

WHEN GIOVANNI reached the age of nineteen, he left Coeur d'Alene. Seven years had erased the war, which, despite its emphatic gestures of having orphaned and exiled him, had curiously made little outward impression on the boy. He had adapted to his new surroundings tolerably well, and although he might have shown signs of developing into a maverick, who was to say that—had there never been a war, and had he never left Rome, and had he been brought up by mother and father in the way that anyone else with a little fortune smiling on him could reasonably expect to be raised—he would have turned out to be any different? Maybe gregariousness, social negotiability, and all that stuff, is borne in the genes. Who is to say? Perhaps, even having been nurtured by a loving mother and disciplined by a stern father, as mothers and fathers were wont to do back in the forties and fifties, Giovanni Trentas might have wound up a loner. Surely his orbit would have been narrower, his world and reach more limited. Though, from what I have been able to piece together, he seems to have been born with a pragmatic head, even if in his teens he developed, at least for a while, a wandering heart.

The man I would sketch stood on the shoulder of the road, his valise beside him, his thumb raised in the hope of hitching a ride to the coast. He was tall, lean, sinewy—with dark eyes that were both calm and penetrating. Whoever might observe him through the windshield of a car that perhaps braked to pick him up would see a strapping kid with large head, a musician's ears, abundant black hair parted on the side but tousled. They would note hollow cheeks and prominent chin before admiring his great handsome beak of a nose, raptorlike, with nostrils opened wide as if to breathe into himself the thin air of Coeur d'Alene before diving into the world. Above all, they would observe the grace of this angular creature who lifted his luggage into the back and then joined them for the ride as far west as they happened to be going. They might even find, I would imagine, that his voice, a gentle tenor, rose to mind for days after they'd let him off.

In the box, a photograph of him from this period showed him to possess these features, and though it was taken in the year 1952, a decade before I was born, when I stared at it in the morning, before heading downstairs, I closed my eyes and listened hard and found I could without any effort remember that tenor voice, and could see him walking across the hayfield with Henry, talking, smiling, arms swinging, strides long and sure.

Later in the day, helping Edmé harvest, then spade over and mulch spent rows in her garden, I asked how she and Henry had met Giovanni Trentas. I realized that while, on occasion, I'd spent time with him—helped with sheep shearing more than once; followed him around Ash Creek trying to get him to converse in our mysterious shared language of Italian; it was he who taught me to ride a bike, but never pushed me to ride a horse—just how Giovanni had gone from the hinterlands of one state to those of another was part of his history I would not be able to derive from the box.

His persistent role as an outsider, however, was one with which I could identify. Edmé spoke freely about the subject, but not before noting, in a quietly disapproving way, I seemed to have disregarded her advice about Helen. There was no arguing the point, so I didn't.

Henry was attending the university on the other side of the

mountains, down near the capitol, and was in his last year, when he had his winter epiphany and decided that designing buildings in which people would live and work was more interesting than anything else a man could do with his life. He had already made up his mind by then not to return to Ash Creek but continue on to graduate school, and had made a list of schools where he would apply after military service—which responsibility he satisfied after getting a diploma, grateful he had just missed the war, being only sixteen the year that saw both Germany and then Japan surrender.

"Are you sure you want to hear all this?" she interrupted her story.

"Yes, yes—please," I said, failing to suppress my eagerness.

Sometime during his service days, he got it into his head that the only way to understand architecture was to know how to use a saw and hammer, and given there were many jobs available to fellows who wanted to do construction work, he labored for a while building houses in the suburban outskirts of the city. This was where he met Giovanni Trentas, then an itinerant worker who had hitchhiked down the West Coast all the way to the tip of Baja, ventured across the southwestern deserts and up the front range of mountains until he arrived here, having experienced adventures that belied his years. He talked about having worked artichoke and lettuce fields, hopped freight trains in the middle of the night, served on a fishing boat out of San Felipe, even spent a week in jail in San José del Cabo— though he'd never say what landed him there. He must have been just twenty.

"Well, your uncle Henry," Edmé went on, "worked side by side with this young rambler, and proximity and time turned them into friends. It wasn't until Henry's accident that this friendship deepened into what I always saw as a kind of fraternal love."

There was nothing unusual about the accident, as such. Henry made the mistake of failing to secure the end of a roll of metal webbing that was unfurled in a rectangular crater, reinforcement grid for concrete that was to be poured for a cellar. As if it had suddenly sprung to life, the tense heavy wire he had just unrolled surged back at him the moment he let go of it to retrieve some tacks from a bucket, in order to nail it to a wooden framing. The cut tips of the reinforcement wire flew up at his face and caught him across his cheek and in the eye. Giovanni witnessed the whole horrible instantaneous event and with ice from a cooler assembled a cold compress, got Henry into a car, and drove him to the hospital, hardly before Henry had recovered from the shock enough to know what had happened. For years, the blindness was partial; later, however, it worsened, and although for reasons of pride he would likely never admit it, the deterioration of his sight might well have had something to do with the decision he made to resign from his firm in San Francisco. The immediate upshot of the injury, however, was that Giovanni Trentas and Henry Fulton got to know one another during the latter's convalescence. Edmé had already met and begun dating Henry by then, too, of course, and so she remembered this youthful, handsome migrant as well.

"How did he wind up here?"

"Your great-uncle was always needing help on the ranch. Those were the days when Ash Creek still was very much an active spread, with cattle and sheep, even swine. They were always hiring seasonal workers. Giovanni came up to the mountains with me and Henry one time, met everyone, and just became part of the family. It was that simple. He lived sometimes on the ranch, sometimes in town. This place became the center of his life, I think it's fair to say, before the days you started coming here. I remember when Henry's father, your great-uncle Wesley, died, how upset Giovanni was. That must have been half a dozen years before you first saw Ash Creek. Henry and I'd gotten married and moved on out to the coast by then, and in a way Giovanni'd become an adopted son. More than part of the family: a real, trusted member. Well, you can see where he's buried, right up there with the others. Your uncle dug his friend Sam's grave with his own hands. I never saw him more sad in his life. He was as decent a soul as there ever was."

Margery came to mind if only by her noticeable exclusion from the story. Why had Margery left Giovanni? Not that people don't leave decent souls every day. But still, I asked.

Edmé said, "Well, poor Margery. Your uncle knew her better than I ever did—"

"Knew?"

"Knew, knows—she's not dead, if that's what you're asking. But from what I gather, her situation's almost as if. Margery used to be the most beautiful girl. But with four brothers straight out of *Grimm's Fairy Tales,* believe me. The grimmest of *Grimm's.* She took care of them when their parents got older, and I think maybe one of them fell in love and moved out, but the others just stayed on. When Giovanni and Margery met, you can imagine how threatened these lugs were, not that they *cared* about him, or her. They would tell you a very different story, no doubt, but what it came down to was simply that they didn't want to lose their nanny, maid, nurse, cook, aide-de-camp, mother figure, and whatever else they'd managed to make of the poor thing. I think she and Giovanni really did love each other, so after sneaking around for a year or two, one night, between Thanksgiving and Christmas, I believe, she eloped with him. They had it all planned out, had Justice Phelps prepared with the license, had the wedding rings all ready in secret."

"And soon after that, I guess, Helen was born," I interrupted, while wondering why they didn't all live happily ever after.

Edmé paused, glanced over at me from where she was gathering heaps of pungent basil leaves into a basket. She had on her face the queerest look, querying and forswearing at the same time.

"Sorry," believing I was being chastised for distracting her.

Edmé continued, the look suddenly having vanished. "Margery and Giovanni lasted longer than any of us expected they would, but it was sheer willpower on their part. Those brothers are lunatics. I mean, with screws loose and bats in the belfry. They took it as a challenge, almost like jilted lovers, to get her back home."

"They finally succeeded, I guess."

"I don't know how they did it, but they did, convinced her to come home. If I remember right, they'd made some offer for Giovanni to move in, too, with Helen as well. He refused, kept Helen, and one day Margery was gone. I don't think they ever bothered getting a divorce."

"That's quite a story," I said, wondering how Margery could leave her daughter for some covetous brothers, understanding Helen's resentment.

"Giovanni raised Helen by himself. She couldn't have had a better father or even mother. Margery never treated the girl like a daughter, anyway. She resented her, I always thought. The three of them tried that winter to live in a little place they'd taken somewhere between here and town, but it didn't go well, and by the time spring came, Giovanni was put in the position of having either to break off with Margery, or put the baby up for adoption, or something crazy. That was very near the end."

We each took her last words to mean that she had no more to say about Margery and Giovanni, and so were silent for a time. Then I broke the quiet with, "Can I ask a question? It might seem a little off the wall. But can you remember what kind of cigarettes Giovanni smoked? or what brand of paper he rolled with?"

"What kind of question is that?"

I shrugged. My own exhausted cigarette dangled from my lips, and I imagined how unhealthy I must appear to my aunt, smoking in her wholesome garden, spilling worthless ash on its rich soil, the smoke fouling this pristine air—not to mention how neurotic she must have thought it was of me to ask about the cigarettes of a dead man.

Edmé gave me a look, eyes smiling, lips frowning. "Not all of us share in that bad habit, Grant."

"I know," I said, extinguishing it and depositing the butt in my shirt pocket. "One of these days soon I promise I'll quit, but what are you saying—surely he must have smoked?"

"No, he didn't smoke. Didn't drink, either. They both cost money, and though Giovanni was always fairly paid for his work here, he never had much. That is, never had much for himself. He always seemed to have plenty for Helen, sending her overseas, buying her nice clothes—Helen grew up like some kind of aristocrat, comparatively speaking. I don't know how Giovanni managed it, if you want to know, except by sacrifice. Anyway, he was always too concerned about his health to do things like drink and smoke. Why do you ask?"

"No reason. Just thinking maybe I've been doing a little too much of both recently, I guess." Such was my lame equivocation, though her answer raised more questions than it resolved. Why the rolling papers and that handwritten recipe for dandelion wine among the preserved artifacts of an ascetic? Why an aristocrat's daughter to a pauper father?

WHAT CAME as the strangest surprise to me—there in my sunny room, by myself in the early afternoon, this fragrance of raw basil leaves on my fingers from helping Edmé mix the basil with pignolis and garlic, olive oil and parmigiana—what came as an astonishment was that I missed Helen Trentas. No: rather, was that I missed her this much. And not merely missed her but found myself longing for her. And, again, as part of this surprise or astonishment, was just *how* I missed her, in what ways longed for her.

These were not the hollow affections manufactured in my baser heart, say, or even baser parts of me than that—though I would be less than honest were I not to admit that I longed for Helen Trentas there, too. This was not the way I'd felt toward that girl I'd picked up near the Spanish Steps, and fucked—that's the word for it, truly—in the very sheets where my wife and I slept the night before. Nor was this the sometime manipulator's devotion kicked into life once more, as it had been when I was a boy threatened by the specter of divorce between my parents. This degree, measure, variety, manner of yearning that came over me as the trapezoid of sun poured warm and brilliant on my back was altogether of a new order. Even compared to my flawed but genuine love for the women in my past, this *thing* which clutched me like an exquisite fist about my heart was undeniable, wonderful, and frightening. Was it possible I unselfishly cared for Helen?

I sensed that those several compass points in my incomplete map were about to be rendered meaningful, as this fourth direction rose into view, and to prominence. If, say, north stood for Daniella, then north had been a bit chilly. If south had been my compass point for Jude, that would mean with Jude everything had gone south, south toward the overhot tropics, south being a tormented direction. And if Mary, whom I met in the East and with whom I traveled farther east to salvage the unsalvageable, was that third point, then what was left in this personal metaphor for Helen Trentas if not west? West where my own wayward feet perhaps had come to find something more permanent, more substantial, more earnest, than what I had known in times past.

But then, I thought, here was a unique way to leave Ash Creek: by not going. While Edmé, with the help of her deficient *sous-chef*, poured the fresh pesto into plastic pint containers and sealed each for the freezer, I mentioned to her that my earlier idea of leaving after Labor Day had come into question. I had nowhere really to go, I told her. "I can move to a room in town, if I'm in the way here," hoping not to sound somehow pathetic.

Edmé gave me a lovingly horrified look. Always her paradoxical gazes.

"Don't get me wrong," I said quickly. "I don't want to be underfoot is all. I don't like the idea of being a burden to you two—it's not why I came."

"Grant, this is your home. You stay here until you want to go elsewhere."

I thanked her, and as I did I recognized that what I failed to mention (though Edmé may have surmised it) was that the magnetism of this place was now irresistible to me, the curiosity it aroused in me was overwhelming, or something else altogether was at play—even I couldn't be sure. Whatever drew me, any thought of moving on from

Ash Creek, was for the moment erased by my unexpected feelings for Helen, and also by what I'd discovered tucked beneath the pretty rubble in Giovanni's box. For once I found myself grateful that nothing and no one awaited me outside Ash Creek. It left me free to pursue phantoms as I pleased. It left me free to be with Helen.

My fingers trembled when I opened up the box, because for the first time I began to understand there might be more to its contents than just a repository of beloved flotsam, of mere memorabilia, as I had presumed a couple days before, when I first undid those ribbons that corseted the thing. I lifted, for one, the packet of *Papiers Mais* and held it up in the light, studied the gold ears of corn stamped on the cover, confirming that these were the same that Noah had used, then opened the packet and saw that more than half the papers were missing. I set it on my bed, rummaged around again in the box. For no particular reason other than that it came first to hand, I read the recipe for dandelion wine, which, like the rolling papers, had no obvious place in Giovanni's trove—*Take 3 quarts dandelion blossoms, 4 qts. boiling water, 3# sugar, 4 lemons sliced. Pour boiling water over the blossoms*—and winced at how horrid this weedy concoction must taste. I placed the recipe beside the *Papiers Mais*, and regarded them together. Neither of the little talismans made much sense to me. So, like the collage artist who must lay out his raw materials before beginning work, or the jigsaw puzzler who spreads before him all the differently shaped pieces to begin to assemble them into a coherent picture, I set out, one by one on the bed, all the other objects. Surely, I thought, there was something here for me to understand if I had but eyes to see.

Two feathers, the joke book, pennies . . . all the stuff was spread out. The brass plunger, whose shiny barrel flashed sharp light straight into my eyes, did begin to seem familiar. What was this thing? I held it like a tiny rifle in the palm of my left hand and drew back the ring on the end of the plunger, then pushed forward, pulled again and pushed. It was not an air pump. The nozzle end wasn't shaped right, I didn't think.

A little brass gun, I wondered, *a little brass gun*—

Then memory raised an image up before me of Giovanni. He was crouched down next to this young boy, who had the serious role of helping the man, by holding a wrench or a can of oil. Both of us idled beside a beat-up bicycle I used to ride around on paths here during summer months. The memory was of Giovanni smiling at me, speaking gently while he worked on my bike, allowing me to believe I was helping him, greasing the chain and rusty sprockets with this little brass gun.

—Good as new now, see here? I could almost hear his voice, as he stood, steadying the bike for me while I climbed uncertainly aboard. His front teeth were marvelously gapped.

—*Grazie,* I might have said.

—*Niente, prego,* as he let go and stood back to watch me ride wildly down the hill toward the horsegate and road along the creek.

Happy, in a wistful way, at the memory and the fact that I, too, was represented among the puzzle pieces in the box—for it did seem a puzzle to me, a rebus of sorts—I laid the radiant apparatus with its companions, wishing I could ask it just one modest question, which would be, What are you doing here, my trifling friend? why on earth would Giovanni Trentas set aside and thereby memorialize such a paltry widget as *you?* Instead, I touched each of its companions, with a reverence one might show toward inanimate things when in church, where often the inanimate represents the animate, where wafer and wine become flesh and blood. I couldn't help but chide myself, in the midst of all this small pleasure, with a question that *could* be answered, however. What if the box was simply a box, a pretty cigar box kept by a charming eccentric who used it not as a treasure chest or an assemblage of mute but eloquent symbols, but merely as a dump for discards and junk? And what kind of fool would spend time trying

to make order of such chaos? Good questions, but not good enough
to dampen my interest.

Not until I read several other of the penciled trysting notes from
the anonymous correspondent, who was, I thought, surely Margery,
did I notice something about the ticket to the dance recital. One
note read:

> *You know I love you and I will do it but I can only do it when
> they're not here, so I will call and I hope you forgive me for all the
> trouble I do cause, it will be sometime this week, I love you.*

Which seemed more of the same, really.

Another was further along in the affair:

> *Dearest yes, I do want to be with you for ever, and sense there is
> no way on earth they will go along with it, I will consider what
> you say, and will see you next Tuesday.*

And then there was this:

> *On Sat eve then, and it is kind of your Henry to offer to shelter us
> till the storm clouds pass over, I know that one day they will for-
> give, but I cannot continue on like in this manner and must grab
> my own chance at life with you, how much I love you dearest,
> soon soon.*

So that was what happened, or was it? Edmé had left out of her
story the crucial detail of Henry's offering the newlyweds Ash Creek
as sanctuary from these ridiculous men who were her brothers, apparently. The dance recital card was, as I mention, what came to my
attention next, having read my way through all the notes from
Margery, and what intrigued me was that it was made out not to
Giovanni Trentas and Margery, though it was dated the twenty-third

of March, 1965—which was, I gathered, about the time the two of them met and fell in love—but rather to Henry Fulton and Willa Richardson. My uncle and Willa together at a dance recital? and in March, when I'd thought he was always out on the coast, his stays at Ash Creek at that time confined to summer months? Moved as if by a force outside myself, I swept the objects before me into a heap, and tossed them back into the box. My earlier elation was eclipsed now by bewilderment.

Maybe there were things here that I really didn't want to know. I retied the ribbons and put the box away in the armoire. I left the room in something of a hurry, assuring myself that it was my own corrupt imagination that would cause me to think for even an instant that Henry and Willa Richardson had ever been anything but distant acquaintances, as I'd always assumed they were. Just look at how they behaved at the Labor Day gathering, I reminded myself as I emerged onto the porch. Elegant, proud Willa, the wife of Tate. This was a false lead. Nothing in the box meant anything; so I now decided. I walked far up into the gorge, with the fishing rod I had taken down from its perch of nails in the eaves of the porch. From placid springheads I caught several rainbows, including a great long one— all of which I put back into the cold water, where I watched them each as they drew from the current molecular liquid through their white gills, recovered their sense of place, then bolted out into deeper riffles with several hard swipes of their muscular tails.

That evening for dinner we ate fresh "pesto macaroni." Henry and I discussed the stock market and other ultimately irrelevant matters with a kind of warm enthusiasm that belied the sketchiness of our various points. Five rather than six cigarettes were decimated by me on the porch that evening. Maybe two not three liqueurs were consumed on the veranda, as we—or rather Edmé—noticed the first of the fall warblers settling for the night in the tops of trees, having begun their migration south toward points beyond both Mexicos, headed equatorward. We retired, as usual, though while again I found I wasn't sleepy, I had no desire to go back to the taproom. Tonight Hawthorne would do fine, I thought. And so he did, with a desperate tale about Midas and his poor, loving daughter, whom, through his own greed and by a fateful accident, he temporarily murdered with his touch, turning her to a statue of gold when she ran to embrace him. Midas's stock market, I reflected, trying and more or less failing to work out an anagram, *Dim ass's mock rakett.*

I lay on top on the bed, fully clothed, arms crossed in the ambient glow, staring ahead at the complicated golden angles of this dormer and that wall. Thinking or dreaming of Helen, in the most abstract way. Not awake but not asleep, either. Just alone. By myself on that bed where I'd slept as a boy. Where now I dozed, the volume of Hawthorne on my chest, until I was awakened by the subtlest sound coming, or so I believed, up the creek road. Subtle, meager, the grinding unoiled metal, tires which rolled on the moist earth to a halt.

Tonight I would not panic. Instead, I set my book aside, on the table, having folded the corner of the page so I could find my spot when I returned. I extinguished the lamp by the bed and slipped into my shoes, went to the door, downstairs, and onto the porch, where I stood, listened. A walking stick of ash that was left beside the screen door frame I grasped and held as a demented king would his scepter. No one stirred in Edmé and Henry's bedroom, so I assumed it was only I who'd been awakened. The moon did not shed tonight the light it might have only last week, when it was full, but by this time my feet knew the way better than they had when I walked toward Henry's studio the other night, groping through drenched grass near the creek. Hearing nothing, seeing nothing, I decided to make my way down to the front gate, by now wondering whether I had simply dreamed those few noises of iron, rubber, dirt.

The foreyard gate at the end of the pebbled walk, which I had skirted, was ajar and thus I needn't have worried about how to swing it open without disturbing the garrulous bells that hung from it. A cool autumnal breeze serenely ascended the valley. By next month, if not sooner, I would be able to see my breath in a cloud at this time of night. Summer was near its end. Fiery yellow lochs of aspen would very soon appear in the green conifer seas as the season gave way to autumn and then to my favorite: beautiful, mesmerizing winter, when the world is softened by snow.

I reached the gate, which glowed palely under the starlight, and as I did, the presence of another was plainly in the air. I could almost smell someone, almost taste a vitality on my tongue. Up my arms and neck this recognition registered as my hair stood on end and goose bumps rose. My fear was, in a superficial way, irritating, even painful. I breathed in slowly, silently, as if by drawing the cold into me I might restore my calm, and as I did, I was reminded of the fish that brought themselves back to life from their own terror, earlier that day, by a similar process. The horsegate also stood ajar, and though it was not unusual for the sheepbell-laden foreyard gate to be left unlatched up by the house, this lower gate never was left unbolted. Something was wrong here.

I wedged myself between gate and post, stepped down the road a few yards. The creek whispered words I couldn't understand, and as it did I discerned the outlines, or rather the substance and bulk, of my prey—it *was* prey because I stalked it—at the side of the road, some hundred feet farther along. Or was I the prey? Without pausing, I walked on, toward it, quietly but steadily. Once I was sure of what I beheld in the midst of all this darkness around me, darkness that lay like some filthy shroud over the hollow and hill crests and mountaintops beyond, I found my voice, then heard myself ask aloud, "Is someone there?" Foolish enough question, I suppose. Nevertheless, it was what I said, and then pronounced similar words again, maybe with more authority the second time: "Who's there?"

The answer, which came from behind, startled me. "It's me," is what she said, and although I hadn't known her all that long, I easily recognized Helen, as I turned on my heel and glimpsed her silhouette, dark black against a vaguer black backdrop. She stood, in fact, by the horsegate.

"Helen?" I murmured. "What are you doing here?"

She was walking toward me. A shiver released my welled-up apprehension; it was as if my body involuntarily shook off fear the way some beast might shake off water. I was grateful this darkness hid from her my odd spasm.

"I had to see you," she answered. Even as she spoke I felt her arms around me and found myself absorbed in a kiss more impatient than deep, more severe than pleasant. The urgency of her tongue and hands was nearly as startling as her presence here in the first place. I dropped the ash stick to the ground. When the embrace ended, I asked, "Are you all right?"

"Let's go up to the house," she said, taking my arm.

"I'm not so sure that's a good idea."

"We won't wake them up, don't worry."

"But if you want to talk—" I said.

"I *don't* want to talk."

Despite everything—despite that rational, wiser part of my character telling me, This is not what you want to do, Grant—I walked beside her, more or less swept away by the strong current of her will.

"Don't you realize how dangerous it is to come up here in the middle of the night?"

"You mean because of those music men you were telling me about?"

"Well, them too, but I meant you come unannounced and you risk having Henry take his shotgun to you. I know; he almost shot me not so long ago."

"It doesn't look like you learned your lesson, does it? You're out wandering around in the dark. Anyway, I can handle myself. I'm not afraid of night visitors, or Henry, for that matter."

"Your father wasn't afraid, either, and—well—"

"The gorge is a dangerous place."

We neared the foreyard gate, and I said, "Helen, what're we doing?"

She stopped, turned, and kissed me once more, somewhat less panicky, more deliberate this time, and whispered, "Didn't you miss me, too?"

I admitted that, yes, I did. We passed through the gate and up into the house. She knew her way through the rooms as well as I, and within minutes we found ourselves in my bedroom, unclothing one another in the hushed but charged atmosphere, a harmony of fingers unbuttoning shirts, unzipping pants, removing underwear, until our bodies were naked and entwining on my sheets. She was my aggressive lecheress tonight, sat in the splayed fork of my legs and lifted my hips toward her face with a strength I might never have predicted. Her tongue and mouth moved in long methodical arcs around from thigh across the flat plain of my stiffened belly over to other thigh, and I lay back with no doubt a grimace on my face, as this physical ecstasy was excruciating to me. My palms cupped both sides of her precious head when she finally took me inside her mouth and lowered herself over me, her hair spread like fibrillate waves across my middle. Time passed, supple and plastic time bent from its normal regularity. When I moved to kiss the top of her head, maybe press my lips into the mysterious soft spot that centers the parietal juncture where, at the crowns of babies' heads, the new blood pulses, she lifted her mouth to mine and I tasted the sweet saltiness of my own body on her lips. She took both my hands and pressed them out away from me and above my head, as we lay down, so that I stretched out beneath her like some intoxicated martyr being prepared for his lascivious crucifixion. Though we tried as best we could to do all this in silence, there was a moment in which nothing mattered anymore, and the rest of the world disappeared from consciousness. The oblivion that drew upon me and blanketed my exhausted body in the wake of climax was sudden and total, and so whether the springs creaked or not, or whether the bedstead whacked against the wall, or whether Helen may have allowed herself to giggle when I found a ticklish notch in the flesh of her neck with my tongue, or even whether we cried out in the moment of abandonment of everything, I couldn't say.

That I woke up alone, with no sign that Helen had been there other than the scent of her on my skin, somehow didn't surprise me. Indeed, my first feeling was of relief at not having to appear downstairs in front of Edmé and Henry with Giovanni Trentas's daughter at my side. I didn't really understand, still, the nature of Edmé's warning regarding Henry, his probable discouragement of our liaison. Despite the several objections I already mentioned, none of which seemed of great merit so far as I could see, especially in light of the fact that I was falling in love, and had no intention of hurting her, I felt I had every right to be with this young woman—felt that surely we were *meant* to be together, that our separate childhood roads had finally merged. Having thought that, I drew the blankets up over me, screening myself off from those many lightening predawn clouds that skimmed the window-framed horizon over the eastern ridge, and slumbered awhile longer, peacefully ecstatic that such an encounter had just taken place, without our having inherited any shame or confusion, or opened ourselves up to judgment the morning after.

DAVID LEWIS knew where he would find Henry that morning. He knew Henry's several defining obsessions and where they took him after dawn, or were likely to take him noon or night. So that when he pushed his hands down the sleeves of his barn jacket and settled a hat on his head for the walk, he sensed there would be no need for him to relate his news to both Edmé and Henry at the same time. He would find Henry, whose business this was, in his opinion, insofar as it pertained to the ranch lands, and tell him—the son of one steader to the son of another. Let Henry go and grieve or complain about it to his wife, as he would: that was none of David Lewis's affair. Instead, as he stepped outside into the crisp mid-morning, he pictured his neighbor up in the studio, like always, intent upon that curious chipboard and foam-core utopia of his, the blueprints of indeterminate shapes, and clay models conforming to wise organic curves. As Lewis walked across the bridge that took him from his own lands over onto the creek road, he called out to his dogs, two black Labradors. They bounded ahead when he turned north and up the road, climbing its mild incline with ease.

He would miss this. The road, the very greenness of the valley and familiar purity of the air, the dogs leading the way, up to Ash Creek. His gait was not as spirited as usual this morning. The quickness of his step, the resilience, was not there. Nor did his hands swing freely at his sides, as they always had over the many years Lewis had tramped here. Why should they? After all, what Lewis had to confess to Henry troubled him, too. These were circumstances he had averted for the longest time, as Henry well knew. His heritage, his own personal history, decades of both hard and sweet toiling, had been at stake. His family had lived in this valley bordering the Fultons for as many decades as anyone alive could remember, and therefore he believed his regrets were every bit as strong and earned as what Henry would no doubt feel. Times change, he reminded himself as he reached the horsegate and shot back the bolt. The dogs had long since figured out a way around obstacles like gates, and rejoined him momentarily, coats wet with creek water from their wading around the terminus of the fence.

Lewis ran his fingers through his hair and glanced up at the bright roof of the house where it mirrored morning light. Smoke from the near chimney meant Edmé was in the kitchen. All these intimate nuances, the tiny particulars he was able to interpret from living in such proximity for so long, all the simple knowledge he would miss having at his disposal . . . he shook his head, then turned away toward the east, where he crossed the rickety bridge into the farther meadow. Let Henry tell Edmé, he thought. By the time he did, Lewis would already have returned down this same road, following these rampant dogs across the narrow wood trestles, back home.

He was there: Lewis knew his man. When he rapped fist against doorframe he heard, —Come on.

—Henry? he said, and to the dogs, —You two sit, *stay*.

—Lewis? Heh.

He stepped inside.

—Take your coat off, man, said Henry.

And so he did.

—What have you got to say for yourself this morning?

David Lewis had this to say: As Henry knew, he'd avoided it for some years now, but the inevitability of the numbers—the loans and second mortgages he could not carry, the taxes he could no longer afford to pay, the ranch revenues or lack thereof—made the place untenable. He was forced to let it go, was selling it off in its entirety. He'd been approached by a broker who brought him an offer he could not sanely refuse. The contract had been signed, and it was only a matter of some weeks before they'd go to closing.

—I either sell now with some dignity, or foreclose sometime soon without, and I like what dignity I've got, Henry, just like you would if you were in the same spot.

Henry sat tacit. He stared at the constancy of the water out the window—moving and falling, pooling and moving and falling—up at the gorge aperture. He said, at last, —This is all done, then?

—I'm afraid so.

—Thank you for telling me.

—I'm sorry, Henry. I know you think of this as a kind of treachery, but who's to say? Maybe they'll do something better with the place than I'm doing.

—You made no deed restrictions?

—Well, I tried to get some language into the contract that would serve as a restrictive covenant against building or doing anything unfortunate with the land, but they weren't going for it. Like I say, I'm really sorry. I didn't have a choice.

—We always have choices.

—No, not always, he said.

—Are you at liberty to tell me who's buying?

Here was the one question Lewis might have hoped Henry would not ask, for wasn't it unnecessary, really, wasn't it finally just a little cruel to force him to state the obvious? Given how Henry felt about Tate, how he represented a kind of leisurely, methodical evil to Henry, through his patient acquisition of power over the years and his equally unhurried dispensation of trouble to anyone who happened to find himself in Tate's path, why would he want Lewis to speak the name? Or, that is, the corporate mask for the name, since who or *what* had already paid a percentage of the substantial sum for some thousand acres of stream, valley, and hills was not in fact Tate, but one of any number of anonyms. Lewis must then have wondered why every year, without fail, Tate had been invited to the Labor Day function, allowed to mingle among them, dine upon Henry and Edmé's fare and drink their wine, possessed of an arrogant bearing that might suggest to any uninformed bystander that all this was *already his.* But there it was, come he always did. Possibly he was invited for Willa's sake—a vestige of days, perhaps, when Henry and Willa were closer, or when Giovanni Trentas was alive and among her best friends, however odd the friendship seemed to anyone who paid attention to such matters. Or else he was invited so Henry could remind Tate just how handsome was Ash Creek, this place which he'd never be able to own.

Lewis hesitated as he thought about all this, and within that instant Henry first gave him a look of burning hostility—almost as if Lewis had metamorphosed into Tate himself—and then, as quickly, Henry's grace returned to him, and he apologized by saying, simply, —Never mind. Thank you again, David, and good luck to you.

Henry then smiled with resolute composure at Lewis.

That was it? Lewis must have thought. That was all?

He accepted Henry's hand, shook it, then turned, retrieved from the horn coat tree his oilskin jacket, and left.

My uncle did not watch him make his way across the meadow back down to the ruined bridge at the end of the trace. From his stool he could hear one of the dogs bark. He remained alone in the studio for some long while, before coming over to the house to deliver the news to me and my aunt.

I might have had some inexplicit handle on the meaning of the sale of Lewis's lands, but conceived my role was to remain silent, an observer, though it did occur to me that David Lewis had never been visited by the night people. Was this because he had been seen as eventually willing to sell, without the spooky, cheap, midnight tactics to urge him along? Was what was going on here a reprise of the Posner story that Edmé'd told me? These seemed obvious questions, except that had not Henry said he'd never been approached with any offer for Ash Creek? Well, then, of course, there would be another question—questions always beg questions—and that is: was Henry telling me the truth? And again: was *this* question planted in my mind by that note left on the gate, what seemed a lifetime ago, or did it have merit on its own? Questions and more questions—the significance of the possible answers to these questions hadn't yet struck an emotional chord within me. That would come.

"The way we are going about dismantling the world," Henry was saying, "turning timber to boards, rivers to dams, ore to metal, and so on and so forth, is just like a cancer working its way across a system of healthy cells."

I listened to my uncle, heard the crackling edge in his speech. Edmé betrayed none of her disquietude—the fear and the anger, the belief that somehow things were drawing down toward some irrevocable finish—while I was still with them in the room.

As it was, I left, sensing they wanted to talk alone, but also needing to get away. I hiked up to the long ridge where I'd come to read that letter from Mary announcing her wish that we divorce, and sat and looked down over Ash Creek valley, whose brilliant expanse dwarfed the house and outbuildings. My thoughts came to a halt, for a moment, and I felt healing gratitude for this small reprieve. It was a calmness, however, before the tempest that now began to storm within. What was going to happen down there? and what effect was it to have upon me? My old room, what minuscule claim on history I had anywhere on earth, was in that house. Edmé and Henry, sole survivors of my limited family, were there, too. And across the valley, nestled in a high pasture to the east of where I sat, the cemetery where Helen and I made love that first time. All these delicate ties, last remnants of past and future, were coming unloosed, little by little

tearing apart at seams that only last night had appeared to be reliable, solid, even *seamless*. Was it because I had not slept much that
my eyes were suddenly warm and tearing? Surely it wasn't because I
feared that this small foothold on the world was about to be taken
away from me? Surely this veteran rambler, this Grant who'd always
enjoyed being uprooted, wasn't worried, or needy, or afraid?

WITH THE BLESSING of Wesley Fulton, Henry's father, Giovanni Trentas had tried to restore the old homestead cabin at the bottom of the meadow, way back when he first came to live at the ranch. It would appear *tried to restore* was the operative phrase for his handi-work, because in fact there was no restoring the place, so unevenly had the walls settled down there by a freshwater spring which fed into the creek, and so green had been the timbers they'd originally used for building that when they dried they bowed and curled and pulled free of their square nails. Another, much smaller outbuilding, which dated from roughly the same period, stood on the far side of the creek, and though it was less convenient, Giovanni saw that he stood a better chance of pulling it into shape than the other, and so he began work there. Across the bridge he carried tools, and wood appropriated from old outbuildings around the ranch that had fallen into disuse. He planed and renailed, replacing boards that were alto-gether rotted or twisted beyond repair, battening the outer walls of the hut and laying fresh courses of shingles on its roof. He reglazed its broken windows, chinked up breaches in the frames, and did his best, with little money and in spare time, to make for himself a place of his own, a home. He brewed coffee on the small coal-fed stove way before the sun rose, well before anyone else on the place was up. He improvised for himself, with what was given him, a decent residence at Ash Creek. Whenever Henry and Edmé returned to the mountains, however, he was happiest, at least during those early years. With them, he became a different man altogether, came forth from his hermeticism, showed the capacity and even the appetite not just for hard work but pleasure. With them, he would go into town to sit on the trampled grass and listen to a summer-evening concert, say, at the band shell. Or attend a production of Shakespeare or Thornton Wilder at the little theater, put on by some regional company with good intentions if meager craft.

His sister, Paola, it seemed, disappeared from his life. In the box was a letter from her, which apologized, though not profusely, for her decision against making the journey with her two children and husband to see him. They wanted to come, she wrote. But money was tight and the children were too young for such an undertaking. *Forse anno prossimo,* she wrote. Maybe next year. But it would appear she never made the trip out. Nor, for that matter, did Giovanni journey to Coeur d'Alene. Two exiles, exiled from one another— these things happen. Despite this, his life at Ash Creek seemed embraced by contentment for some years, was of elemental simplicity, and any reconstruction of his biography through these years might best do no more than follow the seasons, painting his image into scenes of snow and first buds and summer heat and the brilliant dying of the leaves in anticipation of new snows. One cannot help but think he was at peace during those years, loved as a son by my great-uncle and aunt. But, surely, he was lonely.

Which is why I believe the entry of Margery into his life must have been monumental in its impact. One of the reasons we cherish being in love is that our paradoxical needs—for solitude, yet not to be isolated—are simultaneously satisfied when we *fall for* another person. We set ourselves apart from the world, but yet are rarely by ourselves, when in love. And what happens between lovers remains an inviolate secret if they wish it to be. The minutiae of Giovanni and Margery's passion are unknown to anyone now, except perhaps to Margery, and thus here is a fragment of the story I cannot narrate other than in broadstroke.

Suffice it to say, they met when two of Margery's brothers had been hired as temporary hands to help with autumn roundup, one of those last years when Ash Creek was still a working spread. Even as recently as thirty years ago, they would drive several hundred head of cattle from the lower fields down through a funneling gate, where they were counted, and then guide the animals along that narrow creek road. Past the place where the river widened, the noisy procession would flow, then out onto the paved highway, headed southward until they reached a crossing, dozens of miles distant from the T-junction of dirt and asphalt, where railroad tracks intersected their path. Here they recounted and loaded their living shipment, up steel ramps into livestock cars of a freight train that seemed to extend from horizon to horizon. This drive took the better part of a week to organize. The first few days of it were passed at Ash Creek itself, bringing together herds from different high pastures in the mountains.

And, as I understand, on one of those first days, appeared at the main gate a shy but vigorous young woman who had brought, in a basket, dinner for her brothers. Neither of them was about, however, and Giovanni, who by that time occupied the little creek house, noticed her in the early-evening light, perhaps casting a long shadow across the meadow, and asked her if he could be of any help. What a handsome figure he must have cut, with his soft-spoken, mildly accented eloquence and gentle bearing, so unlike anyone Margery had ever met; and she, this flushed beauty with her raven locks tumbling across her shoulders in lustrous counterpoint to a practical, simple, maybe even austere dress, maybe of gingham or maybe linen—though who knows now, now that he is gone and she would surely not remember.

They met during the next days, too. Her brothers, it would seem, ate well that week, even better than they usually did. After they took the basket and left to sit with the other men back in the bunk-house to eat, Giovanni would walk over from the hut, overcome his reserve, and continue whatever conversation she and he had begun the evening before. Their dialogue didn't end when the work was done and the brothers returned home to Red Hill. No doubt, Margery was forced to hide her friendship with Giovanni Trentas—not so unlike Helen and me—at least in the beginning, for fear of criticism or even worse, that they might try to forbid her from con-tinuing to see him.

—But nobody *owns* you, I can hear him saying, as summer burned itself out and autumn hoarfrosts whitened the higher meadows some mornings, just as now they soon would here. —You are a grown woman. You can do what pleases you, no?

—You don't understand.

—Why don't I understand? You like me?

—Yes.

—You like to talk with me?

—Very much.

—You like to be with me, no?

—I do.

—*E 'llora?* and so?

Margery's excuses, the elaborate, tangling fabrications given to explain her more frequent and lengthy absences, must have begun to wear down to a sheer transparency at home. In due time, the brothers probably would have begun to talk among themselves about her odd behavior. Maybe, yes, she did still manage to look after the house in Red Hill and keep things running, more or less—but surely they noticed a difference in how she dressed now, how her patience with their overwhelming expectations had grown as tenuous as all these alibis that seemed to flow from the once-quiet lips of their Marge. The disharmony and the quarrels would continue for quite some time, once Margery and Giovanni discovered they preferred being together—even if only for a few hours at a time—than separated. Giovanni was thirty years old, Margery was twenty-three. The year was 1963. Each was the other's first love. It would make perfect sense that Helen was born in 1965, or so I might have thought. She was, too; though here the ambiguity darkened their personal histories and had never allowed of any bright regard. That dance recital ticket in the box came back to mind, as I reconsidered all this. But: no. It had no connecting significance that I could see. At least, it was nothing I felt able to ask my uncle about. Nor Willa, whom I didn't yet know. Nor Giovanni, who could not answer.

LET ME not give a false impression about my uncle's architectural models. I may have done so, and I'd rather not.

This utopia of his is not the project of some hopeless idealist. The Italian architectural visionary Paolo Soleri has his Arcosanti excavation down in Arizona, with its molded forms and dyed earth; Frank Lloyd Wright tucked Taliesin West against a range of mountains not so far distant from Arcosanti; Buckminster Fuller drew earnest plans for entire metropolises to be sheltered from the elements under massive geodesic domes of steel and glass. Examples surely abound beyond what little I know about such things. Though, then, my uncle's passion might seem odd to some, to others it was unremarkable. And there had always been talk of his raising the money to build, as did Soleri and Wright and others, scale versions of some of the structures, organic spaces that would fold themselves unnoticed into the landscape here at Ash Creek. It was a dream, he knew. But one with which he loved honing his mind.

What's more, Henry wasn't forever building fantasy cities. When one owns things—old truism—they break. As the poet put it, Things fall apart. On the ranch, given the harshness of the winters that visited these mountains, there was forever a new list of what required attention, what needed to be fixed. And since my arrival at Ash

Creek, one of Henry's travails was to get that old jeep up and running, so that I would have the freedom to come and go without stranding them. When he first mentioned his intention to do this for me, I told him not to put himself out on my account.

"It's not a problem," he'd said. "I've been meaning to get that heap going, anyway."

The morning David Lewis brought his news, Henry, unable to concentrate on utopias, finished his work on the jeep. I sat down in the barn with him, as he worked, half waiting for him to broach some serious subject with me. Helen Trentas, David Lewis, someone or something. But he didn't. He asked for a wrench and I handed him a wrench. When the engine turned over at last, there was visible a momentary sparkle in his good eye (the other, as always, gazed ahead into unknown distances). I climbed in and we drove over the western saddle, then down beyond that ridge, forging through the natural alleys in the forest. His fundamental knowledge of the lush and difficult terrain bespoke itself as he easily invented our path through the unmarked woods. Seeing his oneness with this rough geography, I understood implicitly and precisely why he would want none of these woodlands to be razed, rebuilt, ruined.

There may have been much more that ran through his head as we drove through a ravine, then doubled back, retracing our impromptu tracks, toward the house, but this was how I read the expressions on his face, right or wrong. Maybe he'd built enough in his life and had left his profession because he no longer had either the eye or the stomach for it. Perhaps his philosophy was more selfish, in that it had been fine for him to help others with their aesthetic devastation of this or that or the other natural landscape, just so long as civilization didn't darken *his* door. I wouldn't know, per se, and would not ask, at least not this morning.

He handed me the key, and patted me on the shoulder, my dear uncle. I did manage, "Is there anything I can do?"

"You can stay out of trouble," is what he said.

"I'll do my best," perhaps believing at that moment I would not follow through on what I had in mind.

My first venture was into town, to get gas. Thence directly to Graham Tate's offices, on the second floor of the bank building, where I told a hesitant secretary that no, I had no appointment, that no, Mr. Tate did not know what my visit was in reference to, and that yes, I would wait. While my demeanor may have been set to convey intensity, purpose, tenacity, nothing of the kind had any residence within me; oh, there was a decided *turbulence,* wrenching in its way, that played through my limbs, even made my hands quiver some, but nothing more resolved than that. I was shepherded here solely by instinct, the intuition that Tate *knew things.* How more plainly to express it? Tate had things for me, and like some gauche, grabby fool, I had come by here so that he could unburden himself of these things, whatever they were. Plainly, I wasn't thinking. That he proved to be engaged with prior commitments that afternoon but would be able to schedule something in a few days, he was terribly sorry etcetera, was of course a blessing. Even now, I can only imagine what might have happened in his wainscoted and bookcased office, had I been ushered in, shaken his hard hand, sat myself down to respond to his congenial if aloof question, What brings you here? None of this would have come to any desirable end. I made my appointment with heart darkening, and left, still tremulous.

As I opened the door that led from foyer to hallway and stairs, I found myself observing the molded brass handle, the insufficient locks, and even turned around to gaze at the corners of the ceiling for motion sensors or other evidence of an alarm system. What did I think I was doing? My recent excursion through the woods with my uncle had left fresh images in my mind, which somehow collided with this man Tate, and what he was about. I stared at his door, and couldn't help but feel a deepening hostility toward the man whose work went on behind it. But still, the question remained.

My face must surely have been pale as I descended the broad

hardwood steps that led toward another windowed door and the street beyond. Within minutes I found myself back in the mildewed cab of the jeep, breathing shallowly and considering two other destinations to which I had not been invited: the homes of Helen and Margery. I had, in fact, a better idea where the latter was than the former. Margery lived over in Red Hill, about thirty miles due south, a negligible town at the upper end of the great valley. Helen, on the other hand, lived in town somewhere. It occurred to me I could look her up in the telephone book and arrive unannounced, just as she had in the middle of the night, not so many hours ago. But I didn't want to think through the possible responses she might have to my appearing at her door so soon after our encounter, didn't want to consider whether she'd be unnerved by my perceived neediness, by my evidently greedy appetite for more from her, more *of* her. Instead, the decision made itself. I would try to find Margery Trentas.

Along that same narrow black highway that had taken me to the St. Clair—which I soon passed without giving in to the thought of stopping, sitting still for a moment to consider the purpose of these sudden, erratic urges somehow to *connect* . . . with whom if not with Giovanni Trentas—I continued toward the village of Red Hill.

The road widened after I passed the hotel and found myself speeding along an open stretch. Concurrently, the valley narrowed, as a ring of mountains rose up to pierce the precipitous shapeless clouds that cramped and burdened the sky. The radio in the jeep didn't work, so I listened to the heavy fingers of wind rapping against the tattered canvas roof and heard when every fissure and sill in the road shocked the suspension; even the mundane process of getting there was imbued with an exhilaration of peril. So I told myself as the road vaulted into a sudden vertical canyon cut by the river that ran below, then reemerged into a higher flats where a motley assembly of houses called Red Hill came into view. A cinder-block structure with flat roof drew up on my immediate right. Its crude painted sign, indicating coffee was served within, stood on the sod before it like plywood hands tented together. Here I pulled over, climbed out, breathed in the crisp mountain air. Inside, I ordered the coffee not because I wanted to drink but to earn some chance at finding out where Margery lived.

Within ten minutes I found myself standing before a grim tan stucco palace of two stories with a weathered mansard roof of gray slate and multitudes of windows tucked in it, echoing the grand Victorian manner of another time and, to be sure, place. Framed in one arched window jutting from the mansard roof was the pale face of a woman looking down at me in the milky afternoon light, her hair done in a loose chaplet of silver plaits. Both hands thrust into my trouser pockets, I stood there not quite knowing what to do next, returning her frank and somewhat apprehensive gaze. Even from this certain distance, staring up through smudged, hazy glass, I was able to see that Edmé was right. Here had once been a woman of considerable beauty, the forehead hieratic, the whole visage simply filled with light, only the eyes veiled by shadows. She might have looked like a ghost to me then—a day ghost, too shy to haunt the place after dark, too introverted, for hers was a face marked by reticence—but that she suddenly smiled and gestured in the most inviting way. After this, she withdrew into the dim interior, and I made my way up the narrow stone walk to the front, where I waited. When she opened the door, and welcomed me inside, I doubt that if I *had* seen a ghost I would have been more surprised: She spoke my name, "Grant?"

"Have we met?" I asked as I stepped into a large, moist room which was empty but for some wicker chairs and an ottoman.

"Listen, dear, if you don't remember me, what brings you here to visit an old lady you don't know?"

Fair question. "Well, I—"

"Maybe you were too young. But I recognized you right off."

Hers was the kind of face that seemed extravagantly old when creased by its natural frown, and limpidly youthful when punctuated by her smile. It was one of those faces easy to imagine weeping. I did not recognize it, however, nor did I witness there in it Helen's lineaments and character. What was more, I hadn't understood that here was yet another reason for having driven this distance to encounter Margery, until that shimmer of *non*-recognition made itself known to me. She led me through more sparsely furnished rooms to the back of the house, where there was an arboretum of sorts, with dirty glass walls and ceiling, humid and aromatic, thick with blossoming plants. We sat.

"So," she said. "What brings you here? Have you come all this way to tell me what a bad person I am? To tell me what I already know you and all of them think?"

"Hold on. What makes you say that?"

I thought, weren't there pleasantries she and I ought to be mincing around with first, before rushing into the past with such precipitous honesty? I liked this woman already, for her lack of congenital social grace.

She said, "Why shouldn't I say it? Ever since Giovanni and me went our ways, I've heard things. I've known what they say about me over on the other side of the valley. There may be miles between here and Ash Creek, but rumor never did respect distance."

"Look, I don't live on the other side of the valley, and what's more, nobody has said anything bad about you." My ears warmed and undoubtedly reddened at the falsehood, but I persisted, nevertheless wondering for the second or was it third time that day just what it was I hoped to accomplish here beyond simply *seeing* her. "Let me tell you the truth," I said. "I'm not even quite sure why I came. I suppose I came to talk about Giovanni."

"Giovanni," flat, unavailing.

"Giovanni, yes. And about your daughter, Helen."

"I don't have anything much to say about Helen. I don't know her.

You could probably tell me more about her than the other way round. And as far as Giovanni goes, why should anybody care about my opinion? I wasn't even invited to the funeral, if there was one. He was still my husband, after all."

Again, I wondered how had we managed to come so far so quickly. She presumably had some similar reaction, and rose—which led me to wonder whether I was about to be invited to leave—then left me in the greenhouse annex for several minutes alone, before returning with a tray on which was an antique crystal decanter of sherry and two delicate matching stemmed glasses. She asked about Edmé and Henry, about David Lewis, whom I gathered she got to know during her time at Ash Creek. And I answered, as best I could. When she inquired about Helen, her voice fell off so that I barely heard her words. She feigned, I saw, supreme reserve, but did after all want to know.

I said, "Helen's tormented by her father's murder, and so am I. But you tell me you don't have anything to say about that."

The house was noiseless but for the distant ticking of a clock.

"Well, I would have things to say, but why should I, is my point. How do I know you're not one of *them,* anyway."

"One of *them?*"

Her face metamorphosed from pugnacity to skepticism. Her mouth transformed from that frown in which both ends were drawn down, to a smirk in which one corner perked shrewdly upward while the other remained resolute, somber, as if burdened by memory.

She tipped her head to the side, birdlike.

I said, "Margery— Do you mind if I call you Margery?"

"It's my name."

"Margery, I have *no idea* what you are talking about."

"You are right about Giovanni being murdered; that much I can tell you. And I may be wrong about you being one of them. Either way . . . ," and she failed to finish the thought.

Rather than plead for some absurd absolution, I simply drank, sat there, diffident as a stump, and waited for her to finish judging me. After a long interval, she whispered, "Everything could have been very different. And you know what else? What else is, you think you want to know about these things, don't you."

"Yes," I said.

"You don't, though. You don't want to know, Grant."

"How come?"

"Why do you think I left Ash Creek and moved back over here?"

"I haven't any idea."

"Well," she said, "it's not because I fell out of love."

I waited; and as I did I couldn't help but look at this pale, forceful woman, and wonder at Helen's animosity toward her.

"Giovanni was a decent man, as you know. It wasn't so much him as the girl I just couldn't live with. Not even the girl herself but, that is, all the difficulties that went with her."

"Difficulties? She was just a baby."

"Well, so was I, for that matter. The point is, she wasn't *my* baby," said Margery. "She'd grow up one day, wouldn't she? And then what would happen when she found out I wasn't her mother?"

A numbness came over me. I'd known this in my heart of hearts, hadn't I. Something Edmé had said, maybe, something about Margery and Giovanni living together that winter at Ash Creek with the girl, which didn't add up, something about the dates not fitting together right. I had no thought what to say by way of response, but was sufficiently shocked that it didn't occur to me to ask who Helen's mother was, then, if not Margery. Whether or not such a question would have been deemed improper is, now, anyone's guess. Margery simply continued to speak in the absence of anything from me, beyond my quiet, "What? I'm sorry?"

"I said, I was young, what can I tell you. At Ash Creek, the future seemed uncertain at best, and the more I learned, the less I felt I could ever belong. Henry's father was so devoted to Giovanni that he knew Ash Creek would always be a place he could feel was home. For me, this was my home"—raising her hand. "I never ran away *from* home, I ran away *to* home. It was a long time ago."

By not pressing Margery, I may have experienced a moment of unwonted grace. So I would like to believe. Because when I left her, I did so with the knowledge that Giovanni's young wife had abandoned him—if that is the right word for it—not from madness or malice, as Helen had suggested, not from some kind of misplaced love for a gang of helpless and callow brothers, as Edmé'd told me, but from an ingenuous fear of some day of reckoning that seemed to lay ahead for all of them. I liked Margery, couldn't help myself. Although one has a hard time understanding the compromises chosen by others, especially when they're informed by doubts and terrors, it was no more my place to question her decision of that spring of 1966, three years into their romance and not six months after they'd finally eloped, than to question her further about who Helen's real mother was, or is. Margery had, after all, welcomed me into her house, spoken at least a little with me. Enough was, as they say, enough. Throughout the hour I spent with her, I kept waiting for the famous brothers to appear like expectant wolves out of one of Hawthorne's tales, but no such creatures manifested themselves. I left, convinced she lived in that grand, ruined old place utterly by herself, serving the roles of both patient and caretaker, one living in regret for the past, the other modestly grateful for what good life had afforded her.

I went back to the jeep. I had to see Helen. My fear about appearing needy, or whatever, seemed irrelevant now. I did want to call first, and so at a junction where the road branched—one that would take the traveler north through alpine valleys toward state lines, the other that returned to town—I pulled over, having seen a telephone booth.

Finding only an empty metal folder where there ought to have been a directory book, I dialed information, asked for Helen

Trentas's number, was told no one was listed by that name. "There's a listing for a"—the operator spelled this—"*Giovanne* Trentas, if that's any help." Having penned the number on my palm, I thanked the operator and replaced the handset, wondering why on earth Helen would leave the misspelled name of her dead father in the directory, and hesitated before I dialed.

Where are you? I could almost hear her voice asking me.

Can I come over? I would ask.

But then, rather than hearing, Of course, please come, Grant, followed by directions to her place, I could imagine her saying, You're just as deceitful as the rest of them, I never want to see you again, once she knew my whereabouts and the fact I'd visited Margery. No, I would appear, just as she appeared, and leave others aside; I telephoned Edmé and told her not to hold dinner.

An uneventful, blind journey back, one of those stretches of time in which you travel from here to there without much process of consciousness occurring, within which you steer without really seeing, you respond to curves in the road without noticing them. Surely I saw a kaleidoscope of distinct images, some before me, some behind, but most present was a continuous queasy texturing of thoughts, an intermingling of Margery's words with those of Helen, a melding of Edmé's words about Giovanni with those of Noah the other evening at the Hotel St. Clair—into whose parking lot I now pulled, regaining consciousness. It was as if I'd dreamed but could not remember what the vision had been, as I walked into the taproom, empty but for the bartender, who was engaged in resetting the balance of a pinball machine down at the far end. I asked him, first, did he have a bottle of champagne he could sell to go—perhaps drinking too much, again, but I asked anyway—and, second, did he happen to know where Helen Trentas lived? The drive had revived me somehow; I was inspired to continue with my wandering day.

The champagne was a vintage I didn't know and can't recall, and the directions to Helen's house involved the briefest distance and a couple of simple turns. The sun washed the air orange as it descended behind the violet sawtooth range beyond her cottage. I admired the mowed yard edged with dying flowers, and the ascending walk overhung by the thick branches of old trees. The paper bag rustled under my arm as I walked toward the front door, painted azure blue to match the shutters, contrasting with the natural wooden shingles, blackened by weather and honeyed by hard sunlight. The cottage was set apart from any other house, and up behind it rose a field at whose remote edge several horses cropped, red flecks in the dwindling light. I was nervous. My stomach churned. Perhaps this wasn't such a wise move, showing up here uninvited. My edginess served to remind me how very negligible was my knowledge of Helen, how little I finally knew about her personal life. She understood much more about me than I her. What, say, if she had another lover, who might even now be nearing me on the other side of this door? What if she had a child, for instance, that no one had the nerve to mention? So ran my thoughts when I knocked and waited, as dusk breezes toyed with the paperlike leaves in the shrubbery that hedged this cobbled rock stoop. The answers to those questions were all the same: Why not find out now, before I became even more deeply involved with Helen than I was already? Again, I knocked.

The champagne, the misgivings, soon seemed for naught. No one answered the door. Suppressing my urge to prowl around to the back of the cottage and peek through her windows, I turned toward where I'd parked. Sunset apricot light blazed like fiery glaciered crowns in those high mountain snowfields above and ahead of me. Staring at the reflection off the never-melting snow, I felt a perfect emptiness.

Behind me I heard my name called then, and I turned to look again at that door, but saw it remained unopened. You stupid fool, I mumbled kindly, Hearing voices now, are you? and started to turn again when I did hear her, distant but distinct. Squinting out across the field, with my hand shading my eyes in a kind of informal salute,

I saw her riding toward the house on one of the horses I'd noticed earlier. Pale dust rose in her wake.

She was beaming as she dismounted, tied reins to a post.

"You're industrious," she shouted.

"What?"

"I figured you would find me."

"That's why you never invited me over?"

She kissed me, took my hand, and we went through a tack room at the rear of the house, into her kitchen. "I hardly know you. How could a decent lady like me invite a man of uncertain background to her house?" She smiled, and I with her. "What's that?" she added.

"Champagne."

"I can't drink champagne in filthy jeans," and she got glasses down from the hutch and left me alone in the kitchen. I peeled the foil, popped the cork, filled both glasses, which effervesced as I carried them. Circumspect, silent as any burglar, I toured Helen's downstairs: the kitchen that led into a dining room and beyond that into a greatroom whose appointments seemed—how else to put it—so *mature,* unexpectedly organized. Evidence of her daughterly devotion was present in the form of framed architectural etchings, probably from the nineteenth century, of Italian origin: triumphal arches of Severus and Titus; another showing the system of Roman aqueducts, with marvelous cutaway views; yet another displaying columns from various periods, Ionic and Corinthian orders with ornate acanthus leaves and fanciful godlets and sweet little beasts etched in their entablatures. I took a sip from my glass, just a little, so that we might still make some kind of toast when she came back downstairs, and wondered whether Giovanni himself had given her these, maybe some inheritance from the old country. Helen seemed so parentless, it dawned on me there, gazing in the failing light at this series of prints hung in her living room along the length of one windowless wall, that I liked this idea, that Giovanni's family might once have

owned these images and hung them in Rome in their own flat, having left Valle d'Aosta, or in Velletri even, way back when they were
all still together, before the war had pulled them apart forever. She
really was her father's daughter, in fact, I realized, hearing her footsteps above me—although rather than being packed off to a foreign
country when young, in Helen's case it seemed more that she was
born in a place truly foreign to her. How unthinkable it might seem
to one who hadn't gone through a parallel experience himself, to be
ultimately so different from those you grew up with, from the other
kids who struggled for identity and preeminence on the playground.
For Helen *did* have a childhood, of course, though even I might have
a hard time imagining what it must have been like, here and sometimes even up there at Ash Creek with that exotic and in some ways
defiant custodian of her welfare, of her fate really. I sat down on a
dark-green couch whose leather was old but supple, that faced a
matching one centered in the long room, and placed the glasses on
the reflective face of the low table between. On a small round table
in one corner was a stuffed raptor, an eagle whose wings were spread
as if it were about to take flight; on the wall of the dining room was
hung the handsome skin of a wolverine, its sensuous, protracted
claws curled at the ends of its forepaws, its blank black eyes staring
hard at the floor. Giovanni Trentas surely had lived here with his
daughter, yet even in his absence the atmosphere was not traditionally feminine. Helen was no girlish woman. The many masculine details in these rooms—these taxidermic trophies, the abundance of
firearms in that antique gun case on the wall opposite the etchings—
seemed as much to her taste as what might have been her father's. I
found myself content being here in her reflected presence, *their*
presence. She appeared again, dressed in a simple dark tunic
cinched at the waist with tied lengths of bright scarves, barefooted.
Her hair flowed arrant about her wide shoulders.

"Hello again," she said, and took the champagne. We toasted, and she sat beside me. "I'm sorry I left without saying goodbye this morning. You were asleep, dreaming, I think. You were making these little moaning sounds, like this"—she teasingly re-created a series of sobbing sighs—"and your face was twitching. Sort of like this," and then she burst out laughing.

"You were watching me while I was sleeping? That isn't fair."

"What can I tell you."

"Well, it's probably for the best you left, truth be told. Edmé suggested to me some time ago that Henry wouldn't necessarily be all that supportive of you and me—"

"You're not serious."

"Edmé mentioned it, for what it was worth. She knows very well what's happening between us."

"It's none of his business."

"Henry? I'm sure it's just that he cares about both of us."

"What you and I do is no one's business but our own." Helen's face changed so quickly, it was as if she were another person for some unmeasurable brief squib of time, then returned to its original complexion of humor and warmth.

"What can I tell *you*," I said.

We sat, mute. Feeling awkward, maybe, she rose, went to the kitchen. I scolded myself for having mentioned Edmé's dissuasion. But why not put the matter before her? A voice within asked back, reasonably enough, What matter? And besides, her reactions would allow me to know her better, if I was able to interpret. Helen returned with the champagne bottle in one hand and in the other a shot glass which she filled.

"Who's that for?" I asked.

"Sam," she said.

"Sam?"

A quizzical glance as she walked to the mahogany tripod table which accommodated the great beaked, feathery relic there. "I call this fellow Sam, for Uncle Sam, bald eagle. It's bad luck not to share an offering." She set the oblation at the base, near its very yellow talons.

"I thought bald eagles were a protected species."

"They are. Sam was snared in a trap by mistake, by your uncle, in fact, before eagles were endangered. He gave him to my father years ago." She tenderly smoothed its back feathers. "You have to have a license for these, even if they were mounted before the ban. I think he's so beautiful."

"Kind of sad."

"Only in so far as he messed up by getting himself caught in the trap in the first place. It was set there for a lynx or some other small game, a winter trap, Henry said. He must have been desperate for food, is all I can guess. Eagles prefer to kill for their own meat."

"You ever get the itch to leave this place?"

She came and sat close. "That's quite a non sequitur."

"Want to hear another?"

"Outside. Let's walk."

"All right," and I followed her to the door. We strolled into the field where she'd been riding. The minute flecks, those horses that had been there before, were gone now. Twilight was held at bay still by a sky marked with luminescent filaments of cirrus, and pile upon pile of cumulus edged with wondrous pigments overhead.

"You were saying?"

"You never answer my questions, you know."

"That's a dirty lie," and slipped her arm around my waist. "Answers are, One, Yes, not only do I get the urge to leave, but two, I know that one day I will. It's a matter of figuring out what direction to go when I do decide to leave."

"You can come with me," I said.

"Where?"

"I don't know yet."

"When you figure it out, let me know."

We soon came to a wide slow river, whose rilling surface reproduced fluid chinks of the last dying gold-pink sky shades. A bridle path followed the bank. She mentioned that Ash Creek was tributary to this river and that back when she was a teenager, after Giovanni and she had moved down here during the summers when Edmé and Henry returned from the coast, she would sometimes place a crudely carved toy boat in the running water by the bridge at Ash Creek, and then spend hours down on this very shoal, waiting for the boat to reappear. She made this experiment many times, she told me, but the boats never made the long passage from the mountains down across the valley flats, over here to the far side of town, where the river widened out into such a massive and majestic flow. "Stupid game," she concluded.

"You know what I wanted to ask, the non-sequitur question?"

"Aren't I the one who has a third question coming?"

"It was about your mother."

"I have no answers for you on that front."

"Look, for once in my life I don't want to keep secrets or lie or anything of the sort."

"Why not? I mean, don't get me wrong. I hate liars more than any other thing on earth."

To explain my sudden embrace of truthfulness would be difficult; instead, I simply plunged forward into the truth itself: "I wasn't going to tell you, but well—I went and visited with Margery Trentas."

"That's not her name. She's no Trentas. And now I suppose you're going to tell me she's a lovely lady and I have no right to hate her."

"From the little I've seen, she is."

Helen removed her hand from mine, and halted beside a bend in the river. I could see the evening star beginning to glimmer in the violet dark above her, very faint still. "We all have hard lives. She's got no special claim on the difficulties of being human. I don't get you."

"Well, that's kind of my point, I suppose. This is one thing I really don't get about *you*. You told me once you're not even sure she's your real mother, but you hold this grudge against her as if she were."

"Listen. Do I go around asking questions about your parents, your background, anything of the kind?" She was quietly crying out at me. Her face was flushed with hostility, yes, but fear, too.

"Helen, don't be mad at me," I said. "I'm just trying to understand."

"Your trying to understand gives you the right to stick your nose in other people's business?"

I thought back to my imaginary conversation with Helen in that phone booth back near Red Hill and was reminded how accurately I'd predicted her outrage, a fact that gave me pause. If she hadn't the right to be offended, of course I would never have been able to prophesy it. "I'm sorry, Helen," I said—not words I'd often heard out of my mouth in an argument.

"You're not sorry for an instant. Look. I'm not going to tell you how to behave or not to behave. I don't have a mother, and I'm not about to be your mother. I'd rather—" and she just turned and began to walk away, back toward the field and the house.

As I followed quietly behind, the hollow that had been carved in my chest seemed more capacious than the chest itself, and the drafts of dismay, of confusion and shame, that gusted through that sudden hole at my center made me tremble. If the skies had abruptly opened and snow begun to fall, I would not have felt a colder chill.

THE DOCUMENT was not meant perhaps to be hurtful. The man who dictated it to some innocent amanuensis might have been staring out a window as he worked through the specifics of the contract. All this was so everyday to him, no doubt, and these words must have come by rote. To him, as to any other lawyer, this was just a writ notifying a person (or *party*, as we are ironically called—no party, this) on behalf of a client regarding the commonest of suits. And yet the wistful melancholy that this divorce document generated in me, even in light of my new romance with Helen Trentas, went beyond what I might have imagined. I had known it was coming. I had time to prepare. But I was not prepared.

Edmé'd left the express envelope on my bedside table, by the Hawthorne. It awaited me when I returned home that evening, beat and bewildered by the events of the day. I thought back to Helen's rebuke, how I had caught up with and walked beside her—my arms dangling, hers crossed—returning along the river and over the field to her house. She calmed down some during the hike back and, by the time I left, had forgiven me, after her own fashion, for my overzealousness.

"Nobody likes to be gawked at, *watched*," as Helen put it, "and I'm the kind of person who dislikes it even more than most."

What I'd said that broke through her resentment was that my Margery visit had more to do with learning about Giovanni than his daughter. "Look. Regarding your father's daughter: I don't need any convincing or disclosure or any—I don't know—information. I just don't see how I could hear that a man who I remember from my own cast-to-the-seven-winds childhood—"

"It's four winds."

"Four winds, seven winds, whatever. My point is, if Giovanni was murdered—and Margery agrees with you that he was—"

"How would she know?"

"—how could you expect me not to ask around about it? I'd have thought you'd want me to share an interest in the matter."

"I do," she said.

"In fact, if I had to guess, I might have imagined that you *meant* for me to pursue the idea that your father hadn't died in—in an uncomplicated way."

She did not deny this. She said only that she might prefer it if I let her know what I was going to do before rather than after the fact. "If you're serious about it, then I can tell you what we have to do."

"Yes?"

"Graham Tate. He knows. I believe he knows everything there is to know about this. And I think Henry knows, too."

"What would Henry know?"

"I don't have the answer to that question. I don't have answers to many of these questions. I just know."

"You *suspect,* you mean."

"No. I *know,*" and she held her fist against her temple and gently tapped her head there, as if by such a gesture she might conjure from some chasm in her imagination the traces of a hard knowledge, the recognition of what precisely she meant. Without thinking, I reached out (we stood, still outdoors, at the foot of her kitchen porch, in the new dark) and took her fist in my hand. She resisted at first, then slowly relaxed—I could feel the muscles in her hand give way—so that I brought her fist to my lips and kissed her knuckles, then pried her fingers so that the fist exfoliated. I whispered I was sorry to her palm, and her palm now was on my cheek. We embraced as some vesper bird arabesqued over us, and she said, "I get crazy, I get crazy because there's such a tangle here, and I won't ever get free of it until I know what really did happen."

"I don't want you to be crazy. I want you to be happy, trite as it may sound."

She said good night, and I watched her disappear behind the dark door of her cottage, before I returned along a path to the jeep.

Haggard, I drove home. The porch light was left on, but Edmé and Henry had gone to bed. Then found this, took it downstairs to the kitchen, where I put on some water for tea. Devils love to work in spurts, making clusters of trouble, I thought as I slit open the envelope with a knife, knowing full well what was inside. And no, the papers came as no surprise, as I say, this cold, hard *thing* that required my signature agreeing to the division of property as stipulated here below in a brief attachment, and further agreeing . . . well, no need to detail the various points that were laid out, because what I found myself focused on were simple words, like *division* and *brief attachment*. Three years with Mary; a pretty brief attachment, and now the inevitable division. With the pen that lay beside the telephone I signed the documents, initialed the attachments, slid them into the envelope enclosed for return of the various materials, licked and sealed it. I spit the gluey taste out of my mouth into the sink, removed the tea bag from the cup, and went outside on the porch. The chamomile warmed me. A drowsiness settled through me. Soon enough, I climbed the stairs and into bed. No Hawthorne tonight, no dreams good or otherwise, no visitations or nocturnal music, no unexpected midnight encounters of any kind—nothing but a profound, needed sleep.

The morning following, I woke with an idea. From the bottom of the armoire I retrieved Giovanni's box, opened it, ferreted out what I was looking for, and discovered I was right. One of the feathers was a small breast or head feather from the eagle that had been caught in that trap set up in the gorge for some other animal. I brushed the feather back and forth beneath my chin, against the fresh stubble, and pondered once more what these puzzle pieces could mean. Half asleep still, I riffled through the love letters from Margery and tried to imagine her, back when she was a young woman filled with desire and purpose and hope and fear, too, writing these few trepidatious words to her handsome suitor. One by one I reread them, wondering if Giovanni appreciated how much she loved him, tracing the words with the tip of the eagle feather as I studied the notes that were obviously meant never to be seen by any eyes other than his.

And then I detected something so inappreciable, so subtle to my unstudied eye, that I hadn't seen it when I first read through these letters. The briefest among them, penciled on a small piece of paper—*When he goes I can come to see you but not before. I don't want him to see me. Until tomorrow, then*—was not in the same handwriting as the others. Now that I noticed this, it was plain as the daylight that streamed through the dormer window, and I wondered how had I missed it. The calligraphy was somewhat more refined, even though it was obviously written in haste, and the words themselves carried a meaning rather different than that of the other notes. For one, Margery had more than one man who opposed her romance with Giovanni—all those nasty fairy-tale brothers—which did not reconcile with the references here, *When he goes* and *don't want him to see me. They* were not a *he.* I was wide awake now, and turned the bit of paper over. Maybe in the excitement of finding these letters in the first place, I had failed to look at the other side; maybe I'd looked but the light hadn't been quite this bright. In any case, I now read on the reverse of this note, in script faded by time and possibly never very boldly inscribed at all, the letters *H xxx W.*

H for Helen? What else could it be? I thought. But then, no, of course not. I understood without having to think further. The *H* meant Henry. And the *W* meant no one other than Willa—Willa Richardson, not Willa Tate.

This was more confusing than anything yet I'd discovered in the box. And the man mentioned there, the poor *he* who was meant to be kept in the dark about a meeting? "Tate knows and Henry knows, too," as Helen had said. Could the reference possibly be to Tate? I wondered. Did Henry's relationship with Willa go back as far as Tate's? Was my imagination simply running wild?

I packed Giovanni's box away, as if by getting it out of my sight, the tales it began to disclose might also disappear. They didn't, though. Indeed, yet another question was stirred to life. A voice within me asked with lurid hilarity, Just what was Giovanni Trentas doing in the first place with this dark little confidence, this tattered trysting note between Henry and Willa—if that was truly what this proved to be—hidden in his cryptic box? More than ever, it was clear to me that Giovanni's box held the whole story.

THE NEXT DAY was overcast; a cold wind whipped the dying grass. A covey of black birds was driven along by the gusting from north to south, in the low sky. Summer was surely gone now, and it seemed as if a season was to be skipped, that we might arrive abruptly into the first snow. To think that only the day before I had passed so many hours outdoors, working the fence line with Henry, making repairs where barbed wire had broken, or rails had rotted. How many times during that day together I'd wanted to broach all those questions with him, have some answers straight from the source; but was held back by my fear he'd consider it an insult that I would dare pry into his past and the histories of people to whom he was close. What I did, instead, was enjoy the company of my uncle, engage myself in our work. I let Giovanni and Helen and Mary and Willa and Tate simply float up and away from me, during those late-morning hours—after a quick run into town to mail the papers—and through the afternoon. I allowed any thoughts of Giovanni's box to dissolve, as Henry and I tramped from the horsegate up west over the saddle ridge, hauling cat's-paw and hammers, snips and staples and saw, and a wreath of lethal thorny wire wrapped in a mantle of heavy old hide with us as we went. Even when I was in town I resisted the chance to drop in on Helen. It was a day to stand back, to work with my hands, not my head.

The only moment in which Henry and I touched upon a subject other than fence mending was when he encouraged me about my life in the wake of a second divorce, an encouragement offered now but which would later be revoked. "You're young for two divorces," he said, one eye staring me down even as I saw in it his concern, "but you have all the time in the world ahead of you, just remember that. Go easy. You'll be fine if you just go slow."

When I thanked him, I couldn't resist wondering whether these words referred to me and Helen. "That's never been my strong suit," I remarked, as we fitted a fresh-hewn rail into position.

"Never been divorced, you know. But I bet I know more about these sort of things than you'd think. The only thing I know for sure is that slow and steady's the way to any happiness in this world. It's worth remembering."

"I'll remember," I said, then clopped the timber to square, lifted the bale of wire over a shoulder, and we moved along the margin to the next breach.

And now the new day had come all bluster and blowing wind and grayed heavens and withdrawing birds. Although today I had intended to meet Helen, who'd promised to give me lunch if I came over, I wound up telephoning her to cancel. For the first time since I'd arrived, my uncle could really use my help here at Ash Creek, and my obligation was to stay; his studio roof had been damaged by the high gales that hurried down, whistling as they shook the windows and made the trees quiver and bow, and we had to go over, lay down some fresh asphalt tiles, in case it did begin to snow, or settle into freezing rain, as it threatened. She understood, told me to call later, but not before wondering aloud, "Why does he insist on keeping that studio in such bad shape as it is. It's a little perverse for somebody who designed so many beautiful buildings to retire to such a hovel."

"I don't know," I said. "Talk to you later."

Henry lent me an oilskin and gloves, and for the second day in a row we marched off together, across the creek, and began to work. The wind had ripped several odd bundles of asphalt shingles off the saggy roof, and the tar paper had here and there torn away, exposing sheets of plywood beneath. Wind thrashing us, we unrolled paper and stapled as best we could, then nailed courses of fresh asphalt where the defaulting had occurred—hasty nails in a formerly nailless building. Our faces were cold, and so were our fingers. The change from yesterday's mild sunshine was marvelous for its gross extravagance. When the first pellet of hail, tiny as a seed, rigid as stone, struck my wrist, and then another my cheek, we were almost finished with the patching, but not quite. The storm advanced from above in the gorge as a wall, or sheet; when I looked over my shoulder to witness it, I was impressed by the distinctness of its contour, and its weird chartreuse hue. It was upon us within minutes, there on the mildly pitched roof, as we worked quickly as we could to complete the job.

"Hard snow," my uncle shouted.

"—can say that again." Our words were blown in circles by the busy driving winds.

"No, don't mean it's snowing hard. I mean this's called *hard snow*—freak, different from hail, colder."

"Yeah?"

"Don't see it too often. That's good enough; let's get back to the house." We clambered down the ladder, stowed it alongside the building, made our way—Henry half running before me—down the bank, across the narrow bridge, up the already whitened rise past the garden, the grainy snow percolating in the grass and percussing off my stiff jacket. "Won't last long," he said, once we managed to get back to the porch.

We removed our jackets, shook them, pulled off our soaked shoes, even left our trousers at the doorsill, so wet were we both.

Edmé had towels for us, and while it might be true that this was a moment when we stood together as a family, a moment when after a couple of days' laboring side by side I might have been fairly given to feeling connected, even emotionally contiguous, with my aunt Edmé and uncle Henry here at Ash Creek, I had the oddest apprehension of just the reverse. What I felt in the kitchen by the door was my extraneousness, an intrinsic alienation. What was I thinking?—that I would simply continue to live on and on and on here with them? It was the sudden squall that brought this upon me, I knew. Somehow, with the weather still warm, I had been enjoying with my father's sister and her husband just another of my summers at Ash Creek. But now, the air having turned gray with hard snow, however early in the season it had come, I glimpsed that my stay could not continue forever. It would have been an upsetting revelation under other circumstances, but its precipitant character—the fact it barreled down on me with exactly the speed of the storm itself—made it all the more intense. The house had become abruptly very small, to my mind. The three of us, moving around in the kitchen (Edmé'd lit the cast-iron stove in the corner and Henry had gone below, dressed in socks and a long coat from the rack by the door, to fetch up fresh coal from the bin), seemed now to bump into one another. When I climbed the stairs to change into dry clothes, even the staircase was, I swear, narrower than it had been only a few hours before. To be sure, this was *in my mind*. But just because it was did not mean the thought was specious. Out the dormer you could not see the tree line along the creek, so thick was the storm with vapor from the warm soil and with flying snow as well. In a lifetime punctuated by moments of feeling myself destined to be a perennial vagrant, occasionally pausing to build my own nest before finding some nice way to tear it apart, more often than not just camping out in someone else's roost, I had never felt quite as bereft as this.

Get a grip, I warned myself. In the armoire, where I'd gone for some corduroys, I encountered the green and gold corner of Giovanni's box winking from beneath a stack of clothing. "Fuck you," I whispered to the box. Unchallenged by its contents, I might never have gotten into this tangle with my uncle and the pasts of others; it did not occur to me that I was now in the middle of just what I'd come here for in the first place. Diversion from my own worries. The irony was that mine were now enmeshed with those of the very others I had hoped to use as a distraction, a gloomy frolic of sorts. I changed, returned downstairs.

The storm did not pass through as quickly as Henry'd predicted, and if anything it seemed that although the wind had died down, the freak snowfall was even steadier than before. Because the earth was warm, the snow did not accumulate except in shady places, so when it finally petered out, we looked across the fields and down along the creek and what we saw was like a negative print of a winter scene. The fields seemed blackened, and so did the trees and barn roof and so forth, but beneath the boughs and eaves, and along the lee of stone walls, the sheltered places where usually it was dark with shadow, now it was white with unmelted snow. Only the sky, which was low, and which dropped occasional tardy flakes that corkscrewed their way down instantly to thaw on contact with the world there, did not fit into this negative-print image: neither black nor white, it was the most peculiar gray-green any of us had ever seen. It was as if a whole new color was born that day, mixed from equal parts beauty and grotesquerie. We had soup in the kitchen, and I drank so much tea my head spun.

After lunch, I wanted to be alone. From my bedroom I retrieved *The Wonder Book*, then came back downstairs to ensconce myself in a deep-cushioned wing chair in the greatroom, which ran the length of the back of the house, by which I mean to say the room that runs adjacent the steep rise. My uncle's game trophies hung on the walls here and on the floor was a bear hide, with claws and a head whose mouth opened as if in a languid if stiff yawn. When I was young, one night wandering around in the dark, I'd managed to step into the lower jaw of this august stuffed head, hard as that may be to believe, and got for my efforts a handsome puncture wound that necessitated a visit to the doctor for a tetanus shot the morning following. Ever since, I believe I avoided this room because of that incident (the mounted prizes of the hunt never much caught my fancy, either). This afternoon, however, here was where I wanted to be. I settled in, opened Hawthorne to the next chapter, entitled "The Paradise of Children." Just enough light now came through the window at my back that I could read without a lamp.

Long, long ago, the story began, *when this old world was in its tender infancy, there was a child, named Epimetheus, who never had either father or mother; and, that he might not be lonely, another child, fatherless and motherless like himself, was sent from a far country, to live with him, and be his playfellow and helpmate*—yes, I will admit I misread, *playfellow and bedmate* first, then reread the words and saw them for what they were—*playfellow and helpmate. Her name was Pandora.*

"No," I whispered to myself, a smile breaking on my face.

The first thing that Pandora saw, when she entered the cottage where Epimetheus dwelt, was a great box.

In fact, I'd never really known the story, but merely known the image of Pandora's box, and the tradition that once it was opened, all the demons who'd been tenanted within would escape, never to be recaptured. Breaching the box was an act that had marked the divide between an Edenic time, when everybody was a child, and the world we live in now, according to this version of the tale. This was something I hadn't known. I read on, intrigued. Epimetheus and Pandora lived in perfect splendor, as the story had it—*No labour to be done, no tasks to be studied; nothing but sports and dances, and sweet voices of children talking, or carolling like birds, or gushing out in merry laughter, throughout the livelong day.* Troubles of any sort were unfamiliar in this paradise; that is, of course, until Pandora developed such a persistent interest in the mysterious box, and became so obsessed that one day she declared, *"I am tired of merry times, and don't care if I never have any more!"* You poor little idiot, I thought, knowing just how she felt.

Remarkable, too, was the description of the box—of dark wood, with the most beautiful face carved in the center of the lid, a face with a garland of flowers about its brow . . . which was uncannily like that on my own wicked box upstairs. How could I fault Pandora when, left on her own in the house, after Epimetheus decided to go outside and play with the other children, whose interests ran more to games like gathering figs and grapes than fixating on a box, she began to curse it, push it, kick it, even, before setting to the task of unknotting the gold cord that held the lid down tight? How could I not feel some shared trait when I read how, once she was engaged in trying to undo the knot, she heard the voices of the other children outdoors, happily calling to one another in the sunlight, even while her fingers took on a will of their own, busied themselves with the golden thread. *But just then,* as Hawthorne wrote, *by the merest accident, she gave the knot a kind of a twist, which produced a wonderful result.*

The result we all know, and we know also what happened once the lid was raised—buzzing winged ugly creatures, the whole family of earthly troubles, was loosed into the room, evil passions, dread and sorrows, plagues and pestilence, the whole lot—and I sat there huddled into the corner of the wing-back chair and read as some child might, enraptured by the story. It was just before the last of the creatures emerged from the box, a sunshiny figure who would announce she was to be called Hope, that the telephone rang and Edmé called my name.

Leaving Hawthorne on the seat of the chair, as I had one more page to read before the story was finished, I walked around the luckless bear and made my way toward the kitchen, only now noting that the sun had begun to emerge again and that the world outdoors was back to normal. A feeling of contentment, even exhilaration—why not say it?: of *hope*—washed through me when I took the receiver from Edmé, whose face displayed anything but contentment or these other pleasant thoughts.

"Grant?" I heard from a voice I didn't know, but which seemed familiar.

"Speaking."

"I understand you've been asking around about Giovanni Trentas and some rubbish about a murder, and hear you were even up at the office, and thought to myself, Tate, if young Grant's so interested in the history of our community he'd go all the way over to Red Hill and ask Margery, who doesn't remember what pair of shoes she put on this morning, and has gone down to the Clair to speak with Noah, why not get together with this interested fellow and let him ask some questions right from the source?"

"I—"

"Seeing as you asked for an appointment—next week, was it?— why not let's skip formalities and meet tomorrow, you come on over and have a drink at my place in the evening, where we can talk about whatever your heart desires in privacy, man-to-man, just the two of us."

"I don't want to cause any—"

"What time's good for you?"

"Well, whenever."

"Let's say six."

"All right."

"I'm sure your aunt Edmé, or your girlfriend Helen, even, would be happy to give you directions to the house."

"All right," I again began to say, but he was gone, and a dial tone was what I heard.

"What did he want?" Edmé asked.

"Nothing; he just wants me to come by for a drink."

"What for?"

"I guess, well, that he wants to talk about Giovanni with me. He's

heard I'm interested. Where's Henry?" and with that avoided any
further inquiry from Edmé, leaving the kitchen, wearing another of
my uncle's coats, to join him down at the studio, where he'd gone to
inspect the roof.

Once outdoors, I changed my mind. Henry could examine our
handiwork without me. I began to hike up behind the house, ascended the knoll, which was a little slippery from the blizzard, and
rounded the crest path that hugged the hillside edge, and continued
on past the mouth of the gorge, up into the gorge itself. Though it
wasn't all that cold, I could see my breath steam before me as I
walked. The sky was brilliant blue in patches now, and festooned
with great scraps and tatters of clouds at every periphery. Below me
a hundred feet, the creek raged. It was as if twice as much water
roiled in its banks as usual. All the branches of all the trees dripped
black runoff and glinted silver when the sun struck them. I must
have climbed for an hour before realizing the shadows were growing
longer and the afternoon waned. Turning back toward Ash Creek,
I thought of Tate, and the sureness of his voice, and thought of
Pandora and the stubbornness of her whimsy, not to mention the
consequences of her persistence. Maybe it was possible my every
trepidation was ridiculous, my running around prodigal and absurd,
my romance with Helen doomed because ungrounded in anything
other than the fear of getting on with my life, an interest in studying
trouble—like some modern male Pandora who would rather petu-
lantly fiddle the ribbons of a forbidden box than take his chances out
in the real world.

Was this Hope whispering in my ear, or just plain sanity? In either
case, I arrived back at Ash Creek resolved to disentangle myself, if
Tate was able to convince me that nothing unusual had happened
here. With an open mind, I would give the man my honest benefit
of doubt.

Henry's news that the shingling was a success and no water had
leaked through into the studio came as an independent verification,

somehow, that things were on the right track. I tried Helen on the telephone, after Edmé and Henry had gone up to bed, but there was no answer. Whereas I suppose some concern about her absence might have been the more apt response, instead I felt a kind of relief at not having to tell her just then about my upcoming meeting with inimical Tate. In bed later that night, I finished the final page of Hawthorne, and was not surprised by its auspicious ending, where all but one of the fantastical creatures had fled the box, and the last then finally emerged as expected—*that lovely and lightsome little figure of Hope! What in the world could we do without her? Hope,* I read, *hope spiritualizes the earth; Hope makes it always new.* Yes, what would we do without her? I reasoned then, as I fell asleep, book splayed open like the wings of a fallen bird on my chest, and with the bedside lamp unextinguished, as had become habit with me.

I remember all this so well: When I awoke some few hours after, to the stunning sound of a heavy object like a baseball bat or tire iron bludgeoning and crashing above my head, pommeling the raw tin sheeting on the roof of the house, my heart sank even as my adrenaline raced. It was so clear to me, as I moved quickly to switch off the lamplight, that the same pretty figure of Hope disappeared into the darkness now, too, and once more demons were loosed on the house.

III

GIOVANNI'S GIFT

For nothing is secret, that shall not be made
manifest; neither any thing hid, that shall not
be known and come abroad.

—*LUKE 8:17*

LIKE HELEN TRENTAS, Willa must never have seemed a true native of this place. As one of the Richardson family, the wealthiest in the valley when she was growing up, she lived a more privileged life than most. But it was her manner, her sweet imperturbable presence, that set her apart more than, say, her clothing, her governess, or any of the other characteristics that might be associated with one of her class. Willa was never haughty. Never arrogant. Indeed, she was a guileless young girl with a bit of a faraway look in her eyes. —Willa just has *something about her,* parents of childhood friends would say, a uniqueness that made her seem an outsider. She did her best to ignore the feeling of being estranged. But all who knew her assumed that once she was old enough, she'd leave the valley behind in a heartbeat.

Their predictions could hardly have been less accurate. Of anyone, Willa was least likely to renounce this place as home. She adored the rural ranchlands and outback mountain villages connected by slender highways. She loved her pastoral and somewhat provincial life. She knew, from as early as she bothered to contemplate such things, that this was where she would always live. Every walk she took down avenues of the so-called great cities of the world, every time she ventured away from the valley—her parents were persistent in their efforts to educate Willa, to give her access to culture and history and things they thought were valuable—she always returned, only appreciating home the more. What its quirky culture of husbandry and hymnals, of rodeo and radio and a thousand homespun folk rites, might have lacked in urban elegance, it more than made up for with plain old natural *soul*. Willa loved this valley and these mountains, and though her bearing might have suggested to the casual observer a sophistication more often associated with the city—the urbane as urban—it would be the observer's mistake to believe Willa wasn't through and through a country woman.

The life she led with her husband was by all appearances not unhappy, either, no matter how different from Graham Tate she was, how utterly dissimilar were their backgrounds and even their values. Willa had always been full of surprises, and marrying Tate suddenly upon her return to the valley after a year away was not the least of what she was capable of doing. Without a doubt, her friendship with Giovanni Trentas, which was taken by some to be outrageous in light of her husband's open animosity toward him, was one of her most sterling displays of independence and, to some, eccentricity. Even then, however, those who clicked their tongues barely knew the half of it. Willa went her own ways, and kept her own counsel as she went along. No one, even Tate, was going to tell her how to behave. Not that she hadn't made certain sacrifices down the chain of years. She had.

Because he'd graduated from high school and gone on to college before her, Henry never knew Willa when they were growing up. He knew of her family, of course, and had met her brother once, a boy who'd gone to Vietnam in the early years of the war, only to return in a box. By the time Willa left to attend that same university where Henry met his future wife, Edmé, he'd moved to the coast to complete his graduate work. It was when she came home in summer 1963, after three years of diligent study but with no interest in going back to finish her degree, that she was introduced to this poised man, Henry Fulton. To Willa he was a romantic older figure who, in his early thirties, was designing libraries and theaters and other metropolitan buildings for a living but kept returning to his childhood home because, like her, he had this place in his blood. Henry was mysterious and familiar at the same time. His wife, Edmé, was in her way mysterious, too, with a brother who was a diplomat of some sort in Europe, with a name that sounded French and proved to be Scottish. And with their young friend and compatriot Giovanni Trentas, who was adopted by the Fulton family, this chaste *ménage à trois* attracted her intense curiosity.

How much time she spent with them I cannot say. What they did together, whenever the four were out on some social evening, I can only guess. More likely than not, their activities centered on such innocent things as hikes, picnics, hunts for arrowheads or edible mushrooms—something Giovanni was expert at, having learned early on from his father the rudimentary skills of distinguishing lethal soma from those they might toast over coals and eat for dinner. Or they might go to the county-fair mudshow, ride the transient, rickety carousel trucked in one week along with the convoy of other circus machinery—bump cars; the wobbly Ferris wheel, held together with chewing gum, string, spit, and prayers; the booths for pitching balls and shooting painted tin ducks in a cheap gallery—and then trucked out, in the night, not to be seen again until the following season. They fished together, Henry and Willa being more adept at reading the streams and matching the hatch than the others. They swam naked in the river on the hottest July nights, and sat afterward on the stony beach by a driftwood fire and got quietly silly from a bottle of wine they shared.

Graham Tate, several years younger than Henry and several older than Willa, must not have taken too kindly to these excursions. It was said, by voices more cynical than mine, that Tate had fallen in love with Willa the day he met her father, and not a moment sooner. Cynical maybe, perhaps unfair, such a comment—not least because he has proved himself devoted to Willa over time, has never been known to cheat on her or in any way show other than complete loyalty and even obsessive protectiveness, as we will see. But there was some truth to the thought that, in the beginning, Tate fell in love as much with where she came from as with who she was. Tate himself was from a family neither rich nor poor, but austere. "My father believed that a man ought to earn just enough to make sure smoke always came out of his chimney and a meal was set on the table, but never a penny more," he'd been heard to say. At an early age, Tate decided that this approach to life was not for him. When he fell in love with the daughter of the richest man in the region, he further became enamored of the dream that one day *his* son would be heir to the two largest fortunes here—that of his mother's family and the even greater estate of his father. That Willa did not, at first, return his affections didn't deter Tate—who had the sturdy patience of a dealmaker—but her inability to bear him the son (or even daughter) who would be beneficiary to all that he managed to amass over those years that passed since the mid-sixties, after she finally did agree to marry him, skewed his fond plan. Some would say it skewed the man himself.

But in any case, what concerns me most, as now I have learned more about those times when Henry, Edmé, Giovanni, and Willa were inseparable from late May through Labor Day, is the relationship that developed between not Giovanni and Willa but her and Henry. Seeing only the swiftest exchange of glances between them on Labor Day this year, I didn't dare read too much into what I sensed might be there. But on discovering the dance recital card, I was duly entrapped, duly curious. I was reminded of that note Henry and I had discovered the morning after the studio door had been removed with such symbolic melodrama from its hinges: *Tell the truth.* Was reminded of how he'd requested I keep it to myself, and how I had even in the most haunted moments of the following weeks managed to refrain from asking myself, Why? Why would the simple petition to *Tell the truth* prompt him to ask of me a complicitous vow of silence? Willa and Henry, I'd now become convinced, had been involved. How involved, I wasn't sure. Whether or not Edmé knew, again I wasn't sure. But either way, Tate had poured gas over the flames of my suspicion that evening, and by the time I left, my confusions about his hatred for my uncle were heightened, even as my certainty of his wickedness became clearer. That Graham Tate was *at least* wicked I might have known before I parked the shabby jeep in his immaculate driveway, there before his impressive stone house with its many chimneys and lighted walkway to the grand portico. Just how wicked, and what that wickedness was capable of producing, were as yet unknown.

Confusion, in fact, surmounted confusion. What had Tate said to me that night? For one, it was what he didn't say: how he didn't reveal to me just why or how he knew every last move, it seemed, that I had made since my arrival at Ash Creek. I asked. He smiled only, and continued with something else. The look in his eye was as if to say to me, What? do you think I *wouldn't* know your various doings? Why would I fail to observe you, even when you thought that you weren't being watched? What would give you the right to plunk yourself down into my little world and move about unseen? Green as I was with inexperience, such questions—obscure to me but obvious to him—had never encumbered me. After all, how would a rambler know about such things as the inalienable rights of the propertied and rich, or the exemptions from law or rules or simple good manners (like allowing me *my* privacy) that the powerful naturally presume for themselves? And that he behaved like some isolationist hick at the Labor Day party—how was I to know it was only one of the many useful masks such an elaborate fellow as Tate might don on a given occasion?

Willa was not there when I rang the bell, and Tate himself swung open the wide door to let me in. "She's gone to town to have supper with one of her friends, sends her regrets," he told me, as he led me down a hallway and into an impressive library lined from floor to ceiling with books. Tate said, "You like to read?"

"You obviously do," taking the whiskey he handed me.

"Me, read? God, no. I don't have the time for distractions, and books are just that, I don't care what anybody says to the contrary. There's nothing much in books that wouldn't be better learned out in the real world. I like having them around, though. They give comfort of sorts."

"This must be your favorite room."

Coolly, he smiled and motioned me to sit, then sat across from me in a club chair draped with an old Navajo blanket. "That's too bad what happened up at Ash Creek last night."

I pitched my head to one side, waited.

"About Henry's little city, whatever that was. Noah told me. Seemed like pretty gratuitous vandalism."

"Gratuitous in what way?"

"Seems to me that if you want to destroy a city you'd best wait till it's built—why fool around with toys?"

"That isn't what I meant."

"I know what you meant. You meant it was calculated, that there wasn't anything gratuitous about it, right?"

"That's closer to what I might have thought."

Tate paused, as if to take in not just what I'd said but the way I'd said it.

I corrected myself, altogether too late, with the words, "That is, Yes, that's what I meant."

His next pause seemed even more testing, throwing me more off balance, so that when Tate's words came forth in a confident stream, I felt as if they might sweep me away.

"Let's cut to the chase, Grant. That's how they say it in books, isn't it? Little inauthentic words like that?"

"What chase?"

"You think I did all this, don't you. Everything points to Tate, that's what you're thinking. You think I'm behind Trentas's death and that I'm behind all the vandalism and the harassment and every other goddamn thing that's gone on up at your uncle's. But you're not right, Grant."

I winced at the sound of my name coming from his mouth, again waited for him to continue, sensing that whatever I said would be dismissed or misconstrued or distorted. My wait wasn't long. Tate preferred the music of his voice to any silence.

"Tell me, Grant. What do you *do?*"

"What do you mean?"

Looking away as if speaking to someone else, he said, "Answers my question right there, doesn't it," before turning back to me with his great hands folded together into a powerful fist as he leaned forward and continued: "You a slacker, Grant? I think that's the word your generation uses for it, slacker. We had other terms for it, less appealing than slacker."

"I teach English to foreign diplomats' kids, do translation work, things like that. Nothing that has much use here, but overseas—"

"You don't have a job."

"Well, no," I admitted.

"You want one?"

"So much for cutting to the chase," under my breath.

"I always got work for a man who's willing to work."

"I'm fine for the moment, thank you," amazed he could move so quickly from accusation to bribery.

"If you intend to stay on here, since this isn't *overseas,* you might want eventually to bring home some income. Keep it in mind, that's all I'm saying."

Nonplussed, I managed to thank him again, then said, "About what you mentioned before? About what's been going on up at Ash Creek?"

"Yes, yes. That's why you're here. Well, like I say, you believe that Giovanni Trentas was murdered, and I bet you want to blame it on me, don't you. So I gather from my friends. Is this a valid analysis of your point of view?"

Now was the first time I really looked at Tate, truly *saw* him. During that hour I passed in his company on Labor Day, dining al fresco beneath a flawless sky, my thoughts had swirled from having just met Helen Trentas. Now I noted how arctic blue were his irises, how vast and furrowed his forehead, how straight was his nose. He was a ruggedly handsome man with stern mouth and ruddy pocked complexion, and with angular athletic shoulders to match those great square hands. His black sweater set off the silvering hair, whose length and unruliness belied his unambiguous love of order. The trappings of success—his thick tweed trousers, surely tailor made, and polished calf boots, and the heavy silver and gold wristwatch with its several dials that would give him notification of phases of the moon and international dates and Christ knows what else besides—he wore with the ease of someone born to such luxurious trinketry and fine apparel. But they were there, the signs of the struggle as well as the scars of success: the sunkenness of those icy eyes and the puffy flesh that collected beneath them surely were the residue of thousands of nights worrying, like Hawthorne's Midas, about assets, and the softening of the jaw and curl of the lip suggested to me the consequences of prosperity. Moreover, the ambitious, nervous boy he must have been, once, showed, I swear, in the wince he made in the wake of my silence.

"Well?" he was saying. "Is it or is it not?"

"You expect me to deny it, don't you."

"I don't have any expectations."

"Why don't you tell me, since you seem to know everything else around here. If you weren't behind it"—couldn't bring myself to say the words *death* or *murder,* not here, not sitting alone with him right before me—"then, well, who was?"

"No one was behind anything, of course."

"So Helen's insane?"

"I haven't heard Helen accuse me of anything. And you haven't heard me accuse *her* of anything, either. This is why I'm beginning to get a little cross with you, Grant. You seem to like accusing people of things they haven't done. Not a good personality trait." Tate smiled, "You throw darts?"

"What?"

"Look here," as he rose and I followed him to a room furnished once more with trappings of privilege—the vast green baize of the antique billiard table, the vintage movie posters in frames, and so forth. "Wonderful sport, darts. How much simpler can it get? You pitch a weighted object with a sharp tip in the air, and you either hit the bull's-eye, or you don't. You win or you lose, period. I like that," and he handed me a clutch of darts. "After you."

"I didn't really come to play darts, Mr. Tate."

"For chrissakes, ease up, Grant. Can't you do two things at once? We're talking, aren't we? Go on, let's see you hit that bull's-eye."

"What makes you think I can't?"

He laughed. "But I know you can. Otherwise I'd never have asked you in here to play. What fun would there be in that?"

Turning to face the circular corkboard with its concentric rings of red and green, its clock-face bands radiating out, and the small round plug at the center, I said, "And Margery's crazy, too?" as I squinted, held one dart aloft, sent it flying, watched it punch the target close to its heart but drop to the floor, the tip not having penetrated the cork face deeply enough to stay.

"You've got to put more energy into it than that," Tate said, unnecessarily. "See, there you go again with accusations. I'm not saying they're crazy. I'm saying they're mistaken. Altogether different, being mad and being mistaken. Nothing wrong with being mistaken, unless you hurt others by retailing your mistake all over the place. And I'll tell you something else. It isn't something I really planned on saying, but since you want to push"—and here he introduced the idea that if Trentas was murdered, what made me think he, Tate, was the only one interested in Giovanni's permanent silence? Did I think I really knew my uncle that well? "None of us knows anybody as well as we think we do," he said. I listened with combined disbelief and fear as Tate suggested Henry himself might not stand so utterly innocent of any responsibility in the death of his best friend. "Remove just one little letter from the word *friend* and you have *fiend*," he leered, then—seeing my discomposure—said, "Give another toss, why don't you."

I launched the other darts, stepped aside for Tate to take his turn. Naturally, he placed two near center and the third on the bull's-eye. I didn't congratulate him, but retrieved the darts, including mine that lay on the floor. We threw several more sets, and the results were about the same each time. "All kinds of variations you can play," he was rattling on. "Sudden Death, Killer, Shanghai. An ancient sport, damn good sport."

"If you say so."

"You know, Willa adored your friend Trentas, and that fact alone exculpates me, or should, because I myself would never in a million years do anything that would hurt my wife. You hear me, Grant? You been listening?"

His tone had changed radically through those last words. Our game was over.

"Clear as day," and handed him the darts.

He glanced at his watch. "How'd it get so late?" though of course it was not late.

"Well, thank you for the drink," I said.

As he led me out through the library, my eye caught on something I hadn't noticed there before. A surveyor's map lay unfurled on the desk, edges pinned flat by several of Tate's unread books. Unthinking, impulsive, I stopped to look at the pale-blue surface of the map, and was seized by what was before me. The territory encompassing all the acreage from the county road up into the valley formerly owned by Lewis and, yes, continuing up through Ash Creek and the gorge north, all the way to state lands above, was depicted on the map. That this would be of interest to Tate, who I assumed had just gone into contract with David Lewis, was not what startled me, of course. Nor, really, should I have been shocked by what I did observe. I was, however. Not only was David Lewis's name absent on this map, replaced by the surveyor's legend *Lands of Tate Trust,* but Ash Creek was absent as well. The entirety of the tract depicted carried that legend, in fact. I knew but didn't quite know what it meant. When I glanced up from the map, I found Tate standing beside me, unfazed, expressionless. I said, "What kind of monster are you?"

"You can't fault a man for dreaming," and in the foyer he gave me my jacket and pointed at the bandage on my left palm. "I've been meaning to ask, Grant. What happened there? Looks like you took quite a fall."

"It's nothing," I managed; all I wanted was out.

"Maybe you ought to be more careful about where you're going."

Driving the switchbacks down the pass from the hillside aerie, lighting a cigarette with my injured but free hand, I grew furious with myself for having agreed to meet with Tate. How ridiculous of me to think he would offer anything other than lies and flamboyant deflections. His tender assertion that he would never do anything that would hurt his wife rang hollow as a cracked bell, not to mention his factitious concern about my hand. Above all, the map, which Tate must have laid out for me to see—or, even worse, had left on the desk in complete disregard of whether I saw it or not, utter indifference—this map focused my impotence, my helplessness. Tate was not a man on whose shoulders a pair of angel wings looked very good; but neither was I. Are the greedy and vengeful any better than the inept and traitorous? And I was traitorous—wasn't I?—because I had no intention of telling anyone about this map. How could I tell, even if I wanted to? What was I supposed to do, go narrate to Henry that during a pleasant game of darts, Tate shared his covetous dreams with me? Not hardly. Grant, what a fool you are, I thought.

The lights in the valley below were sparse, and burned like the reflections of the brightest of the stars above, so that for one moment I experienced the sensation of being in space, surrounded by cold fiery stars. As I descended toward town—my left hand, the injured one, lay in my lap—I thought back over what had happened just the night before, and how I'd come by this painful bruise. I wondered, was there any way on earth that Tate hadn't known exactly what had transpired up at Ash Creek? or, more to the point, who was there, last night, armed with a crowbar and either rancor or a twisted sense of humor?

There had been the pounding on the roof that awoke me from my sleep. There had been soon afterward voices in the hall, which I recognized as those of Henry and Edmé. Then there had been a brief silence followed by half a dozen rapid jolting whacks. Never had I heard my aunt Edmé scream before, but now I heard her scream. As if by rote, I'd turned off my lamp and sat unmoving in the blackness, convinced this was a nightmare. Quiet then for another interval, in which I found myself counting out the seconds—one pause, two pause, three pause, four—and yes, there'd been more hammering, lashing hard with metal—surely that was a tire iron—on metal. And now I was up, too, out into the dark hall, and downstairs, hearing the hoarse whispers of my uncle and aunt, as the pummeling echoed down through the walls and window glass. Somehow, I had dressed in the interim, had pulled on sweater, pants, shoes without socks, and as I rushed past them, silhouetted in the pale light that gave through the windows from the tentative sky outside, I did whisper to my uncle, "Don't shoot," as I bounded onto the porch and noisily marched the length of veranda toward the rise behind the house. "Who's there?" I shouted in a voice so hostile it seemed like someone else's, as I stomped along, and "Get down off there—*come on, you son of a bitch.*"

The bludgeoning percussion had ceased. I stood at the end of the porch, now very quiet, listening. Behind me, the kitchen door opened and rattled shut. Henry was out here, too, I assumed. Above, on the eaves, all was still. Only the eternal wash of stream water in the lowest folds of the valley gave up any sound. This standoff lasted, again, for some incalculable length of time. It seemed unusually foolhardy of the night visitor to have climbed onto the roof, where he could be treed, so to speak, cornered in his arrogance without any easy path of escape. I could hear Henry down in the yard below, and shivered from the damp chill. Henry trained a flashlight on the roof; I saw the single bright beam sweep slowly from south to north, though could not see what it illuminated on the eaves above me. No shouting, no cursing, no threats. All was eerily calm—so much so that I felt emboldened by the quiet and left the relative security of the veranda for the footpath at the base of the knoll. Having walked it so recently, my feet recalled its first switchbacks in the lightless night. Breezes stirred the leaves of trees, the atmosphere upset, I supposed, from the earlier quick blizzard. I turned around twenty, thirty feet up the rise, from where I could now see the rooflines.

"Come on, man," I muttered. "Come on down."

No sooner had these words settled themselves into the air than I heard a scraping, scratching sound on the far side of the house, to the west, and just instinctively moved toward the clamor there. Henry clearly heard, too, and out of the corner of my eye I noticed his flashlight bobbing past the pebbled walk that led to the front gate, up the gentle grade between the big pines south of the house and the long front porch. Myself, I stumbled blind across the base of the rise, through the kind of natural alley between the back gable and scrubby hill. There was the squeal of torn tin, which I presumed was a rain gutter peeling away from its moorings as the prowler came sliding off the roof and, having caught himself on the lip of the gutter, plunged to the earth, bringing the conduits down with him. This was it, I believed; he would break a leg in the fall, or else be knocked out cold when he hit the hard ground, and now we would finally learn what all this was about. I hurried, tripping, catching the butt of my hand on stone, hoping to arrive around at the west end of the house before my uncle, in case there was a scuffle.

When I came to the corner, I stopped momentarily, caught my breath, listened. It seemed darker around on this side than on the other. Faint as something nearly forgotten were the footfalls I heard— or, rather, the rhythmic brush of someone's legs combing fast through grass, running away from the house, up into the long field that rose toward the saddle ridge and fenced boundary beyond. Wary, I took some steps out into the black open yard. Henry arrived from around the opposite side, and I called out to him to shine his flashlight up into the field. The ghostly sphere leapt over grass and ground as he swept back and forth across the darkness, bringing into view small chunks of landscape at any given instant. Nothing, nothing, and no one. And then, yes. The figure was quite distant already, and running with surreal agility and haste. But still, there he was, embraced at least for the moment in a luminescence by which we could see him. I was off, in pursuit without the slightest thought of what I would do should I happen to catch up. Henry, too, chased him across the field— the figure was already half a hundred yards ahead of us—but it wasn't long before both the intruder and I had left him back alone in the field, catching his breath while continuing to hold the flashlight on the pursued, until both the night visitor and I had sprinted beyond its range, where the pitch blackness of the night encompassed every shape and form, and the only senses left to me to trail him by were hearing and taste, for I swear to God I could taste the person on my tongue, as one would taste a bad penny placed there. It was a taste impossible to describe, not acrid nor tart, nor sweet nor sour. Tasted of nothing, tasted of a thousand subtle poisons.

My voice cried out, "Stop," but the man kept running—I could hear the crashing footfalls not so far ahead of me—and it was as if, again, another voice proclaimed, in a rough imitation of my own, "I said *stop*. I've got a gun." The voice that came from my mouth, that bellowed those words and that lie, might as well have been the devil's own, for what they provoked. I myself now stopped, because I no longer heard those comfortable sounds of the intruder escaping my pursuit. What I heard now was the very faraway sound of my uncle laboring up this long ridge, as I stared hard as I could into the blackness ahead, and tried to hold down the clamor of my gasping breath. Something here was going wrong, I knew. This was the first time I felt the searing panic rise through me. The first understanding that now, here, I was in serious danger. Or could be.

Then it was I fell hard on the outcropping of stone, having been broadsided, knocked down full force without warning. Far too startled to react with anything approaching intelligence or swiftness, I sat there stunned, in total darkness. The ache in my hand suggested to me that my skin was torn away. Instinctively, I touched the palm to my lips to see if it was wet with blood. My back throbbed, my shoulders stung, pain irradiated through me. Even my pride, such as it might have been worth at that juncture, had been bruised. I heard the intruder—the assailant—running fast in a new direction, down along the fence line toward the east. Henry was still too far behind for me to bother calling out to him to shine the light toward the horse-gate, where apparently the intruder was headed. It occurred to me that I might as well remain where I was, curled into a seated fetal ball. Why stand if there was any chance of being knocked over again? And why believe that, even if the man who'd assaulted me was half-way down the slope by now, making his escape, some other person didn't lurk nearby, ready to come at me? Hadn't I mistakenly thought the person I'd been chasing was far ahead of me? I decided to remain right where I was, since the hillside had become populous with night visitors, at least in my imagination.

The morning after, my uncle discovered the scene in his studio that Tate would refer to when I met with him later at his house in a room full of books he would never read. My uncle's utopian city of board and paste was demolished, leveled most likely with the same length of iron that had been used to pound the roof and wake us all from our sleep.

Henry was apoplectic. He was grim and unnerved and enraged at the same time. As well, he seemed beaten. He entered the kitchen, where Edmé and I sat, having just finished putting salve and bandages on my hand, ourselves still in shock from the visit during the night, and collapsed slowly into the chair beside the telephone stand at the doorway there, pale and staring blind ahead into the room.

"Henry, my God, what is it?" Edmé said, rising to approach him. Her hand was delicately extended in his direction, the fingers, I saw, tentative, even trembling. Edmé's reaction to Henry was difficult for me to watch. She knew this man; it was clear she'd not often seen him this distraught. Even David Lewis's news had not caused in him this kind of response. My mind, beginning to race, imagined this was just the look he had on his face the day he came back from his hike into the gorge after having discovered Giovanni's mutilated corpse.

"They just wouldn't do that," he said, casually.

"What?" said Edmé, her voice lowered. She moved toward him as one might approach a hurt animal, tenderly but with a kind of slow caution—as if he might jump from catatonia into a frenzy.

"They wouldn't."

"They who? Henry?" Edmé asked.

Henry turned abruptly toward me, and locked his eye on mine. "You answer that question, Grant."

"You're asking me?"

"Don't you see your responsibility in this?"

Now I stood up. "Wait just a minute. This was going on long before I got here. You can't blame this on me."

"It was never this bad. They came and woke us up, maybe, with their music. They'd do things like that. Pranks, kid stuff. It wasn't until you came that it turned violent, burning buildings and vandalism and—"

"I haven't done anything," I said.

Edmé placed her hand on Henry's shoulder, interrupting his concentration. He glanced up at her, but then right back at me.

"Grant hasn't done anything, Henry," she echoed, quiet, firm.

"They completely destroyed it. It wasn't like it meant a thing to anybody else. I don't see why they had to do that."

Truly he was talking like a child.

"Edmé?" I asked; though I had no question other than a vague query, I suppose, about what to do.

Henry continued on a different tack, "Parading around with Helen like you are, can't keep your pants up for two minutes, is it any wonder you're in another divorce? Your father would be ashamed; your mother, too. You don't even know Helen—"

"Henry, stop," Edmé breathed.

"—and what do you care about Giovanni Trentas, going around asking about his murder? Who the hell do you think you are? You think people don't talk to each other, you think this hasn't gotten back to me? *Now* look. They break into the studio and do this. You're going to make it so they *do* win, so they push us out of here. You're on *their* side."

"Edmé," I said, myself trembling at this outburst. "Tell him again I didn't have anything to do with whatever it is."

"You heard Grant?" she asked him.

"I heard," he shouted, then quietly, "I heard."

Finally, averting his eyes, my uncle wept.

He would find me later in the day and apologize. I accepted the apology and made one of my own, but knew that a profound change had taken place between us; or rather, a schism that maybe had been there for some long time without acknowledgment had been unveiled, revealed to us both.

And now, not so very many hours later, here I was, hearing the voices of Henry and Tate commingling in my head, speaking to me as I made one last turn in the road, which delivered me again into the long valley. The stars were all above me, as well they should be. The road was straight, which I preferred, for once. I rid myself of the voices by listening to the wind rushing around the edges of the old jeep. It was chilly, and the heater did not work. I found myself shivering a little and thought quite seriously, for the first time since I'd arrived in Ash Creek, about driving and driving all night in any direction that might carry me away from here. My usual fantasy under such circumstances was to wonder how I might go about finding Jude, and then give myself over to a Jude reverie. But that seemed less palatable than in times past. And not because I'd promised myself I'd leave my direction to the whims of chance, but because that promise seemed more and more one which, if I had any wisdom left in me, I would go out of my way not to keep.

Why? For one, I missed Helen anew, despite any warnings Henry might have made about such feelings, and it seemed to me if I left, only to change my mind and return—I knew this is what I'd do if I ran away—she'd have every right never to speak to me again. I didn't want that. I didn't care about warnings and threats. She had been abandoned enough in her life, I thought, and had no need to experience it once more, not at my hands. For another, I had a growing if uneasy sense of compassion for Edmé, though just what motivated this I couldn't articulate. And for yet another, I knew that there remained someone with whom I must speak, sooner rather than later. I was too enmeshed now. There was no driving away from this. Only Willa Tate could tell me who Willa Richardson had been, back in the days when she and Giovanni Trentas made their bond, and she and Henry Fulton made theirs.

"CURIOUS THAT Willa would stay with somebody like Tate," I said, and as the words left my mouth I could feel Helen subtly stiffen. Her unclothed arms and legs were woven around mine in a warm tangle of sheets and blankets. Though the sky was still dark outside her bedroom window, I figured it must be nearing morning. "What's her story?" prompting her, after she moaned by response to my remark.

"Come on sweet let's don't talk now just sleep," she blurred.

I closed my eyes, kissed her forehead, which was already pressed against my lips, inhaled the exquisite smell of her, and held her close as I tried to clear the question from my head. She caressed me in a dreamy way, again relaxed, and I listened to her breathing slow, then deepen, until it was apparent she was asleep again. How I wanted sleep, too, but the harder I tried, the more it eluded me. A perfect silence reigned throughout her house, and in that peacefulness I began to worry in a manner possible only at night—a kind of strew of disconnected cares came parading by—while at the same time I marveled at where I was, and who lay here with me flesh on flesh. Henry's claim that I didn't know Helen rose like a specter to haunt me; as much as I might want to disagree with him, of course his claim resonated with truth. Here I was, finally sleeping with this young woman, trying to sleep, anyway, in her house filled with her objects—her vases, furniture, bric-a-brac—and those of her mythic father. Henry was not wholly wrong. I didn't know her, except in this tenebrous way.

At some moment, I discovered myself in a subcellar I didn't recognize, and seated nearby was my mother, who was speaking with me, though I couldn't quite see her face in the wispy shadows. She was worried for me, concerned about my *sick shoes,* as she put it, uneasy about how worn their soles had become and that my toes were exposed from the leather having been eroded by the bad weather, or something of that sort. I assured her, my mother who sat there prim, with her knees together under a print dress of black vines on a white ground, her hands folded gently in her lap, assured her not to worry about my shoes, that I was fine and my feet weren't so very cold. Though I knew I was dreaming, nevertheless I continued to scold myself for remaining unable to sleep, and for a time I must have drifted back and forth from half-conscious wakefulness to light dreaming, until I did awaken, hours later, with the sun in my eyes and Helen no longer in my arms.

Given her penchant for disappearing, it wouldn't have surprised me if I'd gone downstairs to find Helen had left a note on the table and taken off for the day. She was in the kitchen, however, of all things whisking eggs. Espresso stood in a Mellor pot, blacker than the ripest fig—strong coffee such as I had not drunk since leaving Italy. Toasted English muffins lay in a basket under a cloth. Fresh grapefruit juice. She turned, set down the bowl of eggs, embraced me, smiled her rare smile that was nothing less than a crucible of brilliant, warm light, and said, "Scrambled or some kind of fall-apart *faux* omelette. Those are your choices."

"This is a side of you I don't know."

"Which is?"

"The domestic Helen."

"I'm *very* domestic." She smiled again, and poured the eggs into a pan. "What was so important you were trying to wake me up in the middle of the night, anyway?"

"Nothing," as I poured coffee. Barefoot in my jeans and untucked shirt in Helen Trentas's kitchen, I thought to telephone Edmé to let her know I was all right, but imagined she knew precisely where I was. The most unpleasant, curious feeling of having triumphed over Henry passed through me. "I was just wondering about Tate and Willa—you never talk much about her, you know."

"You woke me up to say that?"

"I thought you were awake."

Helen carried the pan to the table, served the scrambled eggs. They smelled of olive oil, rosemary, sage. Giovanni's legacy. Like that pesto Edmé and I'd made. If Giovanni Trentas had never become friends with Henry all those years ago, would there be rows of brave basil plants in the Ash Creek garden?

"You already know what I think about Tate. As far as Willa goes, she was always closer to my father than to me. She's been kind to me over the years, sometimes kinder, more generous than I could understand, really."

"Nothing wrong with kindness, not in this world."

"I guess sometimes she would dote on me too much, and it made me feel uncomfortable, like she might expect something in return. But I'm afraid that's the way I am. You give me something freely and there I'll be, looking it over for the strings attached. I'm the kind of person who if you give me a gift horse I'll look it right in the mouth. Not my best quality."

"Maybe she just was being nice to you to help your father, you know, since he was left to raise you himself."

"No doubt. But it made me suspicious."

We sat side by side, and I held her hand, so that we each ate breakfast with our free hands. "Did she ever ask you for anything in return?"

Helen said, "Willa? No, never."

"You're paranoid, then. Simple as that."

"Master of the obvious."

"Well. Just remind me never to give you a horse."

"Speaking of which, look at this," and she lifted away one side of her white robe to reveal a bruised thigh.

I touched it gently, said, "Jesus."

"Got rammed into the stockade yesterday. It never happened to me before. I don't know what got into the horse I was working with, but he'd never been skittish before."

"Did it hurt last night?"

"You mean, when we? no, nothing hurt last night. Last night was wonderful. I bruise more easily than most. Another bad trait."

"I hadn't any idea you had so many bad traits."

"Deal with it," she smiled.

There were times when I was unable to distinguish whether I was being teased or provoked by Helen, but this wasn't one of them. She fed me a piece of toasted muffin spread thick with marmalade, and I said, in the ridiculous way lovers prattle, "I'll deal with it."

The subject of Willa came up once more, after breakfast. What Helen said was that she had to watch herself, in fact, and refrain from feeling competitive with Willa in mourning Giovanni's death. "Everybody in the small circle who knew him was sad, of course"— not mentioning Tate, who I imagined did not share in the grief— "though your uncle seemed more grim than sad, I thought. But Willa, she was grieved beyond any of us. I remember thinking, Listen, he's *my* father, let me do the crying. Crazy, eh? As if there isn't plenty of room for all of us to cry oceans of tears. She loved him, that's all."

"You ever see Willa yourself?"

"She keeps a horse. Tate owns the stables where I work."

"Of course," I smirked. "Pajarito?"

"Pajarito, yes. I see her there on Thursdays every week, like clockwork, and sometimes we talk and sometimes we don't, and that's about it."

"You know what I think?"

"What do you think?"

"I think you ought to let her be your friend."

She said, "By the way, you didn't want to talk last night about why you showed up here in such a state, what happened to your hand. But maybe you can tell me now—what were you doing?"

"Helen, you'll just be mad at me. Don't ask."

"I won't be mad, promise."

"We had another night visit up at Ash Creek. I got knocked down in the dark by somebody. He actually climbed onto the roof, if you can believe it."

"What for?"

"The usual. To hammer at their rest, punish them, my aunt and uncle. Somebody'd already been over at the studio, and done a good job wrecking Henry's projects. You wouldn't believe how maniacal he was after he found out in the morning. He wanted to blame some of this on me, and I'll tell you, we made up in the afternoon, but I'm not sure how much longer I'm going to be able to stay there."

She sat looking at me, waiting for more, even as I sat waiting for her to say something, perhaps invite me to stay here with her if need be (did I want this? no, not really, not yet). Breaking the silence, she said, "Why would any of this make me mad?" She seemed visibly disquieted, although her voice carried her words along very smoothly.

"I didn't call Tate; Tate called me, and asked me to come meet with him."

"And you did?"

"He didn't give me the chance to accuse him of anything, not really. He accused and exonerated himself before I hardly had the chance to get in a word edgewise."

"Does he know about us?"

"He knows about *everything*. He's the ultimate Argus. He must have a spy in every bush. I kind of hate him and respect him at the same time."

"Respect him?"

"The same way you respect a snake."

"That's fear combined with common sense, not respect. Did he say anything about me or my father?"

"Nothing about you. But he did say that he, meaning Tate himself, was innocent of anything having to do with your father. In fact, he implied that Henry wasn't so innocent, and that I should ask him, or something along those lines."

We sat again in silence, and prompted perhaps by the word *lines*, I reviewed that surveyor's map in my head, then dismissed it, furled it up and tossed it imaginatively into one of the drawers of Tate's leather-topped desk. It was I who broke the silence this time.

"Let me ask you, why would the night visitors leave a note behind with the words *Tell the truth* on it?"

"First of all, who's supposed to be telling the truth?"

I deliberated whether to dig myself in any deeper by breaking my promise to Henry not to discuss that note with anyone—though hadn't he said not to discuss it with Edmé? I couldn't remember anymore. "Henry," I said. "I guess that's who it was left for."

"What's he supposed to tell the truth about?" and as she said these words, I could sense she was pondering whether or not to let *me* in on something she knew in this regard. The downward glance of the eyes, chewing at the corner of her lip.

"This is where my knowledge comes to a dead end," I said, then ventured, "but I think you know more than you're saying. Is that true?"

Helen surprised me with her composed "Yes."

"And?"

"It's just that Tate told me—"

"Why believe anything Tate says?"

"—Tate *showed* me a deposition in which Henry told a somewhat different story about the death than what he told me."

"How'd he get his hands on a deposition?"

Helen shrugged. "You're the one who said he knows everything. But Henry makes me furious how he thinks that just because he can disappear into his little studio and build his fantasy utopia and live up there at Ash Creek, he gets to be excused from any responsibility in the world by simply declaring himself absent from it. The world will always find its way to your doorstep, no matter where you live. He ought to know that. The deposition gave a story that wasn't all that different, but just different enough. Henry's been like a god-father to me all my life, but he's always managed to keep himself at a distance. He's always been loving whenever we're together, but still, I couldn't believe he could tell me that there might have been foul play involved, then turn around and tell Noah it looked like an acci-dent. I think it drove him crazier that the police were crawling all over his precious mountainside for those couple of days than it did that my father was gone. Sometimes I just want to go up to him and scream, Fuck you, right in his face. I know that Tate wants him off that land, and that there's bad blood between him and Tate, always has been. So it doesn't surprise me Tate would try to implicate him. But I also know that though he couldn't have committed that mur-der, he probably understands exactly what happened up there that afternoon in the gorge. And he won't tell."

With this, she began to cry. I sat there dumbfounded at the sight of Helen Trentas weeping, her hazel eyes darkened as I reached out to comfort her and, as I did, realized that within the space of less than a day I'd witnessed Helen and Henry both weeping, the two people least likely to display such emotion of anyone I had ever known.

MONEY. For weeks I had done my damnedest not to worry about it, but perhaps having seen such a dramatic display of it in the form of Tate's mansion in the mountains, maybe even witnessing how Helen lived, not ostentatiously but certainly in comfort, made me aware of what a derelict I'd become. The word *slacker* continued to resound in my head. When I left Helen's I noticed that a button was missing from the cuff of my shirt. Even the dream of my mother, her concern about my shoes, regathered some strength as I started the jeep—my uncle's jeep, the jeep registered to someone who was not altogether happy with me: Lord, it all came together in a bundle of sudden anxiety. I parked near the bank building, another property no doubt mortgaged by Graham Tate or else owned by him free and clear, passed beneath its great round clock into the lobby, and sat with a young assistant manager, who helped me open an account. I wrote a check that closed out what little was left of my balance, and filled out the necessary forms for my savings to be wired from the bank in Rome to my new account here. The sums transferred were even smaller than I might have guessed. I, who'd already considered myself, shall we say, unprosperous, realized I was in fact quite broke.

Given my general indifference to money—a trait I think I must have picked up from my father, who, like his own father, always paid more attention to the capital interests of countries than to his own—this was a state of affairs which normally wouldn't upset me. But it did, this morning; it troubled me. That I couldn't withdraw from the wire transfer for another several days annoyed me the more. Not that I had anything in mind I wanted to purchase. Just the sinking feeling of indigence. And dependency.

Giovanni Trentas came to mind as I left the bank and began the drive back to Ash Creek. It seemed more and more I was following in his footsteps, all these decades after he'd first come here, from Valle d'Aosta via Rome via Coeur d'Alene, into a community already established with rivalries, attractions, jealousies, and with histories all woven into one great impossible maze. So many willful souls, so many silences that required interpretation—and not a sibyl in sight. It reminded me of one of those Greek dramas populated with gods and goddesses, each more pigheaded and grabby than the next, locked in struggles that were decided by maneuvering naive mortals around, pitching us from this horrid trap to that hazardous fate, from their comfortable remove of, say, a cloud palace or mountain peak. To someone like a Tate or, now I'd begun to believe, like Henry, the primary conflicts always outweighed what must be considered lesser—and that gift of focus served to define their greatness, but also their impurity. What was always the pity—it seemed to me as I ascended the dirt road along the creek, which danced, as ever, vibrantly along in the hollow of browning flowers—was that those gods of Greek and Roman mythology never did seem to learn a lesson, no matter how horrible was their mistake against humanity. Gods never learn because they always emerge unscathed.

Sure, Giovanni may well have died at the hands of some stupid, drunken hunter who had just enough of his wits about him to scramble back out the top end of the gorge after he'd had an altercation, say, with this man who was intent on throwing him off the land, who with his halting English told the poacher to leave, and whom he'd pushed, for instance. Pushed a little harder than he'd meant to push, and saw that the poor fellow had fallen hard, then decided to flee, hike fast back up toward the mountain pass over the summit, where he would find his truck and get away, unseen by a soul. This was, ironically, a scenario that Henry and Tate might well agree upon in the absence of any real proof the death could be pinned on the other. This hunter fable, however, wouldn't explain Giovanni's foot having been removed, unless one were to suppose an accidental murder was made to look somewhat more intentional, or at least weird and ritualistic, by using a deer knife on the innocent remnants of the victim. Noah's presumption that some wild scavenger had done the work seemed no more liable to be the truth than this.

I drove on, for a few minutes, without much further thought. And then I began to see—or, rather, to *feel empathetically*—the filaments that bound Giovanni into a web that had been spun by less merciful and serendipitous weavers than a phantom blundering hunter or ravenous animal. For the first time since I arrived here, I got some insight about just how easy it was to be drawn into the wars of others and to go down never knowing what hit you, or why. Surely this is what happened to Helen's father: he got caught in the middle of a struggle between others, most likely Henry and Tate. I could just *feel* it. What struck me, then, like a blow to the chest, was this: There was no reason the same thing couldn't happen to Helen's lover, if he continued to set himself between them. And this thought carried me back to my original concern, money.

To think, when I'd left the bank, within this hour just past, I had actually considered taking Tate up on his offer of work! Lunacy. Would money have bought me out of my problems here, anyway? Yes, maybe. For one, wouldn't some money buy me a proper escape? (Yes, *that* thought again.) I had just enough to return to Rome, reestablish myself in some small flat, do some tutoring. Why not get out? Simply because of Helen? And if that was the case, then money was not my problem, but love. My head was whirling and I might in my distraction have run him over, if David Lewis up ahead on the road, walking his dogs, hadn't waved his arms to catch my attention.

"Grant," when I pulled up beside him.

Allowing the engine to idle, I said, "Morning."

"Glad I ran into you."

His black hair was loose of its binder this morning and hung to his shoulders; his face glowed in the crisp air.

"Listen. Jenn and I are having a farewell dinner and I've phoned up to the house and spoken with Edmé, but she says no way will Henry come down for it."

"Well, he's not likely to listen to me."

"He and I've known each other a long time. I mean, we don't see each other all that often. Neighbors here don't. But if you'd come by with your aunt, it would mean a lot to me and Jenn."

"I don't know, I—"

"We'd hate to leave the valley with bad blood behind."

I caught myself looking hard at David Lewis, thinking, How much of your soul has been foreclosed? but scolded myself, even chuckled at my obsessive suspiciousness.

"What's funny?" he said.

"Nothing, I'm sorry. Look. It's up to Edmé. If she'd like to come, and she wants me to come with her, we'll be there."

"Friday, about seven."

Today was Wednesday. Something else now came to mind—and I didn't think but simply spoke: "I don't know you, and it's none of my business, I suppose, but may I ask why you're selling your place? Seems too beautiful for anyone to sell."

Lewis was as awed by my impertinence as I. He said flatly, "It is beautiful, and yes, it *is* none of your business, if you don't mind my saying so."

"No offense," I said.

"None taken. I knew Henry was not going to be happy about any

of this. I put off telling him as long as I could, because I didn't want
to deal with him. The bottom line is, this is the real world, the practical world. Just because somebody wants to develop Ash Creek
doesn't mark the end of Western civilization. The homesteader days
our fathers knew, where you could settle down on a big piece of unspoiled land for a hundred bucks—those days are long gone."

"If I understand him, though, I think his position is that there's
plenty of land, plenty of valleys where there are people who'd be
only too happy to let them bring in the bulldozers. Henry knows
Tate must be behind your sale, that Tate wants to move Edmé and
Henry out of there for personal reasons that have nothing to do with
development."

"That's not my quarrel. All I know is, the money they offered me
was too substantial to walk away from. I don't think we had a choice.
I have no evidence they're even going to make all these changes
Henry seems to fear so much."

I could think of nothing to say in response.

"I'll see you, then, if Edmé can come. If not, good luck."

As I opened the horsegate, farther up the road, parked the jeep,
and began to walk toward the house, a cloud of dread settled in upon
me like none I'd ever experienced in this place. Ash Creek had
always meant serenity to me, distance from the troubles raised by
the rest of the world, distance even from my own unhappiness
and errors.

This was the oddest sensation. Now I felt I'd been traitorous to
Henry and Edmé—but the facts were different, weren't they? I
walked up the field and imagined here what Lewis had been unwill-
ing to confirm, a future of shorn forests and pistons, lifts and lines of
heavy steel strung between towers, winter carnival sports and other
inanities. Or else another vision: this one of more shorn forests and
road after road winding up through the fields into building lots,
hither and yon, each and every meadow transfigured into lawns. Or
even another: this wild earth not tempered and trampled, but all

encompassed under the name Tate. Tate's Valley, say, or Tate's Basin—*Tate's Trust.*

No doubt my thoughts were given to wandering because I was edgy about what sort of reception I might expect, having now stayed out all night without calling. My parents had always been liberal in regard to my childhood rambling, and were never ones to scold me for coming in late from a friend's. So long as I wasn't in trouble with the law, they figured everything was all right.

My worry was confirmed by Edmé's greeting me with a dark hello. When I asked where Henry was, she said he was in the studio, asked to be left alone, had begun to rebuild his maquettes. A man on a ladder could be heard on the far side of the house, installing a new rain gutter. I'd been so absorbed in fatuous thoughts of Ash Creek ruined that I had failed to notice the workman's truck parked at the upper edge of the field. Life went on here, night visits or not. The pertinacity was impressive. "And so what did Tate say?" Edmé asked.

"Tate is an innocent. A chaste and decent saint who never hurt anyone in all his born days. And he's generous, too. Offered me a job during our game of darts."

"You played darts with Graham Tate?" she asked, in disbelief.

"We discussed books. It was an education."

The map no longer existed, I decided.

"And you stayed with Helen, I presume."

"I stayed there, yes," glad she'd changed the subject, while at the same time amazed I would welcome discussion of Helen over Tate. Moments passed, measured out by the pendulum of the wall clock. My hands were shoved down into my pockets, and I shrugged, "Maybe it's best I go." I found myself studying the bowl of oranges at the center of the kitchen table. A beautiful touch; this was a home, I thought. "Surely you don't disagree I've worn out my welcome here, at least with Uncle Henry."

"Of course I disagree. And where would you go? Helen's?"

"Don't think so. But I'm in the way here. You two are used to your privacy, and ever since I showed up, uninvited, it seems to me you haven't had a minute of it."

"Grant. I won't stand in your way of going, if that's what you want to do, but until you've found a place to stay, you're staying here. You're blood, that's that."

"Even blood wears thin, Edmé. If you and Henry'd be kind enough to let me continue to use the jeep—"

"You can *have* the silly jeep, Grant. You and your uncle both are at a difficult place, for different reasons. Your father would never forgive me, though, if he knew I let you leave like this."

"He would say I got myself here, now it's my responsibility to get myself out—and that you and Henry have been perfectly generous to me, and kind."

"Where do you propose to sleep? In the jeep?"

"I don't know. Maybe."

"Whatever your uncle said yesterday, he apologized and meant it. We're family. I was thinking last night, when you didn't come back, why not move into Giovanni's cabin until things settle down some— you'd still be here, but at the same time you'd have a little distance, sort of a place of your own. Everybody would have the chance to cool down a bit, and if you wanted to find your own place, if you're thinking of staying, it would give you some time. There's no phone down there, but the woodstove works and the place is clean—I looked this morning—dusty but clean, and you would eat with us when you wanted, and always can use this phone. What do you say? I really don't want you to go. How'd that work for a compromise?"

Edmé walked down with me. I with my half-packed bag, to which Giovanni's box was the only addition since my arrival; she carrying blankets, sheets, a pillow. We made the move before Henry returned from the studio later in the afternoon, because Edmé didn't want him to talk me out of accepting her compromise arrangement, as she said he would lobby for me to stay where I was and she didn't want to risk hearing more words between us other than words of agreement. The cabin stood just on the other side of the creek, not so far from where the old log structure had burned on Labor Day night. Grass had grown up around its rough timber walls sealed with white oakum, and the boughs of water spruce, which had overhung its roof when I was a boy, now canopied the modest dwelling in an embrace of foliage. For the most part, as I remembered, Giovanni did not occupy the cabin during those innocent summers when I visited Ash Creek, but stayed with his daughter in town, in order to give Edmé and Henry their space. Nevertheless I'd always kept my distance, sometimes watching the cabin from afar, like kids do, for no particular reason. We approached, in other words, a locus of mystery about to be unveiled.

"See?" Edmé said, when we entered the haven, and yes, soft sunlight flooded the room, whose spartan chairs, table, bed were veneered by a fine dust film but otherwise quite immaculate. Through the closed windows, perhaps through the walls themselves, you could hear the burbling creek, very nearby. Sounded like so many voices engaged in slippery, gentle dialogue. It occurred to me, fleetingly, that Helen might not like my moving in here—ever protective of anything having to do with her father. But no other alternative presented itself, had it. Edmé had made the best possible proposal. I told her so, smiled as we sheeted a narrow bed, swept the checkered linoleum floor, then mopped it with cold stream water, and just passed a couple of pleasant, mindless hours together, working to make the place comfortable. We carried in some kerosene from the storage shed, filled the two hurricane lamps, replacing the tapers, and I lit a fire in the corner stove, which filled the place with smoke at first. Once the chimney flue had warmed and whatever spiderwebs silting the passage there were burned away, the fire drew well. After the smoke cleared, we shut windows and door, and to all intents and purposes I was established down here, where already I felt a little freer, much less a burden to Henry and Edmé and even to myself.

Up at the house, during dinner that evening we spoke tangentially of my meeting with Graham Tate, though I remained mum with regard to his accusation of Henry, of course. Nothing new was disclosed about Tate, nothing I hadn't heard before. But when, tongue loosened by wine, perhaps, I mentioned my confusion about why Willa would stay all these years with Tate, locked in barren marriage to a powermonger, withdrawn like a Bluebeard mistress jailed in his opulent but coarse castle, Henry's face clouded with a subtle, unrecognizable pain.

"I'm sure Willa has her reasons, like any of us, for doing what she does," Edmé remarked, not having noticed Henry's expression (or did she not need to see it in order to fathom it was there?)—and proceeded to litanize Willa's charity work and other involvements that showed a good woman doing good things, no matter who she was married to or how she otherwise chose to live her life.

If I hadn't been so fascinated by Henry, I might have felt properly scolded by Edmé. As it was, I commented, "I didn't mean to belittle her. Just the opposite. She seemed like a remarkable woman, the day I met her."

"She's been very kind to your friend Helen over the years," Edmé said.

Which did snap me out of it, not used to Helen's name being evoked here all that often. And certainly not in association with me. Hoping, I suppose, to deflect any chance of discussing Helen, I asked, "Are her parents still alive?"

Henry himself seemed to awaken, too, and said, "You know as well as anybody that Giovanni's dead, Grant."

"I don't mean Helen's parents. I mean Willa's."

What had that glazed look in my uncle's eye been about? I felt protective of the man; he seemed increasingly like one possessed or haunted or bewildered. I didn't want to contribute to whatever this was that seemed to bother him. I said abruptly, "Just idle curiosity on my part; we can change the subject. So tell me," with as warm a smile toward my uncle as I could project, "did they finish fixing up that rain gutter?"

The question was answered, the supper discourse meandered along, and all seemed as copacetic as could be expected among us. Though it was cool outside, cooler than those half-dozen weeks ago when we first sat after dinner and smoked on the porch, we enjoyed brandy and cigarettes, and Edmé joined us. Henry's wayward look had faded completely, and he spoke with his usual measured spirits, saying that it wouldn't take him that long to have the studio and the maquettes back to where they were before the harasser did his handiwork. "It is the ideas that take time, not the icons," he said, which made me appreciate his resilience. He saked about my hand, and I told him it felt better, though in fact it throbbed this evening, perhaps from the work in Giovanni's cabin. If he had some opinion about my having moved from the house to these new quarters, he didn't express much of it: only when I bid good night to them both, saying I was exhausted and it was time to give this new bed a try, he proposed, "You want to borrow one of the rifles, just to have it there?"

"No need," I answered.

"You sure?"

Instead, I asked for a good flashlight, and after Edmé placed one in my hands, saying, "Maybe this wasn't such a good idea, Grant— you know you really are welcome up here if you find you don't feel comfortable, the door'll be unlocked," I smiled in the darkness on the porch and assured her I felt grateful to them both for putting me up. Henry shook my hand—formal of him, I thought—Edmé kissed me, and off I went down the field, crossing the same narrow unstable bridge Helen and I'd crossed on our way to the little cemetery, back in those simpler days which now seemed so long ago. Orange coals still brightened the grate in the belly of the corner stove, and I stoked them before adding several fresh chunks of dry wood to the fire. Kneeling, I blew gently into the glow until it caught again.

I considered lighting one of the lamps and reading from Hawthorne the next story, which was about the golden apples of the
Hesperides, but instead I sat on the edge of the bed to allow my
mind to drift. Thoughts of what Giovanni must have felt here, way
back when he himself was not much older than I am now, turned
through me, nearly visceral, like golden apple-tree leaves which
surely must have resembled back in olden times those of the quaking
aspens in these mountains surrounding me. Leaves all fluttering
about, having been plucked from the branches by a muscular wind.
And as those thoughts—more thoughtless than reflective—whirled,
I removed my clothes and climbed into the icy bed, and even shivered a little until the sheets began to warm against my skin. The
room flickered with shadow figures cast from the stove fire, and
whether asleep or awake, I heard myself say to Giovanni's ghost both
hello and good night, as the voices in the creek continued to prattle
and chatter and sigh.

And I slept. Money and golden apples, love and jealousies, rivalries and estrangements and every other worry drifted further and
further from my dreamless mind than they ever had, or would.

ON WAKING, I heard the stream continue with its monologue, which must have resembled, I thought as I rose to rekindle the fire, the meaningless babble Giovanni heard when he disembarked the ship with his sister, Paola, and entered America. Myself, I was not unfamiliar with such estrangements; again, what I felt this morning was such affinity with him, a deepening fondness. The man's simplicity, of which I'd had some small knowledge, mostly from those who knew him far better than I ever did, was manifest in this pure plain shelter. Little had been disturbed here, I gathered, since he left the cabin for the relative grandeur of the cottage where Helen now lived alone. And now, these years later, Edmé and Henry seemed still to have kept it as a rustic shrine in honor of their departed friend. This table of pine, its top a palimpsest of scratch marks, some of them no doubt carved in moments of boredom by his girl, and now mine, two decades ago or better. This chair, timeworn but solid. These battered aluminum pots and chipped plates and the bent silverware in the cabinet near the stove. All these artifacts vouched for the simplest kind of life. It didn't take much of a leap of faith for me to imagine how central to Giovanni's existence his daughter had been, how considerable his love for her: what else did he ever bother to care about? His daughter, his friendships with a few who became his kin. That was all.

Out the window, the field steamed. I dressed, knocked shut the stove grate, walked up to the house where I had my coffee, answered Edmé's questions about Giovanni's hut with truthful words of assurance, and asked if I was needed for any sort of work around the place. The day stretched before me, unusually worriless, especially in the wake of these last couple of nights.

Willa Tate was who I wanted to see. Before I left, with no plan for how I would set about fulfilling my wish, I mentioned to Edmé my encounter with David Lewis. "I'll do whatever you want," I added. She said she'd think about what was best and let me know.

The morning was warmer than it had been for some weeks, the sky a succinct blue trimmed with layers of cirrostratus. In the east was a sun pillar, like a candelabra of light in clouds that soon would burn away. Water droplets like silver pearls fell from the telephone wires along the creek road, and the hood of the jeep was beaded with dew. In a rucksack I'd brought along Giovanni's box with me; I wasn't sure just why, other than that I'd begun to fear someone might take it away from me. I'd placed it on the seat beside me; the beautiful *doña* in the oval portrait returned my quick gaze but didn't look away from me as I did from her. Dust, gasoline, and damp canvas scented the interior of the jeep. Once more I turned from the dirt road onto the narrow highway, past the mailboxes affixed along the crossbeam of the rustic crucifix there, and headed toward town in complete ignorance of how I might go about effecting this proposed meeting with Willa Tate.

Then the stables came to mind. If I went to see Helen, there was some chance (*chance* was just the word) Willa might have chosen a warm morning like this to ride. Today was Thursday, and Helen had said Thursdays were Willa's riding days. Given the lack of other prospects, other than simply driving the juniper-lined route back up to the Tates' aerie and ringing the bell, this seemed best.

I knew my way there because when I was younger, my uncle Henry had brought me to the stables more than once to watch the horse shows that took place from spring through fall. Men and women and many horses, Arabians and palominos and other breeds, horses for sale and at stud—I remember these exhibits and how fearful those great powerful flanks and necks and flaring nostrils were to me. I remember finding it incomprehensible how boys and girls no older than I discovered in their hearts the courage, arrogance, poise, it required to climb aboard a beast so much stronger than they. We came and watched, and I noticed Henry would regard the show with a kind of nostalgic infatuation—I was not too young to make such a refined appraisal of him—that made me understand, even then, how he missed this world of his own youth. Edmé never joined us, and so the horse show had been one of those boys'-time-together experiences, and one which despite my fears I'd always looked forward to each visit.

The stables had, naturally, changed some since those days—I noticed immediately the much vaster configurations of white painted fences that mazed the flats out east of town, just on the far side of the river. More paddocks, sheds, stalls, too. Twenty or thirty horses exercised out in the main ring. Whatever funky rural spirit might once have obtained here was now gone: this was an impressive concern. The very lot where I left the jeep, having stashed my Pandora box beneath the seat, was—though still of hard-packed dirt— somehow more *serious business*.

And serious business this was, even to one with as untutored an eye as mine. I wandered the length of an extended barn, open at either end, and saw that each of the stalls bore a chalkboard with feeding, medical, and exercise instructions, as well as placards giving the individual's name, pedigree, trophies and other awards. The sawdusted dirt floor was raked, the equipment immaculate; an air of professionalism washed up and down the corridors of the building. Not having seen Helen's car back in the lot, I didn't expect to run into her, and didn't—but now was approached by a man wearing a red logoed tee shirt with the stable name, *Pajarito,* in white on his chest, and blue jeans and boots, who asked if he could help me. I told my name, and asked whether Willa Tate was around this morning.

"Already come and gone," he said. "Well, no—hold on. Maybe she's still back there in the tack room. I know she's done riding for the day. You mind waiting here?"

Barley, hay, clovery smells, and the smell of horse piss. These were scents, in fact, I liked. I paced back down the center passage toward the brightening light where huge sliding doors had been pushed open to let in fresh air. Some doves coodled above me in the rafters. And then I turned and there she was, tentatively smiling and presenting me with her handshake, solid though not vising like her husband's, whose was meant to wrench the blood from your hand rather than exchange warmth and respects. "Grant? This is a surprise," she said. "You ride?"

"No, no," laughing, embarrassed. "Horses frighten me. I'm a great disappointment to my uncle for never having learned."

We walked together back toward the lot.

"Never too late," Willa said.

"That may be true for most things, but not for me and horses."

"I'll bet I could have you riding decent English style before Thanksgiving. How are Edmé and Henry?"

"Fine," I said, but the falsehood tasted awful in my mouth and so I quickly added, "Not fine."

"Oh, really?" and she turned toward me, a concerned expression crowding her eyes, brow furrowed. I considered that look, and the classical beauty of this woman, her eyes so clear, such *presences,* and intuited, without much evidence to support my thought, that this interest she displayed was genuine. None of the convolution her husband seemed so much to enjoy was evident in Willa.

"Not altogether fine, no. You and I don't know each other, and I'm probably being presumptuous talking with you about it. But I've kind of reached a dead end, and to be honest, I didn't know where else to turn."

"Go on," she said.

"Maybe we should go somewhere else?"

"Helen says nice things about you," Willa said. "Did you know that? Not to me, but to others here."

We walked slowly along. I waited for her answer.

"It's too late for breakfast and too early for lunch."

The coffee shop I'd gone to when I first arrived in August came to mind. I proposed we meet there, figuring—rightly, as it would happen—that Willa Tate did not often frequent the place. This way, at least, we'd be on more equal footing. We drove separately from the stables back the several miles to town. Different parts of the sky displayed different weathers. Over there was cloudless and sunny; back over here was stirring with silver-edged stacks of darkening clouds; and just ahead ran a mingling of clear blues and clots of froth, as if many seasons had taken hold of the heavens at the same time.

It wasn't until I found myself in town, looking along the curb for a free space, my own disquiet returned. Just for one, anxiety about my frail finances was reawakened by that hateful bank clock, pendant and casting its thin shadow on the sidewalk where I walked directly beneath it, hoping to summon some healthy defiance, as if it were a ladder and I the least superstitious man on earth. Then I thought, Are you really going to ask her these questions that are needling you, obsessing you? Are you that far gone?

She had already taken her place in a booth, not near the window but quite far back in the room. She sat facing the wall. Was she smoking a cigarette?

I lit one myself after sliding in opposite her, and she laid the immense plastic-sheathed menu before her when the young woman, May, whom I'd nearly forgotten, came to take our orders. She smiled, perhaps recognizing me, perhaps not, and Willa ordered tea while I indulged in bread pudding and coffee. After she left, some moments passed, while the wooden paddles of the ceiling fan carved the air and light above us, and late-morning customers raised their mild voices here and there as they spoke to one another.

"Helen's an interesting girl, don't you agree?" Willa said at last.

"She's certainly that."

A pause, then, "You're enjoying your stay with Edmé and Henry?"

"Ash Creek's always been special for me. And they've been like parents. I don't suppose you get up to see them all that often, do you. I mean, besides Labor Day."

"When I was younger I went there a lot. Giovanni and I would play cards—canasta, even poker, if you can believe it. He was the best person to walk in those mountains with I ever met, knew the name of every plant, every stone, every bird. His English was never all that good, but he knew Ash Creek inside out. It's still one of my favorite places on earth. Have you ever been up in the gorge?"

"Pretty far up. Never all the way, though."

"It's a different world up there, a fantasy world. You half expect the trees to take on life like in *The Wizard of Oz*, reach out and wrap their arms around you. And the springs at the very head of the gorge, where Ash Creek literally comes pushing up out of the earth—well, I used to hike there often with Henry and Giovanni and Edmé. Not anymore. Not for years."

"That's too bad. To give up something you obviously like so much."

Willa read me easily, in part because I wanted to be easily read. Her face was arranged into the most sorrowful smile, elegant and defended, sentimental yet tough.

"So what is it you wanted to talk about, Grant?"

Remembering this was not Willa Richardson but Tate's wife, I said, "I assume you probably already know. But for the sake of argument, I should say that I've been given a present by my aunt that maybe wasn't mine to have. Giovanni's box. Did you know about it?"

"I haven't the vaguest idea."

The pudding was like manna from some Hawthorne heaven.

"You ought to try this," and pushed my plate toward her. To my surprise, she took up her spoon and sampled some. "Good, right? Well, he kept this cigar box—"

"He never smoked a cigar in his life, always was telling me I ought to give up cigarettes."

"And in this box he kept a lot of knickknacks and mementos and things."

"That doesn't sound like my Giovanni. He was never a hoarder, couldn't have cared less about material things. Are you sure you understood Edmé when she gave you this box?"

"Oh, yes, very sure. And it's definitely Giovanni's. There's a stash of letters in it, written to him from overseas, and letters from his sister."

"Paola wrote Giovanni? I always felt bad they were estranged during his last years."

"Yes, and letters from Margery Wilkins, later Margery Trentas, in the box, brief frightened little notes, more like, but love letters written under duress. And there's another note, too, that I guess I wanted to ask you about, but maybe I shouldn't."

"Why not?"

"Because it involves you."

"Involves me? I see. There are no love letters in your box from me to Giovanni, I can tell you that much. I think there are people around who would like to think differently, because he was one of the best friends I ever had, and people adore nothing better than to create dirty stuff where there was only good."

"That's not what I said, though. The note isn't from you to Giovanni. It's from you to my uncle."

Silence; that smile, and what did she do but say, "I'm not surprised. There was a time when Henry and I were very close. It's no one's business but our own, and besides, it was a lifetime ago. Why would such a thing interest you, anyway, Grant?"

"Because, to answer your earlier question, if I do love Helen, that letter from you has something to do with her, doesn't it? And until there's some closure regarding her father's death, she's never going to be free to love me, and so I'm interested in seeing that closure come to pass."

All of which was sort of news to me, too. That is, these ideas might have been cognitive play toys worried at, in an amused though terrified way, these past weeks. But setting them out, one by one, in words, to be heard by this woman whom I barely knew but who I could sense was deeply enmeshed in the lives of those for whom I cared, made the thoughts themselves condense into *real dispositions.*

"Do you expect me to say something now?" Willa asked. "What would you like me to say to you?" She held her cup with both hands before her face, so that all I could see was a look in her eyes I couldn't fathom. Surely somewhere there must have been wariness in that look. Dismay, maybe, at this news she'd been discovered— though I had not truly discovered anything, nor had she as yet admitted anything, either. What I saw, instead, was warmth, if you will, like affection, and relief, perhaps. As if some absolution was suddenly available to her, if she chose to embrace it.

To my amazement she did, more or less. She told me that her friendship with Henry back then was, yes, close—closer than merely close—and as she continued, she asked aloud, as much for her sake as mine, "No reason not to tell you, is there? because surely you agree there's nothing to gain by going with this to Edmé, not after so much time. It would only hurt her, for no reason. Henry knows, my husband knows, Giovanni knew, and now you know, and that's the full circle. Are you happy now?"

"Edmé and Henry were married, right?"

"They were. I was young. I made a mistake. So did your uncle. We had the choice of going on with the relationship behind Edmé's back, or telling her, or stopping. And we stopped. I went away for almost a year. That was how I broke it off."

"Edmé'd be devastated."

"Would she? They say women *know*. And I think we do. Edmé needs to believe otherwise, and Henry's gone out of his way to provide for that belief. So have I, by the way."

"Don't you feel guilty?" knowing myself hardly to be in the position to question someone else's morals, considering my own past behavior, but asking away nevertheless.

"Why should I? It's over now. I'm an old married woman with a forgiving husband and a memory that's uncomfortable, tormented even, sometimes. I've made my mistake, I've suffered, I've done what I could do to keep that suffering from spreading out into others' lives. And like I say, it's over now."

She rose, went to the rest room, and when she returned, I asked, "Want to go?"

"You know what I want?"

I stood, placed some money on the table, followed her out into the bright daylight, which stung my eyes. Outside, I said, "What?"

"I want you to consider giving me that note. Giovanni'd want me to have it. You know now, you know what you wanted, and I'm not even unhappy about having shared it with you. But let me destroy the note. Nothing good can come of keeping it around."

"I'm not sure."

"Have you told Henry about this?"

"No. I doubt he'd be anywhere near as forthcoming as you've just been, and besides, let's just say he's not very happy with me right now as it is."

"Think about it, Grant. I've been honest with you, be fair with me. I'm not ashamed of what I did. I loved your uncle in my way, but it's been thirty-some years. We've all made our separate peace with what happened."

"How'd Giovanni know?"

"Because I told him."

"Why'd you tell him?"

"That's enough with questions, Grant. Think about giving me the note. It's not much to ask. And never let on to Helen about this. If you do, nothing but pain will come from it. I think if you bring it up with her, you can forget your romance. Helen won't be grateful. Trust me on that score. And thanks for the tea and sharing the bread pudding." We shook hands, accomplicelike, as business people might, and parted.

Having crossed the street, I sat in the jeep, across from Tate's office on the second floor of the bank building, toward which Willa had walked, and savored the last white warmth of the retiring sun through the scratched windows. I understood by my abstracted sense of grief that Willa had confirmed something I'd preferred to think of as a bad fantasy, something I myself, guilty and prurient dreamer, had invented with the harmless box as my muse. But look: *Seek and ye shall find.* Wasn't that how the adage went? Although what she revealed about her relationship with my uncle was disturbing, I was grateful to have the knowledge in hand, because for the first time I felt I had some inkling about what that note, *Tell the truth,* might have meant, and why it was important to Henry that I not mention it to Edmé. Here was one possible truth the night visitor might want Henry to admit—though, of course, as Willa'd rightly said, it was a long time ago, and one might fairly question what good could come of digging up such dead issues. None, to be sure, unless these dead issues were attached to living ones. Lord, I thought. I wasn't a bit closer to any answers than before; perhaps if anything was a little further afield.

The warning Willa had laid out about Helen bothered me, more than anything else. It didn't jibe with what Helen herself had insisted from the first mention of such matters. I remembered her words, could hear them echo in my head: *I get crazy because there's such a tangle here, and I won't ever get free of it until I know what really did happen.* Willa said just the opposite—she'd counted on my never telling Helen about her doomed affair with Henry, based on a forewarning that she would not be grateful for such knowledge.

I didn't get it. Was it possible two distinct, contradictory truths were at play? I believed that both Willa and Helen had been honest with me, but the ledgers when run together refused to add up. I felt a spasm rush through me, an ache of perplexity. I didn't get it, and didn't like it that I didn't get it. For a moment I was persuaded the only sane move for me to make was to take the note out of Giovanni's box—it was, after all, right there—and run upstairs, find Willa, and put the piece of paper into her hands. Instead, however, I just sat there, paralyzed. It was as if *I* could find it in myself to do such a thing, but the *box* wouldn't allow me to begin parceling it out, would not consent to any schism in its integrity. The temptation passed. The box remained unbreached.

AFTERNOON HAD TURNED gusty, wind fingers combing through the wild grasses. Storm clouds fumed at the mountain fringes. The sky had settled upon an endless gray.

Helen was not home. I took a walk along the river, where we'd argued recently, and tossed stones into the water. When I returned to the cottage, I saw she still wasn't around and so let myself in with the key she kept hidden in the stone wall beside the back door. I'd grown disheartened and cold waiting for her to turn up. Going inside seemed the natural move for me to make. I assured myself she wouldn't mind.

Inside, transient light filtered through the windows, making the surfaces of the kitchen ghostly, softly fuzzed and thereby a little unreal. It was as if a new faculty were aroused in me, as I stood in her rooms alone, free to smell Helen's scent, which marked them, at liberty to explore if I dared. I guess I should have felt more of an intruder than I did, though it would be a falsehood to suggest I didn't feel the nervous flutter one gets in his gut knowing he is doing something transgressive. I set my rucksack, with Giovanni's box in it, on the kitchen table. Glancing now and again out the windows to warn myself if Helen was about to arrive, I meandered from kitchen through dining room through living room. An unearthly silence abided, an exquisite calm.

Upstairs. I had to go upstairs. What drew me there was plain curiosity and what bade me to open the drawer to her desk was also curiosity, although the wiser sense of foreboding, which before had led me to glance continually out windows, to be certain I was still alone, was forgotten in my lust to rummage around, see what there was to see.

The usual junk any of us deposits over years into our drawers rattled together—more spare keys, some tarnished silver jewelry, a broken seashell. What interested me were some photos she kept in no apparent order. Helen with blue ribbon and a grand wreath of flowers, standing next to a magnificent stallion. Helen in tan jodhpurs and black velvet jacket. Another of Helen, in Italy with women who appeared to be kin surrounding her, though their faces were so different from hers, their clothing, their smiles—not kin, though the next photographs would lead me to believe she was in Velletri, standing with these women in the Piazza Cairoli, with the Trivio tower rising behind them no different now than it was in the fourteenth century. And here was yet another of Helen, a girl about ten years of age, a tomboy in overalls and with hair shorn—quite different from her pinafore garb in that photo in Henry's studio—once again surrounded by people, though I couldn't immediately make out who they were. Where they were was easier—the knoll to the right and the long veranda which stretched from south to north and thereby paralleled the creek were plainly Ash Creek's. Some caught in the shot looked directly at the camera, others didn't, and after a moment's reflection, telling by the number of people there, I realized this was a Labor Day feast from a couple of decades ago. Giovanni Trentas had his hand on her shoulders and stood behind the girl, I now recognized. On her left was a woman whose face was altogether bathed in shadow under her flamboyant black gaucho hat. To her right, I could see, stood my uncle Henry, his arm over Giovanni's shoulder, placed there as a brother might, but his gaze off away toward someone outside the view of the camera. It wasn't my imagination that led me to believe he had a look of deep sadness or even apprehension on his face—once more, the two Henrys of Ash Creek caught in a single instant, one the comfortable paterfamilias and host posing with dear friends, and the other Henry gazing away toward problems on some immediate horizon. Little Helen smiled, openly, as only children can, at the person taking the shot. She was beautiful, a dark angel even then. Nothing was written on the reverse of the print, unfortunately. I would have liked to verify who the woman was at Giovanni's side.

I put the photographs back into the desk, tried to arrange them so they appeared to lie there haphazard, just as before. I listened hard and heard nothing, and was persuaded by the silence to open yet another drawer.

Here were receipts, business documents, phone bills, that sort of thing. None of this much interested me, but I found myself sifting through the papers, anyway. Who did Helen write checks to? Nothing very unusual; to the gas company for propane, the electric company for the power that would allow the lights to shine were I to come to my senses and shut this drawer and hurry downstairs to the kitchen, having turned the lights on there, where I might rather innocently sit and await Helen's return rather than continue with this folly.

Then my eye caught a glimpse of something unexpected. Graham Tate's name printed on a series of documents; mortgage receipts, they appeared to be. The amounts were substantial, at least from my purview, and though my fingers went cold and numb at the vision of his name here in the house of Helen Trentas—for what could this mean but that she had been hiding from me the extent of her involvement with Tate?—I continued to lift sheet after sheet of these bank statements, and gazed in disbelief even as I began to realize that I was probably standing in the second-floor bedroom of a house owned not by Helen Trentas—nor left to her as part of the estate of the late Giovanni Trentas—but by Graham Tate. The omnipresent Graham Tate, the omnivorous Tate. Here he was again. I pushed the drawer shut and went slowly downstairs, sat on the couch facing Sam the stuffed eagle. The wind at the windows whistled, calmed, then whistled anew. My mind raced similarly, went blank, raced. When I laid my head back into the pillow of the sofa, I remembered seeing an eagle during a family excursion to salt marshes on Long Island, a few hours east of New York City, near Sag Harbor; remembered the sight of the bird whose wingspan was tremendous and head imperial, as it flew steadily across the low sky, carrying the fish it had just caught in its talons. The fish faced forward, its tail jerkily wagging and snapping. It was a vast fish, with mouth jutted open and a look of shock registered there. Sleek, with its silver sides caught in the claws and spurs of the fisher bird. Prey and predator journeying toward their final wrestle in the nest where chicks equipped with their own beaks and claws would render the fish into mutilated strands of meat and skin, fin and bone. And before I closed my eyes, I gazed at Sam and knew he'd made many similar kills during his brief time on earth—just a fact of nature, as Helen might say, in that same calm voice she used when telling me about trapping bear. But the remembrance bothered me, just as the witnessing had, back near the salt marshes of that boyhood junket. I felt a curious kinship with the stupid twitching fish. What a ludicrous fate he suffered. Or was it? Maybe he'd been in an ecstasy, soaring toward his ruin. Maybe it beat being caught in a yellow tide and washing ashore poisoned, or cannibalized like most in the deplorable food chain, condemned by fate for being slower or smaller than the next.

Despite my uneasiness, my concern about being here uninvited, despite my memory of that eagle and her hostage, and of these new dismaying discoveries upstairs, I nodded off to sleep, there on the sofa, as the wind went on blowing.

My awkward nap wouldn't last long. Soon Helen was standing over me, a smile awry on her lips. "Burglar," she said.

I yawned, stretched casually as I could, smiled back with the words, "Caught me."

"Breaking and entering now, are we."

"It was a crime of passion, and also it was cold out. Punish me as you see fit."

"Don't think I won't," she said, smile gone as she sat beside me, fluently wrapped her arms around me, kissed me with a kind of rough levity. "Your cheeks are cold," I whispered; but they weren't cold for very long, neither of us was cold for long, as I found my way inside her there on the davenport, while the first grains of what would begin as a light shower percussed against the window, grains that would develop into fine hail, then settle into a steady drizzle driven by capricious gusts.

"So tell me the truth," Helen said, as we gathered ourselves up and faltered toward the kitchen. "Did you snoop around before I got here? Truth now."

It would be easier to trap a tempest in a bottle than describe the next moments, such a chaos of subtle lies her questions evoked, even as she surprised me with goads, like, "Closets are the best places to look for things people don't want you to find, the backs of closets, and under stuff at the backs of shelves. Only mediocre cat burglars look in people's drawers. Nobody hides important stuff in drawers; too obvious."

"Is that so," as neutral as I could manage.

"Or else they put things there hoping they'll be discovered."

"I see."

"If I had to guess—"

"You don't—"

"If I had to guess, I'd guess you were one poor burglar."

"I'm not the thieving kind."

"Sure you are, everybody is."

"I don't think you are, for instance."

"Naive."

"Look, why are we talking about this? I didn't steal anything, and if you have something to hide, why not just tell me what it is, and that would save us the trouble of playing word games."

"I just missed you this morning at the stables. They said you were talking with Willa."

"You didn't answer my question."

"Grant—you want some tea?"

"Whisky, more like," I said.

She filled two glasses neat with Scotch whiskey, handed me one, then said, "Let's run away to Rome."

"Anywhere but Rome."

"I don't care where, just away."

"Cliché. I'm naive and you manufacture clichés—quite a pair."

Hours later, when we sat at the St. Clair together, drinking with the fervor of sailors on brief leave, I confessed. I told her I had looked at photographs in her desk drawer. Not in the closet, I assured her, nor elsewhere in the house. I couldn't fess up to seeing the Tate documents, so it was a quasi-confession, but still, both of us were surprised by the burst of honesty. And rather than chide me, she said, "You're a decent guy, Grant."

"Not that decent."

She said, "Decent enough."

We were in a booth, sitting close side by side, holding hands, sometimes kissing. This was our *coming out,* I supposed, and we didn't have to wait long before Noah and Milland Daiches walked in together, saw us, then sat at the bar, heads inclined with fraternal familiarity, speaking or softly laughing, bemused or amused, I couldn't tell which. Helen, rather than growing tacit or shy, became even more animated than before. "Tell me about the photos, burglar. What did you learn about me?"

"That you were in Italy, and stop calling me burglar."

"Visiting cousins and second cousins and twelfth cousins twice removed, yes. What else?"

"What else?" I echoed. "Nothing really. It's embarrassing to talk about it. There was a photo of you when you were young at one of the Labor Day feasts." I wanted to ask about the woman with the gaucho hat, but when we glanced up Milland Daiches was standing there. "Buy you two a round?"

"No, thanks," Helen said at the same time I said, "Thanks."

Milland sat across from us, having shouted the word "Round" to the bartender, and slurred, "Rotten out, boy. Good night for bein' inside with friends. Looks like we all got the same idea. Helen's got herself a boyfriend, looks like."

"Shut up, Milland."

"So now, Grant. Mr. Tate says you'll be comin' to work with us." It was apparent Milland had already indulged before he and his brother came to the Clair.

"Is that true?" Helen turned to me, horrified.

"He offered me work. I didn't take him up on it."

"You will, though. Tha's what Tate says."

Milland thanked the man who brought over the drinks clutched together in both hands. After he left, I said as calmly as I could, "If that's what Tate says, then you can be sure I won't."

"We'll see, boy. Tate says you're broke, says he'd pay better than anybody else around here. Says you will."

Helen said, "Milland, you heard Grant. If he doesn't want to work for Tate, he isn't going to."

"First of all, I'm not broke," I lied. "And second, how would Tate know whether I was broke or not, anyway?"

"He's smart, Mr. Tate. Knows things."

We've all had too much to drink, I thought. "What else's he know about me?"

"Tate prob'ly knows the way your asshole's put in."

"You're an idiot, Milland," Helen said with disarming evenness.

Not looking at her, he muttered, "You don' even know how smart I am."

"Oh yeah? What makes you so smart?"

"Nothin' you'd want to know," he said, still smirking at *me* rather than Helen.

"What sort of work you guys do, anyway?" I asked.

"Whatever needs to be got done."

"Let me rephrase. What is it exactly that needs to get done around here that you boys do? Just say, like, if I went to work for Tate, what sort of work would I be doing?"

"Well"—drawn out long, Milland's attempt to create suspense—"next week we gonna be workin' up by you people, widenin' out that road to Lewis. Want to get that done afore the snow flies."

Helen interjected, "What did you mean by that before?"

"Huh?"

"When you said nothing I'd want to know is what makes you so smart. What did you mean when you said that?"

"Didn't mean nothin'," he smiled.

Milland did truly seem half-witted, I thought, though he had managed to provoke in me precisely the dismay he must have intended, with his unreluctant comment about the creek road. Tate was, if nothing else, blatant in his prideful display of power and ascension. Was he really going to drive his crew right up to Ash Creek's gate? Yes, I answered my own question; why not? Did it have to do with land and development and all that? Yes, again, I thought; but that must have been a small convenient element in his larger purpose, which I finally began to understand as having much more to do with rivalry, jealousy, personal revenge, the usual human stuff, the pitiable motives that fester at the unquiet center of nearly all folly. Wars have been waged over such matters. Murders have been committed over much lesser disputes.

Milland was saying, "Sometime there's things for some people to know and for other people not to, and that's all."

"What are you talking about?"

"You wanna know what I'm talkin' about?"

This was more or less shouted at Helen, though he continued to look at me. Milland was a touch walleyed, irises chaste brown but whites ambered by time, and drink.

And then Noah was suddenly there with us, saying hello to all, sitting beside Milland, who became instantly silent, even childishly sullen, I might have thought, contemptuous—but of whom, and why? Noah asked how I'd been, nodded to Helen, and inquired about my aunt and uncle. "I think Henry ought to let me come up there, spend a couple of nights maybe in that studio of his, see if we can't bring this business to an end."

"I doubt Henry'd ever go along with anything like that," I said, watching Milland, just as he'd watched me while speaking to Helen; his mood had shifted so abruptly from the high spiritedness of his cryptic intimations to what now seemed to be muted ire. Fascinating, even a little frightening. Noah had his arm over his brother's shoulder, I noticed. This was not the first time the older brother had been forced to jump in and save the younger from making an outrageous mistake, I thought. It wasn't difficult to imagine them as a pair of kids, their faces hewn and hard even in their youth, nor to draw a mental picture of the elder with his arm cast over the shoulder of adolescent Milland, steering him off the field, say, where a group of tough boys had gathered to watch a fistfight between the Daiches boy and some youngster who was about to cream him with a flurry of knuckles for having opened his big mouth, said something that wasn't supposed to be said. Even then, Milland must have been a bit like this, I believed. Such a fantasy made me like Noah a little more than I already did. But also made Milland more murky to me— murky, ambiguous, unintelligible—than ever. What was he capable of, this man? Besides, I didn't like the way he leered at Helen.

Noah and Helen exchanged a few words, nothing I could hear, as my head was saturated not only by too many drinks but, now, with one overwhelming idea. Not an idea that was new to me this evening, but one which, in the wake of Milland's provocations, had become wholly compelling. When Noah said it was nice to see both of us, and that he and Milland would leave us alone—he turned to Milland, shook him a couple of times as if to awaken him from a coma, and said, "These two have better things to do than sit here talking with a couple old dogs like us"—I reached over and shook his hand, then extended my hand to Milland, too, though he rose and left without having noticed. They had hardly withdrawn from the booth before I whispered to Helen, "You think I'm a burglar, well, I got an idea that'd prove you right."

Helen looked at me with eyes that suggested she was returning from another world altogether. I was reminded of the first day I met her, when she'd stared at the sky while we were sitting in the cemetery. Just as I did then, I kissed her, and afterward she asked me what was I talking about.

"Tate's office," I said. "He's arrogant enough to have a bad security system."

"How d'you know?"

"I happened to look, don't know why. Was up there, and you see, I happened to look around on the way out. Wasn't sure why then, and now I know why. There's something up there in a file, I just know it. I don't like it when people take it upon themselves to know my private business, and seems to me, best way to respond?—you just know their private business *right back at them*."

Helen had neither agreed nor disagreed, but we paid for our first few rounds, before Milland had joined us, with his largesse and torments, and left the glowy, liquorish but dry Clair for the night that was quite the opposite: black, sobering, and drenching with sleet. When I failed to make the turn at the road that would take us back to Helen's house, and continued instead toward town, toward the bank building at its center and Graham Tate's offices there, Helen did not disapprove or protest, but held my free hand tight as the headlamps illuminated numberless pathways of frozen rain. What's to lose? I thought, spurred on to continue in the reckless directions of the drunken evening. As we drove, Helen told me a story about Milland and Tate and my uncle, which made me realize that whether we wanted to do this or not, it was unavoidable and necessary.

When we reached the outskirts of town, saw the lights along the main street blurred by the torrents of rain, the perception came upon me in a flash, the realization that I, too, had become a night visitor. I, who used to be so devoted to the bells ringing the noon angelus in Rome, had become a midnight man.

INTUITION IS the most mysterious art. Even now I cannot say for sure that intuition was really what motivated me, compelled both of us, the night of the black rain, to coerce the door that kept Graham Tate's world safe from that of others. Arm in arm, unsteadily we climbed the dim stairway of the bank building, footsteps resounding and clothes dripping wet. I wasn't altogether surprised when Helen produced a credit card and slid it down between frame and door until the bolt eased away and we were inside Tate's office. No alarm or siren sounded, no security lights flashed in our eyes. As we moved into the dark rooms, whose furniture was palely illuminated from the streetlamps outdoors, we began to laugh and talk to one another, still drunken, somewhat astonished by where we were and what we were up to.

"His files are in here, I think," Helen said, as wind thrashed against the windows of Tate's inner sanctum, facing the main street. I followed her silhouette, and noticed how beads of rain ran in swift descending patterns down the great panes of glass beyond her, back-lit by neon and a steady apricot light from the street.

The shadowy raindrops projected their impressions on the wall opposite, where legal file cabinets stood in a row. "I'll look under Daiches," said Helen, who surprised me by turning on a desk lamp, a gooseneck with green shade on a low brass stand. "You look under Trentas, why don't you."

I pulled open the heavy drawer, wondering how so many files could accumulate with respect to business in such a small burg as this, unnerved by the fact that these cabinets bore no locks and my fingers picked their way through alphabetical files which of course Tate would not want me, or anyone, to read. Should we have been wearing gloves? Too late now. Helen had already pulled a file and was riffling through sheets of paper under the lamp behind me, when I found what I was searching for. I pulled the manila folder marked *Trentas, Giov./H.* from the drawer and paused, took a breath, before opening it.

Intuition had led us up the stairs and inside—but never would I have dared guess at the images and scenes that would spring from words on the few scraps of paper I now found. Nor would I have been able to foresee that one of the most breathtaking of conjurings came from the most humble of these fragments. A shred, a tatter, just half a leaf of foolscap, there at the front of the file: and from it, this torn scrap, what a scene arose in my imagination. Ripped down the middle from top to bottom, only the left-hand side of the piece of paper was here, held between my quivering fingertips. The other half, I recalled, was at the bottom of Giovanni's box, where I'd stuck it, assuming so wrongly that it'd had no meaning, having given up weeks ago on interpreting the half-phrases and divided words that were split along the serrated edge where Tate—or someone close to him, for here it was in his file cabinet—had torn the sheet in two. While I held it in the dim light, it seemed as if both halves became whole again in my suddenly focused gaze, so obsessively in weeks past had I studied that remnant in the box before relegating it to the bottom of the heap.

What this was, what *these* were, had been written by Giovanni himself in a diminutive script, in ink. The account of a meeting, a shorthand digest. I deciphered, and as I did, words and letters be-

came phrases in my head, and phrases soon rose into figures—the figures of Giovanni Trentas and my uncle, on a morning half a decade
ago. *Late spring,* I read, and thought of spring, when the world was
blossoming and soft clouds decorated the lovely blue dome over their
mountain, over the valley and the town, over the gorge and creek and
house where Henry and Edmé lived. Mid-May, in fact, and late
morning.

A man, an old friend, someone whom Henry trusts above every
other friend he's ever had, walks up the rise from the horsegate, re-
considers, doubles back down to the bridge by the cabin where I
now live, hikes the green muddy field to the studio. He knocks on
the plank door, and a familiar voice asks, —Who is it? and he says,
—It's Sam, and he is of course invited to come in. —How's all? he's
asked, and he answers, —All right, but knows that what he has to
say here, this morning, will not make the other man, my uncle, very
pleased.

Earlier that same morning Giovanni had already called on Willa,
his other closest friend, to let her know that despite appearances,
he'd not been feeling well lately. He had always taken such care of
his health, knowing that his mother died pretty young from pul-
monary disease and that his family had never been long lived, but for
some months he'd experienced pressures in his chest, he wasn't sure
whether heart or lungs or both, and the doctor who examined him
didn't offer an auspicious diagnosis. —You're hardy as a horse, my
uncle would have said, and Giovanni must have smiled and shaken
his head from side to side, then said, —There's no problem for the
immediate future, but just for the fact of Helen's future.

Giovanni, who pronounced the names of his daughter and best
friend with his residual accent, said *elen,* said *enry.*

—What do you mean? Henry asked.

—I've talked to Willa, and she agrees with me it's time the three
of us sat down with Helen—

—No.

—Time has come. *Time as come.*

And I can see Henry, although it would be difficult to put myself in his position, impossible really, in order to *feel* the multifold weave and complex layering of his years of apprehension that this day, a day of generous reckoning, would finally arrive. What I see is a combination of perplexity, fear, resignation, love for his unwell friend, his betrayed wife, his estranged lover, and his hidden and unclaimed daughter, as—enveloped by some fierce will that would insist that none of them was ready for the truth yet—he implores Giovanni not to ask this of them now.

But that isn't all, because I also see Edmé working the garden for spring planting, spading over ice-pocked soil and nipping out the first budding weeds, sorting out her rows, content in a profound way I myself have never known, utterly oblivious to what is being weighed between Henry Fulton and Giovanni Trentas across the creek. Further, I can imagine Helen Trentas, the child of three people, a radiant, skeptical, beautiful woman in her middle twenties who is devoted to the idea that Giovanni is her father and that Margery, the jackdaw crow woman, as she'd have it, had abandoned her and her father so long ago, and can imagine—as Henry is now explaining to Trentas—that she might not ever want to know all this about her heritage.

—At a certain point, Sam, what good comes of it? She'll wind up hating us all.

—She'll understand.

Giovanni must have continued, too, gone on to explain that whether Willa's husband likes it or not, and whether Willa's family likes it or not, Helen Trentas should someday be the rightful heir to several estates, not the least of which would be Henry's own.

—Back when we were young, secrets were more important than anything. They had good cause. I believed in it, and I still do. But look at us, Henry. We're old now. We wanted to save one marriage and make another possible, to protect the girl. My life has been better with Helen in it. In the end, it worked out. What's left to do is put Helen's good above our own.

—You spoke with Willa.

—She will do it.

—And Tate? What does he think?

Trentas was always plainspoken, and said, —He doesn't want anything to do with it. But Willa said she would, with or without his blessing. It's up to you.

—Willa may be ready but I'm not, my uncle said, with finality.

—Think about it, Henry. I don't say do it tomorrow, or the day after tomorrow. But the time is coming when we've got to bring Helen in on her own life. Trying to protect her, we manage just to hurt her. You know this is the only fair way.

These words spoken quietly, and having finished saying what he came to say, he shook his friend's hand, left the studio, then undoubtedly crossing Ash Creek to join Edmé, exchanging comments about what kind of weather they might expect this summer, that sort of thing, before making his way back down to the horsegate to return home.

How strange it must have felt for Henry and Tate to realize that they, who had disagreed about everything under the sun over the course of their paralleling lifetimes, finally concurred about something. Tate, who always held Henry responsible for a barren marriage, knew all too well about Willa's difficulties in giving birth during her year in exile from the valley. He remembered that year of secrecy, which ended with her poised, proud, if despondent homecoming, and also her suddenly agreeing to marry him, so long as he would tolerate in absolute silence the fact that her secret daughter was to be adopted by Giovanni Trentas and that she would never be able to have another child, having "secondary infertility," as her doctor put it—a terminology, not to mention disorder, that would continually gnaw at Tate, become a private canker to one who loathed the word *second* as much as he adored the word *first*. Still, he recognized Willa's stipulations and her saying that if, in fact, he loved her and could accept these constraints, she would love him, too, and be as dedicated a wife as she could.

Tate had agreed to this: wealthy wife over blood heir. But he never made any real peace with it, not then, not now. He agreed, knowing that one day Henry Fulton would have to pay for his intimacy and betrayal—if possible, in some way so that Willa could not reasonably fault him. And, of course, she could never reasonably fault him for pursuing his avocation as a businessman. Therefore, if Ash Creek was the necessary piece in a larger puzzle he needed to assemble for development, for some kind of resort, or to become, say, part of a land trust that would one day be given away in order to keep it out of *everyone's* hands, though emblazoned for time immemorial with his own name, then Willa would have no right (or ability, finally) to criticize such a venture. With patience, with time, Tate would exorcise Henry from his own family grounds. Tate's name would have to serve as his sole heir. That would be sufficient, or nearly so. But though he might have been willing to help Helen, in clandestine ways, and look out a little for her financially— she was, after all, Willa's daughter—he was not prepared to suffer the shame, as he saw it, of what the town would then know: that he, Graham Tate, was Willa's second choice.

Neither did Henry want to have so many years of difficult, tentative harmony thrown into discord by Giovanni's proposal. And this is where the most unhappy component of what I came to learn during my stay at Ash Creek would eventually rise into view.

As I slipped the torn fragment of Giovanni's account into my pocket, a phrase that Milland used back at the bar came to mind. *Sometime there's things for some people to know and for other people not to.* How much of our lives is spent, I marveled as I glanced over to see Helen working her way feverishly through a file, sorting out for ourselves what to say and what to hide. It was as if I were metamorphosing into a repository for everything people wanted no one to know. As if the night had a volition of its own now. Why had Helen told me, on the way over from the Clair, that story about Tate and Milland and Henry, if not intuitively to pry their secrets free?

I imagined Helen's surprise that quiet evening, after ten, she'd said, home alone, when there was a knock at the door of her cottage. She'd taken to spending more and more time by herself those days and nights after Giovanni had been laid to rest, not that she'd ever been very sociable. She might have known it wasn't the healthiest response, to mourn, hidden from the world. But it was everything she could do in the wake of what she saw as obstruction and repression among those around her, all she could manage since she believed herself to be alone anyway, given no one seemed to lend the same credence to the possibility that Giovanni's death was unnatural. The knock at the door was gentle. She might even have thought it was the wind disturbing branches of a tree, thus imitating the sound of someone knocking, if it had not happened again, this time somewhat more insistent.

Graham Tate smiled at her, face bathed in the pale porch light, and she must have looked as startled as she felt, because she would remember later, when she finally told me what Tate said that night, her words.

—What're you doing here? she asked.

"Not a very nice way to greet somebody at the door," she'd tell me, with an acerbic laugh.

"Not very," I'd agree. "So what did he say?"

—You have a minute? I've got something I want to tell you I think you'd find interesting.

She waited for him to continue, then realized he meant for her to invite him in, so she did. Across the threshold he walked, and sat himself down, laying his hat on the table before him.

—Well? she said, arms crossed, eyes undoubtedly darkening. —What brings you here in the middle of the night?

Tate smiled. —This is hardly what you'd call the middle of the

night, Helen. How come you hate me, anyway? You have no reason
to hate me. Quite the opposite. I'm worried about you.

Helen didn't speak, didn't move.

—Milland told me something this afternoon. Told me something
interesting.

—What did Milland possibly have to say that was interesting?

—You scoff, but Milland's a good man. He doesn't mean harm.
He's hardworking and honest.

—He doesn't have enough intelligence to be dishonest.

—You underestimate people, Helen. You overestimate and underestimate. It's probably your greatest fault.

—Say what you've come to say, why don't you?

—Milland told me he was up at Ash Creek a couple of days before they found your father. Said Trentas had invited him up to hunt
with him, and that he took up into the gorge on the east side of the
creek where that studio of Henry's is.

Tate paused.

—And? said Helen.

—Nothing much, really. He just said Henry saw him walking up
into the gorge with his pack and gun and all, but that he never did
mention it to Noah when Noah came around asking Henry if he'd
seen anybody up there.

—I don't see the point.

—Milland said Henry saw him, looked him right in the eye, said
he looked like he saw a ghost but just turned his back. Didn't go out
and ask Milland what he was doing, or anything. Just turned his
back like that.

—Are you telling me Milland had something to do with my father's death?

—No, not that. Milland said he started up into the gorge and kept
hearing somebody tailing him, and so he got spooked and doubled
back down, and never did join up with Trentas.

—Noah knows all this?

—Of course. Doesn't change anything, not really. Except we found it interesting that Henry never mentioned Milland was there. Makes you kind of think Henry has something to hide, doesn't it?

—That's all? You came all the way over here to tell me *that*?

—Willa says you've been meaning to go up to Ash Creek and get some of Giovanni's effects out of that cabin of his. Why not use it as a chance to drop in and have a few words with Henry about all this? Just some friendly advice, for what it's worth.

—I'm tired, Helen demurred.

—I'll just be going, then. Glad we had this chance to talk.

With that, Tate reached out his hand to place on her shoulder, but she jerked away before he was able to touch her. He may not have been able to bond with her, as such, but left knowing, Helen's indifferent facade to the contrary, that he had planted the worm in the rose. She withdrew for several days even more than she had in months gone by. She didn't leave home, didn't telephone anyone, was paralyzed by the ideas which had taken up residence in her mind.

Then, as she went on to tell me, one warm summery late-July morning a year ago, she finally had gathered her strength and made the drive up to Ash Creek. Whether she'd have the temerity to confront Henry with Tate's questionable revelations she didn't know, but she understood the time had come for her to retrieve the remnants from Giovanni's hut—Sam the eagle he'd kept there, for instance, among other belongings—and so she drove across the broad valley, along the creek road, and parked by the horsegate, as she often had in the past. She was surprised to discover the padlock on the cabin door, and realized that because of it she had no choice but to walk up to the house and ask for the key. Her relief at finding Edmé there rather than Henry was great, as she remembered, but the gratitude would not last for long. Edmé asked Helen if she wanted any help, and Helen had said no, that she thought she'd like to be alone, so she strolled back down and across the creek, and opened the door to the cabin.

Sam the eagle was there, in his corner perch. Some other things were right where Helen had seen them last, back when Giovanni was still alive. But something was different; she sensed it immediately on entering the room. She went about her business, carting things across the ramshackle bridge over to her car, then returning. She decided to leave most of it, as Edmé'd told her everything was hers to have whenever she wanted—Edmé having forgotten, perhaps, that Giovanni's box was upstairs in the house, tucked away in her own chest of drawers. And so it wasn't until she went back to re-lock the door that she found a shoe, a right shoe with a tarnished buckle, the old shoe which had been missing the day her father was found in the gorge, placed neatly under the cot—almost as if Giovanni himself had left it there upon retiring for the night.

Not a week passed before the night visits at Ash Creek began.

"Look at you," I now said, seeing that Helen had made herself comfortable in Tate's leather chair, going through the records he held on Milland. "Like you own the place." Intent on something she had discovered, she neither answered nor even glanced up. For myself, feeling queasy, I wanted to put Giovanni's file away, but then I saw it, buried deeper among the papers, and couldn't resist—this unexpected photocopy of a birth certificate. Helen Richardson's birth certificate, with Willa's name given as the baby's mother, but no listing for a father. How was it possible Helen didn't know this?

My fingers froze in the damp room, as I recalled that dance recital card in Giovanni's box. Helen's birth date, two days before Christmas 1965. That dance recital, March twenty-third, I remembered, and made the inevitable nine-month count in my head, as I closed and reinserted the telling folder where it belonged.

Nine months down to the day. Impossible, I thought, and when Helen glanced up finally and asked, "Find something?" an irrevocable deceit, my "No, nothing," was the best I could manage. All I wanted now was to get out of this place before someone down in the street happened to glance up and notice lights and movement in the bank building office, but when I asked Helen, "How about you?" she said, "Look at this."

At first, I didn't get the point. Cash receipt made out to Milland Daiches in the amount of a thousand dollars, *24 Aug 92.* "So what?"

"Don't you get it?"

"I guess not."

"Milland Daiches murdered my father," Helen said, in a voice so calm there was no connecting the meaning with the speaker. "Daiches and Tate."

"Based on *this?* Sorry, Helen, but that's ridiculous. Nobody makes out receipts for murder contracts. Let's talk outside, why don't we. I think we ought to go."

"Can't believe it," she whispered to herself as she folded the receipt and slipped it into her pocket. Standing now, she carried the file to the cabinet, but then changed her mind and returned to the desk, where she laid out the folder, open to the place where the receipt had been, right at the center of Tate's writing pad.

"Put it back, Helen."

"This is better," and she turned off the light.

We left without having pushed the file cabinet door closed. Helen's further idea of a signature. The drive back to her cottage was silent. She didn't ask me to come in, which was fine, as I myself wanted to be alone. We kissed good night and I drove away, exhausted to the point that the world beyond the window seemed hallucinatory. Low running clouds were violet, the highway had a postapocalyptic emptiness about it. The earth, it seemed to me, was wholly tenanted by shades, leased by obscurities, franchised by deception.

All I wanted was to be back home, quiet in the quiet recesses of Giovanni's dwelling, where I would wed two halves of an old piece of paper that had been torn in two; for I, like Helen, had stolen from Tate. Where also, before I fell asleep, I would be appalled by the fear he must have felt, here in this very bed, when he returned to the little cabin one night and found his record of the meeting with Henry ripped down its center. The ceremonial nature of the gesture, leaving him half his story, must surely have made him suspect he was in danger for what he knew, and what he wanted for Helen. Did he guess that Tate had been behind the vandalism—rage renewed perhaps at a barren marriage, or at the threat of disclosure of truths Tate's pride would have him keep forever buried—or did he sense his best friend had turned against him? I hope it was the former, since my now having found the missing half at Tate's proved it so, at least to me. But I can easily imagine Giovanni suspected the latter, and for that reason would entrust Edmé with this rebus of what he knew.

Either way, it must have been on that desperate night the idea to shelter his memoirs, to house and protect his suspicions within a fragile wooden cigar box, was born.

A FACE was at the window—and Jacob's ladders of sunlight spiriting down into the curtainless room—as I awakened into a morning that was already more or less finished, as burnt out as I now felt. At first, I didn't recognize this face, which peered in at me, unmistakable as it was, with its purposeful frown, hard blue eyes, sunken cheeks, flinty edges. The head disappeared from the window as the man made his way around through the hedges of grass to the door. The moment I was able to connect a name to that face, the name Noah Daiches, I understood why he was here—though it seemed too quick for Tate to have discovered Helen's impudent signature, called in Noah, and deduced that I had something to do with last night's break-in. Since I'd slept in my clothes, I had no need to get dressed. I opened the door and asked him in.

"You're living down here now, Henry tells me. Independence over comfort, eh?"

"Something like that."

"I remember when Trentas used to live here."

I lit a cigarette, would have offered him one but saw that he was already smoking one he'd rolled—oh, yes, *Papiers Maïs*, no doubt, thinking how canny Giovanni had been to add some classifying element, some *thing* that identified each of those who he sensed had played and would play a part in the resolution (is that the right word?) of his challenge to Henry, Tate, Willa, regarding Helen. It was then, as I rekindled the fire in the cast-iron stove, having offered Noah a cup of instant coffee, that I experienced what was nothing less than an epiphany about Giovanni's box. Of course, of course, I thought. Those *papiers*—*Papiers Mais*, and the Prince Alberts— actually *meant* the Daiches brothers, and the typed sheet of paper which bore those columns of numbers accruing into millions must surely have *meant* Tate, even as the little black leather change purse holding its ten lire, two wartime pennies minted in alloy, and all those pennies that I would wager numbered forty-seven—ten lire for ten years in Italy, two tin cents for his two war years abroad, and one penny for each of the years he had left to him—*meant* Giovanni Trentas. But what did those meanings mean?

Noah interrupted my streaming epiphany by saying he had a couple of questions he'd like to ask me.

"Ask away," was how I responded, effecting innocent cheerfulness with probable mixed results.

"I know you were out with Helen last night, of course, having seen you at the Clair, but I'm wondering where you went after you left there. You mind telling me?"

"We went back to her place."

"Went back there directly?"

"Why don't you ask her?"

It wasn't too bald an attempt, I hoped, to get him to reveal whether or not he'd already spoken with Helen, so that I might know if I was in the midst of contradicting her account of the same events.

Noah wasn't going for it, however, obvious or not. His face quite unmoved and unmoving, he said, "Because I'm asking you."

"We went back to her place, then I came home."

I thought to ask him what this was all about, but kept quiet instead, to see what he would reveal on his own. Noah was far too shrewd not to see through such bosh from the likes of me.

"Came straight home, did you?"

"Straight home."

"All right," he said. "Thanks," and stepped toward the door.

"Don't you want that coffee? This water will be boiling any minute now."

"I'm fine. Sorry to bother you."

After he'd crossed the rotted threshold and was outside again, I changed my mind about not asking Noah the purpose of his visit. After all, wouldn't it have been peculiar of me *not* to ask? I stepped outside, barefoot, called his name, and asked boldly as I could manage, "Hey, what's this all about?"

Noah half turned round, his angular silhouette against the pale autumnal foliage along the creek beyond him. "You think I believe you don't know? You think a sorry old unsophisticate like Noah just don't get it, is that what you think, Grant?"

"I'm lost." Although I felt increasingly uncomfortable about these homely lies of mine, this particular pronouncement, which came forth in something of a raspy whisper, had an element of truth about it. So much so that I repeated myself, spoke up: "I'm lost."

"That I believe," he said. "But if you're lost you might want to spend a little time thinking about getting yourself *unlost*, before you go straying any deeper into the dark than you already have."

Nonchalant, even serene, he turned away, as my mind pinwheeled and fingers thoughtlessly tugged at the collar of my rumpled shirt, which had been dampened by night sweats. My feet were too cold against the new October ground for me to remain there watching Noah Daiches recede into the distance down the hill, where he crossed the broken bridge. My mouth was dry, eyes ached. He was unarguably right, Noah was, as right as he could be. No matter what his own involvement with Tate might have been, or not, no matter if I'd just contradicted word for word what he earlier extracted from Helen, and no matter what earnest, even virtuous motives might lie behind my activities—Noah was correct. I was lost and had better find my way out of this abstracted lostness, but quick. The sun had a bony pall to it that morning, I thought, those Jacob's ladders having transformed into glowing spines of light, as I returned to the cabin, cursing myself for not having come up with better responses to his simple skepticisms. Noah wanted to like me; he with his love of lacrosse and I with my hatred for all sports—we were mates of sorts. I sensed it the evening when we drank together at the St. Clair. And now I had let him down.

My head ached and my stomach complained. I decided to go up to the house, shower, and see if I couldn't get something to eat. More than ever, my antics with Helen of the night just past seemed absurd and even dangerous. As I walked up the rise, it became clear that more than anything, I wanted to talk to my aunt Edmé about all this, but I *couldn't*. Not without upsetting decades of secrets and un-covering God knows what other histories were best left forgotten in the process.

Henry, not Edmé, was in the kitchen. He was waiting for me, I felt, sitting at the empty table, his large hands set out before him, fingers knotted together, thumbs tapping against one another. Sun-light spilled through the windows and bounced off the burnished floor. This light was reflected in my uncle's eyes, which gazed over at me, rather expressionlessly but with something about them that stopped me in my weary tracks. How could Edmé and Helen have missed this all these years? How could I myself not have seen it that first afternoon when Helen came walking up the very hill I'd just now climbed, full of confidence and fire and maybe just a little apprehen-sion, too, and stared me right in the face until I had to look away?

The hazel eyes. The shared hazel eyes. Their hue and glimmer and, yes, their hauntedness, too. My uncle here before me—Helen Trentas's father—would never be the same to me. He was different to me now, and would be different from this moment forward. He was my uncle, yes, but he was the father of the woman I made love with just yesterday, the woman into whose enigmatic past I'd agreed to search without any thought to eventualities such as *this*.

"What did Noah want?" he asked me.

"Is Edmé around?"

"Upstairs. What'd Noah want?"

"Wanted to know what I was doing last night."

"And what were you doing that Noah would want to know about?"

"Nothing," as I tried with perfect unconcern to select an apple from the bowl of fruit at the center of the table and then sat down. Everything felt so different here all of a sudden; even the apple tasted different, salty somehow, of cinnamon. I couldn't bring myself to meet his gaze. "Helen and I had a drink with him and Milland at the Clair. I took her home. I came on back here myself."

My nose was lengthening to Pinocchio proportions. Once more I asked about Edmé—was he sure she was upstairs, because I had a question I wanted to ask.

"Remember that sign someone left on the gatepost that night a while ago, the one that said—"

"I remember."

"What was that about? If it's none of my business—"

"It's not. Not really, Grant."

"I just feel a little weird keeping secrets from Edmé."

"Secrets aren't there to make people feel comfortable."

"I'd have thought that was just exactly what secrets are for, so that everybody can stay nice and comfortable and not know the truth about each other."

"You don't like secrets, then, do you?"

"Not particularly," as I bit into the rock-hard apple.

"Well then, why would you lie to Noah like that? It's one thing to tell lies to your family, or your friends, but another when you're talking to the law." The statement was unchallengeable because so peculiar. Before I could respond, however, Henry said in a deeper, quieter voice, "Tate called this morning. He knows what happened, and he doesn't like it. I can't say I do, either."

"What happened?"

"For God sakes, Grant." His hands broke apart, and one of them slapped the table. "What do you want from me?"

I found myself staring at the framed photograph on the wall behind Henry, a group of men working side by side on a decaying pier, taken in Sicily or perhaps Greece, island fishermen together mending their lissome nets. Edmé had managed to capture both the shiny fragility of the netting and the rough capability of all those knowing hands at work. Only one of the men had noticed they were being photographed, and as he'd apparently glanced up just when she opened the shutter, his face was a gray smear, a shadowy haze. Just behind him was a very young boy, or maybe a girl, whose delicate fingers were hard at work on repairing the net. The son or daughter of the blurred man. Edmé's small genius was to distract this man—*just him* and no other—so that the photograph became not a routine illustration of picturesque villagers, seaside along their charming breakwater, but a portrait of a father's concern, his protective vigilance, which forced him to leave aside his work for a moment—this moment, the moment caught in Edmé's image—so as to check out this stranger, assure himself she posed no threat to his child. "I really, honestly, don't want anything."

"What are you doing in Tate's office in the middle of the night, then? He thinks I put you up to it, naturally. I lied for you. I told him you were here. But he didn't believe me any more than I believe you, Grant. Is it Helen who's got you doing this?"

A day for vistas opening upon vistas, I thought, drawing my gaze down from the black-and-white photograph to my uncle. He was right, of course; and it only then occurred to me that Helen left her "signature" so Tate would contact Henry and Henry would talk to me and . . . could she be *that* manipulative? No, I thought. My adoration proposed I allow her every benefit of doubt.

Yet Henry's question was still there for me to answer.

I said, "I don't want to hurt anybody. Least of all Edmé or you. But not Helen, either. I don't know what to say. That's about as honest as I can be, Uncle Henry."

"We have the same objective, then, Grant," he said, and a faint smile broke across his lips. "If I were your father, I would tell you something brilliant, no doubt. But I'm no diplomat, I'm afraid. I'm not sure what your father would say if he were here—maybe he'd be able to help us both—but as it is, I don't have anything to offer other than that you must let people undo their own tangles—" and he made a backward nod toward the photograph, which he'd obviously noticed me staring at.

"My father would probably say, sometimes when we protect those we love, we risk becoming confused and unfocused ourselves."

"Don't think I'm not aware of that."

The evocation of my father, the anniversary of whose death was coming up soon, brought us both to a point of silence. Even if Henry hadn't mentioned him, my poor father, we two had reached the inevitable impasse.

Henry, in a voice suddenly sanguine, asked, "Don't you want more than just an apple for lunch? Or, what is this for you, is this breakfast still? You look terrible, by the way."

"I don't feel so great, either."

He got up, lifted a copper skillet down from the iron rack where it hung, and lit the gas stove. "Go wash, and when you get back down, I'll have something ready for you. No guarantees about what. It'll be warm, whatever it is. Fair enough?"

"Is that all we're going to say about the other topic?"

"What more's there to say?" and with this he offered me the most ambiguous look I'd ever seen—combining dread, hardness, love, distance—before disappearing into the pantry, where the refrigerator hummed steadily and pleasantly. I listened to the reassuring sound of it for some moments before going upstairs.

MY AFTERNOON walk into the forest above Giovanni's hut, and my visit to the venerable cemetery on the knoll beyond, were meant to clear my head. With Hawthorne in Giovanni's loden pocket—Edmé gave me his old ranch coat, as I had nothing appropriate for the coming season—I intended to take advantage of the day's having turned warm. I settled myself facing south toward the great valley below, leaning against the wrought-iron fence. The sun warmed my cheek as I opened my book. I didn't want to think about the consequences of all my choices this past month. Rather, like a child, maybe, preferred to enter Hawthorne's fairy-tale world for a respite from considering what must surely lie ahead.

The scent of mothballs mingled with the sweet decaying odors of fall, and as I read about the three golden apples that grew in the garden of Hesperides, and the miraculous pitcher of Philemon and Baucis, from which you could pour endless rivers of honey-milk, my thoughts drifted away with the little breezes which finger-combed the grasses around me. The mothball smell brought Giovanni into mind, and when I closed the book, not quite willing yet to read the last story in it, one about the Chimera, I closed my eyes as well, and fell asleep.

What I dreamed seemed so real, so *lived,* that when I awakened an hour later the fantasy, the projective vision, seemed stronger than my solitary reality here on the knoll. We were all present, Giovanni and Helen, Tate and Willa, Henry and Edmé, my parents Maria and Matthew, in this meadow. Noah was dressed in priest's garments, black cassock and surplice, white tippet draped around his neck, muttering in what seemed to be Latin. Milland Daiches and David Lewis stood on either side of the casket, themselves dressed in some kind of coarse cloth robes, each holding the ends of two sets of straps that were hitched under the front and back ends of the box. Willa had her arm around Helen's shoulder, Henry and Giovanni stood side by side, as did my mother and Edmé. The lid of the box had not yet been nailed into place, and when I looked down at my hands, I discovered that in one was a clutch of long penny nails and in the other a hammer. When Noah finished, he waved his right hand over the casket, and stepped back. He looked up at me and nodded, by which I understood he meant for me to seal the box for burial.

Of course it was I who lay in the casket. I was dressed in Giovanni's coat and a pair of black trousers. My eyes were open, but rather than eyes there were small gold apples in the sockets. My hands—which seemed rather larger than my own, more the magnitude of Henry's—were folded across my chest. A wedding ring I recognized as my father's glimmered on my finger. I glanced briefly over toward Helen Trentas, whose face I could not see although I knew it was she, and saw the matching band on her finger. The other me, the man who gazed down at himself, went about his business like any good sexton, arranged the pine lid over the coffin so its edges lined up properly, then began nailing it in place with disinterest.

What woke me up was the hand on my shoulder, which was my own hand, I saw, upon turning around and looking up, a little annoyed at the interruption. Several minutes must have passed before I was able to reorient myself. I didn't know what the dream *meant,* if it meant anything whatever, but I didn't like it. The sensation that had

visited me in this place in the past came again—the feeling of being
watched. Spooked, I got up quickly and found myself jogging across
the clearing toward the trees.

That night allowed me only the most fitful sleep. No dreams, or at
least none I could remember. Only recurrent images of Rome—of
cats walking the Aurelian Walls; of the crumbling Colosseum and
Byron's silly poem with its prophecy *When falls the Coliseum, Rome
shall fall; and when Rome falls—the world,* which fails to fathom that
the world has no intention of waiting that long to crumble; of the
bustling Campo de' Fiori, with its pretty name belying its drug dealers and spirits of those burned at the stake there, and Mary's charming if disgusting love for campari at one of the outdoor tables at La
Pollarola in the piazza nearby—and other images of what memory
tricked me into thinking were such happy days in the ancient city.
You see, I liked feeding the scrawny cats, watching the marketplace
motleys of the Campo, and adored teasing poor Mary as she sipped
her horrid neon-red drink. Only these half-invented remembrances
of good times there allayed an otherwise haunted night.

It didn't help that, sometime before dawn, I remembered I'd left
Giovanni's box in my rucksack over at Helen's house. Edmé had told
me earlier that evening, after we had finished dinner and she and I
sat for a while in the living room, that the two of us would be going
to the Lewises' farewell party without Henry. "Would he prefer we
didn't go?" I asked her. "I don't care about David Lewis one way or
the other."

"It's less for David Lewis than the others who'll be there—and for
myself, too. I've given it some thought. Henry needn't come along,
but you and I should at least put in an appearance. Things change,
people move on, it isn't the end of the world. Your friend Helen will
be there, no doubt. Tate and Willa, too."

"Tate'll be there?"

"He's bound to come, if only to gloat."

"Then we're going for sure."

"Grant," she scolded.

"Best behavior, promise."

Why my drive into town to retrieve the rucksack was so fraught with dread was not hard to guess. But Helen greeted me with no less enthusiasm than ever. And so, relieved, I assumed she hadn't looked in my pack, and that the contents of Giovanni's box remained my own secret. "Did Noah talk to you?" she asked.

"Sure did."

"You deny everything?"

"Of course. I assume you did."

"Well—I did and I didn't."

"Oh no, Helen."

"Don't worry," she smiled. "I didn't implicate you. I left it open that I *may* have gone in on my own, but that on the other hand I may not have. What're they going to do about it, even if I did? Arrest me? I don't think so. Who's going to turn over a stone if he himself is the slug who's hiding under it?"

"You going to the Lewises' tonight?"

"I am."

"Let's go together, with Edmé."

Helen was serene. She seemed to have been liberated from the anger of not knowing about Giovanni's death, freed from suspecting but not being quite certain. That the receipt she'd discovered in Tate's files wouldn't begin to carry the burden of proof required to convict Milland Daiches—even to arraign him on murder charges— didn't seem to dampen this fresh calm. When I mentioned that Edmé had said Tate would likely be there, she didn't flinch, but added, not only Tate but the Daiches brothers as well. "Many of the same people who were at the Labor Day party up at Ash Creek will probably come," she said.

"You can face Milland Daiches?"

"We'll find out."

As I left, I noticed a black gaucho hat on the rack by the door, which I commented on as attractive. "Willa Tate gave me that one day years ago," Helen said, and while I couldn't at just that moment remember where I'd seen it before, sometime during the drive back across the long valley I did. Helen Trentas, I thought—was it possible she'd always known more than she'd let on? Maybe not, but a singular woman either way, and not someone to have for an enemy.

The evening was cloudless. No breeze provoked the leaves along the creek road where we walked, the three of us together. Parrish blue hastened toward black over where the sun had set, and out to the east above the dark ridge, the stars glistened dry and limpid. Edmé brought a flashlight but kept it in her pocket. We could see well enough without. The last flycatchers of the season—tenacious little souls in their feathery array—dove through the tender air and peeped, though surely most of their venturing forth must have been in vain, as the swarms of mosquitoes and gnats were gone by now.

Helen spoke in high spirits and even laughed with Edmé about nothing in particular. She had never seemed before so peaceful and gracious and, yes, happy. Edmé watched the two of us leave the house and descend the stone stairs hand in hand, and seemed herself to have reached some kind of harmony with the fact of our being a couple. Henry, it was true, remained adamant about not attending the dinner, but even he—though he didn't come over from the studio when Helen arrived—had been a benevolent specter that afternoon when I returned from town with Giovanni's box back in my possession. I still marveled at his having prepared me some fried bologna on toast the day before, which I ate cringing but happily, as it was the first time he had ever done such a thing for me in all the years I had been coming to Ash Creek. Delusion or not, I felt a measure of tranquillity had settled over those around me, who had each seemed so recently to have been mired in every variety of turmoil. The lights of David Lewis's house were so festive down in the distance, as we strode alongside the creek, that for a moment I hardly remembered what the dinner was about. It seemed more a celebration than a farewell. That was, at least, how I read—or misread—the atmosphere.

Until we crossed the bridge and began to climb the road up to the Lewis house, which was set behind a cluster of bushes and trees, situated so that it faced south and west at an angle that conformed to a long knob, it had not dawned on me that I'd never been inside. Indeed, I knew very little about David Lewis, and nothing about his wife. Edmé once told me about a tragedy that had struck their family, an accident that took their only son from them, but I'd never been clear about the circumstances of the child's death. As I have mentioned, Lewis was a recluse among recluses, minding his own business as his father had before him, and as we neared the lit porch of the squarish board-and-batten ranch house, I recognized that part of the reason his selling off this land and moving away had made so little impression on me—and, thus, part of my not fully appreciating the impact it must have had on Henry—was this very ignorance. I wanted to ask Edmé to tell me again about what had happened to the boy, but before I had the chance, Jenn Lewis opened her door and welcomed us in.

Half a dozen cars were parked informally on the grass out front, and when we entered I saw the party was under way.

Helen showed miraculous pluck by going right to Tate, who stood with a group of men, several of whom I had never seen before, and kissing him on the cheek, as she said just audibly enough for me to hear, "Noah tells me there's been some trouble down at the office. I hope nothing serious."

"Nothing serious," Tate said, confidence unshaken. Did that curling at the fleshy corner of his lip signify insolence? or was it really meant to be some sort of smile, as he reached out his hand to me, saying, "Grant, have you found employment yet? How are you tonight?"

"No and fine," I said.

"There are fugitives from the law running around free," Helen told me, eyes wide open, with mock drama coloring her voice.

Neither Tate nor I rose to it.

"Where's Willa?" she continued.

It seemed interesting to me that Tate did not introduce any of the several men with whom he'd been holding court. They closed their own circle, conversed among themselves, turning their backs to us three. "Willa didn't feel well enough to come tonight," Tate answered. "She asked me to send her best to both of you." That curl, that carnal gnarl at the corner of his mouth, ascended again.

"I don't blame her," Helen said. "What's to celebrate here?"

David Lewis scuttled Helen's dissidence, or whatever it was, by coming into the conversation himself, offering drinks, asking me if I wouldn't mind helping him get something for Edmé and Helen, and sending us all off in different directions. I followed him into the modest kitchen—the house was very old, wide-planked floors and rough-plastered whitewashed walls punctuated by natural wooden trim everywhere—and saw that boxes stood in corners of the rooms in anticipation of the movers. Its fundamental barrenness, coupled with the fact that many of its chattels had already been wrapped in newspaper and crated, lent the house the feeling of a prematurely struck stage, one populated by many characters still at odds with one another, aware that they had arrived at the final act without having memorized, let alone rehearsed, the scenes left for them to play. Helen, it occurred to me, was improvising a splendid Hamlet in her search for a father, and here we were gathered together for some play within the play. I asked Lewis, as he made drinks, where he and his wife were going, what they were doing next.

"We have decided to put everything in storage and follow the summer around for a while."

"Sunbirds I think they call them."

"Yes, that's it. We're going to be sunbirds. And what about you, Grant? Have you decided to live here?"

"No, no," I said. "I mean, I don't really know."

"Have those trespassers been around?"

"Well, except for the last visit, which was pretty insane"—and I held up my hand, which though unbandaged was still bruised, as if it were proof—"things seem to have calmed down."

"Isn't that why you came out here?"

"I hardly remember anymore, but that was the idea. Maybe I should become a sunbird, too. In a way, that's all I've ever been."

"Helen," Lewis said, and handed her a wine glass.

"What's a sunbird?" she asked him.

"A creature who can't chart his own path, so just follows the sun," he answered. "Tell me something, Grant. Have you been able to figure out why all these night disturbances go on just up the road from us but we've never been involved, never seen or heard a thing in all these months?"

"I haven't."

"Any idea who's behind it?"

"Somebody who knows the terrain pretty well, somebody who has something they want to get from Henry—that's who. But beyond that I don't understand any better than anybody else—"

"Maybe David's been behind it all this time," Helen said.

"That's not even funny," he frowned.

As I watched him I noticed something about him seemed changed. He'd cut off his ponytail. Leaving it *all* behind, it would appear.

I said, "I can tell you one thing. Henry hasn't been idle these last couple of days—"

"It's too bad he couldn't come."

"Would you have?"

"—you'll be interested to hear this, Helen. Remember that bear trap I asked you about that time? He got it down, scraped it clean of the rust, filed the teeth, greased it, and set the thing."

"You're kidding," Helen said, abruptly serious.

"But isn't that against the law, to set a trap like that for a human being?"

"No more than it's against the law to trespass, assault people in the middle of the night, vandalize their property. Anyway, Henry says he found bear tracks near the house and that's why he wanted to set the trap."

"I suppose if I were in Henry's situation I'd do the same."

"Or else pick up and move away."

"Helen . . ."

She half smiled, composure regained, her radiance obscuring—at least from my eyes—the spite that lay behind a taunt such as that.

"Well," muttered Lewis, "let's hope this is the end of it for them."

"If the intrusions stop after you've left, we'll know where to look for the culprit," I said, unwittingly mimicking Helen.

"In that case, I'll be sure not to let you know where we are. Shouldn't we join the others?"

For someone who was about to leave the valley where he had been born and raised, David Lewis struck me as being remarkably composed. He bowed, with imponderable old-world manners that seemed ironically fitting in this old house, and left with a glass of wine for Edmé in hand. "What does he do?" I asked Helen, after he'd gone.

"Not a thing," she whispered. "Henry thinks he's just now sold off his land, but I have reason to believe he's been mortgaging it in little bits and pieces for years. Everything his grandfather put together, and everything his father managed to keep intact, David's been living off all this time. They say ever since his boy drowned in the creek he hasn't been able to work. The bank, Tate, they've kept him afloat in a life raft made out of loans. And finally, the collateral ran out. Everybody's being quite civilized about it all, it looks like to me."

"Since you know so much, what's Tate intend to do with the place?"

"You'd have to ask him. Anyway, I don't know so much."

"Sure you do," and I kissed her on the cheek.

"So Henry set that old trap, did he?" kissing me back. "Even if there were bear tracks near the house, he wouldn't set it because of that, would he?"

"I don't know. But I wouldn't go walking in the dark around his studio if I were you."

"I'll have to keep that in mind."

"Is Milland here?"

Her face clouded.

"That must mean yes."

We returned to the front room, and circulated. Parties were never my preferred method of human intercourse, I think it safe to say—my father was a genius at such gatherings, had developed some system whereby he managed to leave everyone with the feeling of having truly communicated with him, no matter how vast the function, or how brief the encounter. My mother and I—on those occasions when I was invited to attend—flowed in his genial wake through rooms small and grand, and I remember how even when a boy I marveled at his grace and skill. Now I flowed behind Helen—as she conversed with various people whom I didn't know any better than I'd known those diplomatic consuls and envoys at parties years ago— impressed by her élan and wicked charm, and reminded oddly of Matthew Morgan, my father. Nothing she or any of the others said was memorable to me until we inevitably came upon Noah Daiches, who did not return my ersatz ambassadorial smile.

Even Helen seemed at a loss for words.

Noah asked after Henry.

"He's made his feelings pretty clear about all this," I said, "and it's not my place to question him."

I suppose Noah was meant to read between these lines some kind of remonstrance for his having had the audacity to question *me* the morning before.

"I'm tempted to go up there and get him to come on down. Lewis here is no enemy of Henry Fulton. Man has a right to move. Just the same way Tate has the right to buy."

"Well, if you want to know the truth, I think he might best be left alone. Maybe he'll change his mind on his own and show up, but if you go up there and try to force him to do something he doesn't want to do—"

"Runs in the family, stubbornness, is that what you're saying?"

Helen said, "Grant's not so stubborn."

"Neither he nor his uncle's ever taken one piece of advice I've given them."

"That may be true about Henry, but what advice have you ever given me I've not taken?"

Noah looked at Helen as he answered, "Can't follow it if you can't remember it. I told him he better get unlost before he gets more lost—more or less the same advice I gave his uncle some months ago."

I said nothing; neither did Helen. Through my mind raced many comebacks, none of them of any particular worth. Our impasse was broken by Tate, who appeared at Noah's side. Rather than entangle myself with Noah then, I asked Tate the question that had been on my mind, the one about what he intended to do with the Lewis ranch. "Milland said something about widening the road, bringing in some crew before winter?" I asked.

"Did he now. Well, let me tell you. I don't know what we're going to want to do. And that's the whole truth of it. There's a lot of financial mess here that's got to get cleaned up, and the land itself is going to have to pay its way. You could mine it, could log it. The town's growing every year, and power one day soon is going to be scarce. This here's a pretty narrow hollow, with a good strong constant flowing water supply and only one couple living on the land now. I don't know. I could imagine a day where it mightn't be better for the welfare of the community to dam up Ash Creek and harness the energy off it."

"You wouldn't," Helen said.

"Least number of persons would be displaced off this particular tract than anywhere else I can think of. But then who knows. We may just turn around and put it on the market."

As I listened to Tate's marvelously unveiled threats, I found myself thinking back to that day when David Lewis first told Henry about his decision to sell, how Henry had foretold Tate's purposes with unnerving accuracy, even going on to equate this stripping of the world to a kind of disease. He had, I remembered, recited just precisely this list of transformations—logs into lumber, earth to metals, rivers to dams, and so forth. When I thought about just how far back these men had been engaged in their rivalry, their small war, I wondered how much of the world's history had turned on such rivalries. Here was a valley settled a hundred years ago by a couple of families, a marginal but beautiful narrow valley that had been carved by a marginal but persistent creek over the course of eons, which fed into the vast valley below where many such creeks collected themselves together into a river, which graced the wide, verdant plain down there and supported the growth of a town and many ranches. Yet for all its isolation and insignificance, this valley was host to the depravity of human history, just as iniquitous as any grand and famous setting of war, rebellion, subversion, and riot that raged elsewhere. I looked at Tate, at Noah, at Helen, and understood for just a fleeting moment the profundity of the notion that history is merely the saga of small jealousies and struggles, individual conflicts in these brief existences of ours, writ large on the canvas of life. I lifted the glass to my lips and realized I'd finished my wine. Helen saw this and used it as an opportunity to bow out of the conversation, saying, "Let me refill that for you."

"I'll go with you," I said, but Tate interrupted my own escape, saying, "Grant, can I have just another minute of your time?"

I shrugged at Helen, who left. Noah, too, took this hint and drifted away, leaving Graham Tate and me more or less alone at the periphery of this room of partyers. He spoke in a lowered voice as he handed me an envelope, "I want you to take a look at this when you get home tonight and consider carefully what's inside. You think you know what happened to Giovanni Trentas? What happened to him can happen to somebody else."

"Did I just hear you confess?"

"You just heard me give you some very good advice, and I suggest you take it. Your welcome here has long since worn out."

His smile, inappropriate and overbearing, backed me away from him. I said nothing. What more was there to say?

In the kitchen, Helen asked, "What happened? You look white as snow." When she put her hand on my shoulder, it was as if I'd been shaken awake from yet another dream.

"Maybe Noah's right," I said, lighting a cigarette with my now unsteady hand.

"About getting unlost?"

"Yeah, maybe he's right."

"You're not lost, Grant. They're the ones who are lost."

"And what about you?"

"Grant. You want to go home?"

"I'm all right," taking a deep drag off the cigarette.

"You're sure?"

"I'm not sure about anything."

"Look, you've done your duty. Edmé looked to me like she was ready to go, too."

"We just got here."

"You walk Edmé back to the ranch when she wants, and I'll catch up with you later."

"But Tate's going to think—"

"Since when do you care what Tate thinks?"

She was right about Edmé, and maybe not wrong about me, and

though we did stay on for another half hour or so, the two of us thanked the Lewises—Aunt Edmé embracing Jenn Lewis and genuinely wishing her nothing but best luck wherever she found herself in the future—and said good night. As she and I walked back up the creek road, we found again we needn't have brought the flashlight. The moon had risen, round and full and bright enough to cast shadows on the ground beside us. We stopped at the gate and stared at it for some moments before ascending that last meadow hill. There it soared, absolutely distinct in the cold spangled void above, so bright we could see its mountains, its luminous seas, its craters, its broken and irregular face, with such heightened clarity that it seemed impossible we couldn't reach out and impress our fingerprints on its dusty face.

WESLEY FULTON, the man who had erected with his own hands the first structure at Ash Creek, had lived a long and decent life before he passed on to what he was certain would be an even longer and more decent life among kindred spirits above. The winter of 1965 was harsh, and the heavy blanket of snow which covered the fields and forests made it impossible to carry out his wishes to be buried on his own lands, beside his dead son, who would have been in his thirties by then had he lived, and who—he'd been convinced—would have stayed on the ranch, unlike his younger brother, Henry. For six weeks, then, the body lay in a temporary coffin, wrapped in winding sheets, and placed in the frozen barn until the snow should melt enough that Henry could come back and manage the burial.

Snow still clung in patches everywhere that March, but the time had come to put the poor man to rest, and so Henry and Edmé made the trip from the West Coast out to Ash Creek. With spade and fence-post digger, Wesley's only surviving son and Giovanni Trentas hammered their way down past the frostline, and got the plot ready. The funeral was attended by twenty stalwart souls, including Willa Richardson and her parents, a young, ambitious Graham Tate, and others.

After the funeral, Edmé returned to the coast. She and Henry had decided that she had best keep things going back home, while he stayed to help his mother put things in order, and figure out what to do about the administration of the ranch. What had passed between Willa and Henry at the funeral, an exchange of looks that ran deeper than anyone might have noticed, or some few words from Willa, which gave Henry the perilous impression that she and he shared this loss in a way that maybe Edmé and he did not— whatever had aroused them brought the beginnings of their affair to fruition much more quickly than even they could have expected, or desired.

Henry called her the night Edmé left, I learned later from Henry himself, when so much that had been dark became light, after those last few days of my own stay thirty years later at Ash Creek. The romance must have been impetuous and explosive. His judgment was surely mired by grief and obscured by the misgivings he must have felt at having the responsibilities of the ranch fall on his shoulders, since he went ahead with it, knowing he risked losing the love of his life in order to pursue Willa Richardson. Most details of their affair will always remain lost fragments in a secret story, but not all of them.

The decision to place Ash Creek in Giovanni's reliable hands followed Rebecca Fulton's insistence that she had no intention of moving into town, as Henry'd suggested she do, at least during the rough winters. She wasn't all that old, she said, and between her and Giovanni, with the help of outside labor, they could maintain much of the basic functioning of the ranch. Henry's idea to call on Willa's father to seek his help with arrangements for partnering annual livestock sales and other such things—for a commission, Richardson's concern would oversee for a time most of the market transactions having to do with Ash Creek—was not, of course, based only on business.

After Richardson and Henry were finished with their talk, maybe

Willa came into the room to bring them refreshments, or maybe she simply asked Henry if he would like to take a walk and see their family operation. Then the flirtation would have continued, the downward glances and thoughts in both their minds: Is this only happening to me or does he feel it, too, does she feel it? And I can imagine the guilty self-doubts would come forth like a pattern on the loom of this inevitable weave. Remorse, shame, sanity—none of these feelings ultimately could have restrained them from the greater one of passion. Willa had a fierceness that would be reborn in her daughter one day, and Henry was guided by an intelligence which understood how precious this woman was, and that these days and weeks were theirs to seize.

Death was temporarily vanquished in the swirl of love. They met as often as they could. They maintained as socially chaste a disguise as was possible to protect their sudden friendship. If anyone in their acquaintance wondered about the propriety of this married man going to a dance recital with Willa Richardson, while his wife awaited his return home, no one brought it to their attention. Rebecca Fulton hadn't a clue, nor did the Richardsons, that Willa wasn't merely being supportive of a friend who'd lost his father.

Two people did find out, however, as did eventually a third. Giovanni, I believe, gave them a place to be alone together after that dance. He would have conspired because Henry was his best friend, but reluctantly since his friendship with Edmé was also close. He and Margery had averted their gaze, so to speak, knowing that soon Henry would go back to his wife, and hoping when that time arrived, the lovers would come to their senses and realize the madness of allowing it to go any further. Tate was the third person who would know of this adultery, or at least suspect, but given he had no claim on Willa then, nor any power over Henry, there wasn't much he could do about his suspicions other than watch and wait. His designs for the future involved maintaining the good graces of Willa.

He pursued a young woman who was blind to him, quietly, with strategic slowness, believing his day would dawn.

Giovanni's hopes weren't altogether misguided. By the middle of April, Henry had done everything there was to do at Ash Creek, and the moment had come for him to go back to work and to Edmé. Neither he nor his lover could have known on the last night they spent in one another's arms—down in the very cabin where I stayed those weeks in the fall—that Willa was pregnant with Helen. But when Henry and Edmé returned that summer, Willa understood all too well what had happened. Giovanni had become her confidant, and while she may have tried to keep up a good facade for some weeks as the four of them were reunited, the front couldn't last for long. Willa arranged secretly to meet Henry one afternoon up at the cemetery, a place which had the advantage of privacy, and which was where she felt their liaison began and so was an appropriate place for it to end.

She told him she was pregnant, then went on to say, —I love you enough to know that it wouldn't be right to put you in the position of having to make some awful choice, so I've made a decision for both of us.

Henry was petrified, no doubt. A chill must have gripped his heart as he listened.

—I'm going away to have the child. Don't even try to contact me. Let me do this my way.

—But then what? It's *our* child.

—We put it up for adoption, and we never say a word about any of this to anyone.

—What about your parents?

—I'm old enough to go away for a while; they're always trying to get me to go abroad; maybe I'll have it overseas. But you're already asking questions. When I come back we'll be friends like we were before, but never lovers again. I'm going to be married, too.

—You are—to who?

—I have another idea, too. Maybe it's something that will work and maybe not. But like I say, this is my problem now. Let me solve it and you go on with your life. Edmé is good and decent, and I won't be a part of hurting her. I should have thought of this before, but better to set things right later than never.

With that, Willa strode across the field and out of Henry's life for over a year. Everything she promised to do, she did. She gave birth to a baby girl, married Graham Tate, and, unable to give the child up for blind adoption, arranged clandestinely for Giovanni Trentas and his wife to raise her in guise as one they had adopted. Time passed, healing some wounds, leaving some scars. For the most part, Willa's plans worked well. She did her best to right wrongs, put the world she'd unwittingly been drawn to destroy back together as carefully as she could. She supported Giovanni's parenting of her daughter by helping him financially, always in absolute secrecy. She watched Helen grow at a remove, always grateful that she was able to follow her progress and her life as closely as she did. Giovanni often shared with her all the little stories that go along with childhood, so that Willa knew when she first spoke, first walked, first went to school. A silent mother, she managed to find ways to participate in Helen's upbringing—enough so that she felt like Giovanni's tacit partner, she acting more like the traditional father, the distant breadwinner, while he performed the role of mother, nurturing and immediate.

Henry and Willa kept their promise and their distance, and Giovanni, Margery, and Tate, each for different reasons, kept their silence. The only dilemmas Willa had not been able to predict and thereby preclude arose from Helen's own suspicions as she got older, and the slow rage Willa's husband would come to nurture toward the true father of her only child. Henry Fulton's ruin became so dear to Tate's heart that if he *did* have a child, he couldn't have loved it any more than he loved, cherished, cultivated this bitterness.

And when Giovanni Trentas, so many years later, sensing that his own mortality was soon to have some impact on Helen, told them he wanted her to know these truths, Willa couldn't have foreseen that, either. Giovanni's abruptly being silenced, before he'd been able to force the issue further, was not the end but rather the beginning of a new allegory none of them seemed to be able to govern.

HERE WAS a piteous howling, shrieks that seemed neither human nor bestial, but from some other world, one that no one should ever be obliged to visit. They came from across the creek, cutting the soft, chilly night air as concertina wire might slash the supplest flesh; came in barrages, heaves of pain, bursts of breathless anguish.

I looked around me and found that I'd dozed off in the kitchen of the ranch house, waiting up for Helen. The porch lights were on, and so was the light above the table on which I'd laid my head down in my hands like some small boy might. Upstairs, I heard the frantic whispers of my aunt and uncle, and even as I rose to my feet, lifted the loden coat from where I'd placed it over the chair back, and threw it on, Henry was coming downstairs, and erupted into the kitchen, shotgun under his arm and a rifle, too.

"Here," he said, handing me the latter. "It's loaded. Only shoot up in the air, you hear me?"

"Yes."

"Unless you need to protect yourself. This is the end. This is it."

With that, he got on his own coat and hat, and went to the door.

As we made our way quickly down the hard stone stairs from the porch into the yard, and ran past the garden and the stick figure of the scarecrow, which looked in the moonlight like some emaciated angel, I wondered what time it was and how long I had slept. Could that party down at the Lewises' still be going on? Had Helen gone to the cabin to meet me and, not finding me there, decided to look for me at the studio? No, that couldn't be right. But, still, I thought, Please God, don't let it be Helen.

By the time we crossed the creek, the excruciating howls had ceased. The creek rustled along beneath my feet, the moon glowed brightly overhead, having risen to its apogee and swollen to a fullness that seemed impossibly great. Hard to believe the moon was only a couple thousand miles in diameter, so huge it was tonight. I stayed on Henry's heels, wasn't about to fall behind, or get lost. His urgency, and the urgency of those screams, gave me my own sense of need. Whatever lay ahead had to do with me now, too. It wasn't that I was here any longer in the role of patronizing nephew or fool or fuck-up—this had to do with *me* tonight. Where such exigency suddenly came from, I wouldn't have been able to say. But it was there, in my legs and arms, in my lungs and beating heart. Henry shouted something inarticulate upon arriving at the studio, near the doorway. "Get back, Grant," he seemed to say. But it was too late. I was beside him, looking down at the image captured within the periphery of whiteness cast by his flashlight.

Milland Daiches had the silliest look on his face. The eyes were bulging and a clownish smile spread on his lips, a dark smirk accentuated by that red grin of blood his toothy mouth had formed. I never knew blood could be so florid. But there it was, and coming forth in profusion, as the heavy jaws of the bear trap, rigid and unarguable, had clutched him about his lower belly, biting down on him below the waist and around there along his back. His hands had seized upon its uncompromising embrace, where they'd tried with no success to pry the thing apart and free himself from its iron teeth. I would have thought his coat and pants might have protected him some from the thing, but this was not what I saw before me. They'd been sharpened to a fine edge and had done their work.

Henry was kneeling, trying to force the spring bows—as Helen had taught me these jaws were called—away from their victim.

"Milland?" he was asking, oddly.

I got down beside him and grasped the opposite bow, and the two of us pulled against one another—I couldn't believe how strong the spring was—and managed to get the body out of the apparatus. My hands, wet with gore, caught him up by the sleeves, and it was some struggle to lift him into the studio, Milland at dead weight being surprisingly heavy.

"Get that light," Henry said.

I wanted to speak, but even the word *Okay* wouldn't form itself.

In the light, lying on the plank floor of the studio, in this environment of books and paper and fresh clay maquettes, the corpse looked much less real than it had outside.

"Jesus God," and Henry backed away from the body. We both did.

"What you want me to do?" I heard myself ask.

"I—well—"

"Maybe we better call down to Lewis's, see if Noah's there?" now finding my voice.

"He was trespassing," Henry explained.

"Don't worry about that. You didn't ask him to come and do this to himself."

"This is—Tate did this."

"Uncle—"

Milland's dying here did seem to bring matters to full circle, though something I sensed was terribly wrong still. Here was our night visitor, yes, and that receipt Helen had discovered in Tate's files seemed to take on fresh meaning, but then we heard something beyond the studio walls—a quick cry, faint and extraneous—which was even less expected than Milland's last brutal utterances.

Abruptly, we stepped outside and listened under the stars and powerful moon, having extinguished the lights. Now we heard the sharp sound of a stick cracking, above where we stood, up toward the falls.

"Who's there?" Henry asked, confused, his voice vague.

Purest silence reigned; we saw no movement.

"Who's there?" he shouted aloud after clearing his throat.

The silence would have overwhelmed us, I think, if it hadn't been saturated by the continuous whispering of the creek and falls. I couldn't fathom how our night visitor lay dead on the floor, but some form of his degenerate ritual seemed now to carry on without him. Careful to step around the bloodied trap, and with every conceivable nuance of cheap triumph having been wiped out of our minds, Henry and I left Milland's body behind, as we glided along the brief gable of the studio and began to walk across the flat upper end of the meadow. We moved slowly, cautiously, each of us no doubt coming to fresh conclusions about what possibly was happening. Henry stopped, shushed me, and I stopped beside him, and listened. We must have stood dead still for half a minute before we heard the next sound.

A rattling, first, then it crunched and crunched again. The rhythm of it pulsed, supple in the resonate valley.

Someone was running. We could just make out the presence of the figure in the light of the moon.

We said nothing to one another but began to stride quickly out of the relative flatness of the meadow and up toward the mouth of the gorge. Henry stayed with me for a hundred yards or so, but then fell behind. I heard him breathing hard back there, and when I stopped long enough to allow him to catch up, we saw the figure in the silvery light again, climbing higher into the gorge, over on the other side of the creek.

Side by side we hesitated, and if the context hadn't been so bizarre, we might have marveled at the miraculous beauty of these moonlit woods in which we stood like two hapless mortals transported by magic into a wonderland. The moonbeams laced through innumerable branches in their passage to the floor of the forest. The world had converted to two colors, silver and black. But for the fresh vision of Milland impaled in the death trap, this might have been a moment Henry and I would cherish, standing together bewitched by what we saw and by how small we really were in this wild world. But our purpose came rushing in to take its rightful place. I asked Henry, "Why don't you go back and check on Edmé," adding that I would chase this intruder all night if I had to: Like he'd said, this was it.

He refused, saying Edmé was armed and Milland wasn't going anywhere. "Come on," he finished, in a low, hoarse voice.

We hurried forward into the mercurial dark, snaking our way between clumps of shadowy bushes and jagged upheavals of rock. To our left the water spilled and pooled and moved forward to the next rough lip of stone, where it plunged again. This close to the falls, we lost track of the running figure, but assumed whoever it was we were chasing intended to continue climbing on up through the narrowing gorge and escape into the high forest. We crossed at a place several hundred yards from the studio. The creek narrowed to a point where you could leap from a jutting boulder over onto a flat patch of ground.

Water surged, gushed, rose, flooded along beside us. I was angry, and afraid, and committed this time to not losing. After all, I was closing in on my reason for having come here in the first place. I began to lose all sense of time, but was committed only to the chase. My lungs began to burn. My throat was raw from sucking in this thin cold wet air. The muscles in my legs and back were scorched and deadening. Henry was no longer right behind me. I stopped for a moment to get my bearings and catch my breath, knelt down on both knees with my hands still clutching the rifle on the earth before me, as if bent in prayer before some false idol, and listened for him. I thought maybe he had given up, gone back down to the house to attend to the business of telephoning Noah for help—though *that* would be no easy task, telling a man that his brother had died such a death as Milland's. Or maybe he knew some other path up here. Either way, I was on my own now. I looked behind and was startled to see how high I'd climbed. Far in the distance were the faint hazy lights of the town, and here and there, like enchanted jewels spread across the black carpet of the broad valley, other lights glimmered. Wind breathed in the boughs of conifers and made the dry deciduous leaves in the aspens and scrub oaks clatter. I stood again, and began to plod on, not altogether certain of what I was doing. It was quite clear to me that no matter how determined to catch the intruder I might have been, if he chose to slip me, he probably could. But then, just as I'd begun to despair, I saw him again. I felt as if my mind were being read.

The race became considerably more arduous now, the walls of the gorge began to close upon each other, and as they did the sheerness of the ascent increased and the creek path became treacherous. I worked my way up through a rocky passage, so narrow and unstable, where stones clattered out from beneath my feet, and emerged into the primordial forest of stubble pines. It was, I knew, somewhere in this tract of woods that Giovanni met his fate, and for the first time since my pursuit had begun, a stab of panic flashed through me. You could die here, I reflected. *He* did, and unlike yourself, he knew his way around.

Again the morbid image of Milland's grimacing face arose with galling clarity before me. I heard some rocks unloosened above—or was it just in my imagination now?—and I walked on, but not with the same confidence and desire that had got me this far. Bent at the waist, once more bowing as a penitent might, I carried the rifle with barrel forward and finger on the trigger—a savage penitent, less prepared for reverence than for violence.

He was close by. It wasn't as if I could *see* him as such; I rather felt his presence. He couldn't have been more than a hundred paces away—I could swear I heard his breathing, no more calm than my own—and I took those steps like one who was sentenced but bound to continue, locked into an irrevocable journey. Even if the occasional scutter of tumbling scree didn't smack the air, even if I hadn't caught sight of him, oddly spidery in the tangle of boughs and stone architecture, I would have known he was there in the silvery darkness, waiting. I sensed how alert he was, and tried my best not to make any noise that would betray my advance. By moving slowly I hoped to be more invisible. He was within yards, I sensed. Why couldn't I see him? With heart pounding crazily, I moved sideways in the direction of the fountainhead that rustled steadily just to the east. As the creek provided me with neither shelter nor safety, my movement toward it had no purpose other than that it felt like some kind of lifeline connecting me with the ranch below and the world beyond.

The word *"Henry"* was whispered, in a voice I recognized as coming not from the rushing water, which had such a knack for deceiving me into believing it could speak, but from someone right behind me. *"Who am I?"* it breathed.

"I don't know," slowly turning.

"Stop."

I froze.

"Say who Helen Trentas is. Tell the truth."

"I don't understand."

The shotgun blast stung both my ears and for an instant lit the immediate landscape with a yellowish burst. I dropped to my knees, and was surprised to find I'd not been shot. The detonation echoed, and then the forest was quiet again. Terrified, I didn't move.

The voice was still there and spoke once more, empathetic but weirdly calm. *"Say Helen Trentas is your daughter."*

Surely I recognized this voice, distorted though it was by fear and the whispering. "She's—"

"Henry?"

"But—no, it's Grant."

Now the burst of sound just behind me was different. Not the coercive explosion of a shotgun but a cry of disappointment and the footfalls of someone running headlong away from this site of our confrontation. I'd dropped my rifle and, in the rush to catch this whisperer, I left it where it lay among pine needles and broken branches, and ran hard after, heedless of the boughs that scratched at my eyes and the capricious terrain beneath my feet. I could see the figure in the thicket ahead, shouted, "Stop," as it dashed out over the glistening flat rock formations which cradled the head-waters of Ash Creek. It disappeared into the flow, and emerged on the far bank, and in I plunged, surprised by how heavily the current shoved against my thighs. I grabbed down at the surface of the flood, as if it were something to hold on to for balance. Then came a great surge, and a flicker of icy water that scorched my face, and the shock of feeling myself toppled and being swept several yards, maybe, and once more thrown upright. My hand caught something firm, and I was steady again although I couldn't see. I felt myself being pulled in another direction, by the hand that held my own, wrenched toward the bank of stones.

I was out of the current and lay on rocks, and then, as if some other spirit that lived inside me came to life, I found myself on my feet and had my arms wrapped with the last of their strength around this person who had eluded me, threatened me, and now pulled me from the water, too. We went down hard, Helen Fulton and I. Both of us were too exhausted to give much more to the struggle.

Rome is most beautiful on a rainy day. The venerable statuary is shrouded in mist, and mystery. The Baroque palaces along the Corso, once residences of privileged aristocracy but now given up to banks and boutiques, wrap themselves in the melodrama of drizzle and for a moment, despite the shop windows with their displays, seem again restored to their original grandeur. The Rococo stairway ascending to the Trinità dei Monti glistens with its puddles of water, which reflect the pale scowls of kids in ponchos who've come from around the world to idle, to *hang*. Every piazza is taken over by pigeons, and the face of the Tiber is delicately pocked by falling droplets. Back in this city of possibilities, I inhale the gentle northern wind, hoping it will revive me after another insomniac night alone in the hotel. Already it's been a morning of wandering, one of my last before giving myself the chance at a different life, and now I ramble past the Pantheon, down the Corso, vaguely toward the Palatine, with Hawthorne in my pocket and nothing before me today but a café where I might sit for an hour with the book. I promised Edmé I would send it back to her after I'd read this last story, one about the Chimera, and then signed my name on the endsheet, thereby completing finally an endeavor I'd begun as a boy. Edmé'd said, "Keep the book," but I see no reason to break her set. Indeed, of all the people I have ever known, Edmé might be the one who deserves wholeness, completeness, unbrokenness, because as I understand things now, she had, through her capacity for forgiveness, tried to keep so many lives unbroken. This is nothing I could ever communicate to her in so many words, of course. She would look at me with wondering eyes. But, as I say, while I have no desire to part with *The Wonder Book,* I haven't it in me to want what's not rightly mine. No more breakage.

Someone at the hotel said that yesterday was Veterans Day back in the States, a Saturday in early November. While I don't have a calendar and don't really care what day it was yesterday, I feel that though I've come home wounded—veteran of a war not of my making—I have some chance at healing, too. Maybe even of finding some health I never knew before.

I put up at a decent hotel; nothing with stars, but nothing with fleas, either. Though I can barely afford to stay here, a newfound pride didn't allow me to check into some run-down pensione, as I might have done in times past. If I'd taken Tate's money, I would have sought out something far fancier—but just because I chose not to sell out doesn't mean I have to wallow. Some people claim that even the filthiest, most tainted money should be managed with *some* care, if it's the only money you've got. Tate's money was just too filthy, though. Until I know what I'm going to do, until I discover what *she* intends to do, this hotel suits my needs fine. Besides, the room has an eccentric dormered ceiling, not unlike my room back in the mountains, and looks out over thousands of rooftops, duomos, cupolas: quite a different sight than I'd become accustomed to at Ash Creek, but one I like nonetheless.

Not that I spend much time looking at rooftops. In the past, I would have thought to come back to Rome to brood, would have delighted in the delicious sadness of these distracting streets, as I mused whether to try to find Jude, make up with Mary somehow, even search out Daniella. *Domi manere convenit felicibus:* how I'd have turned that maxim once more on its proverbial ear. But now who's to say that happiness doesn't come to many who do know home, embrace it wherever and whatever it is. There are those among us who seem destined to look for it beyond, out *here,* outside. It's up to me to learn which is for me. Not that any of this will come easy. Just this morning, while I gazed out at the Roman vistas softened by balmy drizzle, I knew I had to get down into the streets one last time, as I start work tomorrow on another kind of existence. Maybe the finest solitude was not to be had there, as I'd always thought, but a final wandering seemed appropriate. To rephrase what Mary wrote in that last letter to me, *Old habits die hard.*

There were moments during these past months when I'd have thought I might never walk the Corso again. My involvement with Helen, Edmé, Henry, Tate, and the others had reached an intricacy, a deepening involvement, from whose knotty web it'd begun to seem I might never escape, even if I'd wanted to abandon them all. But for what was in the envelope that Graham Tate passed me during the farewell party at the Lewises', I might still be in Ash Creek. What it *meant,* however—what everything which culminated in the aftermath of that party *meant*—brought me finally to this understanding of what was no longer good for me. And to think that in the midst of so many other developments which claimed my attention that violent night, the envelope had temporarily slipped my mind.

I'd been anxious to open it when Tate had first given it to me, but during my walk with Edmé back to the house, I simply forgot it was there in Giovanni's—now my—loden coat. Edmé and I marveled at the full moon. We strolled up to the house. We told Henry a little about the party he'd boycotted. And, as the clock ticked steadily on the wall, I fell asleep at the kitchen table, until Milland's anguished cries awakened us all and sent us off in pursuit of what would turn out to be *both* night visitors. Why the envelope wasn't swept away by the rushing water of the creek that nearly drowned me in the gorge, I don't know. When I finally picked my way back down to Giovanni's cabin, after answering questions Noah and others had for me in the kitchen of the house, I was a mess. Sick at heart, bewildered, sore, frightened, wet, and all alone, I threw myself on my cot.

That was when I remembered. I touched my pocket: the packet was still there.

Hundred-dollar bills, fifty of them, held together by a rubber band, were inside. No note, of course, nothing to incriminate him—nor was there any need for one to explain the five thousand dollars Tate had given me to go away. If Helen hadn't abandoned me, after helping me out of the creek, Tate's lousy money might not have meant anything. Not even for the briefest moment would I have considered taking this bribe, this blood bread. But some part of my uninnocent spirit fractured up there in the gorge, after Helen shed both light and focus on so much that was happening around me.

"Don't you realize what you've done?" I'd cried out at her.

"What *I've* done?"

"Milland's dead."

Even in the subtle light shed by the moon I saw her disquietude—not a look I was used to seeing on Helen's face.

"You knew about that trap. You led him there, didn't you."

"I didn't force him to step into any trap, he did it all on his own. Besides, if you heard what he said to me—"

Her voice was more vehement now.

"At the party I saw he was really drunk and so I asked him about something I happened to find, a receipt for a thousand dollars that dates back to the day after Giovanni died. I asked him why was it that receipt had his name on it?"

"What did he say?"

"He told me to meet him behind the house, we needed to speak in private."

"You went?"

"Of course I did. Milland said Tate was mad, and wanted that receipt back. 'You can make it easy or you can make it hard,' he said. 'I

bet you have it on you right now, don't you?' he told me, and before I
knew it, Milland's filthy hands were all over me. I started fighting
him and then he came out with, 'Don't make me mad now, don't
make me do what I did before. Mr. Tate made me swear I wouldn't
do it to you, too.' "

"Do what?"

"He came out with it *like it was nothing*. He said, 'Don't you get
why Mr. Tate had to have Giovanni roughed up a little? How else
would everybody see he meant business?' I asked Milland what the
hell he was talking about, but he just kept on with his drunken
babble. He said, 'Shit, the old man was dying anyway, but he put up
quite a fight.' Milland told me everything. It got out of hand up there
in the gorge, he said. He even bragged, 'The foot was my idea, but
Mr. Tate knew where to have me put that shoe to get you going,' "
and then he smiled that idiotic proud disgusting smile of his. 'Giovanni wasn't your real father anyhow, so what do you care?' That's
what he said."

I was speechless.

Helen finished, "So I set it up with Milland to meet me at Henry's
studio. I told him I'd hid the receipt there."

I didn't move.

"Helen," I said.

She was crying.

Quietly, I asked, "But why lead me up here? That's what you were
doing, isn't it? You could have escaped me without half trying, if you
wanted."

"Henry was supposed to catch up with me, not you. This was
where Giovanni died, and this was where Henry was going to tell
me what really happened to him and why. I've listened to Tate for
too long."

"Tate?"

"Don't you understand? It all got out of hand, those nights with

Milland running around in the dark. I never meant to hurt you that time—"

"That was *you* who knocked me down?"

"It was when that happened I knew I had to get out of this loop, that Tate was lying, lying like always, telling me Henry did it, that Henry had his reasons and it was never going to come out, and the only way to break the truth out of him is—"

"Stop, Helen."

"I told them I wanted out, but Milland wouldn't ever have let me; Tate, either. They were both getting what they wanted. Tate was getting his revenge, and Milland, I don't know, he was getting money and Tate's attention and—"

I kept listening behind me for Henry, who I imagined would have arrived by now, summoned by the shotgun blast his daughter made, but heard nothing more than the perpetual deafening rush of spring water. Helen's confession was disturbing for so many reasons, not the least among them indicative of the choices I must face. It was then I got it, understood with lightning intensity that my love for Helen wasn't counterfeit, or unreal, or contrived. Her last words, before she broke away from me and disappeared into the shimmery woodland, were heartbreaking to hear.

"Now you're the only one who knows. Do what you think is fair. That's all I want. Nothing more."

What was there to say in response to such a torturous edict? I should have told Helen that I was in love with her and all this was unimportant in the end, this forcing people to unearth secrets from their pasts they'd rather leave buried. I should have told her that the secret of her appointment with Milland was safe with me, that we'd ride out whatever would be the consequences of the evening's disaster and, after that, go away together—back to Rome, even—and live anonymously, quietly, happily, and so forth. I would stop with this wandering, stop with the lassitude, do something with myself. I should have *said something,* no matter how banal. Yet, at the same time, wasn't it true that when we parted, each of us knew what the other desired? And didn't those desires interweave? While my last hours at Ash Creek were struck by bewilderment, they were also charged with insight, and clarities I had never enjoyed before.

Noah had arrived at Ash Creek with several men, and though I first emerged from the gorge disconsolate, with teeth chattering and fingers going blue, I maintained some presence of mind, and continued naturally my own pattern of protective dishonesty. The red lights running with supernatural speed around the bowl of the valley were menacing. An ambulance was parked by the gate, the white lights emanating from the opened rear doors spreading an eerie glow over a block of meadowland. Several other cars were parked down there. Some men had gone up into the gorge to have a look.

I had never seen Noah looking so tired as that black morning. His approach to me was more paternal than suspicious. When I came into the house, he offered me his leather bomber jacket, as I was shaking from the cold. It was I who ought to be comforting him, it might have seemed, here in these hours after his brother's accident, but Noah's undoubtable grief was not something he was going to show any of us; and what was more, I wondered how many years he had known that this day of his brother's reckoning might arrive. I sat in the ranch house kitchen with his jacket thrown over my shoulders and drank hot tea and tried to mold my spinning thoughts into some consistency, as he asked questions. *Truth is freedom, secrets are pain,* I thought, however paradoxically, as I began to weave Helen out of the story, hoping as she herself had hoped that all this madness might find its way to an end with Milland's death.

No, I told Noah, I never caught up with the guy. No, I never saw his face. Yes, whoever he was seemed to head out of the gorge and continue northward up toward timberline. My answers never once strayed into the light of fact, and in retrospect I wonder if Noah was really buying any of it. Was it possible that even he saw the chance that Milland's ruin could somehow be a martyrdom? Maybe not, maybe not.

The riskiest of my fabrications was that I heard the intruder taunt me, in a voice I did not recognize. I didn't understand what he was trying to say, but yes, it was definitely the voice of a man.

Noah's attention, after he'd finished with me, was directed to Henry, who freely admitted to having set the trap, saying that of course he never expected anything like this could happen. It was fortunate, I suppose, that Henry had the shrewdness—was this the word? or *had* he acted innocently, out of habit?—to bait the trap pan with fresh raw meat. This allowed Henry to warrant he'd set the device for obvious, lawful purposes, against which no one could responsibly claim otherwise. That Milland had been trespassing his lands, drunken and uninvited, in the middle of the night, made it all but impossible to bring up charges of wrongful death or anything else, even if Noah had wanted to, which as I say I suspect he didn't. By prosecuting Henry, or for that matter going after Tate, Noah might only succeed in further disgracing his brother. Matters had suddenly arrived at a restive equilibrium.

"I doubt we'll be having any more midnight intrusions up here," Henry ventured—a brash scrap of accusation that Noah did not fail to disregard. Surely he understood the framework and dynamics, the political and psychological rivers which ran beneath these surfaces better than I or anyone could suspect. That hard arbiter's face of his, I thought, was shaped by moments such as this. I thanked him for the use of his leather jacket, handed it back to him. I felt spent now, spiritless and frazzled, as first light began to redden the eastern ridge.

My impulse just before dawn, when I'd finally gone down to the cabin and opened Tate's envelope, was to grab the cheap freedom it would allow me. I never felt so alone as when I lay there on my side, in the firelight from the old stove, and counted those moist bills. Edmé had tried to convince me to stay at the house, to sleep upstairs in my old room. But I craved a dense, thorough withdrawal from everyone and everything—and that is what I got in spades. Exhaustion finally overcame me as the sun broke over the trees, and I fell asleep, though not before hiding the money in Giovanni's box under the bed—a gesture whose impropriety went unnoticed by me that morning, so tired was I, ready to vanish into whatever anemic consolation was to be had from sleep.

The sky was overcast later that day. Autumn was unpredictable, and the weather would change from hour to hour. But I, at least, woke up with some resolve, some clarity. For the first time in memory, I knew with assurance a few commitments I must make if I was to leave Ash Creek without my spirit entirely shattered.

First and foremost, Tate was going to get his fucking money back. How I would adore shoving it down his vile throat. When I recalled where I'd stowed the envelope, a wave of shame washed over me, but there was no time to bother with scolding myself. I did a funny thing when I unnotched the brad, lifted the lid, and removed the money: I apologized to Giovanni, asked him to forgive my stupid transgression. I promised him I'd take good care of the box now—I knew what to do with it—and not make a mistake like that again. I promised him I'd do what was within my power, to care for Helen, too—if that was what she wanted. For just a fleeting instant, I felt him there in the hut, his certain presence, evidenced by an indescribable warmth. What was communicated, I swear, was some benediction, a gift for having, in my absurd, unfocused, backward way, managed to bring matters so long left tangled toward resolution. For being, a gift for better or worse, a kind of catalyst. I gathered myself together and walked up to the house.

Henry was downstairs and still wore on his face the look of shock. Nothing so disturbing as getting what you think you want—here was an adage which spoke of such bitter ironies, was it not? I caught a glimpse of myself in the front-hall mirror, and noticed how my hair had grown. Noticed, too, that the countenance on my own face matched Henry's, although I couldn't see how my shock came from getting what I wanted.

"You lied last night, didn't you," were his first words.

"What do you mean?"

"Grant, I would never repeat anything you told me, not if it would bring any harm your way. But you were lying. I could tell. Who was it up in the gorge?"

"I think you know who it was. I don't think you need me to tell you. Is that why you disappeared on me?"

"It *was* Helen, then?"

"One of these days you're going to have to deal with it, face her. You can't go on like this, none of you can."

Henry brushed his flattened hand across his cheek.

"That's what she wants?"

"You don't need me to answer that, either."

"She didn't have to do things this way—"

"This is where you're wrong. I can't help you, if you really believe she had other ways to go about getting the truth. She still doesn't really have it. Milland gave her a hellish version of it—she deserves better. If you won't talk to her, then I will."

Henry said, "You wouldn't know what to tell her, because you don't know all that happened." It was then he confessed to me about Willa, their brief love, and the story of Helen's beginnings.

"She needs to know this, and straight from your lips," I said, quietly, once he'd finished speaking. "Again, if you won't tell her, I will."

"It's not for you to do," he said.

His voice and his eyes told me this was as far as we would ever venture together down this line of thought. Henry and I discussing somewhat openly his *true* relationship with Helen—this was both much further than I'd ever expected us to get, and not quite far enough, because neither of us had a willingness to broach a deeper dialogue about the meaning of *my* relationship with her. I didn't myself want to ponder the vocabulary of intimacy, and therefore had

scant interest in discussing it with my uncle. I did tell him that unless Noah Daiches, or some other authority, meant to bind me over
for further questioning, I was going to return to Rome. A job had
been in the offing there before I left, something I wouldn't have considered before, because it would have involved a burden of time
and energy I wasn't, then or even recently, able to embrace. This employment, if still available to me, was nothing anyone else would
consider particularly special—working for an import-export company—but meant a livelihood, a pursuit.

Winter was around the corner, I told him. I couldn't remain in the
cabin much longer and didn't want to be underfoot at the house. If
Edmé and he needed me to help with any winter preparations, any
repair work, anything at all, I would stay as long as necessary, then
be on my way. Henry thanked me, said he and Edmé would take
care of whatever had to be done with Ash Creek and whatever else
needed restitution.

"We'll find out where the road leads," he said, by which I assumed
he promised to begin the process of setting wrong to rights.

With that, he left for his studio, and I went upstairs to find Edmé
to say goodbye, to thank her for letting me stay with them and for
calling me in the first place.

Edmé looked radiant to me this morning, somehow unburdened.
"I'm off," I said, rather unnecessarily, as she embraced me.

"You'll be all right?"

I nodded, then, without having pondered my question, asked,
"Why did you give me that box?"

She spoke in even and quiet tones. "Giovanni would have wanted
you to have it."

"I don't understand."

"I saw the rootlessness that scarred my brother—your father—
and even you, Grant. I've always loved my husband, my home. I did
the best I could, by giving you the box."

Once more, Edmé's riddles.

"Certain things had to be said which I couldn't, wouldn't, say. Don't you understand? Giovanni wasn't able to speak in so many words, either. We can love people and know what they've got to do to be whole and healed, when they've broken themselves, say. It's the oldest truth in the world that we can't take their actions for them, walk their road for them. But it doesn't mean we can't alter the landscape through which the road passes, help them see their way." The look on my face—one surely of astonishment—must have been misread by her as critical, while she stood there revealed before me, because she finished with, "I hope you won't think ill of me, Grant."

"Never," was what I said, and kissed her on the cheek.

I spent a few minutes alone in my cherished room before driving the jeep down the creek road and across the ranging expanse of valley.

Phalanxes of dark heavy clouds marched low overhead, and to the east a column of gray smoke rose up into them—someone burning off a field for winter. It looked as if the sky and earth were connected by this pillar, as if heaven were supported by the earth. Given it was the weekend, I assumed I'd have a better chance of finding Tate at home than in his offices.

When Willa greeted me at the great door of the aerie, her first words, "I warned you," were no different than I might have expected.

"You're wrong—I did exactly what you said, Willa. She's known all along, in her own way. Helen's only been waiting for you to step forward and tell her."

A silence passed between us.

Then I spoke again. "Here, I think this is yours," and I handed her the note she'd asked for that day we met at the coffee shop. "And this is for your husband," giving her the envelope of money, which I had placed inside another envelope and sealed. "Thank him, if you would."

We shook hands, uneasy intimates, then parted. A time would come, I hoped, when Willa and I would see each other again.

My next stop was the post office, to complete what was perhaps the most unorthodox of my parting deeds. I was compelled to release back into the world all the pieces Giovanni'd assembled into this reluctant collage. It seemed a necessary gesture. I had chosen carefully objects for each of the individuals who'd been part of this portrait, and wrapped for them small parcels. As I'd gone about my business, deconstructing Giovanni's box behind the closed door of my bedroom upstairs at Ash Creek, I thought of the paradise of children that had existed before the god Mercury got it in his head to leave that box in Epimetheus' house—in Hawthorne's version of the myth—of a world with no danger, nor trouble of any kind. Eve's daughter, Pandora—or Pandora's, Eve—seemed so *richly human* to me, as I went about my business there. Hope was born in the shadows of clouds of demons, according to all versions of the old myth, and in that I saw there was a familiar human dark-edged radiance.

To Noah I sent the packet of *Papiers Mais, Bestest 200 leaves, Verdadeiro papel Francez*, as well as the Prince Alberts, wondering whether he would simply use them, roll tobacco into the supple antique yellow leaves of paper and smoke his way through them one by one, never knowing who or where they came from. To Margery went her precious letters, some photographs and keepsake cards, along with the affection of a stranger and my admiration for one who made a tough decision and stuck with it. Tate I mailed the typed column of numbers, nothing more. The miniature diary for 1942 had no owner, as such, but I thought that the Lewises, beginning their own migration, ought to have it. The pair of rusted spinner hooks went off to Henry, in memory of those times with Giovanni spent in quiet friendship along that creek they'd loved; as well as the dance recital card, which was meant not to challenge him but to put his mind at ease, allow him to make his own decisions about responsibility. The pieces of foolscap I'd taped together also were Henry's to have, sent by me in the strong hope that he would take it upon himself to share with Helen what Giovanni wrote there. Finally, the black leather change purse and one of the two feathers I wrapped, tied with string, and addressed to Edmé, in the belief that they were fetishes very close to Giovanni's heart and that he, who entrusted all these secret objects to her, would want her to have them.

This nearly emptied Giovanni's box. But not quite.

For myself, I would keep that brass cylinder, I decided, and the recipe for dandelion wine. I also treasured the joke book, the exterminator's card, and some few other inexplicable odds and ends, not least among them that old subscriber's receipt to *True Detective*. It was for me to clear out any detritus so that when I gave the box itself to Helen, it would contain two things only, one placed there by Giovanni, the other by myself.

The drive to Helen's cottage was unhurried. The closer I got, the more faulty and precarious became my resolve. Having gone this far with her, I didn't want to lose her, although what had happened so recently gave me every fair reason to believe she wasn't mine to lose. At the same time, Helen frightened me—*there,* now I have said it—frightened me by her passion. It awed me in a way no passion had I'd ever witnessed. There was faith in it, a kind of hope bordering on madness, and there was fury crackling at its edges. When she withdrew the night before, the emotional fracturing I felt was easy to reduce to diagnosis. No, I didn't *want* to be in love with Helen Trentas, or Helen Fulton, or any other Helen—but I was. I would have preferred my unreachable Jude, or my heartsick Mary come for another reconciliation to be followed soon after by one more sad deception, disagreement, and divorce. Such again were my thoughts, as I arrived at her house. Helen was terrifying because she had my respect. I'd loved women before, had loved trying to make them happy and felt desire for them, kindness toward them, and tender anger, too. More than once I believed I'd found someone suited to me. But what had always been absent was such thorough respect.

No one responded to my knocking on the side door, and when I tried the knob, for once it did not turn. I walked back around to the front door, knocked again. Again nothing, and a locked door. I knew of course where the key was hidden, but this time I wanted to be invited in. Still, I wasn't going to leave here until I'd said the few things I wanted to say, and given Helen my present. Because the temperature had fallen and the sky lowered, I decided to wander out across that field toward the river. Better than sitting on the stoop. A walk at least had the advantage of getting my blood circulating.

Out at the far edge of the pasture I crossed, a solitary horse stood, head lowered to crop at grass. Magpies picked their way over hummocks of dried mud and tufts of vegetation. Above, a flock of small birds bounded southward, calling to one another with voices that whistled *pee-pee-bee*. Behind me, back toward town, the random barking of a dog broke through this private atmosphere, this heavy silence. As I neared the horse, it raised its great chestnut head, shook its mane, fixed one wary eye upon me, and as it did, I felt the strangest urge come over me. I wanted to touch it, for some reason. I, who had never known anything but the deepest fear of these creatures, had got it in my head I wanted to see what its dusty, gray, velvet muzzle felt like. As I got closer, I began to speak to the horse. "It's okay, don't worry." Gently, slowly, I murmured, approaching the mare, which surprised me by not retreating as I expected it would. "Good girl," I sang as softly as I could. "That's right."

And she did stay there, she did allow me to touch her. I ran my hand along her neck, amazed by the animal warmth of her coat. I continued to speak to her, marveling at her indulgence. At the center of her forehead was the most perfectly formed white star marking, which I stroked. She smelled of home, I thought—whatever *that* meant. The world surrounding us was, for those few moments we stood together at the margin of this long field near the river, the most completely hushed I'd ever heard, or *not* heard, it.

When I glanced up, raised from this serenity by the sound of someone approaching, I saw Helen. She herself had been walking along the river trail and, having seen me in the field, turned back to meet me. "Should I believe my eyes?" she said.

"I know."

"What's got into you?"

I shrugged. The horse sputtered, then broke away, leaving Helen and me behind.

"Are you all right?" she asked.

"I seem to have survived."

"No thanks to me."

I looked down, then up again.

"You hate me now, don't you."

"What? Of course not. Why would I?"

"Because you probably should."

We'd begun to walk side by side toward the house. I may have shown the temerity to touch that mare, but could not bring myself to take Helen's hand. Not that she took mine, either.

"Because?"

"You've got to believe that as much as I hated Milland Daiches, I never meant for him—"

"You didn't?"

"Are you going to tell them?"

"I had my chance last night when I got back down out of the gorge. Noah was right there, some others, too. They wanted to hear all about who I'd chased, if I found somebody."

"What did you tell them?"

"Told them I'd heard a man's voice. Told them it was somebody I didn't recognize."

"Grant, I *did* mean for Milland to get hurt, didn't I. Why lie about it?"

I didn't know what to say.

"Can we do something, make a covenant? Can we never talk about this again? I have to make this right, and you can't help me.

You've already done what you can, whether you meant to or not. But you and I, if we're still going to talk—"

"Of course we are."

"Then we've got to look—and talk—beyond, forward."

I took her hand, which was cold. "Let's go inside. I've got something I want to give you."

She tightened her grip and we walked the rest of the field in silence. The banks of dark fleshy clouds continued to roll like waves, low over the valley. The mountains were shrouded in dense fog. We entered by the side door, she having produced a key from the pocket of her pea jacket.

Helen put up water for tea, and as she did, we were enveloped by our silences. Her hair was knotted into a loose bun, revealing her sharp profile, and as I sat at the table in the kitchen, I studied her beauty with the same intense fascination I'd felt that late-summer day up at the cemetery. She wore the simplest black turtleneck and black jeans, no jewelry, no adornments whatever, and as I watched her concentrate on pouring the hot water from kettle into pot, I understood that no one other than Helen would ever make any sense to me as an intimate, a companion. She filled the silver tea egg and lowered it into the pot, laid a knitted cozy over. As she sat down to wait for the tea to steep, I felt saturated with affection, and content that my recognition of Helen's importance to me was not mistaken. I reached down into my satchel on the kitchen floor beside my chair and pulled out Giovanni's box.

"This is yours," I said.

She admired it without reaching out for it; she kept her hands in her lap, sitting directly across from me.

"I don't understand," she said.

"Edmé gave it to me. It used to be your father's, Giovanni's. Now it's yours. I hope you don't mind, but there were some things in it he was holding on to for different people, and I took the liberty of returning them. There are a couple of things for you inside, too. Here—"

She took Giovanni's box from me, set it before her quite formally, and raised the lid. She smiled as she reached in and lifted out first the feather, saying, "Poor Sam will be pleased to have this back." Then she took the photograph I'd placed in the box and held it up to the cream light. Edmé had given it to me that very morning, after Henry and I had our talk and said our farewells. She'd said she had known it was around somewhere among her thousands of prints. "It's not a very *good* photograph, as you can see," she had apologized as she handed it to me. "But I think it's one you'll find interesting."

It didn't take Helen quite as long as it had me to recognize whose three faces those were in the image. I, who was all of eight, stood on the timbers of the bridge with feet spread, right hand on my hip and left holding the hand of a small girl. Opposite, on the other side of the girl, knelt Giovanni Trentas, a beatific smile spread on that memorable face of his. He was holding the young girl's other hand, in both his own.

"My God. We *did* meet."

"Edmé said we got along very well, too."

Helen laughed quietly; we both did.

"It's a shame Henry had to keep his two families apart when we were kids. I could have known you all my life."

Placing the photograph carefully back in the box, she said, "This is really good of you, Grant. But are you sure?"

"Sure of what?"

"Sure you want to part with it."

"I don't want to part with anything," I said.

Helen squared me in her sights. "You don't want me, Grant."

"Since when is it your place to tell me what I don't want?"

"We don't even know if I'm going to be brought up on charges of some kind. I did admit to breaking into Tate's office, after all. That's against the law. And it may be true I didn't murder Milland, but it's not like I saved him, either. I wanted to, I tried. I heard that spring clamp snap and I heard him make this awful sound, and I ran back, and I tried to help him get loose, but he grabbed at me and was screaming, and those teeth were into him so hard. I wasn't strong enough. I grabbed the shotgun and I ran, Grant."

"Are you breaking the covenant?"

We just sat there. We said nothing until I repeated to Helen that I had no interest in parting with anything, but that I was leaving— the time had come for me to go back to Rome.

"I can't come with you," she said. "Not until what was happened here works itself through. Truth to tell, I haven't even decided whether I shouldn't just go down and talk to Noah, tell him every- thing, give him that receipt from Tate's files, let the chips fall where they may."

"Whatever you think is right, that's what I'd want you to do."

Helen brightened suddenly, smiled, then took my hands and said, "You remember back on Labor Day when you said I had three ques- tions coming to me?"

"I remember."

"Well, I still have one question to go, don't I?"

"You do?"

"I do, yes."

"Well, then. Ask."

"I'm not completely sure yet how I want to phrase it. I'm going to ask, though, someday soon. You just better be ready to answer."

Her piercing eyes immersed themselves in mine; and after we drank our tea, each cocooned in thought, while outside the cold rain began to peck the windows and roof, we lay down together for an hour once more, upstairs, the rhythm of our breathing there match- ing curiously the pulsing of wind against the panes and rushing under the eaves like sea swells. After, she drove me down to the bus station, having reluctantly agreed to take the jeep back up to Ash

Creek—seeing very easily through my ruse, my clumsy but well-meant manipulation to bring Helen and Henry together, a key passing from one hand to another, setting before my uncle the chance to speak to her. It was a chance I felt convinced he'd not fail to embrace.

On the back of Edmé's photograph of Helen and me and Giovanni Trentas I had written the address of the hotel where I decided I would stay, the place she could find me—La Speranza, of all things. Indeed, "When you can, if you can, please come—find me," were the words I left Helen with as I boarded my bus in the rain, taking back with me both less than I came with and much more.

The rain here now in Rome is tapering, and the haggard sun is trying to find its way through the clouds. I have walked the length of the Corso and found for myself an old familiar café, where I can sit and read this last fable of Hawthorne.

Once upon a time, it begins, *long, long ago.* But then, before I can read another word, I am distracted by the single chiming of a bell, far off in the distance, singing its pure high note from the crown of a medieval tower somewhere in this sprawling city. Soon another bell chimes, lower, and another, much higher than the first, and then more bells, of every timbre and tonality, join in. Bells of every size, weight, mold, material, and epoch are ringing; deep throbbing bells and broken reedy bells, quick clanging bells and bells that toll with slow dignity. More bells and yet others add their singular voices to the chorus, until it seems that, *yes,* all the bells of Rome are ringing the noon Angelus. Enraptured, I close my eyes and then open them on a whole new world.

Mark of the Reader

___ ___ ___ ___ ___ ___ ___

___ ___ ___ ___ ___ ___ ___

___ ___ ___ ___ ___ ___ ___

___ ___ ___ ___ ___ ___ ___

___ ___ ___ ___ ___ ___ ___